MAGIC HOUR

MAGIC HOUR

Susan Isaacs

HarperCollins
An Imprint of HarperCollins*Publishers*

First published in Great Britain in 1991
by HarperCollins Publishers,
77-85 Fulham Palace Road,
Hammersmith, London W6 8JB

9 8 7 6 5 4 3 2 1

A CIP catalogue record for this book
is available from the British Library

ISBN 0 00 223823 3

Printed and bound in Great Britain by
HarperCollins Book Manufacturing, Glasgow

To my best friend,
Susan Zises

ACKNOWLEDGMENTS

I sought advice and information from the people listed below. All of them gave it freely and cheerfully. I want to thank Arlene Abramowitz, Janice Asher, Peter Corwith, Lawrence Goldman, Maddy Kahn, Susan Lawton, Neil Leinwohl, Tony Lepsis, Fr. Thomas McCarthy, Bob Mitchell, Catherine and Robert Morvillo, Saundra and Herschel Saperstein, Cynthia Scott, Abby Singer, Dustin Beall Smith, N. T. Thayer, Sr., William Wexler, and Frank and Lisa Cronin Wohl.

A hug and a kiss to my great pal, Frank Perry, who taught me about making movies.

A salute to the police officers who answered my technical questions. Unlike Detective Stephen Brady, they were all straight shooters and gentlemen. I apologize if I twisted the facts to fit my fiction. Thanks to Detective-Lieutenant Eugene Dolan of the Nassau County Police, Captain William Kilfoyle and Officer Alan Paxton of the Port Washington (New York) Police, Lieutenant William P. Kiley and Captain John McElhone of the Suffolk County Police, and Sergeant William Crowley of the Southampton Town Police.

The staffs of The Hampton Library in Bridgehampton and the Port Washington (New York) Public Library were unfailingly courteous and helpful.

A special thank you to Paul Brennan, who was generous enough to share his memories of growing up in Bridgehampton with me.

My assistant, AnneMarie Palmer, deserves cheers, bouquets, standing ovations, and whatever else she might want for her hard work and grace under pressure.

Owen Laster, my agent, manages to be both hardheaded and kindhearted. He is truly a class act.

Larry Ashmead is a great editor. All writers should be as lucky as I am.

My children, Andrew and Betsy Abramowitz, are no longer children. I thank them for their wise and perceptive editorial comments and, of course, for their love.

Finally, in case anyone is curious about who the best person in the world is, it is still my husband, Elkan Abramowitz.

CHAPTER 1

Seymour Ira Spencer of Manhattan and Southampton was a class act. Hey, the last thing you'd think was "movie producer." No herringbone gold chain rested on a bed of chest hair; there was no fat mouth, definitely no cigar. If you could have seen him, in his plain white terry-cloth bathrobe (which he was too well-bred to have monogrammed), standing on the tile deck of the pool of his beachfront estate, Sandy Court, sipping a glass of iced black-currant tea, talking softly into his portable phone, you'd have thought: *This* is what they mean when they say good taste.

I'll tell you how tasteful Sy Spencer was. He actually might have hung up, strolled inside and picked out a Marcel Proust book to reread. Except just then he got blasted by two bullets, one in his medulla, one in his left ventricle. He was dead before he hit the deck.

Too bad. It was a gorgeous August day. I remember. The sky was a blue so pure and powerful you almost couldn't look at it. Who could take that much beauty? Down at the beach, where Sy was, silver-white gulls soared, then dive-bombed into the ocean. The sand gleamed pale gold. Farther north, out beyond my backyard, potato fields gave off a rich, dark-green light.

It was the kind of perfect Long Island day that makes the summer people say: "Darrr-ling [or *Ma chère* or Kiddo], this is *such* a glorious time out here. And do you know what's so pathetic? All the little social climbers are so busy being upwardly mobile that they never get to appreciate"—taking a deep, sensitive sniff of fresh air through their dilated nostrils—"such breathtaking loveliness."

Jesus, were they full of shit! But they were right. That day, the sun bathed the entire South Fork of Long Island in glorious light. It was like a divine payoff. For the last five years, one of the secretaries in Homicide had been bestowing the same benediction on me: "Have a nice day, Detective Brady!" Well, God had finally come through. This was it.

For Sy Spencer, of course, this was not it. And to be perfectly honest, the day, wonderful as it was, wasn't so nice for me either. Nothing as dramatic as Sy's day. Definitely not so fatal. But the events of that sunny summer afternoon changed the ending of my story almost as much as they did Sy's.

I was home in the northwest corner of Bridgehampton, six miles east and five miles north of Sandy Court, in considerably less impressive circumstances. My house was a former migrant worker's shack. It had been renovated by a hysterically ambitious, pathetically untalented ponytailed Brooklyn Heights architect, who comprehended, too late, that the place would never be considered a Find. He had been forced to sell it cheap to one of the locals (me) because even the most gullible smoothie from New York would not buy a low-ceilinged, Thermopaned whitewashed hovel with a six-burner restaurant stove and aggressively cute fruits and flowers stenciled along the walls and floors, situated on a rutted, geographically undesirable road between a potato field and a stagnant pond.

Anyway, somewhere around the time the bullet blasted

through the base of Sy's skull, my life also blew up. Our two lives—ka-boom!—were joined. Of course, I didn't know it. Unlike movies, life has no sound track; there was no ominous roll of drums. For me, it was still a nice day. A fantastic day. There I was, with my fiancée, Lynne Conway, lying on a blanket on the grass in my backyard, having moved outside from the bedroom for a little postcoital sun, conversation and iced tea. (I'd even thrown a couple of lemon circles into our glasses, to show that, okay, Lynne might have gone to Manhattanville College and known about fish forks, but I could still be a gracious host.)

Of course, if I had been truly gracious, we would have been stretched out on lounge chairs, but in the last few years I hadn't had time for amenities like towels without holes, much less outdoor furniture. So what? I knew all that would change in three months, when we got married. We'd have lounge chairs on a brick patio. A barbecue with a domed cover. Tuberous begonias. I would stop referring to the bacon-cheddar cheeseburgers I ate in the greasiest diners in Suffolk County as dinner; I would come home to poached salmon with parsleyed potatoes, fresh asparagus. I would, at age forty, be a newlywed.

I turned over onto my side. Lynne was so pretty. Dark-red hair, that Irish setter color. Peachy young skin. A perfect nose, slightly upturned, with two tiny indentations on the tip, as though God had made a fast realignment in the final seconds before her birth. She wore khaki shorts that revealed her fabulous long legs. It wasn't just her looks, though. Lynne was a lady.

She came from a good family . . . well, compared to mine. Her father was a retired navy cipher expert. His retirement seemed to consist of sitting in a club chair, his white-socked feet on an ottoman, reading right-wing magazines and getting enraged at Democrats.

Lynne's mother, Saint Babs of Annapolis, went to Mass every morning, where she probably prayed that the Lamb of God would strike me dead before I could marry her daughter. Babs Conway needlepointed all afternoon while she watched *The Young and the*

Restless and *Geraldo;* she was eight years into her masterwork, a gigantic "The Marys at the Sepulchre" throw pillow.

So there was Lynne: a nice Catholic girl. And a good woman. A beauty. Believe me. I knew precisely how lucky I was to have her. My life had not been what you'd call a charmed existence. Happiness was a blessing I'd doubted I deserved and never believed I would receive.

"For the honeymoon," she said softly, adjusting the shoulder seam of my T-shirt, "what would you think—this is just another option—if instead of Saint John we spent a week in London?"

"You want to snorkel in the Thames in late November?"

Lynne smiled, and the smile made her look even lovelier. She offered no wisecracks. No: Do you think I want to spend my honeymoon with some schmuck in flippers? What she said, without a trace of sarcasm, was: "I think I get the point. Saint John." I gazed into Lynne's fine brown eyes.

And then I stopped having a nice day.

Because there I was with a wonderful, kindhearted, titian-haired, honey-skinned woman, and all I was having was a nice day. I wasn't having fun.

This is nuts, I said to myself. I had to understand that Lynne was young. She didn't quite get me yet. To her, I was a man of the world. It was kind of sweet. Okay, I wished she'd loosen up just a little. I admitted it. I even admitted I was a little tense. I should have wanted a drink. But listen, I told myself, I *don't* want a drink. I'm doing fine.

Still, that was why, when Headquarters called fifteen minutes later and said, There's been a homicide reported in your neck of the woods, ha-ha, on Dune Road in Southampton—that's *the* high-rent district, right?—a movie producer, Somebody Spencer, was shot . . .

Jesus H. Christ, I said. Sy Spencer.

You know him?

I know about him. My brother's doing some work for him on the movie he's making out here.

Hey, is it true he won an Oscar a couple of years ago?

Yeah.

I bet I saw him! On TV, you know, one of those guys saying: I wanna thank my agent and my parents and my late cat, Fluff. Listen, it's your day off, but you're the only one who lives way the hell out in the Hamptons, and we just got called in on a mess in Sachem where some computer nerd got into a fight with his old man and strangled him and tried to hide him under the compost heap, so could you get over and establish a presence? Keep the village police eager beavers from playing cops, sticking everything not nailed down into Baggies. You know how they can fuck up a crime scene. Thanks, pal.

. . . Well, I felt a certain gratitude toward Sy Spencer.

I walked Lynne out to her car and kissed her goodbye. "Sorry, but this one sounds like it's going to totally screw up our weekend."

She squeezed my hand and said, "Come on. I'm an old pro by now. I just feel awful about your brother's boss. What a shock!" Then she added, "I love you, Steve."

I thought: This woman is going to be a wonderful wife. A terrific mother. So I said, "I love you too."

A homicide would be a snap compared to this. Which shows you how much I knew.

The night was as beautiful as the day had been. But neither the moon that rose four hours later nor the floodlights from the Emergency Services truck shining on the crime scene could make cheerful what was, in fact, gruesome: a corpse.

Although a corpse in a spectacular setting. Sy Spencer's lifeless body sprawled facedown on his tile deck. These were no ordinary exorbitantly priced tiles; about one out of every five of the deep-blue squares was hand-painted with a different fish, all of them too fashionably thin and richly colored to truly exist in Long Island coastal waters. But as some New York exterior decorator probably explained to Sy, they combined an oceanic motif with tongue-in-cheek chic.

The pool itself was long, luminous aqua. In the cool night air, a mist, like a rectangular cloud, hovered over the water. Sy's graceful, sprawling gray-shingled house, built in the early twenties, in that lost era of huge families and happy servants, rose up three stories high behind the pool. If you turned the other way, you saw soft sand and the Atlantic.

"How's your beautiful bride-to-be?" Sergeant Ray Carbone asked me. We were standing right near Sy's head. Carbone wore a blue serge suit and Clark Kent glasses. With his small frame, potbelly and hunched-over back, he looked more like an overtaxed accountant than a disguised Superman.

"Still beautiful," I said.

"She's a lot more than beautiful. Rita and I were talking about you two the other day. Lynne gives you just what you need. Stability. Stability's the name of the game."

"For me, it has to be."

"Don't think I was talking about the drinking."

"It's okay. You can talk about it."

"As far as I'm concerned, that's history. Look, I know there's no such thing as a re*cov*ered alcoholic. You're always recover*ing*—for the rest of your life. But, Steve, you were classic emotionally labile." Carbone, who had a master's in forensic science, was going for a second one, in psychology. "You'd be Mr. Nice Guy, and then you'd become so withdrawn—like no one was home inside—and then you'd start with the belligerence. But the past few years: what a difference! You're as solid as they come. Trust me. You don't have to worry."

"No. I always have to worry."

"Wrong. But you know what? Your not being complacent is a sign of wellness." That's what happens to a guy after twenty-four credits at the State University at Stony Brook. "Actually," he went on, "what I meant by stability was a fire in the hearth. Good company. A nice bowl of soup. We need something normal, healthy to come home to after what we have to look at." Twenty-four credits couldn't entirely knock out Carbone's basic common sense.

A technician from ID elbowed his way past us, knelt down beside Sy, and slipped bags over the lifeless hands. (Paper bags. In movies, they use plastic. Scary when the camera moves in close, those lifeless hands wrapped like last week's Oscar Mayer pimento loaf. Very visual. But very phony: we never use them. Plastic traps moisture and screws up any chance of doing an FDR test, to see if the victim fired a weapon.)

"What did you find inside?" I asked Ray.

"Nothing. No signs of robbery, no violence. Sy had packed a carry-on bag to go to L.A. for some meetings. There was an unmade bed in the guest room. He could have taken a nap." The button on Carbone's too-snug suit jacket popped open. Not counting his midsection, he was thin. But his clothes were always a size too small for his basketball of a belly. "The cook was downstairs the whole time," he continued. "Nice lady. She gave me a bowl of clam chowder, the red kind. She's making something now for all the guys. All she heard was the shots. Nothing before that."

"Nothing after?"

"No. She looked out the window, saw Sy, ran out to him, saw he was dead. The way his head was turned, she could see that one eye, open." We both glanced down. The hood of Sy's bathrobe was pulled back far enough that you could see his quarter profile and a bit of his hair: short, tight gray curls, cut middle-aged-gladiator style. The one eye that was visible was wide open. Because of the position of his head, the eye stared downward, as though it had found a hideous flaw in one of the fancy fish tiles. "She called the village police."

"From the portable phone?"

"No. She said she knows not to touch anything near a murder victim. She went into the kitchen."

Okay, I thought, what kind of homicide do we have here? Not a heat-of-the-moment crime of passion, a murder arising out of jealousy or a family quarrel. And so far there was nothing to indicate a felony murder, a killing that occurs during the commission of another crime, like a burglary.

I knew I should hang on for forensic results—the autopsy report with photographs and videos, the toxicology and serology reports—but there I was, itching to figure out what kind of a guy/gal (I'm an equal-opportunity detective) the perpetrator was.

Well, it was easy to figure out that this killer wasn't some impulsive jerk who, in a moment of madness, grabbed a stake from the flower garden and turned Sy into a human shish kebab. No, this killer was extremely well organized, bright enough to plan the murder, bring his own weapon and take it away with him. His getaway had been slick too: completely uneventful. Judging from the lack of any physical evidence so far, he hadn't gotten rattled.

Another thing that struck me—from the first minute I saw Sy—was that although the killer had a brain, he had no heart. I always notice how the perpetrator treats the victim; it tells so much. This one didn't seem like any psychopath. I knew I'd have to wait for the autopsy, but it didn't seem like there would be mutilation—no sicko ritualistic marks, no deranged slashing. So he was heartless but no sadist; there was no need to terrify, no gun shoved in the victim's mouth or gut or genitals. Sy had been shot from a distance, from behind, impersonally.

But just as there were no indications of cruelty, there were no signs of decency either: no concern, no remorse. The killer had not covered Sy's face, or closed that awful, staring eye, or picked a flower and tossed it toward the body.

Of course, it could be a stranger murder, a nut case unknown to Sy. "You hear about anybody else getting taken out this way?" I asked Carbone. I did my homework if I was in the mood; he always did his. If there was a serial killer operating within fifty thousand miles of Suffolk County, he'd have read about it. "Rich people? Movie people? People shot from a distance?"

"I'll check with the FBI, but I don't think so. Unless this is number one."

"We've got a cool cookie here," I observed. "An organized fucker." We'd wait for the post-offense behavior, to see if it was a Son of Sam–type wacko who'd want to declare his genius to the police. "Good shot too. Got to give him credit."

"So what do you think the weapon was?"

"Low-gauge rifle?" I asked the ballistics guy, who was standing a couple of yards away, opening his case.

He nodded. "Looks like a .22."

Carbone muttered: "Damn. That's not going to make our life easy."

He was right. Here on the South Fork, .22s were a dime a dozen. Everybody had one; locals used them for target practice, small-varmint shooting. Or anything. If a farmer wanted to kill a pig, he'd get out his .22; my father had owned one.

"What background were you able to get on this Sy guy?" Carbone asked me.

"Fifty-three years old. Dartmouth College graduate. From a rich family—kosher provisions business. The ones with that commercial where they all sit around the kitchen table in crowns: 'Bologna for the Royal Family!' But it sounds like he wasn't all that turned on by lunch meats. He wanted culture. He started a big poetry magazine, *Shower of Light,* about twelve years ago. Put a pile of money into it. But then he seemed to have decided that poetry wouldn't get him what he wanted."

"What was that?"

"Who the hell knows? What do most guys want? Excitement. Fame. Fortune. Superior ass. I mean, who would you rather hit on, a receptionist in a pastrami factory or a poet? Or a movie star?" Carbone the Thoughtful looked like he was actually beginning to contemplate the alternatives. "Ray, the answer is: Movie star with giant boobs."

"I don't like those big, big ones," he said, thoughtfully.

"What do you like? A girl who looks like she's got two Hershey's Kisses glued on her chest?"

"No, but you see a young girl with giant ones, you figure that when she's thirty-five . . ." He shook his head in sadness.

"When she's thirty-five," the ballistics guy interrupted, "you trade her in for two seventeen-and-a-half-year-olds." He chuckled at his own wit, then added: "Move back a little, out of my way."

"Anyway," I continued, as we moved back, "all along, Sy Spencer was pretty much a man-about-town, one of those people who pop up now and then in the gossip columns. No dirt: just some guy with major bucks who gave money to the right causes, went to all those jet-setty charity benefits. That seems to be where he met the movie types who have houses out here. And he got it into his head that he wanted to be a movie producer. Apparently, so do half the people in his world. But he got what he wanted."

"You know, I've heard his name. Good movies, right?"

"No doubt about it. The guy had class."

"So, Steve. Gut reaction."

"It's going to be a media circus. Plus a major pain because we're dealing with hotshots who expect heavy-duty ass-kissing: 'No, thanks, sir, I don't drink while I'm on duty,' when they offer us the cheap-shit Seagram's they've been keeping from before they became famous. And—unless we get lucky in the next seventy-two hours and find someone in Sy's life stroking a warm .22—it's going to be an absolute bitch to crack. Sy was the ultimate fast-track guy; he probably had fourteen Rolodexes, and those were just for personal friends."

"Where would you start?"

"The movie he was producing, I guess. It's called *Starry Night*. They're shooting it over in East Hampton now."

"No kidding! *Now?*"

Having spent my whole life being local color in what people called the Fashionable Hamptons, I was used to rubbing shoulders with celebrities. Well, not exactly rubbing. But from the time I was a kid, besides the regular rich and semi-rich summer people, there'd be famous models squeezing tomatoes at a farm stand, or TV anchormen picking out a toilet plunger in the hardware store in town—right next to you. We knew to pretend they were just plain people, but we also knew it was okay to ogle as they paid the cashier. Neither they nor we wanted them so plain as to be overlooked.

But Carbone came from the *plain* plain world, suburban Suffolk County, a world peopled by ex–third-generation Brooklynites—shoe salesmen and IRS auditors and junior high school social studies teachers—a world that, if plopped down outside downtown Indianapolis or Des Moines, would not seem an unnatural part of the landscape. "East Hampton's only—what?—ten, twelve miles away," he was saying. His eyes were lit by a starry sparkle. "We may have to go over there to question some people on the movie set." Carbone was normally so levelheaded, so thoughtful, you'd think he'd have been glitz-proof, but at the thought of Lights! Camera! Action! he was loosening his tie, unbuttoning the top button of his shirt. If there'd been a straw hat and cane, he'd have grabbed them and high-stepped over to East Hampton, belting out "Hooray for Hollywood." "Who's starring?" he asked, much too casually.

"Lindsay Keefe and Nicholas Monteleone."

"No kidding!" Then, fast, he switched back to his I'm-a-regular-guy mode. "I always liked him," he said. "Reminds me of a young Gary Cooper. Good without being a goody-goody. And she's a good actress." Carbone shook his head in sadness. "But too left-wing for my taste."

"With her body, do you care what her position on disarmament is?"

Suddenly it hit Carbone. "Is Lindsay Keefe *here?*" he asked, his voice a little hushed with awe. "In the house?"

"Upstairs, with her agent. You didn't hear her? He's trying to calm her down."

"Can you believe it? I was *in* there, interviewing the cook. I didn't even know she was here, in the same house."

"The agent brought her back from the set. Heavy-duty hysterics." Carbone's eyebrows began drawing together in sympathy, so I added: "Let's not forget she's an actress. Anyway, according to the agent, for the last six months Lindsay's been living with Sy.

Here, and he has a duplex on Fifth Avenue. They're madly in love. Perfect relationship. Never a harsh word between them. Blah, blah, blah. The usual. Oh, and they were going to get married the minute the movie was finished."

"You believe the agent?"

"He's not a slimeball. He's an older guy named Eddie Pomerantz. Late sixties, early seventies. You can't miss him. A color-coordinated hippo: pink polo shirt and forty-eight-waist pink madras slacks. He was the one Sy was on the phone with when he was killed. Claims they were discussing some minor problem about photo approval. A movie star gets to approve any picture before it's handed out to the press, and Pomerantz said someone on this movie slipped a shot of Lindsay drinking coffee with her hair up in curlers to *USA Today* and she started crying when it got published because it's detrimental to her career to be seen in hair curlers." I shook my head. "For this the guy gets ten percent. Anyway, Pomerantz said he heard two shots over the phone."

"You buy his story?" Carbone asked.

"I buy that he heard two shots. He sounded pretty definite on that. But he kept eating nuts like a fucking maniac. There was a giant bowl of nuts on the table in the library or den or whatever it's called, and he must have glommed two pounds of pistachios in five minutes. I was going to tell him not to eat potential evidence, but he was such a nervous wreck I didn't have the heart. He was upset about Sy, and *very* worried about his client."

"Could it be normal professional concern?"

"Could be."

"Listen, in this situation, concern would be an appropriate response. You know and I know and this Pomerantz must know that murder may mean publicity, but in the long run, being the mistress of a homicide victim isn't going to help anyone's career." I nodded in agreement. "What's the matter? Do you think he's afraid of something specific?"

"Couldn't tell. But we've got to consider if this business is in any way related to Lindsay Keefe. A jealous ex-boyfriend. Or some jealous ex-girlfriend of Sy's who got pissed off that Lindsay came into the picture."

"And we have to find out if things were really that hunkydory between Sy and Lindsay," Carbone said.

"Yeah. Maybe Sy did something so terrible she felt she *had* to kill him."

"Like what?"

"How should I know, Ray? Maybe he left dental floss with last night's corn on the cob on the sink. Who the hell knows what sets people off, makes them kill? Do you?"

"No."

"Me neither. Maybe it was just something boring, like Sy was getting it on with the script girl."

"You can't wait to start with the hypotheses, can you, Brady?"

"No. Now listen: someone on this movie besides Lindsay might have had a grudge. Or from some other movie. Or it could have been a cold-blooded hit. We've got to find out what kind of life Sy had—beyond his movie life. Did he gamble? Was he cooking the books? Into weird sex? Doing drugs?"

A video tech stepped in front of us and, walking around Sy's body, aimed his camera on the white robe. Then he zoomed in on the two small splotches: the one on the hood, where a bullet entered just above Sy's brain stem, and another by his left shoulder blade.

"You'd never think of a man like Sy as a victim of anything," Carbone mused. "He seems like the ultimate winner."

"I know. Look at all this," I said, glancing around the pool area.

White wood tubs overflowed with trailing ivy and deep-purple flowers that gave off a light, spicy scent: nothing too perfumy, nothing too obvious. The chaises lay back, deep, welcoming. Small stone tables were carved like diving fish. You'd put your drink on the tail. White umbrellas on bamboo poles stood tall, like giant parasols. Almost-invisible quadraphonic speakers peeked up from the velvet grass.

"Ray, I bet your wildest fantasy isn't as good as what Sy

actually had. What was missing that any reasonable man could want?"

Carbone started mulling it over, probably thinking something like a cohesive family unit or Self-knowledge.

What I was thinking was: If Sy had stuck with kosher salamis and not had all his dreams come true, would he now be alive, dressing for dinner, buttoning a three-hundred-dollar sports shirt, or sticking his pinkie into the salad dressing to check whether his cook was using enough basil or chives or whatever this month's most fabulous herb was? Why, on this splendid summer night, was Seymour Ira Spencer, the Man Who Had Everything, playing host to a bunch of cops who were swabbing between his toes, tweezing fluff off his bathrobe and cracking Lindsay Keefe tit jokes over his dead body?

Look at a map. Long Island resembles a smiley but slightly demented whale. Its head—Brooklyn—butts against Manhattan, as if trying to get into some hot party from which it was deliberately excluded.

But unlike bubble-brained Brooklyn, the whale's body wants no part of the high life. Queens, Nassau and suburban Suffolk County just swim, eternally, in the bracing waters between the Atlantic and Long Island Sound, yearning to reach mainland America. See how the whale's hump arches up in longing? All it wants is to be part of the U.S. of A., where life resembles a Coke commercial.

Okay, now check out the rest of Suffolk County, the whale's forked tail. The tail isn't swishing a salute to either Manhattan or Middle America. No, it's raised high to greet Connecticut and Rhode Island. The East End of Long Island is, really, the seventh New England state.

See? On the North Fork of the tail, there are Yankee-style farms, fishing fleets and a few intensely quaint colonial villages that lack only a hand-carved "I am unspoiled" sign. And now look at the South Fork, my home. Our accents closer to Boston than the Bronx. Solid Anglo stock, augmented (most would say improved) by Indians, blacks, Germans, Irish, Poles and Others. More farms again. More cute towns. But unspoiled like the North Fork?

No, spoiled beyond comprehension.

For over a hundred years, artists and clods, geniuses and jerks, have been coming out here with their ways—and their money. To the Hamptons. "We summer in the Homp-tons," they say. Do they ever: in oh-so-social Southampton, don't-say-rich-say-comfortable Water Mill, bookish Bridgehampton, belligerently down-to-earth Sag Harbor, show-bizzy East Hampton, home-of-the-boring Amagansett (I think the last truly interesting person to live in Amagansett died in 1683) and I-am-one-with-the-sea Montauk.

This summer paradise isn't my South Fork, though; it belongs to men like Sy and to the legions of lesser New Yorkers who yearn to walk in his footprints in the sand. It is the Eden of the urbane: beach clubs, tennis clubs, yacht clubs, golf clubs; power breakfasts in the designated-chic local coffee shop, power softball games, power clambakes, power naps.

But along this narrow strip of trendy whale's tail, there are also hamlets called Tuckahoe and North Sea and Noyack and Deerfield. And there are people who neither know nor care that the copper beech is the Tree of Choice and the Japanese maple is Almost Out, or that duck is a passé poultry. There are people who are here not to vacation but to live lives: farmers, supermarket cashiers, dentists, welfare recipients, librarians, truckdrivers, short-order cooks, lawyers, housewives, carpenters, lobstermen, hospital orderlies. Oh, yes—and cops.

My name is Stephen Edward Brady. I was born in Southampton Hospital. A few days later, I went home with my mother to Brady Farm in Bridgehampton. It's still there. Not the farm, of course. My father sold everything but the farmhouse and two acres in 1955, a little more than a decade before the big land boom that would have made them rich, the only thing my mother had ever wanted to be.

I was born on May 17, 1949, to Kevin Francis Brady, farmer and (in the great South Fork tradition) drunk, and to Charlotte Easton (of the Sag Harbor Eastons) Brady, housewife and social climber. In 1951, my brother Easton was born.

I went to Sagaponack Elementary School, a one-room schoolhouse. (The summer people say: "I love it! It's so *real*." So okay, A for ambience. C − for education. B for freezing dampness that makes your fingers throb in the winter. And A + for smells from decomposing rodents under the foundation in late spring.) Then I went to Bridgehampton High. And then the State University of New York at Albany.

It wasn't that I'd been such a saint in high school, but at least I'd known who I was and that I'd belonged. Sure, I was a bad boy in Bridgehampton—a little driving while intoxicated, a little breaking and entering. In my heart I knew it was a phase, that someday I would become a solid citizen, buy back my father's farm, sit on the school board.

But I picked the wrong generation, and the wrong genes. Up at Albany, I became just another whacked-out asshole with sideburns. I embraced my generation's holy trinity: sex, drugs, and rock and roll. I was a true believer. I screwed and drank and drugged along with Jim Morrison and Jimi Hendrix and Janis Joplin. I didn't die, though. I flunked out.

So I enlisted in the United States Army. Why? To this day, I have no idea. I can't re-create the boy I was, the boy who could do something that dumb and self-destructive.

On my first day of basic, they clipped my hair with a machine that left it less than a quarter inch long. I remember standing at attention and having a five-foot-three Filipino drill sergeant reach up and grab those hairs between his thumb and index finger, pull at them, and scream up into my face, "Fucking hippie!" All I wanted to do was go home. I knew I wasn't man enough to take it. Except I had to take it. In those eight weeks, the army's goal is to break you down, then build you up again into a machine that obeys all commands without thought or argument. Well, they broke me down. I cried myself to sleep every night. There I was, a big guy, a soldier, boo-hooing into my pillow so that no one, especially all the other crybabies, could hear me.

But I went off to war an infantryman, a master of the M79 grenade launcher. I fought for God and America and the honor of the Brady bunch. No. Actually, I just fought to stay alive. I fought even harder not to feel alive. Feeling dead was a major asset in Vietnam. I moved on from hash and pot to smoking opium joints. And after about a month, skag.

Skag is heroin. Five or ten percent pure on the streets in the States. Ninety-six percent pure in Vietnam. No needles: cigarettes. You just had to inhale, so you weren't a junkie. We were all very clear on that. We were just a bunch of grunts sitting around smoking at night after a hard day's work in the jungle: a little patrolling, a little shooting, and then stacking up stinking dink corpses so we could get our body count and move on for more.

Skag was cheap: three bucks a hit. Skag was good for us grown-up G.I. Joes, better than pot, because pot makes time go very, very slow. Heroin lifts you out of your body, takes you out of time. It got me through those three hundred and sixty-five days in hell. No, I wasn't caught. If you had brains and a little foresight, you could get a buddy to pee for you and were home free. (Ha.) I was discharged, honorably.

I hadn't been doing skag every day. Just almost every day. I said to myself: You're not addicted. But when I landed back in the States after the eighteen-hour flight, I was sick—leg pains when we refueled in Guam, stomach cramps, the sweats in Hawaii. Terrible diarrhea the whole time, banging on the door of the airplane bathroom, doubled over, screaming at the top of my lungs: Please, oh God, let me in!

In San Francisco I had to buy heroin on the street. Three days, five hundred bucks. I couldn't handle a needle. The dealer had me wait in the basement of a burned-out grocery store; after the high started to wear off, I'd stand there shivering in the dark, my head twitching. I could smell the wet, charred wood and the decay, hear the deranged scurrying of rats. When there was a lull in his action, the dealer would clomp downstairs, hold a flashlight in his mouth and shoot me up. He had hunched shoulders and a thrust-forward turtle head, like Nixon. His damp, hot fingertips probed for a vein; there were crescents of green-black dirt under his nails. He told me: Don't expect me to keep doing this. This is a special introductory service.

It was that night I lucked out. I came up for air about two A.M. and ran right into a San Francisco P.D. street sweep. A big, mean-looking black cop grabbed me. He was about to pat me down when he took a second look and said, Army? I said, Yeah, and he said, You dumb piece of white shit, but instead of taking me in, he dropped me at one of those free clinics in Haight-Ashbury.

The clinic was run by a woman doctor. It took almost a week to get detoxed. Then I spent another two weeks in bed—with the woman doctor. Her name was Sharon. "Positive reinforcement," she called it. Sharon panted a lot; I kept feeling her hot, moist spearmint Certs breath. She always gazed deep into my eyes the second it was over. Aren't I *marvelous?* her eyes demanded.

Marvelous? Somehow I was getting it up and, apparently, getting it off. But my dick could have been Novocained; I swear to God I felt nothing.

By the end of the second week, Sharon was after me to go back to college—in San Francisco. Hey! I could move in with her! What a fabulous idea! Together we could bang our brains out! Detox the toxed! Refinish her floors!

I did not leave my heart—or any other part of me—in San Francisco. I was back home for Christmas.

Two days of my mother and brother, and I moved out. I needed a job. One of my buddies from high school had joined the Southampton Town P.D. No degree necessary. Decent pay. I applied, but there was a waiting list, so instead I joined the Suffolk County

P.D. I became Guardian of the Suburbs, Keeper of the Peace for the lawn-tenders and split-level dwellers.

I soon began showing my true Brady (as opposed to Easton) colors, popping a few beers a day. Then a six-pack. I was an alcoholic—not that I knew it—and an armed officer of the law. But hey, I was a terrific, ambitious cop. My job meant everything to me. In the beginning, I was even snowed by the dumb stuff: the uniform, the shield, the gun, the siren. Finally, I was part of something good. Law and order. With a little effort, I felt that my life, like Suffolk County, could be brought under control.

Mainly I worked. I spent my days off in Bridgehampton, picking up women and getting laid or watching the Yankees. (In an ideal world, it would have been both.) In eighteen years, I don't think I had a relationship that lasted longer than a month. I worked my way up to drinking two six-packs and half a fifth of booze a day. Scotch in winter, vodka in summer.

Like every other drunk, I was absolutely positive I wasn't a drunk. My mind was so sharp; I could give you every single stat from Thurman Munson's entire career. And at work, when I was on a hard case, I could lay off booze completely. Hey, I had no problem.

By 1984 I was a detective sergeant in Homicide. I was working eighteen, twenty hours a day. I'd go on the wagon and stay on for a couple of months; then I'd slide off. But I was good at hiding my drinking.

Finally, not good enough. Fourteen years after I'd been an alcoholic, someone in the department noticed that what even my friends had been calling my short fuse might be a bad drinking problem when I got into a fight with some guy from Missing Persons in the parking lot at headquarters in Yaphank. I pulled my gun, aimed and shot out his side mirror. I have absolutely no memory of it. They told me I started up because this guy had parked over the line, too close to my car, an indigo '63 Jaguar, E-type. It could go from zero to fifty in 4.8 seconds. I loved my car.

My commanding officer, Captain Shea, suggested a vacation at South Oaks, the department's favored drying-out spot. Vacation: They took away my suitcase and searched it; they strip-searched me; they took away my razor.

I was so scared. No one else there was. This was the place to see and be seen. Anybody who's anybody is drying out, all the hip guys and gals in sweatpants and slippers seemed to be saying. They all loved group; they loved to talk about their sodden daddies, their stinko moms. They couldn't wait to tell about waking up caked in their own vomit. They cried. They laughed. They hugged each other. They all seemed to think they were auditioning for the lead in their own TV bio-movie: *Debbie [or Marvin]: Portrait of a Long Island Alcoholic*.

I remember always being cold at South Oaks, and talking as little as I could get away with. But I thought all the time. I thought: My life is shit. All I have is work—death—my dick and TV. Listen, when you're sitting in a therapy session at a funny farm with seven substance abusers and a psychiatric social worker and you look back and realize that the highlight of the last decade of your life was getting cable so you could watch Sports Channel, you begin to realize you might be a little deficient in the humanity department.

I dried out at South Oaks. After I left, I stayed with AA. The department told me they wouldn't can me, but I would have to go back into uniform.

That was terrible. No, humiliating was what it was. Forget that I'd once been thrilled to be the boy in blue. Now I was a man. So what was I doing all dressed up like Mr. Policeman for Halloween? Was I doomed to endless, mind-numbing cruising in a patrol car for the rest of my life?

I fought like hell for half a year to get back into Homicide. Besides the Yankees, my work—putting together the puzzle— was the only thing I really cared about in the world, the only thing that made me feel alive. I finally made it back in, mainly because Shea and Ray Carbone knew they needed me and went to bat for me. But I lost my rank of sergeant. I was clearly not a leader of men. Shea said, "Bottom line, Brady. I don't give a rat's twat that alcoholism's a disease. That's your problem. If I hear you even walk within a mile of a bottle of anything, I'll bust your ass for good. Hear me?" Yeah, I said. Fair enough.

In January 1989, on my way home from an AA meeting, I met Lynne, age twenty-three, originally of Annapolis, Maryland, a teacher of learning-disabled kids at Holy Spirit Academy in Southampton, when I stopped to help her with a flat tire. Lynne was intelligent. Serious. Classy. Pretty. And competent: she really didn't need me to help her change the flat. And yes indeed, she was stable. On July 4, we got engaged.

There it is. *My Life*, by Stephen Edward Brady. Not precisely a sterling character. In fact, something of a not-so-good guy. Maybe even a bad guy. But a man who, like all men, holds within him the possibility of redemption. Right?

Anyway, my autobiography until that not-nice day when Sy Spencer was murdered and when I realized that—till death do us part—I would find peace and quiet and even happiness with Lynne.

But I might never have fun.

CHAPTER 2

"Come *on*," I urged the kid, hoping for an argument. "Sy and Lindsay were the perfect couple." Jesus, I wanted *life*. Believe me, I'd worked on enough homicides to know that the first interviews set the tone for the whole investigation. You had to charge up your sources; any passion—rage at the killer, outrage, grief, hostility to the police—was better than slack jaws and lead asses. I paced back and forth. "Sy Spencer and Lindsay Keefe. A brilliant show-business couple: successful, in love, making a great movie."

"No," Gregory J. Canfield whispered. He had actually uttered a word. That meant he was metabolizing. But it was hard to tell; he was about as animated as the average homicide victim. Gregory was Sy's personal production assistant, hired through some work-study deal with NYU film school. Poor guy: not only was his personality bordering on inert, but he was a born creep. He was the world's skinniest human being, and his tight maroon T-shirt, which clung to his rib cage, and his wide-legged shorts with pleats didn't help. Also, he had those spooky blue-white, almost colorless eyes, eyes that belonged to some slime-bellied animal that crawled along the sticky, grape-soda-splattered floors of dark movie theaters. "Uh, Mr. Spencer and Ms. Keefe—they weren't any Irving Thalberg and Norma Shearer." I could hardly hear him.

In comparison, my voice sounded overly strong—like an announcer on a toilet-bowl-cleaner commercial. "What are you saying? They weren't happy?"

"Maybe Lindsay Keefe told you something else, sir," Gregory J. Canfield mumbled. That seemed as close to authoritative as he could get. "But I think, you know, maybe they were headed for disaster."

"What do you mean? Personal disaster?"

"Well, um, more with the film. Maybe the personal stuff would follow." He bent down and ran his finger under a too-tight strap on his leg. He was wearing sandals, handmade things with leather thongs that crisscrossed up his stick legs.

"What was wrong with the movie?" I asked. But I'd lost him; his attention was riveted on Sy and the crime-scene crew. His eyes panned the activity and then bugged out for a close-up of a couple of ID apprentices who were unreeling a tape measure from the corner of the pool deck to the back of Sy's skull. Gregory's skin got a little green; he swayed: a potential fainter. "Let's move," I said, grabbing his shoulder and steering him away from the action, down toward the stillness of the dune heath. "Talk to me. That's it. Concentrate. Now, what makes you think *Starry Night* was in trouble?"

"Uh, the dailies. What they used to call the rushes. They weren't . . . good."

"Not good, or lousy?"

"Um, more than lousy. Actually, more than horrendous."

His head had swiveled back to watch an M.E. tech swabbing Sy's nose with a giant Q-tip. I turned him around so he was facing the ocean and held my hands up on the sides of his face for a second, like blinders. "Stop looking at all the cop crap, Gregory.

You're a movie guy, not a Homicide guy. You'll just make yourself sick. Now tell me about *Starry Night*."

"Lindsay was killing the film. You should have seen Sy's face after dailies: it went from disappointed to . . . traumatized."

"What did he say?" I asked.

"Uh, well, you see, nothing. He was very—how can I put it?—reticent."

"What do you mean? Reserved? Cold? Nasty?"

Gregory swallowed to clear his throat; his Adam's apple bobbled. "No. He just didn't . . . didn't respond. It wasn't one of those comfortable Gregory Peck silences, you know? More brooding De Niro—if De Niro was playing an Ivy League type. Something was going on underneath, but you weren't sure what. Anyway, Sy's secretary was staying in his New York office, so my job was to always be there for him: place phone calls, keep lists of whatever he wanted people to do, run errands back and forth to the set that his personal assistant—the assistant producer—was too important to do. I was in the house a lot, sometimes in the same room. But he never said anything to me unless it was some specific request. Like get a glass of Evian; he liked it plain, no lemon. Or find out what kind of flowers the costume designer likes, because Lindsay had gotten pretty nasty over a red lace teddy; Sy wanted to smooth things over."

"He never talked to you personally?"

"No. Just hello in the morning and goodbye when I left—if he wasn't on the phone."

"Did you ever see him angry?" Gregory shook his head. "Did you ever see him show any emotion at all?"

"Well, he'd laugh at someone's joke on the phone, that sort of thing. One time, when he was talking to someone who I guess was very important, he was doing William Powell. You know, roguish charm. But *nothing* else. Not while I was around, sir."

"Sounds like he must have been rough to work for."

"He was kind of like a combo William Hurt–Jack Nicholson.

Classy-scary-cold. I think if you had some value to him he could be very nice. But I had absolutely no idea if he liked me or hated me."

"But still, even though he didn't show emotion, you say you sensed he wasn't thrilled with the dailies?"

"Yes. The last couple of nights, he was white as a sheet after the lights came back on. He *had* to have known that Lindsay was running the film into the ground."

"But do you know that for a fact?"

"No. I could just . . . intuit it."

"Had Lindsay and Sy been fighting?"

"No direct confrontation. Not that I ever saw. But most of this week, the air was charged. I'm sure, with you being in Homicide, sir, you know better than most people that anger isn't always expressed verbally."

"Yeah, I know that. But if you're trying to sell me a charged-air theory, you've got to give me some substantiation. Come on now. How angry was Sy? How angry was Lindsay? Angry enough to have pumped two bullets into him?"

Down near the beach, there was just enough light from Emergency Services for me to see Gregory's white skeleton arms start popping goose bumps. "Please, Detective Brady, Ms. Keefe may have been wrong for this particular role, but I have the greatest respect for her not only as a performer but as a human being. I'm sure someone of her intellectual stature and—"

"Can it, Gregory! This isn't some NYU film school fucking seminar. Now, you'd been shooting the movie for three weeks. Isn't that early to know a picture's in trouble?"

"No. Everyone sensed it. You know how there's a feeling of intense community? Did you ever see *Day for Night?*"

"No. And don't tell me about movies or actors. Tell me about life."

"On the set, the cast and crew were just going through the motions, talking about all the other movies they'd worked on. Not about this one."

"But what about Lindsay Keefe? How could she stink? She's supposed to be one of the best actresses around, right?"

"She *is* a good actress. But her role calls for vulnerability under a brittle exterior. The *only* thing that came through in dailies was brittleness. And not sophisticated, Sigourney Weaver brittleness. Just hardness, shallowness. Very TV miniseries."

"You personally saw these dailies?"

"Yes."

"Well? Was she bad?"

"Yes, sir."

"Did Sy ever express displeasure over her, either to her or to you or to anyone else?"

"Not . . . really. But he was so circumspect, you never had any idea what he was thinking unless he specifically told you." Gregory hesitated. I couldn't tell if he was trying to come up with something—anything—to please me or whether he was honestly trying to remember something. But just then, Robby Kurz came sauntering down the lawn.

Detective Robert Kurz. Rain, shine, sleet, hail. Gunshot, strangling, knifing, poison. Man, woman, child. No matter what the conditions of a homicide were, Detective Robby lit up every crime scene with his big Howdy Doody smile, his endearing, snub-nosed face and the bright white light of his enthusiasm.

"Yo, Steve!"

"Hi." To get away from his relentless exuberance, I walked toward the beach, pretending I wanted to think. Naturally, Robby hurried after me.

Lucky for me, Robby was thirty. That provided some distance. I'd had almost ten years more on the force than he did. While he was still sitting in his patrol car, waiting for some commuter in Dix Hills to run a stop sign, I'd been the rising star of Homicide. In rank, having been busted, I was his equal. In fact, being lead detective, I was his superior.

He tried not to acknowledge it. Robby—despite the shiny

bald spot he tried to hide by combing his hair sideways and spraying it into paralysis, despite his desperately-eager-to-cheat wife (Mrs. Howdy Doody, with a silver heart dangling in her freckled cleavage) and, more important, despite his arrest record, which was, embarrassingly and unfortunately, almost triple his conviction record—had determined that he was the perfect cop. This notion filled him with pleasure; it was impossible to pass him in the john, on the stairs, at the coffee machine without getting a rapturous grin. Every morning he handed out bagels and crullers and Danish to the squad like the Pope bestowing blessings.

Robby stood beside me near the dune, one foot higher than the other, his body on an awkward slant. He was definitely not an outdoor guy; the security of Suffolk County—issue linoleum was vastly preferable to sand.

"What've you got?" I asked. I ran my hand over the spikes of some tall beach grass.

"Footprints on the grass near the house!" he enthused. "From rubber thongs. The regular, cheap kind. Mitch from the lab says they're a man's size ten or eleven, although obviously"—Robby paused, probably so I could prepare myself for a blast of deductive brilliance—"those kind of shoes can be worn by *anyone*. But if we can track them down—"

"Where exactly were the footprints?"

He pointed past the pool and the lawn, to the corner of the big porch that ran the entire length of the back of the house. I stretched my neck and squinted. A guy from the lab was straddling an area of grass right up against the house. He was just finishing photographing the footprints, getting ready to apply the dental stone we use for making molds of them.

At that particular corner, the crawl space, neatly covered in lattice, rose about five or six feet high, with the porch above it. From up on the dunes, not far from where we were standing, a hundred feet away, it would have been easy to spot a man with a rifle. But not from the house. Unless you were deliberately leaning over the porch rail, looking right down at the spot where lawn met lattice, someone with a .22 could probably crouch in the shadowy safety of the grand old house and you'd never see him.

"This could be *major* important!" Robby announced, nodding his head in agreement with himself. His sprayed hair didn't move.

But despite his excitement, I wasn't ready to have an orgasm over the footprints; good investigators shouldn't come too fast. I wanted to rule out all other possible explanations for the footprints before I wasted two days on a *major* thong hunt.

"See if you can get someone to check out the gardeners," I said to Robby. "Find out if any of them wore thongs. Also, take a look in Sy's closet. I didn't notice any in there when I did my walk-through, and I don't think he'd do anything like wear them, but this could have been the summer that guys like him decided K Mart was *très* amusing or some shit, and he'd have bought fifty pairs." I thought for a second. "Except maybe not a size ten or eleven. He was a little guy: little hands, little feet, probably little—"

I stopped before I even started. It was no fun being immature and dirty around Robby. His idea of humor was Polack knock-knock jokes. His concept of sex talk was to confide that he and Freckled Cleavage had gone on a marriage encounter weekend. "Anything else?" I asked him.

Robby grinned (boyishly) and fiddled with a cuff of his sports jacket, a shiny blue thing that had a half-belt stitched around the waist in back. He dressed as though he made an annual haberdashery pilgrimage to suburban Peoria. "There were hairs. In one of the guest bedrooms, although there weren't any guests."

"Were they all from Sy?"

"There was one pubic hair, probably his. Four head, someone leaning back against one of those wicker headboards. The hairs got caught."

"Any with roots?" With the new DNA typing, you can get a genetic make on someone from any cell with a nucleus. But to test hair, you need the follicle cells that cling to the root, and although you can sometimes make do with one, it helps if you have a clump of ten or twelve hairs.

"Complete roots on two of the head hairs from the headboard. They were *not* Sy Spencer's hairs, because they were black or very dark brown, and longish. He had short gray—"

"Yeah, I saw."

I'd also gotten a fast look at Lindsay Keefe when her agent had half escorted, half hauled her out of the car, and she'd been what I'd remembered from movies. Blond. In fact, the blondest.

"That's all you found?" I asked him.

"Come on," he said. He was so goddamn chipper. "You know how long it takes to get anything resembling an opinion from ID."

"So while you were inside with Carbone you didn't happen to ask if there were any live-in people who might have had a quickie in the bedroom? Maids, valets—that kind of thing?"

"Relax. Where are you going? To a fire? I was just about to ask about servants, but I thought I'd fill you in first." Robby paused. It had been three minutes since he'd displayed any disarming boyishness, so I got a lopsided smile. "Look, we both know this is a major case, Steve. I want the brownie points on this one— and so should you. If we can close this neat and fast, it could mean *big things*."

When you work with a bunch of cops, or any group of people, there are always some who are going to irritate you. Either with lousy character traits, like laziness, dishonesty, sloppiness, or just with irritating personal habits like teeth sucking, cuticle nibbling or superfluous grinning. But Robby wasn't awful. He wasn't hateful. Sometimes, like when he was talking sports, especially hockey, he could actually be interesting; nobody knew as much about the Islanders' offensive strategy as he did. And so what if behind all the smiles he was a self-righteous dick? I just steered clear of him.

But what I couldn't steer clear of was the fact that I thought he was a bad cop. And he thought he was Suffolk County's anointed Good Guy. Days, even weeks, before the assistant D.A.s felt they had a case, Robby would be pushing to arrest, because he *knew* who the bad guy was. And he was going to get him.

The smiles and the crullers he handed out to cops disappeared for suspects; most of his interrogations turned into finger-jabbing accusations. Sure, he could intimidate some kid into spilling his guts. But he'd alienate suspects other detectives had softened up, and instead of agreeing to a videotaped confession, they'd be screaming for a lawyer.

One time, my best friend on the squad, Marty McCormack, and I had a young guy whose new wife had disappeared. I knew— Christ, everybody knew—that he'd killed her and dumped the body. But how could we find out where? We played it as if this guy was the anguished husband; Marty kept him looking for his wife, thinking of possibilities where she could be. I kept him talking. One night, we stepped out for a bowl of chili and asked Robby just to come into the interrogation room and baby-sit. In the half hour we were gone, he came on tough. Hostile. Aggressive. He knew this was a bad guy. Who didn't? But he almost ruined it.

And I'd lost it when I found out, banging walls, calling him a stupid piece of shit in the squad room. "You almost fucking blew it!" I yelled. He'd said, "Just cut it out, Steve," and even managed a boyish shake of the head that said: Jeez, that Brady and his darn ole temper.

It wasn't that I hated him. We were just oil/water, fish/fowl, day/night. And so without making a big deal over it, we'd pretty much arranged our lives—and our desks—so we stayed apart.

Until Sy.

"Steve Brady!" Marian Robertson, Sy's cook, exclaimed. Then she made a twirling motion with her index finger. Spin around, boy, it said. And, obediently, I turned around so she could get the three-hundred-sixty-degree picture. "I can't say you don't look a day older than you did in high school," she went on, "though you are that same boy—but with a man's face. I said to myself the minute you walked in: 'That's the boy who was shortstop on Mark's team,' although I went blank on your name. I do see your brother. Easton Brady's your brother, right?" I nodded. "Such a handsome boy. Could be a movie star himself."

Mrs. Robertson babbled away with the absolute self-confidence that came with the conviction that she was the South Fork's Most Unforgettable Character. In fact, I'd totally forgotten her until I walked into Sy's kitchen.

And what a kitchen—especially if you were a big eighteenth century fan. Strings of garlic, wreaths of herbs, copper pots and straw baskets hung from the walls and the beams. An iron kettle hung in a six-foot-high brick fireplace; it was so gargantuan Sy could have played hide-and-seek in it.

Mrs. Robertson turned away from me to finish cutting the crusts off the sandwiches she was making for the crime-scene crew and began arranging them in a perfect, intricate pile: some creamy-colored cheese on the bottom, pale-pink pâté next, and then dark smoked ham, so the platter looked like a spiffy architectural model of a ten-million-dollar beach house. "Isn't this something?" she inquired. "One of my specialties. Anyway, Steve, the minute you showed me your badge, of course I remembered hearing you had become a policeman, although as you may imagine, between you and I and a lamppost, you were pretty near the last boy at Bridge-hampton High I'd expect to see in uniform, so to speak." She gave me a nose crinkle that (I think) meant: You may have a gun and a badge, but to me you're still a teeno with Clearasil dots. "I see being a detective you can wear regular clothes. Rank does have its privileges, and that's nice, because you are looking fit."

Marian Robertson looked the same as when she sat in the first row of the stands at every high school baseball game: dark-brown skin, short, with rounded features and a cute, pudgy body, as if, through interracial marriage, she was half sister to the Pills-bury Doughboy. The only change I could see was her hair; it looked like she'd slapped a gray wig on her head as a seventh-inning joke to give the Bridgies a laugh. Back in high school, she'd acted Unforgettable too, bringing cookies for "you young fellows," handing each of us a chocolate-chip or a pecan sandy as we trotted off the field, calling out, There's more where that came from!

"Mrs. Robertson, I know you gave your statement to Sergeant Carbone, but I have a couple more questions. What does the maid look like?"

"The maid? She's very plain." Mrs. Robertson opened one of the glass doors of the giant restaurant-style refrigerator, eyed the melons and took out an enormous beige ball that was probably a twenty-five-dollar, genetically engineered cantaloupe.

I glanced at my pad. "There's only the maid, Rosa?"

"That's right."

"Is she black, white, Hispan—"

"Portuguese." Marian Robertson cut me off. "Short, but taller than me. Maybe five foot two. You know, there used to be a song." She cleared her throat: " 'Five foot two / Eyes of blue / But oh what those five two can do . . .' Oh, Lord! Steve, that I'm singing! I apologize. How it must look! But I've been working for Mr. Spencer for fourteen summers, and it's so . . . Murdered!"

"Listen, you're upset. You have every right to be." I paused. "Were you very fond of him?"

"Well . . . fond enough. I mean, he was so polite. That's what everyone said: 'Sy is *so* divinely polite. *So* courtly.' You know how those Yorkers talk." I nodded; all of us who were born here shared the knowledge that we were more decent and more down-to-earth than the slickers from New York City. When you really came down to it, we knew we were better human beings. "Let me tell you, you can double the phoniness in spades for movie types. But Mr. Sy Spencer himself seemed to be genuine silk stocking—not at all flashy or fresh."

"But did you like him?"

"Well . . . now that I think about it, I'm not sure. He was one cool cucumber."

"Was he cold? Withdrawn?"

"No. Very toned down, but decent enough. Smiled a lot. Didn't laugh. Never treated me any different the first summer or the fourteenth. But it was like he had a script of how to act with a cook, and that was that. Teasing, like about how he was going to have to mortgage the house to pay for my chickens; I make a *very* rich chicken stock. But the same joke for fourteen years.

"And let's see. He was indeed polite: a compliment after every dinner party, and if he didn't like something, which was hardly ever, he wasn't rude. He'd just say, 'I am not entranced by chocolate-dipped fruit.' " She opened a plastic container and handed me a cookie. "Viennese almond wafer."

"Thank you. Getting back to the maid, Mrs. Robertson. What does she look like?"

"Short, like I told you. Yellowish skin, but with pockmarks, poor baby."

The cookie was good. I smiled. "What color is her hair?"

"My, are you handsome when you smile! You should smile more often. It lights up your face like a Christmas tree."

"Rosa's hair, Mrs. Robertson?"

"Originally, only the good Lord and her mother know, although my guess is your basic brown. For all the time she's worked here"—she shook her head sadly—"fire-engine red."

"And you and Rosa were the only people who work here? I expected valets or chauffeurs or butlers."

"No. He hired waiters and bartenders for dinners and parties. He had a driver in the city, but he took a helicopter out here and drove himself around in that Italian sports car of his."

I held out my hand for another cookie. As she gave it to me, I asked: "Who was in the guest bedroom today with Sy Spencer?"

"What?" She looked startled.

"Someone used the guest bedroom."

"Besides Mr. Spencer?"

"Yes."

"Really? I have no idea, Steve. You know, he and Lindsay Keefe were living together. But they're in the master suite. What makes you think someone was in the guest bedroom?"

I took another bite of the cookie. "Just some indications," I answered. "Did you hear anyone upstairs?"

"Only Mr. Spencer. He was here all afternoon, packing to go to Los Angeles, on the phone. He had been supposed to leave this morning, but then he had to go over to the movie set, so I guess he was changing a few plans."

"No one with him?"

"No." She thought for an instant and then added: "I mean, I won't cross my heart and hope to die, because to tell you the truth, you can count the times on one hand that I've been on the second floor of this house. But as far as I know, he was alone."

"Where was Rosa?"

"She cleans and does a laundry every morning, then goes home for the afternoon . . . she has a little girl. Takes whatever ironing. She comes back about six, to tidy up from my cooking—scours pots, damp mops the floor, takes out trash, that sort of thing. Then she stays through dinner and does the dishes and sets the table for breakfast."

"Mrs. Robertson, I don't want to embarrass you, but in a police investigation we have to ask some pretty direct questions."

"Go ahead."

"Was there any indication that Mr. Spencer had sexual relations in any other room beside the master bedroom?"

"I go home after dinner. So for all I know, he could be making hay in the sauna or in the screening room or in the wine cellar. All I can vouch for is not in my kitchen, because I would know in two seconds flat. *Nobody*, not the boss, not God himself, is allowed to mess with my kitchen. Got that, Steve?"

"Got it."

"Good."

*   *   *

Local cops—in this case the Southampton Village P.D.—secure the perimeter of a crime scene. One of them, a gangly kid my grandmother would have called a long drink of water, came into the tent on the far side of the pool where we were inhaling Marian Robertson's sandwiches. He called out: "Is there a Steve Brady on duty tonight?" I put down my mug of coffee. "A guy's out front. *Real* shook up about the murder. Says he's your brother."

So I went over to Ray Carbone to tell him about Easton's connection to Sy, even though I had to interrupt Carbone while he was lifting up a triangle of sandwich and eyeing it suspiciously, clearly having deduced that it was, in fact, pâté. "Can we talk outside for a minute?" I asked. He slid the sandwich back on the platter.

The green-and-white-striped tent we'd been in was a three-sided thing. I guess it was either for changing, if you were an exhibitionist, or for just lying out of the sun and wind. It was about ten feet away from the shallow end of the pool, a perfect distance for a police snack—far enough from the crime scene so that you wouldn't have to pretend Sy's body was a scatter rug while you were woofing down his food.

"Listen, Ray, my brother—his name is Easton—he's out front. He wants to see me."

"Let him come back, take a look," said Carbone. In the shadow of Sy Spencer's house, he'd suddenly become Long Island's most gracious host. He even did a be-my-guest sweep with his arm. Then he added: "Easton?"

"Yeah."

"What kind of a name is Easton?"

"My mother's from this Yank family up in Sag Harbor. It was her maiden name. They do things like that."

"I thought you were Irish."

"My father was Irish. About my brother—"

"What does he do?"

"A little bit of everything. Classy stuff."

"Like what?"

"He sold Jaguars. I bought mine from him. Then he sold expensive real estate. Worked in a bunch of hot-shit boutiques around here."

"Sounds as if he never settled into a defined role. How come?"

"I'm a borderline personality myself. How the hell should I know what's wrong with anybody else?" Over in the tent, the men were still swarming around the table laden with Sy's food. "Ray, put a lid on the psychoanalysis for now. I want to get this over with. It has to do with the case."

"The case? Your brother?"

"Yeah. I mentioned the connection when Headquarters called, but I forgot to tell you. Easton was working for Sy. Listen, about three, four months ago he was out of a job: not exactly news. Anyway, he heard about how Sy was going to be making a big part of *Starry Night* in East Hampton, so he wangled an invitation to some jazzy charity party. To make a long story short, he got introduced to Sy and made a big pitch about how he'd been born and raised here and knew everybody and could be helpful. Sy liked him and hired him to be a kind of liaison with the locals— I guess to spread a little money around and keep things happy and get things ready for filming. He did so well that Sy kept him on for the movie."

"Any problems?"

"No. It was really working out. That's the shitty thing; my brother finally seemed to have found something he was enthusiastic about, plus something he was actually good at. Sy had even made him one of the assistant producers, with his name right up there. Not at the beginning, but at the end when you see all those names. Anyway, sooner or later someone will be taking his statement. I'm just letting you know about him because the department's so big on all that ethics crap."

"Well, maybe let Robby take it." I guess he saw my face. "Steve, Robby's not a bad kid. Okay, too bright-eyed and bushy-tailed for your taste."

"He has no balance."

"He has enough, and if not, you'll make up for it. Robby is with you on this one. You'll see, it'll work out. He's really gung-ho. Anyway, it looks better if someone who isn't your closest friend takes care of your brother. But listen, I have no objection if you want to sit in the background. Quietly." He paused. "Is your brother, you know, a stable guy?"

"No. He's a demented twit who took a .22 and blew Sy Spencer away because Sy had become his mentor—father figure and Easton has such a low sense of worth that anyone who respected him and helped him self-actualize was ipso facto worthless and had to die."

I'm not bad. Easton is handsome. Although we resemble each other, I look like an Irish cop and he looks like an Episcopalian lawyer. In other words, my brother is a WASPier, more refined version of me: his eyes a truer blue, his jaw more squared-off, his hair shinier, plus he actually is six feet. I'm just a shade under, which has always annoyed me because girls—women—always ask "How tall are you?" and if I say six feet I feel like a fraud, but if I were to say five eleven and five-eighths, I'd feel like a buffoon.

Easton was standing in the gravel driveway, not far from the stairs that led to the front door. He wasn't in one of his typical getups: a bright-colored blazer, or a pale-pastel sweater, looking more the leisured Southampton aristocrat than the real ones ever did. He was wearing a dark-gray suit with an impeccable paisley tie. His cordovan shoes, illuminated by the unobtrusive low beams that lit the circular driveway and entrance, were brighter than his face. Upset? Even in the dim light I could see he was very upset. Skin waxy. Eyes red not so much from crying but, as I saw as I came up to him, from rubbing them, as if in disbelief.

"Hey, East," I said. He jumped. "You okay?"

"Sorry. Do you know what's so odd? Here I am, actually waiting for you, hoping you were here, but my mind was going in ten different directions at once, and just now, when I heard your voice, my first thought was: What the hell is Steve doing at Sy's house?"

"When did you hear about what happened?"

"When I got back from New York. I drove there today, to do some odds and ends for Sy, and when I got home, there was a call on my machine. From this perfectly awful film school type who's his P.A. Production assistant. Something like: 'Um, uh, you might wish to know that Mr. Spencer was, like, murdered at his home.' " All of a sudden Easton stopped talking. He got the shakes. "Damn. It's nippy," he managed to say. Like my mother, Easton used words like 'nippy' instead of 'cold' or 'cool' or 'chilly,' words to distinguish him from the proles. "Oh, good God." He rubbed his arms, but it didn't help. Then his teeth started to chatter, fast, like those stupid wind-up teeth in novelty stores.

"Did you speak to Sy today, East?"

"Last night."

"Any indication of trouble?"

"No."

"Had any threats been made against him that you know of?" He shook his head in answer—and in disbelief. "Do you have any reason to think he was afraid of anything, or anyone?"

"No."

"Any change at all in his behavior?"

He couldn't stop shaking. "He was fine, I'm telling you." For my brother, trembling was the absolutely perfect, tasteful way to fall apart: so proper. It didn't make any noise, and unlike sweating or barfing, you could have your breakdown and then go right on to a cocktail party without messing up your clothes and having to change.

"They can get your statement tomorrow. Why don't you go home? You look pretty shitty."

"I don't even know why I'm here." He glanced up at the house. "Actually, I suppose I thought I should show up. In the back of my mind I was thinking: With all the chaos—police, God knows what else—maybe I can give Sy a hand. It's an insane reaction, but Steve, I have to tell you, this is such a shock. I mean, to get that message."

"It must have been a real kick in the nuts."

"It knocked the wind out of my sails. I can't believe it. Who in God's name would murder Sy?"

"Who do you think?"

"No one would want to kill him," Easton announced. He was positive. He stuck his hands in the pockets of his New York City fancy pants.

"The facts seem to indicate otherwise, don't they?"

"Probably a burglar."

"No."

"How do you know for sure?"

"What are you talking about? It's my job to know."

"And you're never wrong, are you?"

As usual, after more than sixty seconds in each other's company, we were into our regular sibling routine—being irritated by each other. I decided this was one time I should be unirritated. More than that. He was my brother. He was genuinely upset; I should be gentle.

"There doesn't seem to be any evidence of a burglary attempt," I said, as softly as I could.

"How was he killed?"

"Shot. From some distance. Most likely with something like a .22. It doesn't look like an impulsive act." We had a long moment of silence. "Listen, one of the other guys will interview you, probably tomorrow. Go on home."

He shivered again. "He was really good to me."

"Yeah. Listen, I'm sorry. Oh, East, one more thing. Forget fights, threats. Did Sy give any indication that he was having problems with anybody?"

To give him credit, my brother really seemed to think about it. "I've only been working with him for three and a half months. I can't set myself up as an expert. But from what I've seen, when you're producing a movie, you have problems with *everybody*.

You're dealing with a cast and crew of a hundred prima donnas—
and their agents, and their unions. And then you have the moneymen, who always make life a living hell. A producer has to be
tough-minded—and tough. And Sy was. He never backed off from
a confrontation. He just kept going." A small, affectionate smile
passed over Easton's face for a second. "Sy was like a steamroller.
He wouldn't stop. You either moved or got crushed. At some point,
just about everyone involved probably told him, or wanted to tell
him: Drop dead."

"Son of a bitch!" Carbone blew up in front of me and Robby Kurz.
He was yelling about Eddie Pomerantz, Lindsay's agent, now safely
on his way home, who, two minutes earlier, had informed him that
Lindsay had taken a couple of Valium and was out like a light,
but who then admitted, when Carbone started screaming at him,
that she'd had four or five. Possibly six, although he wanted it
clearly understood that his client was seriously not into drugs.
Carbone explained to us: "I had that doctor from the M.E.'s office—the one with the Dumbo ears—go up to her room. He says
she could be genuinely knocked out for more than eight hours.
Passive-aggressive bitch."

We sat in Sy's office, a room on the second floor that had
probably been a kid's bedroom. You knew it was an office because
there was a phone with so many buttons that it looked like it could
launch a satellite, and a small computer. But that was it for modern
stuff. The rest of the room looked like some fish-crazy English
gentleman's study: there was a stuffed marlin on the wall, some
washed-out paintings of salmon leaping out of the rapids, a bunch
of gleaming, never-used rods, perfectly, casually arranged in a
corner.

Carbone scanned his notepad. "Now listen, no matter when
we get out of here tonight or tomorrow morning, I want both of
you back at ten to interview Lindsay Keefe. I'll probably be stuck
in a meeting with Shea on how to handle this thing. This thing's
bigger than *Newsday*. It's national. International. Now, Robby,"

Carbone went on, "before ten, get what you can from Steve's brother, Easton. Then meet Steve here, for Lindsay. After you're through with her, you work on Sy's business associates. First from this movie. Then start working back.

"Steve, you concentrate on all the nonbusiness-type movie people. Oh, and his women. Look into if he was currently involved with anyone besides Lindsay. And check his ex-wives. He had two of them. One lives in Bridgehampton, so maybe you can get to her before ten." He glanced down to his pad. "Bonnie Spencer."

I shook my head. It sounded vaguely familiar, but I was sure it wasn't anyone I'd actually met.

"A movie writer." He handed me a piece of paper with an address. "You know where it is?"

"About two minutes from where I grew up."

"The other ex lives somewhere in the city. She was the first, and we'll have a name and address on her by tomorrow. All right? We'll use Southampton Village's squad room as a command post for the next day or two. I'll meet up with the two of you as soon as I can get out here tomorrow." He stopped, looked right at me, and sighed. "I think this is going to be it. The case where I find out that I'm too old for this kind of work."

I stood in Sy's gym, talking to Lynne from his wall phone. All the not-fun stuff I'd been bugging myself about since the afternoon now seemed stupid. Engaged-guy nerves, a last-ditch defense of bachelorhood. Because, objectively, Lynne was so terrific.

One of the things that had always knocked me out about her was that she acted as though I had a normal, not-terribly-exciting job. I could be a manager of an Aamco transmission franchise. She deliberately did not focus on what I actually did. I understood why; homicide is the ultimate breakdown of law and order, and Lynne's whole life, as a teacher and as a person, was dedicated to being constructive. She was there to give someone a chance, not take it away. Murder wasn't exciting. It was sinful, and it was also outrageously unfair. In the deepest sense, killing wasn't nice.

Another thing: despite her career and her really astonishing competence, she was enough of a traditional female not to want to hear the details of a fatal beating, or how the scalp is peeled back from the skull during an autopsy. So she concentrated not on the subject of my work—the dead and how they got that way— but on the living.

So we were not chitchatting about the murder, other than the briefest summary of what had happened and where I was. Instead, we were talking people. We'd done thirty seconds on how Carbone managed to be an intrusive pain in the butt and a terrific guy at the same time, a minute and a half on why I couldn't stand Robby, and now we were on to my brother.

"Did you say anything like: 'Gee, Easton, I'm sorry about Mr. Spencer. I know how much you liked him and how important he was in your life'?"

"Don't bust my chops, Lynne."

Except for the floor, the entire gym was mirrored. I was the only thing in the room that didn't gleam. Besides a stationary bike, a treadmill and one of those stair-climbing things—all with glowing red or green digital displays—there was a bunch of Nautilus equipment. I stood up straighter; either Sy had a lot of vanity to work out in front of all those mirrors, or he needed tremendous incentive.

"Steve," she said patiently, "did you say anything at all to comfort your brother?"

"Yeah. I said I was sorry."

"That's all?"

Just when I thought I looked okay in one mirror, I'd see my reflection in another. I pulled my shoulders back. I knew I didn't have a gut, but in the ceiling mirror I seemed to, so I sucked it in. "Don't get on me about Easton now. I just called to say good night and I love you."

"Well, good night and I love you too. It's just that I know how much you want a decent relationship with him. Wouldn't this be the perfect time to reach out?"

I told her I guessed it was, and then we did the good night

and I love you business again because I'd been on with her for almost five minutes and wanted to get back.

After we hung up, I lay down on the gray-carpeted floor and closed my eyes for about ten seconds, probably my total rest for the next forty-eight hours. I know it was sentimental—and probably inaccurate—to say Lynne had saved me, but I really felt she had. Sure, I'd been staying sober with AA. And since getting back into Homicide I was working better than I ever had before.

But by the time I met her, I was feeling scared. I was standing all alone, no crutches. No booze. No drugs at all. Two months after I got out of South Oaks, I got the flu. I sweated out a hundred-and-four-degree fever rather than risk becoming a Tylenol junkie. Hardly any women either: I had lost almost all desire. In the old days, almost anything that produced estrogen could get me going if I was in the mood to get going, but most of the time now I couldn't seem to find anybody who made me want to unbuckle my belt. And yeah, there was football—the Giants, who I liked a lot. But no Yankees: it was January. I was running at least five miles a day to stay in shape and get that chemical going in the brain; I forget the name of it, but at South Oaks they told us it was the body's natural narcotic and was okay. Running ten, twelve, sometimes fifteen miles on my days off, to get that high—and to exhaust myself because I was nervous about what I'd do with too much time and energy.

See, at the funny farm the shrink talked to me about what deep down I always knew—or, if I didn't know, sensed. That the drinking and the drugs and the womanizing were all pretty much the same thing, part of what he called my self-destructive pattern. Sure, I had been going for the high, but (a big but) the high hadn't been my real goal. What I'd really been searching for all that time was to feel nothing. Oblivion.

So there I was, finally, trying to turn my back on oblivion, to face the world, to take one day at a time.

But all that summer and fall, after those first heady years of sobriety, I started having nightmares: I was drinking again. I'd wake up from a dream about taking a bottle of icy, syrupy vodka out of the freezer, pouring it—almost against my will—and taking a deep, desperate sip. I'd feel panicked, sick to my stomach with despair. Because I knew how fragile my stability was. And I also knew I wasn't a resilient kid anymore. If I lost my grip again, I could fall into a bottomless pit, and I wouldn't have the strength or the courage to try and climb back out. I would be lost for good. I would die. Talk about oblivion.

And suddenly there was Lynne, standing by the trunk of her car, assembling the jack. She was cautious as I pulled over, but she looked me right in the eye and said, "Thanks. I can handle it." I showed her my shield and told her that was fine with me; I'd hang around and watch. I liked watching women change tires.

She handed me the jack, and when I finished I took her out for a hamburger. All of a sudden, I found I was having a genuine, normal conversation. Not just talking to a woman to prove I wasn't only out to screw her. Real discussion. About the emotional problems kids with dyslexia can get. About whether a person's body language can make them more or less likely to be the victim of a crime. About public schools versus Catholic schools. And about how I was an alcoholic.

And two weeks later, we went to bed. I lay there afterwards and thought: Oh my God! I'm having a *relationship*.

CHAPTER 3

onnie Spencer's dog barked with joy: Hiya, hiya, wonderful
to see ya! Its tail made giant circles of jubilation: Whoopee!
We got company! It was a huge, happy thing, like a fat, black
English sheepdog.

"Steve Brady," I called out, and flipped open my ID.

Her dog interrupted its woofing only long enough to lick my
hand and my shield: Hiya! Love ya! But Bonnie Spencer stood
silent and motionless in her front doorway—and gaped. It was
seven forty-five, the morning after her ex-husband had been murdered. She obviously hadn't been expecting condolence calls; she
was wearing turquoise second-skin biking shorts, a huge, shapeless
faded pink cotton T-shirt and sweat socks. A pair of sneakers
dangled from her hand, as if she'd been about to put them on for
a run.

"I'm a detective with Suffolk County Homicide," I added.

Her lips rounded as if she was going to say Oh!, but she
didn't. She didn't do anything, not even glance at my ID. She

simply gawked. "Bonnie Spencer?" The dog poked her leg with its snout, as if to say: Come *on*, talk to the guy. But she didn't.

I put my ID away, stuck my hands into my pockets. Even though it was a warm, end-of-summer morning, the moist, leafy smell of fall was in the air. Bonnie Spencer didn't seem to want to look at me; instead, she seemed mesmerized by my car in her driveway. Listen, the '63 XKE is a truly great car, but when there's a detective from Homicide on your doorstep first thing in the morning, that should be the attention-grabber. "Are you Bonnie Spencer?" I repeated.

She blinked, shaking off her daze. Her eyes brightened. "Am I Bonnie Spencer?" She laughed. But then she did an awkward box step of embarrassment, probably sensing her manner wouldn't win any awards for Most Seemly Display of Wistful Sadness in a Situation in Which an Ex-Spouse Has Been Offed. She switched to subdued. "Of course I'm Bonnie." Then she added: "Gee."

Gee. Bonnie Spencer.

Okay, picture the ex-wife of a celebrated movie producer. What comes to mind? A cold, elegant bitch with tobacco-colored arms who wears jewelry to the beach. A stunner with pointy, polished nails that tap all the time, sending out the coded message: Fuck you; I'm dissatisfied.

But Bonnie Spencer didn't seem dissatisfied. And she definitely didn't come across as elegant, especially with that goof of a dog slobbering with happiness at her side. Looks? No glamour girl, not by a long shot. More like one of those girl-buddy types, tall—five eight or nine—broad-shouldered and clean, probably from some clean town where all the girls said "Gee." Nothing to write home about. Not much to look at. But the weird thing was, I couldn't keep my eyes off her.

Her best feature was her hair, glossy and dark, pulled back into a ponytail. Other than that . . . well, okay features. Deep laugh lines around her eyes. She had the high, healthy color men have more often than women: that rosy brownness that comes to the naturally fair-skinned who spend a lot of time out of doors. In other words, Bonnie Spencer, sneakers in hand, looked like someone you never really got to know in high school: the big, strapping girl jock who gets over mourning the end of field hockey season by spending the winter stroking her lacrosse stick.

Except she was no girl—not anymore. The strong body and the shiny hair were deceptive. At first glance I had put her in her early thirties. But her neck was a little too lined, her lips a little too pale. She was in her late thirties, maybe even forty.

In relation to Sy she made absolutely no sense. To have seen the compact, richly robed, perfectly groomed Mr. Spencer and his exquisite world of hand-painted pool tiles, and then to look at big, all-American Bonnie standing on the planked wood floor of a pretty but definitely not show-stopping old saltbox house . . . The question was not why Sy had dumped her, but how such a man had come to marry such a woman in the first place.

She was staring at me again. Her eyes were dark gray-blue, a deep, mysterious color for such a straightforward girl, the color of the ocean. I looked into them; that how-come-*you're*-here expression had returned.

"Ms. Spencer?"

"Please," she said, almost shyly. "Bonnie."

And then, once more, ka-boom, her mood changed. Suddenly she became friendly, easy. She gave me a smile. A great, generous smile. Perfect white teeth, except for a slightly crooked one in front, as though her parents had run out of money a month before the orthodontist had finished. Listen, it can make you so happy to get a warm, uncomplicated smile like that. But why the hell was she smiling? Why the hell was her face lit up like that? What did she think I was going to do? Ask her to the senior prom?

"You've heard about your former husband, Seymour Spencer?"

"Oh, God," she breathed. The smile vanished. Her eyebrows, the kind that slant up, like a bird's wings, drew together; they were eyebrows meant for a more delicate woman. "It was on the ten o'clock news last night. One of those god-awful stories about famous people you don't know. Except it was about Sy." For a minute, her expression reflected the normal disorientation of the average citizen confronted with murder: a flash of horror, then a fast flare-up of incomprehension. "You probably hear this all the time, but I can't believe it." Her voice was filled with fervent emotion. "I'm *so* sorry."

Too much emotion. Too goddamn fervent. Look, I'd been in Homicide a long time. Every working day of my life was spent with the distraught, the agitated, the grieving, the indifferent. And so I knew that something wasn't right about Bonnie Spencer. First of all, her "I'm so sorry" was overly personal; it's hard to explain, but even the world's most extroverted person doesn't respond to a cop with that kind of familiarity.

And another thing: just standing there in the doorway, she kept changing her mood. Not in the usual way, like a dazed person trying to come to grips with a too-terrible reality, but as though she were searching for the perfect, appropriate emotion to show off to me.

How did I know all this? Any decent detective knows when to turn off his mind and tune in his gut. And my gut was saying: Something's going on with this woman.

So all of a sudden, instead of a routine interview with a dead hotshot's ex-wife to see if I could come up with any leads, I was on the alert.

"Would you like to come in?" she was asking.

"Thanks."

It was a good-size, solid house, built for a farm family. I followed her—and the dog—into a roomy kitchen and, naturally, said "Yeah, great" when she offered to make me coffee. (Saying yes to coffee during an investigation makes people feel you've accepted them; it makes them relax, open up. Unfortunately, half the time you wind up drinking stuff that tastes like lukewarm liquid shit, but in the long run it's probably worth it.)

She cleared the morning's papers—the *Times*, *Newsday*, the *Daily News*—all with their stories about Sy's murder, off the table.

She must have gone out for them when the coffee shop opened, at six; they'd all been read. I tipped the chair back and sat quietly, the way I usually do. I wanted to see what Bonnie Spencer would reveal. But she turned away to put the water up to boil and measure out coffee, so for a few seconds the only thing she revealed was nice thighs—a little overdeveloped, but muscular, tight. Meanwhile, the dog put its head on my lap and gazed up into my eyes— the soulful look a dumb girl who wants to be taken seriously would give in a bar.

Bonnie turned around. "Moose," she ordered, "go to place!" She pointed toward one of those small, oval braided rugs. The dog ignored her. Bonnie shrugged, half to herself, half in apology: "The dog has the IQ of a cockroach." Then she opened a cabinet and took out a little white pitcher shaped like a cow. She was waiting for me to begin questioning her. I didn't. She asked: "Did Sy . . ." She stopped and started over. "The TV said he was shot." I nodded. She held open the refrigerator with her hip while she poured milk into the pitcher. I glanced inside: no chilling white wine or goat cheese in there. God knows over the years I'd made it with enough summer women to recognize that, at least in the food department, Bonnie was not a typical New York woman. She was either on a budget, on a diet, or had given up all hope of visitors; she had a pint container of milk, whole wheat bread and a big, Saran-wrapped glass bowl that looked like she'd gotten overenthusiastic about broccoli. "Was his death instantaneous?" Her voice was high, hopeful.

"We'll know more after the autopsy." Just then, Moose gave a deep, lovelorn sigh and lay down at my feet. On my feet, actually.

"Everything I can think of to say is a cliché—but I hope he didn't suffer."

"I hope not."

"Well," she said, "I guess you weren't just cruising the neighborhood and felt like a cup of coffee."

"I guess not." All of a sudden I realized I had seen her before. Probably at the post office, getting her mail.

"I guess you have some questions," she said.

"Yes."

But I didn't ask any. I got busy pretending to formulate a question while studying her cow pitcher. What I was actually doing was checking out if Bonnie had a body worth writing home about under that big T-shirt. Naturally, when I caught myself doing it, I got pissed because I'd always made it a point never to think about sex during work hours (which is generally a snap, homicide not being generally conducive to hard-ons), and also because wanting to know what was under her T-shirt made me feel ridiculous. If she were in a movie, she'd be the heroine's good-natured girlfriend, a tomboy with a heart of gold. But for someone who wasn't attractive, she was so attractive. Here I was, half hoping she'd need something on a high shelf. She'd have to stretch up her arms; her shirt would rise and I would get to see her ass. It made me feel like a louse. Since AA and especially since Lynne, I'd stopped my bad-boy crap, my automatic concentration on anything female, my reflexive coming on to almost every woman I met.

"Tell me about you and Sy Spencer," I said quickly. "How long were you married to him?"

"Three years—1979 to 1982." She poured the boiling water through the coffee filter. "You don't take notes?"

"I think I can manage to remember 1979 to '82." I'd forgotten to take out my pad. Suddenly it felt like a block of lead in my jacket pocket. "Amicable divorce?"

"Even if it hadn't been, do you think I'd shoot him seven years later?"

"I'm open to all possibilities."

"Well, I didn't shoot him." Her manner was solemn, sincere, proper; if Bonnie Spencer's mouth was from the city, the rest of her had grown up in that nice non–New York hometown, wherever it was.

"Good. Now, do you want to answer my question? How was the divorce?"

"Amicable."

"Fair settlement?"

"I got this house."

"Just the house?"

"Yup."

"Was there any litigation?"

"No. Both of us were just overflowing with amicability. 'Bonnie, *please* take the alimony.' 'No, Sy, but thanks *so* much for thinking of me.' "

"Why no alimony? He was rich."

"I know. But back then, I didn't care about money. Oh, and I was in my wronged-woman phase: 'Do you honestly think a monthly check will make up for the loss of a husband, Sy?' " She shook her head. "God, was I morally superior. You can imagine Sy—and his matrimonial lawyer. They must have been shouting 'Hallelujah!' and jumping up and down and hugging each other."

I didn't like this. At the same time I was being vigilant, trying to figure out just what was wrong with Bonnie Spencer—because I *knew* there was something wrong—I was finding there was something about her I really liked. Maybe I was just intoxicated by the homey atmosphere—being at that bright-polished wood table in the fresh-smelling country kitchen, watching a woman open a cupboard and think for a second before choosing from a bunch of mugs. Maybe it was that big hairy black mop, Moose, warming my feet. I could just feel myself letting go, my brain turning to mush. Bonnie put the cow pitcher and a sugar bowl down on the table and handed me a mug of coffee. The mug said "I love"— the "love" was one of those hearts—"Seattle!" and had a cartoon of a smiley animal with funny-looking flippers.

"I know it's tacky," she said. "It was a choice between tacky and chipped."

"You didn't get any alimony at all?" I tipped the pitcher. The milk came out of the cow's mouth. It was so dumb.

"I never dreamed I'd need it. See, when I met Sy, I was a hot screenwriter. My movie—*Cowgirl*—had just opened. It got great reviews, did decent business. And during the time we were married, I wrote five more screenplays. Three of them were in development." She sat down across from me at the table. "When you're a big success right off the bat, you assume it's going to go on forever."

"It didn't?"

She shook her head. "No. *Cowgirl* was my first and only movie. Nothing ever happened with any of the others. Anyhow, Sy offered to pay me alimony at least three times. But I wanted to show him I could be independent. And you know what? In the long run, it really was better this way."

"Why did the marriage break up?" She was clearly not a New Yorker, because instead of giving me a socio-psycho-feminist analysis of the relationship, she clammed up. "Come on," I urged. "I know this may seem like an invasion of your privacy, but someone's been murdered. I need a picture of this man's life—a complete picture."

It took her a while, but finally she opened up. "When we met, in L.A., Sy was trying to produce his first movie. I guess I was the important one—the toast of both coasts. Okay, the semitoast. He loved coming along for the ride. He met a lot of people. You know, contacts.

"I don't want to make it sound as if he was using me. I think he truly thought I was . . . well, wonderful. And he was so smart and worldly that when he proposed I thought: Gee, if this man is in love with me, maybe I *am* wonderful. Anyway, pretty soon he made his first movie, and then his second. And let me tell you, Sy earned his success. He wasn't just another rich guy who wanted to get into the movie business to date actresses or impress his friends in Cleveland. He was a born producer."

"What makes a born producer?"

Bonnie didn't have to think for much more than a second; she'd done her legwork on Sy a long time ago. "He has to have a good story sense; Sy had a great one. And the ability to get people excited over his vision. And be a trendsetter. If everyone else was making heartwarming movies about farm families with lovable old grandpaws and alfalfa blights, Sy would make something stylized and science-fictiony because he loved the script and believed it would make a great movie."

"So he became a big producer. What happened to you?"

"Nothing much. I stopped needing an unlisted number."

"You're not saying he dropped you when you stopped being a hot screenwriter?"

"Yup."

Yup? "Where are you from?" I asked.

"Ogden, Utah. Is Moose bothering you?"

"He's okay."

"She. Can't you tell? She loves men. She drops me in two seconds flat for anything in pants. She's the town slut." Real fast, Bonnie's doting dog-lover smile faded. She glanced away, up at the wall clock, but she wasn't interested in the time. I made a mental note to check on her reputation.

"How did Sy drop you?"

"How? Not too hard, considering how much he wanted out. He told me—very gently—he had been having an affair with someone. Some society lady, like his first wife, except this one didn't look like she ate oats and neighed. Anyway, he told me he was in love with her and it was causing him enormous pain to be hurting me, but that he would appreciate a divorce so he could marry her."

"But he didn't marry her."

"No, of course not. He just wanted out. He was having the affair anyway, so he used it. I guess he thought it would be easier for me if there was another woman; he knew I could accept love a lot better than him saying, 'Hey, Bonnie, I hate taking you places because you're taller than me and a has-been.' "

"And you weren't angry at this kind of treatment."

"Of course I was angry! If you go back seven years, I bet you'd find twenty witnesses who heard me yelling: 'I hope you die, you louse.' But time passes. And the fact of the matter is, we wound up being friends."

"When was the last time you saw him?"

"I'm not sure." But she was! Damn it, I could feel it. She lifted her chin, examined a pot holder on a hook and pretended to think. "A few days ago, I think. I dropped in on the set."

"And before that?"

"Let's see . . . Oh, about a week before. He asked me to come over, to see his house."

"Did you stay long?"

"No. He just gave me the fifty-cent tour."

"How good friends were you?"

"Pretty good friends."

"Did you spend a lot of time with him?"

"Not all that much."

"Did he visit you here?"

"He dropped by once or twice. But we were mainly phone friends. He was my colleague, my collaborator. See, I hadn't written any screenplays for a few years, but last winter, when I gave it another shot, I sent it right off to Sy. I mean, I hadn't seen him since the divorce, but I knew he'd give me a fair reading. And he really liked it!" She massaged her forehead. "Oh, God almighty, I can't believe he's dead."

"What about the script?"

"What? Oh, we were developing it together. It was a kind of female-buddy spy movie."

"What exactly does 'developing' mean?"

"It means working on a project—the script, the financing, trying to get a good director or a star involved. But Sy never moved on a project until he was satisfied with the script. And mine—it's called *A Sea Change*—wasn't quite in shape to be sent out. But he had a lot of great suggestions. I was rewriting based on his suggestions."

"And then he'd produce it?"

"Yup."

"Was he paying you a lot?"

"Well . . . he wasn't actually paying me yet. But if I'd asked, he would have given me option money."

"Why didn't you ask?"

"I guess the same reason I didn't want alimony. I didn't want to seem greedy. I know, that sounds stupid. No, it *is* stupid. But Sy always worried that people—women—were out for what they could get from him. I didn't want him to think that of me, either time. Anyway, I knew he'd be fair once we got rolling."

"How do you support yourself? Family money?"

She laughed and looked around the kitchen. "Does this look like family money?"

"You live in Bridgehampton all year round?" I was really surprised.

"Sure. Oh, I see; you thought this was my sincere little summer cottage where I go to get away from my forty-room Sutton Place triplex. No, this is it. I support myself by writing. I do the 'Happy News' column for the *South Fork Sun*. I'm sure it's the high point of your week: weddings, babies, anniversaries. 'Penny and Randy Rollins of Amagansett's famed Wee Tippee Inne celebrated their nineteenth anniversary with a gala extravaganza—featuring Penny's world-famous fish chowder!' And I write copy for mail-order catalogs. Stuff like 'White swirls of rayon chiffon set aglow by luminescent faux-pearl buttons.' "

"You didn't resent Sy, that you had to give up screenwriting, give up all that high living for something . . . less exciting?"

"Resent? A woman tends to resent a man who says, 'I don't desire you anymore.' " She looked away, embarrassed. Then she went on: "But that's on a personal level. Professionally, how could I resent him just because other people weren't hiring me as a screenwriter? That wasn't Sy's fault. Eight studios and fifty thousand independent producers rejected my scripts. They said they were sweet. Sweet is movie speak for insignificant. But in all those years I never doubted that Sy wished me well."

"Did you ever talk about anything beyond this new project?"

"Sure. Look, I know his friends, his family."

"Any brothers or sisters?"

"No. Just Sy. Both his parents died since the divorce. But he had aunts, uncles, lots of cousins. I knew them all; we went way back. When I met him, he was still publishing his poetry magazine and trying to get his first movie produced, and his office was still in the Spiegel Crown Kosher Provisions building."

"Spiegel?"

"Spiegel was his name originally: Seymour Spiegel." She shook her head. "He changed it the summer before he went to Dartmouth. I never understood why. I mean, what did he think he would say at graduation? 'These are my parents, Helen and Morton Spiegel. Their name used to be Spencer, but they Judaicized it.' Or if he was going to change his name, why not go the whole route and call himself Bucky? I mean, Sy is not a quantum leap from Seymour."

Just then, Bonnie got stopped by some memory of Sy. Her eyes opened too wide, the expression people use when they're trying not to cry. She stood up and got busy sponging off what looked like a clean stove.

And then it happened again: the imposition of self-control, followed by the conscious shifting of the gears of her personality. When she turned around, she was composed—but with just the appropriate degree of concern. "Do you have any ideas about who killed him?" she asked. Sincere. Saddened. Full of sympathy. Full of crap.

"Do you?"

"No," she said. For a woman her age, she looked like she had a great body. I tried to figure out where I'd seen her before. Maybe running. She had the slim, muscular legs of a runner.

"Think back over the last few weeks. Was Sy angry at anybody?"

She leaned against the kitchen counter and smiled. "Everybody. When he was making a movie, anyone who gave him a hard time was an enemy. It was funny, because for all his charm he was aloof, and always in control. When we were married, we'd have fights where I'd yell, kick the refrigerator, and Sy would watch, like he was watching an actress doing an improvisation: Wife Losing Her Temper.

"But when he was producing—God, that was another story! Goodbye charm. And forget aloof. His money and his reputation were on the line. He never yelled—that wasn't his way—but he'd lace into people in this icy voice. It could really get scary—all that fury expressed in this absolutely cold manner. Let me tell you: he got his way."

"Was he angry at anyone the last time you talked?"

"Lindsay, I guess."

"But they were living together. They were supposed to be in love."

"Well, I've got to tell you: the love part is debatable. But even if they had been, this is the movie business. An executive producer doesn't love an actress who's jeopardizing a twenty-million-dollar project. Sy told me the dailies were awful, which really surprised me because her success isn't just based on blatant beauty; she's a talented actress."

"But you think Sy got disillusioned with her?"

"Sy had a gift for falling in and out of love pretty easily."

"Let's put love aside. Was he annoyed with her? Angry?"

"Furious. He said she was just coasting—not putting any thought or energy into the role because it wasn't an 'important film.' That *really* ticked Sy off, because it was an article of faith with him that any movie that's true, that moves audiences—even a screwball comedy—is an important film. He believed in *Starry Night*. And Lindsay didn't. What made the problem even worse was that she has such a monumental ego she couldn't see how flawed her performance was. And naturally, she wouldn't try to fix what she'd decided wasn't broken. Let me tell you, if he hadn't gotten killed, he would have made her life a living hell."

"So he was ready to steamroll Lindsay?"

"Yup. And the director too."

"What's his name?"

"Victor Santana."

"Why was he mad at him?"

"Because Santana had gone gaga over Lindsay and couldn't or wouldn't get her to change."

"Anyone else?"

"Oh, his usual hate list. The director of photography they'd hired—a French boy genius—was shooting too pastelly. The line producer was bellying up to NABET—the film technicians' union—too much. Sy was angry at *everyone*."

"Okay, then who of the movie people was seriously angry at Sy?"

"I don't know. I'm not part of the *Starry Night* company."

"How about Lindsay Keefe?"

"My guess is if you tell a critically acclaimed actress—a movie star—that her performance is putrid and then, no matter how many little adjustments she makes, that the dailies are still awful . . . well, you figure it out. But even *I* wouldn't believe she'd shoot him because he criticized her work."

"Who else?"

"I don't know."

I looked her straight in the eye. "He was your ex-husband. He could talk to you."

"We didn't talk all that much."

"You talked enough. What else was on his mind?"

"He never really said anything specific."

"Tell me anyway."

"Well, I just want you to know this is my interpretation of what he *didn't* say."

"Go ahead."

"This is a very expensive movie for an independent production. I think maybe he was a little concerned that his backers were upset. The people who invested might have heard about trouble on the set, and they might have gotten anxious."

"Who were they?"

"Specifically? Beats me. I think a couple of them may have been from his days in the kosher meat business." She paused. "You know there are some rough people in that industry."

"Yeah, there's mob money in it."

"From the little Sy said, though, these guys didn't sound like out-and-out goons. More like businessmen in suits and ties, except with five-pound gold ID bracelets."

"Was that all? No one else with a grudge?"

"I'm pretty sure." I waited while she thought. "Nope," she said at last. "No one else. Definitely."

I stood and faced her. She lowered her head so I was looking down at her dark, shiny hair. Her breathing became quick, shallow. I knew I was getting to her. Not just the cop: the man.

"Bonnie, you're smart, observant. Sweet too, and I mean that as a compliment." She tried to look me in the eye—casual. But her face had flushed bright pink. "You're not being straight. I get the feeling you're holding back, and that concerns me."

"I'm not holding back anything." Just for an instant her voice caught in her throat.

I moved in closer. "You could help me solve a murder, Bonnie."

"I can't. Honestly. I've told you everything I know."

"Listen, if things were going lousy with Sy Spencer's movie, with Lindsay, who would he confide in? Who knows the business? Who knows him? You."

"Please. I've told you everything he told me."

"I've got to tell you: something about you doesn't feel right. What are you hiding?" She turned her head away from me. "Come on, do you want me to start thinking maybe you were involved?"

"Why would you think that?" She wasn't exactly scared, but she wasn't at ease either.

"Open up, Bonnie." I stepped toward her. She inched backward, until she was pressed against the sink. I moved in until we were almost touching. "Tell me what you're *not* talking about. Be smart. Because if I start to think you were involved, I'll go after you—and I won't stop."

I had a few minutes after Bonnie, so I drove down to the beach. I hadn't liked the way the interview had ended. A little official charm is one thing. That final minute, that simultaneous coming on to her and threatening her, was another. And I hadn't come on to her just for leverage; I'd really wanted to be close to her. I needed to clear my head.

Down at the beach, a stiff wind was whipping up the sand, blowing sharp, scratchy grains against my face and neck. Summer people were scuttling around, on the verge of hysteria. Nature was behaving badly. They closed their inside-out umbrellas, folded their chairs, picked up their coolers and rushed past me, back to their cars. There could be no grain of sand under gold spandex bikinis, or in eyes that had to be wide open for the next hostile takeover.

I took off my shoes, squatted down by the dunes near a patch of jointweed, pretty much out of the worst of the wind, and watched until all the New York bodies had run away.

Back in the late fifties, when I was a kid, people still slept on the beach, right where I was, on hot summer nights. Grownups would pitch tents, but the rest of us would lug out the blanket rolls we'd learned to make in Boy Scouts. Sometimes we'd tell scary stories about the Cropsey Maniac or whisper dirty jokes, but by eleven, we'd fall silent and just lie on our backs, staring up at the night sky. The stars were so beautiful they shut us up.

I must have been about ten when I started sneaking out of the house one or two nights a week to sleep on the beach after the summer was over. I did it all year round, except for the winter months. Once the house was dark, I'd tiptoe down the steep back staircase and out the door, grab the blanket roll I kept in the toolshed behind the house, take my bike and race like hell for three quarters of a mile over the pitch-black road.

I don't know why I had to get out. Okay, even back then, my brother and I didn't exactly revel in each other's company; but our relationship was more mutual annoyance than animosity. At his worst, Easton was just a pain-in-the-ass prig who ironed his T-shirts.

My mother? A lady. She didn't hit me or scream at me. She just didn't like me, and probably didn't love me. I was the mirror image of the drunk farmer who'd fucked her over and then taken off. Just being myself—dangling my legs over the arm of the couch while I read, whistling a tuneless few notes when I was doing something mindless like washing windows—pissed her off. She'd pass by, and there'd be just a sharp expulsion of air through her nose, an irate snort. When I was younger I'd ask, "Hey, Ma, what's wrong?" Her answer would be "nothing" in the form of a high-society chuckle—a throaty heh-heh of denial. Then she'd say, "Steve, sweetheart, *please. Anything* but 'Ma.' Did I raise a hillbilly?" My mother always made me feel like total shit.

I know. She didn't have it easy. The farm was gone, and so was my old man. There was no way near enough money to feed me and Easton, and keep us in jeans and sneakers, much less for her to lead the gracious-lady life she aspired to. So she got a job— at Saks Fifth Avenue in Southampton, selling expensive dresses to expensive women. And when she wasn't involving herself in rich lives by zipping up their dresses or stroking their embossed names on their charge cards, she was busting her chops doing scutz work for their charity groups. My mother would do *any-thing*—set up three hundred bridge chairs in the midday sun, lick one thousand envelope flaps until past midnight—to be allowed into their swan-necked, high-cheekboned society.

I don't know where my mother got her obsession with the upper crust. Sure, her family was an old one in Sag Harbor, and to hear her you could practically see portraits of bearded Eastons in the brass-buttoned uniforms of whaling boat captains. But there were no portraits; I'd biked up to the Sag Harbor Library in eighth grade and learned there was absolutely no basis for ancestor worship. Early Eastons might have gone to sea, but they'd obviously been ordinary sailors: guys with bowlegs and black stumps for teeth. Her old man, who died before I was born, had sold tickets for a ferry company that had the Sag Harbor and New London, Connecticut, route.

Still, my mother was convinced, despite all hard evidence to the contrary, that she was a gentlewoman. She didn't give a damn about the local South Fork female elite, the wives of lawyers, doctors, successful farmers, or even the moneyed Yanks—maybe because they all knew who she was, or wasn't. No, she lived for Memorial Day, when her "friends" opened up their summer houses out here. Even when we were kids, she'd sit at the supper table and talk about her New York "friends." Quality People.

Her friends, of course, were not her friends but her customers, summer women who came to the grand old houses, "cottages" in Southampton—like the one Sy bought—for the summer. She'd go on and on about Mrs. Oliver Sackett's hand-embroidered-in-England slips ("Divine, teeny stitches!"), or the thirty-one ("Norell! Mainbocher! Chanel!") dresses Mrs. Quentin Dahlmaier had ordered from the main branch in New York, one for every night of the month of July.

Bottom line? My mother felt fucked every single day of her life because she didn't have a driver ("*Never* say 'chauffeur'!" she warned Easton; "it's *nouveau riche*") and a maid and a sable coat. She didn't even have a roof that didn't leak.

And I think that's why I got out from under her roof as often as I could. Sitting over a plate of her *spécialité de la maison*, macaroni and undiluted Campbell's Cheddar Cheese Soup (which, of course, she knew was not Quality, but which she announced was Great Fun), listening to her go on to Easton in her throaty voice—she was a heavy smoker and wound up sounding like Queen Elizabeth with laryngitis—Jesus. She'd talk about how Mrs. Gabriel Walker ("one of the Bundy sisters, from Philadelphia") was mad for nubby linen, absolutely mad. . . . Her conversation was directed to Easton, never to me. But then she knew and I knew that would be a waste of time.

I did not belong in that house. Like my old man, I was not Quality.

"Had Mr. Spencer to the best of your knowledge received any threatening messages or phone calls?" Robby Kurz was asking Lindsay Keefe.

You could tell Robby had gotten up extra early to get spiffy. He'd arranged a yellow handkerchief in the breast pocket of his brown plaid jacket into points. The smell of his double dose of hairspray overpowered the scent arising from a huge bowl of white roses on the table in front of the couch he and I were sitting on.

"Of course there were no threats." Lindsay exhaled, a sharp, pissed-off breath between pursed lips. She was trying very hard to be patient. "What do you expect? That his killer went up to him and announced: 'You're a dead man'? And there were no heavy-breather phone calls either." For a woman in shock, Lindsay sounded clearheaded. In fact, completely self-possessed, not a hint of hysteria. The bat-shit, Valiumed, sensitive *artiste* her agent had described could have been some other person.

Even though I'd caught a glimpse of her the night before, in the back of my mind I must have been expecting a fifteen-foot-tall Goddess of Film, a gargantuan babe with enormous, glistening lips and colossal legs that could crush any man caught between them. But Lindsay, standing by the window, fingering the sheer white curtain, was of ordinary height, although so small-boned and petite (except for her world-famous tits) that she looked as if she'd been created solely to make men feel big, important. In her daintiness, she must have been a perfect match for Sy. Two exquisite pocket-size people: a separate species.

But Sy had been an ordinary-looking man. Lindsay Keefe's looks were extraordinary. No wonder she'd gone from doing Greek tragedies in little theaters in little midwestern cities to making avant-garde films in Europe to being an American movie star. Her features were beautiful. Okay, they didn't add up to perfection, but they came damn close. (Movie stars usually have one annoying flaw—a wen, a strawberry mark that you can't ignore, one defect that makes you wonder why they couldn't pop a few thou for a plastic surgeon. Lindsay had a black mole on her neck, at the spot where a guy's Adams apple is. It was a thing you'd never think about on a regular person, but I couldn't keep my eyes off it.)

Her skin was the palest possible, the kind where you can almost picture the whole blood vessel network underneath. Her hair was some miraculous white-blond, but with half silver, half gold overtones. And the eyes: pure black.

She'd gotten herself up all in white. A long, filmy skirt and a plain, schoolgirl blouse. The living room was all white also, like a stage set designed solely to flatter blondes. There were a lot of what I'm sure were antiques, but solid stuff: fat couches and chairs covered in different materials—but all whites too, various shades of it, so it became a kind of color.

"If you want to know the truth," Lindsay went on, "*nothing* could scare Sy. He was a man in control, at the peak of his powers. Intellectually, emotionally, financially . . ." She stopped for a second. When she continued, it was with disgust, as though she'd caught us sniggering over the notion of Sy's "powers." She seemed exasperated with what she'd decided were our infantile, dirty cop minds. "All right, I'll fill in the blank for you: at the peak of his powers sexually."

Forget that her words were unfair, to say nothing of blunt, brusque and bordering on the stunningly snotty; it hardly mattered. Robby and I sat motionless as she spoke. Her voice had a deep, sensual undercurrent, a hypnotic hum. You wanted to hear whatever she had to say. She could be talking about Sy's death, or reciting erotic poetry, or reading the ingredients off a Kaopectate label. You couldn't resist being Lindsay Keefe's audience.

You wanted to applaud everything. Because besides the Face

and the Voice, there was the Body. She had positioned herself perfectly in front of the window. With the curtains open, the late-morning light behind her was so strong you could practically see what she had for breakfast. Everything was lit up: her legs, the line of her bikini underpants stretched over her flat stomach, her hand-span waist—and most of all, the fact that she wasn't wearing a bra. Incredible: her boobs were flawless, the awesome ones that defy gravity and point north. And naturally, she stood slightly sideways, making sure the sunshine lit her up so you couldn't avoid seeing the pokes her nipples made as they pushed against the gauzy fabric of the tightly tucked-in blouse.

"Sy was a great success artistically *and* financially. You must know that this is not an industry where people wish each other well. But would someone murder him because his last film won the Gold Palm at Cannes and grossed ninety-two million? *Please*."

Robby was nodding at everything Lindsay said, but it was nodding run amok. His head kept bobbing up and down, nonstop, like one of those jerky dolls with springs for necks you used to see in the backs of cars.

I wasn't nodding at all. Because, number one, although I might have been spellbound by the Voice, I still had enough brains to realize all we were getting from Lindsay were words. She was giving a brief (but wonderfully well lit) personal appearance that would satisfy two uncouth cops—without revealing anything.

And, number two, my nodding reflexes weren't working so well because I was genuinely stunned at Lindsay Keefe's absolute indifference to us. Hey, we hadn't dropped in to discuss delinquent parking tickets. You'd think, being an actress, she'd offer a few chest-heaving sobs, or at least sniffle. All she was doing, though, was going through the motions of an interview so she wouldn't get marked down as uncooperative—and keeping us titillated while she was at it, only because it would have been against her nature to be in the same room with a human dick and not titillate. But she totally didn't give a shit about what we thought about her. I'd never come across that before.

Homicide is not a common circumstance in most lives and, therefore, neither are homicide detectives. I'd always gotten *some* reaction: respect, hostility, obsequiousness, guardedness, guile, cooperation. Forget personal qualities: to anyone remotely connected to a murder, Robby and I were figures of authority, symbols of the Law. But not to Lindsay. To her, we were clowns in cheap sports jackets.

She lifted her hair out from under her collar, letting it fall over her shoulders. "Is there anything else you want from me?" Lindsay demanded.

Robby tried to be cool. He didn't get anywhere. He started giving off a sour wet-wool smell; he was in a sweat of nerves and desire. "Did Mr. Spencer ever mention anyone from his past who might not wish him well?" he asked. Lindsay took a slow, deep breath, presumably to show us how she was trying to retain her composure so she could continue the ordeal of questioning. "Miss Keefe?" To be fair, Robby's voice didn't quite squeak, but it wouldn't have won any prizes for resonance.

She left her position near the window and came and sat on a chair opposite us, her legs curled under her, her hands clasped in ladylike fashion in her lap. "Look, I've given you all the help I can," Lindsay said. "I don't know anything more."

That voice! It was one of those voices you read about in old detective stories, which girls with names like Velma have: rich, luscious, like warm cream. Except the funny thing was, for all her cream and translucent skin and superior tits and blond hair and black mystery eyes, Lindsay Keefe wasn't knocking my socks off. Sure, if your taste ran to devastating blondes she wasn't bad. But on or off the job, I was never the kind of guy who gets off on contempt. Okay (to be fair), maybe this was Lindsay's tough act, to hide some vulnerability—or some real or imagined indiscretion she was afraid was incriminating. Or (not to be fair) maybe Lindsay was just an insolent, contemptuous, cold, emotionally defective twat.

"Well?" she asked. "Any more questions?"

Robby wasn't completely star-struck, but he seemed to have forgotten, momentarily, that he was the killer interrogator of the Suffolk County P.D. Homicide Squad and the beloved husband of Freckled Cleavage. He gulped. "I think that about covers it for now," he said.

"Fine," she said, and stood. Robby stood too, although not without banging his shin on the white marble coffee table.

I stayed on the couch. "Did Mr. Spencer ever mention seeing any of his colleagues from his days in the kosher meat business?" Lindsay eyed me a little curiously. I hadn't said anything beyond a "Hello" and an "I'm sorry"; until now, I'd been letting Robby do the questioning. "Why don't you sit down just for one more minute, Ms. Keefe." She sat, and then Robby did too. "The meat business," I prompted.

"No," she answered. "I'm almost positive he didn't see any of them. For him, that was another life. But let me say this, Detective . . . I forgot your name."

"Steve Brady. Did any people he knew from the meat business invest in this movie, Ms. Keefe?"

"Yes. One or two."

"Do you know their names?"

"Just one. Mikey. Michael, I suppose."

"Any last name?"

"I don't know it."

"Did you ever hear of Mr. Spencer meeting with this Mikey?" She shook her head. "Having a phone conversation with him?"

"Sy made most of his calls from his study."

"Right, but did you ever happen to be passing by and hear any call to this Mikey?"

"Actually, once. And I *was* passing by—not eavesdropping. Don't condescend to me."

"Okay. What did you happen to hear, passing by?"

"Sy was reassuring this man that everything was going well."

"Was Mikey worried that it wasn't going well?"

"No, of course not. It was one of those soothing, stroking, you're-*so*-important phone calls. Sy was a master of those."

"No problems with *Starry Night?*" I asked. She shook her head, allowing a curl of her long platinum hair to fall in front of her shoulder. She started twirling it around her index finger; I assume my eyes were supposed to follow the little circles until I was mesmerized. But I couldn't stop watching the mole on her neck; it was so black it looked like an undeveloped third eye. "Mr. Spencer was pleased with how it was going?" I asked.

"Yes."

"No problems with the director? Any of the actors?"

"Nothing that wasn't routine."

"He was happy with your performance?"

"Of course." Emphatic. Clipped. "Why do you ask?"

"Just trying to get the lay of the land," I said.

"Let's be straight with each other, Detective Brady. I don't know what you've heard, but there's always on-set gossip about the star of a film. Sometimes it's more than petty nastiness. I'm sure there are people saying terrible things, like that I'm a tough bitch. That's because I'm serious—*passionately* serious—about my work. Or that my performance is somehow lacking. Or that my relationship with Sy was . . . well, one of mutual convenience. The truth is, yes, I am tough. But I also happen to be a vulnerable human being."

"I'm sure you are."

"And I loved Sy very, very much."

"I understand."

"I hope you also understand that Sy loved my work." She bowed her head for an instant, a second of silence. Then she looked me right in the eye. "And he loved me."

"I don't doubt that for a minute," I said, and thought about the long, dark hairs that had gotten caught on the headboard in the guest room.

"We were going to be married."

I asked: "What do you know about his ex-wives?"

"I haven't met either of them."

"Did he ever talk about them?"

"Not very much. The first was named Felice. He married her right after college. She was getting her Ph.D. at Columbia. Supposedly very brilliant. Came from a distinguished family. A great deal of money."

"What happened?"

"Truthfully?"

"Please."

"Bor-ing."

"Did he have any contact with her recently?"

"No. I'm almost positive. They were divorced in the late sixties. She's remarried."

"What about his second wife?" I asked.

"Bonnie. From out West someplace."

"Do you know anything about that marriage?" Robby asked.

"A mismatch." Lindsay placed the fingers of one hand in the palm of the other; they needed a rest, or else she was examining her nails. "She's a writer. Well, she had one movie produced, and that's when Sy met her. I think he was enamored of what he thought was a lively, unpretentious intelligence. All zip, and hero-worshiping quotes from Joseph Mankiewicz's screenplays. That appealed to him—for five minutes."

"And then?" I asked.

"The truth? She had one movie in her. She was yesterday's news by the time they were married."

"Do you know if he saw her at all?" Robby asked.

"No. Of course not. But she lives around here. When they split, she got their old summer place. Actually, though, Sy did hear from her a few months ago. She sent him some new script she'd written."

I asked: "Was he going to produce it?"

"God, no."

I found myself swallowing hard. "He told her no?"

"Of course. He told me he had to. Kindly, probably gener-ously. But I'm sure very, very firmly. Oh, but wait a second. That's right. I'd forgotten. She came onto the set in East Hampton, *pursuing* him. I didn't see her, but she went and knocked on the door of his trailer. It was awful. But he said he told her in no uncertain terms: 'Goodbye. Stay off the set of my film. And keep your screenplays to yourself.' That may sound harsh, but he had no choice. This business is a magnet for all sorts of unstable people."

"He knew her, though," I said. "She was his ex-wife. Did he think she was unstable?"

"No. As far as I know, he just thought she was a loser. But if Sy had given her the least bit of encouragement, she'd have been all over him: Love my screenplay. Love me. Do for me. Make me rich, famous. Make me a star. People like her are *desperate*. Sy had to get rid of her."

CHAPTER 4

The Homicide team meeting turned out to be six cops sitting around a blackboard shrugging shoulders. Robby hadn't been able to interview Easton because he'd been tracking down the kosher-meat guy, Mikey, who turned out to be Fat Mikey LoTriglio—a real sweetheart. Like the Spiegel-Spencers, Mikey's family had owned a major meat-processing plant, but he also had ties to another family—the Gambinos. He had a dandy record of arrests for extortion and aggravated assault—our kind of guy—but he'd never been convicted of anything.

Ray Carbone announced that all he'd been able to do, because he'd been busy calming down the higher-ups and helping write a press release, was find out that Sy's first wife's name was Felice Vanderventer and she lived on Park Avenue.

Our man at the autopsy, Hugo Schultz, the Sour Kraut, reported that not counting his death, Sy had been in great shape. No diseases. No traces of alcohol or drugs. His last meal seemed to have been bread and salad. There was evidence of recent ejaculation, probably post-salad. Oh, he'd been killed by the first bullet, which had gone through his head; the one that had gone through his heart was unnecessary: Target practice, Hugo said.

The other two guys listened and drank coffee. I briefed everyone on Bonnie's story on her screenplay versus the opposing Lindsay version—and how there was something not right about Bonnie, something that bothered me. Oh, and that Lindsay's claim of giving a stellar performance was countered by both Bonnie and Gregory J. and how I thought *Starry Night*, the twenty million dollars it was costing and, possibly, Lindsay's reputation might be headed for the crapper.

In other words, what I got from the meeting was not much. It was then that I thought about my movie man. Jeremy. Germy.

Jeremy Cottman, the most famous movie critic on TV, was my one rich and famous friend. Okay, so it wasn't exactly a big-ass buddy friendship. In fact, it had been over twenty years since I'd laid eyes on him.

Jeremy had been a Bridgehampton summer kid, the son of rich but not famous parents. His father had been a stockbroker whose only customer seems to have been himself. Mr. Cottman played perpetual golf; his skin had the texture of a grilled cheese sandwich. Mrs. Cottman, who called everyone "cutie-pie," had spent whole summers in a sunbonnet that tied under her chin, clutching a pair of clippers, pruning anything that didn't run away. Their house, a rambling white wood Victorian, overlooked Mecox Bay.

Rich kids like Jeremy played all summer: swimming in each other's pools, going to parties at each other's beach clubs, taking riding lessons in those puff-thigh pants. Kids like me worked. I started out scraping duck shit and sorting potatoes for the farmer who had bought our land. When I was twelve, I graduated to cleaning swimming pools, and later to caddying at one of the local golf clubs.

But in spite of work, summer had always been an enchanted

time. It didn't get dark until late, so we'd grab a bite of supper and rush down to the ball field. We were in the four thousandth inning of a baseball game that had been going on since the summer after third grade: shirts and skins, our shirts getting progressively scruffier as the fifties gave way to the sixties, our skins darkening from the white, stick-out-ribbed chests of nine-year-olds to the broad, tanned, hairy torsos of high school seniors.

It was a strictly Bridgehampton game. Every once in a while, a summer kid would ride past—on an English racing bike. After a few nights of bypasses, he'd brake, knock down his kickstand and get really busy inspecting a tire. Usually we'd ignore him, as in: This is one club you can't join, fuckface. But if he looked like a terrific jock, we'd be a little less exclusive. Sure, the kid would have to have the balls to grunt the opening "hi." But then, if he wasn't too well-dressed, we might ask him if he wanted to hit a few.

Jeremy (I was the one who started calling him Germy) made our team. He was an incredible power hitter, a so-so outfielder, and a cruel and funny mimic. He'd pick some movie star or a baseball player and have them say terrible things about one of the kids, so it was like being dumped on by Marilyn Monroe or Carl Yastrzemski (the greatest human being Bridgehampton had ever produced, even though he'd played for Boston).

I'd never met anyone like Germy Cottman. To be able to hit those line drives. To have discovered a way to say *whatever* was on his mind. God, how good that must feel! We became great summer friends, eventually trusting each other enough to share our most intimate sports fantasies. We were the best of buddies from about the time we were twelve until we went off to college.

Germy went to Brown. I went to Albany State. I looked for him that summer after freshman year, but his mother, clipping roses that were doing something to annoy her, said, Sorry, cutie-pie, Jeremy is in Bologna, learning Italian. I saw him around once or twice after that, but we didn't have much to say; by then, he was an intellectual, I was a druggie, and neither of us was playing ball anymore.

But every now and then Germy's name came up around town. I heard he was in graduate school in Chicago for something; he was working on a newspaper in Atlanta; he was working on a newspaper in Los Angeles; he was writing long movie reviews— film criticism, I suppose—for some high-minded magazine.

And then one night on TV: the Germ! I remember lying on my couch, pretty drunk but not totally gone, slugging down a beer, thumbing the remote control. There he was, swiveling back and forth in a big leather chair, legs crossed, telling us folks at home— in his familiar, clothespin-on-the-nose prep school nasality—why *Out of Africa* was such an overrated movie; then he did a brief, mean, but exceedingly accurate, imitation of Meryl Streep.

Germy was on the map. A celeb. And over the next couple of years, his show actually got better. He wasn't only negative. Sure, there were still his killer reviews and his snide imitations, but he stopped showing off his intellectual superiority and started displaying his real intelligence. He'd run a film clip in slow motion and explain exactly about how a certain shot was done, or describe precisely why So-and-so was a good editor, or a bad production designer. He knew the players too; he'd report how some internal fight at a studio affected a particular movie.

All America watched Germy: seven-thirty, Friday nights. And read about him too, in *People, Time, Newsweek*. I read he'd married the daughter of a famous 1940s director; that he had a house on a cliff overlooking the Pacific; that he'd moved back to New York; that he'd divorced his wife after fifteen years and married some very famous Broadway lighting designer—not that I'd ever heard of her. Around town there was talk that his father had had a heart attack on the eighteenth hole and had died before they could get him back to the clubhouse and that his mother had died too, and Germy had inherited the house. But although I kept up with what he was doing, I hadn't spent any time with him since I'd played shortstop and he'd played outfield.

I felt a little nervous about calling him, but then I thought: I've got to give it a shot. It being a glorious, sunny Saturday afternoon, Germy could actually be a couple of miles away. He might be spending the day practicing a cruel Clint Eastwood imitation or banging the lighting designer or (I smiled to myself as I pulled into his driveway) sitting cross-legged on his bed the way he used to, working neat's-foot oil into his mitt.

A minute later, there he was at his front door, his hands braced against the frame, as if he were defending his house from some intruder who might push him aside and ransack his living room, or demand to know what Chevy Chase was really like. "Yes?" Chilly, about to cross the border into absolute iciness.

"You don't recognize me, Germy?"

Then he did the Oh-my-God! I-don't-believe-it! bit, followed by our mutual finger-squishing handshake. It was for real. We were both pretty touched at seeing each other, although not comfortable enough to follow our natural inclination, which was to give each other one of those acceptable, non-homo, World Series hugs. "Steve! Come in!"

I followed him through the front hall, toward the living room. It was like stepping back into 1959: the blue-and-white umbrella stand filled with tennis rackets, the dark, scratched-up old mirror in a carved wood frame. "I can't believe it," I said. "It looks exactly the same. Any minute your little sister's going to come running in and spit at me."

"That's right!" Germy said in his slow honk. "I'd forgotten. She spent a whole summer spitting at you. She was madly in love."

The Cottman house still had the we've-been-rich-forever shabbiness it had when we were kids: faded flower print cushions, threadbare rugs with flowers that skidded across wood floors, old wicker chairs. Out on the back terrace, there were flowers blooming in his mother's mossy clay pots, and the old, white-painted wrought-iron chairs, chipped in the same places.

Like the house, Germy hadn't changed much. He was tall, about my height, but he hadn't outgrown his round-chinned baby face, with its button nose and wide-open eyes. Sure, his forehead was a little lined, his brown hair had a little gray, but in his horn-rimmed glasses and white tennis sweater, he looked more like a tall kid in a daddy costume than a full-fledged adult. He made a take-a-seat gesture. "Can I get you anything? A cup of coffee?" Then he remembered. "A beer?" I shook my head. "Steve! God! Tell me about yourself. Where are you living? What do you do?"

Germy had much too much class to ask: What do you want? although it must have been in the back of his mind that maybe I was there for a handout, or with some obnoxious request: Can you get me an autographed picture of Goldie Hawn?

"I'm here, in Bridgehampton, north of Scuttle Hole—"

"Married, single, div—" He interrupted both me and himself with his own enthusiasm. "I got married again last year!" He paused as if to give me time to prepare myself for something wonderful. "To Faith Armstead!"

I nodded respectfully, as in: Oh, of course, I'm always dazzled by Faith Armstead's lighting. "Congratulations."

"She's stuck in a theater all day today. Can you believe it?" His second marriage was working; I could hear the pleasure as Germy pronounced his wife's name. And he seemed proud, almost awed by her dedication; she could have been the first wife since the dawn of history to work on a Saturday. "Now, what about you?" he demanded.

"I never got married. I was pretty screwed up when I got back from Vietnam."

"Vietnam," Germy echoed.

"And then I got used to being single, being free. But I finally met a great girl. We're getting married Thanksgiving weekend."

"You were in Vietnam," he said softly. The new quietly-moved reaction. After all those years of being Asian-baby butchers, we had somehow turned into national treasures. "Did you see action?"

"No, you jerk-off. They needed a shortstop on the Saigon

intramural team, so I spent the whole war on the ball field. Listen, I really want to catch up, but I'm actually here on business. . . ." I saw his face fall a little, his round kid-cheeks flatten. "Eat it, Je-re-my. You think I'm going to give you a life insurance pitch?"

"Well . . ." His embarrassment evaporated. "No." He became his real self, his caustic TV self. "You look more like redwood decks, actually."

"I'm a detective with Suffolk County Homicide."

"*You?*"

"Yeah. Never thought I'd wind up on this side of the law, did you?"

"Homicide!" he said. "Steve, that's exciting. Glamorous!"

"Yeah, well, the violence is fantastic, and I've always been crazy about decomposition."

"Seriously, do you like what you do?"

"It stimulates my intellectual processes."

"I said seriously."

"Yeah, I like it. A lot. Now, do you know why I'm here?"

It took him less than a tenth of a second. "Sy Spencer."

"I need background, foreground, whatever you've got. Did you know him?"

He turned his chair so he was facing me; his back was to the bay. "Slightly."

"You didn't hang out with him?"

"No. He ran on that middle-aged fast track: a little old money, a *lot* of new money, and writers, restaurant owners, fashion designers. All those emaciated, face-lifted women and their beefy men."

"Sy wasn't beefy. Five six, a hundred thirty-two pounds."

"He was an exception." Germy hesitated: "Oh. You know how much he weighed from . . . ?"

"Yeah. The autopsy. Listen, the guy was in fantastic shape. I should have his liver. If he hadn't backed up into those bullets, he'd have lived till a hundred. The thing is, Germy, I know more than I want to about all his organs. But I want to know about *him*. So I need you. Even if you weren't his best friend, you must know about him, about what he was doing."

"Of course."

"Okay, what do you know about *Starry Night?*"

"Gossip or substance?"

"Both. Substance first; get it over with."

Germy took off his glasses and gave the earpiece a thoughtful chew. "All right. I actually read an early draft of the script. It's an action-adventure-love story about a charming heel who marries a very rich woman for her money. Superficially she's the frosty, sophisticated sort—a 'Hamptons' type, if you'll forgive me. She's overwhelmed by the heel's magnetism and sexuality. Well, to make a convoluted story short, his past—dealing a little cocaine—catches up with him, and some Colombian types kidnap his wife for reasons the script does not adequately make clear. The heel doesn't care at first. Then slowly he realizes he has fallen madly in love with the wife, and she . . . she's tied up in a basement in . . . I'm a little foggy here, but I think in Bogotá. Maybe Brooklyn. In any case, it dawns on her that he's more than a charming stud; he's the first true love of her life. He goes after her, she escapes, there's a gratuitous car chase, the bad guys seem about to win. But in the end they live happily ever after."

I sat still for a minute, staring out at the shimmering golden reflection of the sun in the bay. "Would a guy like me shell out six bucks to see it?"

"Hard to say, Steve. It's a film about breaking through your shell, discovering your humanity. The script has some of the best dialogue I've read in years. Genuinely witty. And some fine straight moments, before the kidnapping, when each starts to reveal himself to the other and then pulls back, as if they realize they're violating some unwritten Law of Superficiality of jet-set marriages. But it certainly doesn't cover any new ground. And as far as I can recall, the plot is pedestrian. But the characters are unusually well drawn for a postliterate script." He slid his glasses back on. "In case you don't know it, we are living in what is, essentially, a postliterate era."

"Oh, I do know it. It's a tragedy I've got to live with every day of my life."

"I knew you'd feel that way."

We sat in comfortable silence for a minute. When you know someone since you've been kids, you have a kind of ESP. I could sense Germy, like me, relaxing, lifting up his face to feel the sun, and wanting—really, desperately wanting—to talk about all the amazing things that had happened to the Yankees since Steinbrenner.

But I had a your-guess-is-as-good-as-mine homicide hanging over my head, so I made myself stick to the subject. "It sounds like maybe you have a qualm about the *Starry Night* script."

"Well, it could make an exciting, stylish film. But it's all in the execution. Will the actors be credible? Will you believe in the possibility of a great love between Lindsay Keefe and Nicholas Monteleone? His appeal has always been more emotional than sexual. He's essentially a man's man; all his best movies have been about relationships between men—rodeo riders, Amazon explorers . . ." He grinned. "Homicide cops. But the question about whether the movie will work goes beyond the two principals: Will the Colombians be offensively stereotypical Latino greasers or genuinely terrifying? How good a job will the director do on the action sequences? Will the big chase scene come off? Also, the real problem—the reason Sy didn't get studio financing—is that it was felt there is a limited audience for this type of vehicle: Cary Grant *cum* balls. It probably won't play to the under-twenty-fives. It's not moving enough to be another *The Way We Were*. And it's not a sizzler; even if Lindsay does bare her breasts once again, or decides it's time for a change and moons the camera, it won't help. First of all, audiences have seen her body too many times; there's a strong inclination to say: 'Please, madam, keep your shirt on.' In the script, the compelling sex is verbal, lighthearted man-woman word play, not sex play." He leaned back and clasped his hands behind his head. "Is that substantive enough?"

"Yeah. Now what about money? I've heard twenty big ones. Where does that kind of dough come from?"

"Private investors. Or banks who had faith in Sy's track record."

"If you were a bank, what kind of faith would you have?"

Germy unclasped his hands, then crossed his arms over his chest. "I'd invest—although not twenty million. That seems awfully high for a film that will be shot primarily out here and in Manhattan, even with all the lavish set decoration and costumes and an anxious director who's known for a lot of retakes. But forgetting dollars and cents, Sy's films were really good. Bankable. He believed in starting with a polished script. He'd go for the gifted actor over the big name. I always admired his movies."

"Just admired? You ever love any of them?"

He took a minute to consider the question. "No. I can't really explain it, but there was something a little smug about every picture he produced. Each one seemed to be saying: 'Aren't I sensitive? Provocative? Don't I have superb production values?' There was always intelligence and care, but never any real spirit. I suppose his films were like Sy himself."

"From the little you knew him, what did he seem like?"

"Intelligent. Polished but not slick. And for the movie business, where hugging and kissing and screaming 'Dahlink, you're a very great genius' is an institutional requirement, he was notable because he was so restrained. A gentleman." Germy stopped short.

"What are you thinking about? Even if it seems totally irrelevant."

"Well, Sy wasn't definable. He struck me as something of a chameleon. Man-about-town with men-about-town. Lover boy with women. Tough negotiator with the unions—a real dirty street fighter. And full of Jewish show-biz warmth with a couple of the old-time reporters, dropping Yiddish all over the place. The few times he and I talked, he was very professorial—as if the only thing he lived for were discussions of Fritz Lang's deterministic universe. It made me laugh because I knew he had to have gotten me confused with another critic: I never gave a flying fuck about Fritz Lang."

"Which one of his personalities came closest to being the real Sy Spencer?"

"I haven't the foggiest."

"What do you think drove him, Germy? Money? Sex? Power?"

"Well, he certainly seemed to have enjoyed all of those. But he didn't *seem* driven, even though he must have been. He could be pleasant—even charming. But some integral part of his circuitry—the part that reaches out and makes human connections—seemed . . . disconnected."

"What do you know about his ex-wife Bonnie Spencer?" Germy shook his head: never heard of her. "She wrote the screenplay for a movie called *Cowgirl*."

"I remember that one. It was a nice movie."

"What was it about?"

"A widow of a small-time rancher literally puts on her husband's boots. It deals with her relationships with the ranch hands, the neighboring wives. Some moving dialogue about her passion for the land. Beautifully photographed."

"A major motion picture?"

"No. But a really decent minor one." He took off his glasses again and did some more gnawing. "Her name wasn't Spencer when she wrote it. Something else."

"Sy married her after it came out. But then none of her other screenplays ever got made." I had this vivid image of Bonnie in her bicycle shorts and too-big T-shirt leaning against the sink in her kitchen. It was not an image of a person who could in any way be in the movie business. "Ever hear anything about her?"

"No," he said.

"It sounds like he cut her loose when he realized she wasn't the hot property he thought she was."

"That sounds fairly typical. Of the industry and of Sy."

"What about Lindsay Keefe? I've been hearing her acting wasn't very good this time around."

"Well, now we move on to gossip. I've heard the same thing, and I don't doubt it. She's a very cerebral actress. Her characters tend to be focused women, intelligent, passionately devoted to whatever they're doing, sometimes capable of deep emotion: abused women who write poetry, missionaries who join obscure revolutionary movements. That sort of thing. The character in *Starry Night*, though . . . she's different. Soft, endearing, the poor little rich girl. My guess is, Lindsay may be enough of an actress to project endearingness. But she's mostly head, no heart. The role would be one hell of a stretch."

"Will they stop making the movie now that Sy's dead?"

"Are you joking? Making movies is a *business*. For an actor, a director, they'd have to stop for a few days until they could get a replacement. For an executive producer . . . they won't even stop for a cup of coffee."

"Did you hear anything else about what was happening on the set?"

"The usual malicious innuendos."

"Good. What are they?"

"That Sy was dissatisfied, and he and Lindsay may have actually fought over her performance. Or, even if there was no confrontation, she sensed she was in trouble with him. In either case, she took a deep breath . . . and pointed her major artillery at the director, Victor Santana. Made him an ally."

"How did she get him on her side?"

"Her side? Her side was the least of it."

"No shit! Lindsay was making it with Santana?"

"Steve, when the executive producer leaves the set for the day and the director and the leading lady then proceed to hold a script conference in the director's trailer for forty-five minutes with the blinds drawn *and* they don't ask a production assistant for coffee *and* the trailer is observed rocking back and forth, what do you think?"

"Fuck City."

The real question was, what did Sy think? What did he know? And what had he been planning to do about Lindsay Keefe?

We sat in his kitchen eating ice cream out of pint containers, the way we used to. Halfway through, we switched; I got Germy's cookies 'n' cream and he got my coffee Heath bar crunch. Neither of those flavors had been invented when we were kids.

He told me how his mother's cancer had metastasized and how excruciating her pain had been and how she'd finally ended it by OD'ing on the Seconal she'd accumulated over a month. I told him I always thought she'd go on forever with that funny old bonnet and the pruning shears and how truly sorry I was she wasn't around anymore to call me cutie-pie.

He put down his spoon. "Steve, when we were kids, I never had the courage to ask you . . . Your father just walked? Your mother supported the family?"

"Yeah. After he sold the farm, he had a few different jobs, but he'd always get canned for coming to work drunk. I'm not talking a little slurring; I'm talking pissed out of his mind. When you're working over at Agway, it isn't a plus to puke all over the biggest farmer in Bridgehampton. Anyway, he took a hike when I was eight."

"You never heard from him again?"

"No. For all I know, he could still be alive somewhere, although I wouldn't make book on it."

My father was a lazy, disgusting, dirty drunk. He was also, in rare, semi-sober moments, a sweet man, talking sports to me, buying a buck's worth of bubble gum so I could have the baseball cards. And he'd sit beside Easton as he built his model ships and say "Good work," although he couldn't help, because his hands shook with perpetual D.T.s. And once in a while he'd come up

to my mother and say, " 'Ah, love, let us be true to one another,' "
or " 'Shall I compare thee to a summer's day?' "—and for that
second, you could see there had once been something between
them.

"You never let me come into your house," Germy said quietly,
as we walked back onto the terrace. "You always had an excuse.
The painters. Your mother was expecting company."

"We didn't have any money. I couldn't have even offered you
a soda. And the place was falling apart. You lived here, in all
this richness, and this was just your summer house."

We fell silent for a minute because, although we had often
discussed Roger Maris's troubles, we had never spoken about our
own; we had no idea where to take the conversation next. I got
up, walked to the edge of the terrace and, for a minute, watched
the brilliant red-and-white sail of a Windsurfer skim across Mecox
Bay. I turned back to Germy. "Remember your Sunfish? You got
it for your sixteenth birthday." He nodded. "You let me sail it,
and I took it out so far I was sure I was going to die or get in deep
shit with the coast guard. I remember I was more afraid of the
coast guard than of death."

"That was when you were starting to get pretty wild. I remember the next summer, before college. You were drinking too
much, even for a rebellious kid. I started . . . not to feel comfortable with you."

"I know."

"You were bragging about breaking into houses over the winter, trashing them—for fun." He looked straight at me. "Were
you just bullshitting?"

"No. And it wasn't just a little vandalism. I'd gone bad, Germ.
I was stealing. Color TVs, stereos. Sold most of the stuff to a fence
over in Central Islip. I pissed the money away. Booze. Records.
A leather jacket. Except one time I went to Yankee Stadium. Got
a terrific seat, right near first. This was going to be my perfect
day. But we lost. A shitty game."

"When was that?"

"July of '66."

"A shitty year," Germy recalled. "We finished last."

"I remember. The first of many shitty years. For me. The Yankees got better. I didn't. Not for a long time." I separated my thumb and index finger by maybe an eighth of an inch. "This much," I explained. "I missed being dead or in the slammer by this much."

"That must be scary."

"Yeah, it was." I thought for a second. "Still is."

CHAPTER 5

By the time I finished with Germy, it was after three o'clock. And it was a Saturday afternoon and the set of *Starry Night* was closed down. So I had the movie people come to me in our temporary headquarters in the Southampton Village P.D. I'd gotten use of the Xerox/coffee machine room for interviews— with the understanding that I could be interrupted in the event of a catastrophic copying crisis.

The room was no more or less ugly than any other small, windowless, fluorescent-lighted, metal-and-green-leatherette-chaired government-bureaucracy utility room. Its stale air was perfumed with the aroma of prehistoric coffee grounds and the fumes of copier fluid, its floor decorated with the pink and white and blue confetti of torn-off ends of Sweet 'n Lows, Equals and sugar packets, as well as with a dusting of white powder that was not a controlled substance but nondairy coffee lightener. It was no different from any other room where cops work: a place that was habitable yet degrading to the human spirit at the same time.

Victor Santana, the short-haired, thickly mustached, spiffy dude of a director who sat across from me, was willing himself to rise above his surroundings. He was doing a damn good job. He did not seem to belong in the room. In fact, he did not seem to belong anywhere except in a three-star restaurant, a four-star movie or a five-star hotel. The guy was one suave package: a white shirt with a dark red tie, pale gray slacks and a charcoal sports jacket made of some priceless fabric so exclusive a guy like me would never have heard of it.

Santana's name was Hispanic, and he was a pretty intense beige, but his accent wasn't Spanish. He sounded as if he was trying to have been educated at Oxford. It didn't quite work; his diction, like his sideburns, was a little too clipped. My guess was he wouldn't deny his heritage, but neither would he cry *"Caramba!"* to an offer to be grand marshal of the Puerto Rican Day parade.

He came off as urbane, the sort of guy James Bond would banter with at a chemin de fer table, whatever the hell chemin de fer is. But despite his civil smiles and even his I'm-so-accommodating dark-eyed glints, I knew I was getting nowhere fast. He seemed to be spouting the same essential script as Lindsay: *Starry Night* was great; Lindsay was a great actress; Sy Spencer had been a great producer. "Making a film," he was explaining, veddy Britishly, each consonant a pearl, "is a collaborative process. I cannot tell you what a joy it was—artistically *and* personally—to work with Sy and Lindsay."

So I said: "Mr. Santana, please cut the shit. We know for a fact that you and Lindsay Keefe were having an affair."

His torso twitched, as if I had, for an instant, electrified his chair. "That is absolutely untrue!" he declared. He pronounced the word "ab-so-lyutely."

"We have witnesses." Of course, all we had was a secondhand report of a rocking trailer. But it was worth a shot. "Witnesses who can testify to you and Ms. Keefe—in your trailer." Suddenly he appeared to be studying the veins in his hand. After a second, though, I realized he wasn't into veins; he was communing with his wedding ring. Santana was in his mid-thirties and had had a couple of successes. Maybe he was calculating how much each lurch of the trailer would cost him if his marriage blew up. Had Lindsay been worth a hundred thou per hump? Or maybe he just felt guilty. "Why not tell me about it?"

"All right," he sighed. Total mush: here was this cosmopolitan guy who didn't have the presence of mind to ask who the witnesses were and what they had witnessed. It was going to be a cinch, because Santana was dying to Tell All. He settled his perfectly tailored ass back in the chair but leaned the rest of himself forward. "We were having an affair," he confided, real whispery, as if to say: Swear to God you won't tell. "Please understand, this is no superficial run-of-the-play liaison. It is . . . well, it is a love affair. I wouldn't want you to think . . ."

"No problem, Mr. Santana. Listen, normally, what you do is your own business. Two people working together can fall for each other. Happens all the time. It's just that in this case, the lady's boyfriend, fiancé, whatever, was shot through the head and heart. So I have to ask a few questions."

"Maybe . . . Do you think I should speak to an attorney?"

"You can speak to whoever you want. Hire a whole law firm. You're a sophisticated man. You know what your rights are. But why? You're not guilty of anything, are you?"

"Of course not."

"So just answer a couple of questions. Now, to make my life easier. Or later, if you want, with your lawyer." I really wasn't trying to trip him up. I just didn't feel like hanging around until the middle of the following week when some dork in a dark-blue three-piece pinstripe could manage to get here from Manhattan, hook his thumbs onto his vest pockets and give me a harangue on prosecutorial discretion. "Did Sy know about you and Lindsay?"

"No. Of course not."

"How do you know?"

"I asked. I was a bit nervous, but she said she was certain."

"Everything seemed lovey-dovey between them?"

"I'm quite certain he thought so."

"Which means what?"

"Which means he didn't know how Lindsay felt about me—and I about her." You know those hearts-and-flowers stories you read where the hero's eyes shine? Well, Victor Santana's eyes started to shine. He glowed with the glory of love. You wouldn't think a grown-up guy with such an expensive sports jacket could be such a sap, but he was.

"Was Sy happy with her acting?" This clearly was not Santana's favorite question. His glow dimmed. He sat up straight, tense. He tried to calm himself by stroking his tie; it had lots of little shield designs that I guess were supposed to be club insignias, or family crests. "Hey, Mr. Santana, I've been talking to a lot of people. I have an idea of what's going on, so do us both a favor. Don't get creative. Was Sy happy with what Lindsay was doing?"

"He was not thrilled."

"Objectively, how was she?"

"She was *won*derful. I mean that sincerely." He stopped whacking off his tie; he started rotating his wedding ring.

"So Sy Spencer was wrong?"

"Yes. Completely."

"Why would a smart producer like him think an actress—someone who he's also supposed to be in love with—is crapping up his movie? Especially if she's not?"

"Sy wanted total control over every aspect of Lindsay's life. When she started showing the smallest signs of independence, he began to undermine her—so she would be more dependent on him." Santana's script was a little different from Lindsay's, but it was pretty clear from his mechanical delivery who had written his lines. "Sy was terrified of losing her. So he played on her vulnerability. Superficially, Lindsay seems strong. But she's a very vulnerable woman."

"What did Sy say to you about her acting?"

"He indicated that he felt Lindsay was cold." Santana shook

his head as if unable to comprehend such insensitivity—except the gesture was way overdone, like an actor in a silent film.

"What did he want you to do?"

"He told me to warm her up."

"Did you try to warm her up in the acting area?"

"No. Truly, it wasn't necessary. She was giving a smashing performance." Come on, I wanted to say. Get real, Santana. Your old man was probably a building superintendent, and here you are saying "troooly" and "smahshing." "The warmth was there," he was explaining. "Not in words. But in a million tiny gestures. The camera really doesn't lie, you know."

"You saw this warmth in the dailies they show?"

"Definitely."

"Who else saw it? Besides you and Lindsay?" In his silence, I could feel Santana's embarrassment. So I changed the subject before he could start resenting me. "What about your work? Was Sy happy with it?"

Santana let go of his wedding ring and glanced up. "Other than our disagreement over Lindsay, I think he was pleased. This was only our third week of shooting."

"Did he ever have it out with you over how you were directing Lindsay?" More silence. "Come on. Why should I hear a lot of fancy stories from third parties when I should hear the plain truth from you?"

"He said . . ." He shook his head as if refusing to give words to the unspeakable.

"What?"

"He said if Lindsay didn't start showing some real warmth . . ."

"He'd do what?"

"He'd replace me with someone who would be able to . . ."

"Say it."

"He was . . . crude. What do they say about men like Sy? You can take the boy out of Brooklyn, but you can't take the

Brooklyn out of the boy. He said, and I quote: 'Give her a kick in the clit and get her to act like a real woman.' "

"End quote," I said.

"Oh, yes indeed," he agreed. "End quote."

I wasn't really sure why Nicholas Monteleone was such a famous actor. It's not that he was bad-looking. Dark-brown hair, matching eyes. Big lips that critics probably called sensuous. And for a slim guy, lots of muscles, even in unnecessary places, like his forearms, as though he moonlighted as a blacksmith. If he'd worked in Homicide, he'd be second or third best-looking. But that someone was paying him a million bucks a movie because he was such a hunk? I'd seen a couple of his pictures, and he'd never looked like a leading man to me. He had no intriguing dark corners; despite his sleepy, heavy-lidded eyes, he was all sunshine and light.

But he did look like his part in *Starry Night:* a playboy. His thick, almost shoulder-length hair was moussed back on the sides. He'd rolled up the cuffs of his pale-pink shirt just once, and miraculously, they stayed that way. But sitting in the Xerox/coffee room, Nick wasn't playing it smooth. More: Forget I'm a world-famous star. I'm a regular guy. Come on, let's be friends!

Temporary friendship was fine with me. He seemed genuinely good-natured, and what the hell, it's nice to have a movie star trying to grin his way into your heart. But for all his pleasantness, Nick Monteleone didn't seem to know anything worth knowing. Had he seen Sy angry? Hmmm. No, didn't think so. Had anyone been angry at Sy? Ummm, not that I know of. That type of thing for twenty minutes.

"Uhhh," he finally said, "I know this is a serious business, and I'm probably acting like a self-centered asshole, but I've gotta ask. By any chance did you happen to catch me in *Firing Range*? I played one of you guys."

"Yeah," I told him. It wasn't anything I'd go to the movies

for; I'd caught it on cable, although I wasn't about to tell him that. "You were very good." In fact, he had gotten a lot of it right: the camaraderie of a homicide squad, the compulsive twenty-hour workdays and, especially, the fatigue. But he'd worn a shoulder holster—which hardly anyone I know wears—and he'd been physically slow, almost clumsy. By the time he'd have drawn his gun, he would have been dead about forty seconds; he hadn't moved right. And now, watching him, I realized he couldn't even sit right. He was doing the relaxed, manly, lean-back-on-the-two-rear-legs-of-the-chair, when suddenly he lost his balance and almost crashed over backward. He saved himself, barely, but couldn't admit defeat by bringing the chair down on all four legs, so for a minute his feet did a hysterical cha-cha until he regained his balance. Forget his expensive muscles; I saw that Nick had the coordination of a Frankenstein windup toy. When he was a kid, the guys probably muttered, "Not Monteleone!" when they were picking teams.

"Did you get what my character was about?" he asked. "I mean, did *you* buy him?"

"Sure."

Actually, thinking about it, I remembered shaking my head, wondering how come this white Chicago homicide lieutenant (in movies, homicide-cop heroes are always lieutenants) had a combo black—New York—Rambo accent: Yo, mothafucka, put that .38 (which came out like "dirty-eight") on the table and get those hands up high. *Now*, putz.

"I mean, you probably think I'm just another narcissistic actor—and you're probably right—but I am just honestly curious: Could I have been someone you work with?"

What he wanted, I realized all of a sudden, was unconditional acceptance. Not just as my friend. As my colleague. I had to love him totally—and prove my love—or he wouldn't open up to me. So I gushed. "You know, it was the goddamnedest thing! You really were one of us," I told him. "No shit, you could have had the desk next to mine at Headquarters."

Nicholas's entire body eased. He let up on his macho chair

routine. He stretched out his legs, crossed his feet at his ankles. He was wearing some kind of step-in shoes made from lots of thin strips of leather; they probably had some foreign name my brother would know.

"Tell me about dailies," I asked him, now that we were practically best friends, to say nothing of partners. "What are they exactly? The whole day's worth of film?"

"The film has to be processed, so what you're seeing is the footage shot the day before. All the takes. The director and the editor sit in the back and talk—whisper, actually—about which take is good, which isn't, what coverage they'll use, what kind of light and color corrections they'll want to order."

"Who else goes to see them?"

"Actors. Sometimes. Personally, I'm *super*analytical about my own work, and I like to see what everybody else is doing too. You know. Like how is my lighting? My costume? My makeup?"

"Did Lindsay go to dailies?"

Nicholas compressed his big lips. "No. She always rushed back to Sy's house to work out. Swam laps in his pool. Had to keep those pecs toned."

"How come she didn't want to see her acting? She's supposed to be smart. Isn't she analytical about her work the way you are?"

"The real truth? Lindsay is an egomaniac." This said by a guy who went every night to watch his makeup. "She's totally convinced she can gauge her performance as she gives it, so why bother to see herself? Besides"—Nicholas shook his head wearily—"if she wants a reaction, all she has to do is look into Spanish Eyes after each take. You get what I'm saying? She can see her brilliance reflected."

"She really got to Santana?"

"Got to him? She had him in a chain collar, on a leash. 'Roll over, Victor. Good boy! Stay!' A *tragedy* for the rest of the company. The first week, Victor was very strong, full of ideas, energy, really exciting to work with. And actually giving Lindsay a rough time because from day one—well, day three or four—he was under the gun. Sy was not happy with Miss Keefe's work. Naturally, Lindsay being Lindsay, she *immediately* picked up that the balance of power had shifted—away from her. She needed a new ally. So she sniffed out Victor's weakness. *That's* her greatest gift, finding a guy's most sensitive area."

"What was Santana's?"

"Oh . . . being allowed to live in Movieland. I mean, Victor Santana was a damn good cinematographer and then moved to directing. He's directed two really well-received films, right? But beneath his 'I'm *so* sophisticated' façade he's still wide-eyed about being in the business. Deep down, he can't even believe he made it out of East Harlem. And here's Lindsay, with her classical-theater background and her Commie Chic reputation and her half-naked *Vanity Fair*. Supremo nympho. The only guys who get into her are *major* lefties—or very heavy hitters with a net worth of at least fifty mil. So Victor thinks: If the same woman who screws the world's most interesting men—that Latvian novelist, Fidel Castro's minister of defense, Sy Spencer—well, if she wants to screw me, I must be in their league."

"How did she get Sy? What was his weakness?"

"Oh, easy. Sy was the ultissimo intellectual snob. And even though she manages to take off most of her clothes in every movie she makes, Lindsay is still considered a very serious actor; she's convinced everybody she's getting naked as an *hommage* to the First Amendment. She gets brilliant reviews in all the right little magazines—the ones with French names and cheapo paper—and the big ones too. And she was politically correct on Nicaragua before anyone else knew you were even supposed to think about a Nicaragua. Also, she's a genuine beauty. No plastic surgery. And that for-real blond hair."

"No shit. The hair's real?"

"I've been told by highly placed sources that the bottom . . . it's a match."

"Wow." Then I said: "Okay, we'd better get back to the dailies business. Did Sy see them all the time?"

"He had to. First of all, he genuinely cared. And also, they were the only way to monitor his investment."

"Did he ever say anything about being dissatisfied?"

"No. I mean, it depends on the director, but usually it's not just the inner circle at dailies. There's the director of photography, the writer, cameramen, sound men, assistant directors, production assistants, hair and makeup, set designer. The whole cast and crew, if they feel like it. Usually about fifteen people show up, sit around, stuff their faces with trail mix and watch. So Sy—who prided himself on his classiness—wouldn't sit and bitch about Lindsay in front of an audience." The skin around Nicholas's eyes glistened, almost raccoonlike, in the fluorescence. At first I'd thought it was some weird trick of the light. Then I realized it was face cream.

"So how did you know he wasn't happy with her?"

"Well, one day about a week ago, we'd been shooting *very* late. Hardly anyone came to dailies. Most people, Santana included, were wiped; they got the hell out the second after the lights came on. I was kind of hanging around, wanting to get a minute with Sy to talk about something—"

"What?"

"I forget. I'm sure it was nothing important. In any case, Sy starts letting loose to a few of his people. Not loud, and not even angry, which shows you how under control he was, because when you looked at Lindsay up on that screen it was like looking at Big-Tit Barbie. I mean, not one single spark of life. Anyway, Sy was supercool, just kidding about the scene and what a fortune it was going to cost to have an effects man add lightning, and did we really need lightning. Everybody started talking about lightning. All of a sudden, Sy laughs and says how the best thing that could happen to this movie would be if lightning struck *Lindsay*. Then he said, 'Just kidding.' But naturally, everybody knew what he meant."

"What did he mean?"

"If anything really happened to her? It's what the moneymen

always say when one performer is crapping up a movie; if lightning struck, the completion guarantors—the insurers—would have to pay so they could begin production again with another actress. Sy was being lighthearted, but the subtext was: Forget the two-hearts-that-beat-as-one shit; he wished to hell he could be rid of her." Nicholas paused. He was working up to something big. Inhale. Exhale. Inhale. Finally, he got it out: "Can I call you Steve?"

I wasn't any actor, but I flashed my most engaging cop-friend smile. "Yeah, sure."

He smiled back. "And you call me Nick. Now, Steve, just between us. About Sy's wanting to get rid of Lindsay. This last week, I think Sy *might* have been taking meetings off the set." Nick had heavy eyebrows. He lifted them significantly. "Do you get my drift?"

"He had someone else?"

"I'm not sure. But you could see Lindsay trying too hard to please him, and him not interested in getting pleased. I mean, she'd put an arm around him, and he'd put his arm around her. The movements were right, but hell, I'm an actor. Why do I get the big bucks? Because I'm intuitive. I *know* body language, and his was saying, 'I have a headache tonight, dear.' "

"Maybe he was just upset about her performance."

"Maybe. But the first two weeks, he'd always be sniffing around her, hanging around the set most of the day. He knew then that she wasn't doing her best work, but he was so goddamn hot for her he couldn't be angry. I mean, you should have seen him: canned heat. But suddenly he's looking at his watch. He's leaving by eleven."

"Did you hear any talk—vague rumors, even—about this from anyone?"

"No. It's just my theory." Nicholas the Graceful stood up, stretching his arms, and—whammo—slammed his hand against the wall. He sat down again and pretended his knuckles weren't throbbing. "Listen, can I *really* trust you, Steve?"

"You bet." I leaned forward and gave him a light, male-bonding arm punch. "You know you can."

"You know Katherine Pourelle?"

"The actress? Yeah, sure."

"This is not for public consumption, but I used to have a thing with her, when we were both starting out. She was living with this guy from ICM. Her agent, in fact. Well, she was more than living with him. She was married to him. Anyhow, we had this big love, big breakup, big hate. But last winter we met in Vail. New husband—real estate developer. New agent. But you know what goes down. We stopped being silly and became . . . I guess you'd call it friends." I assumed what he was trying to tell me was that he fucked Katherine Pourelle in Vail while her husband was out schussing. I gave him what I hoped was a knowing smile. "Well, I got a call from her Tuesday night. From L.A. She wanted to know what was with the production. At first I thought she'd heard about how lousy Lindsay was doing and just wanted to dish. Kat *hates* Lindsay and *loves* to dish. She did a play with her, years ago. Everybody who ever worked with Lindsay *loathes* her. Fine, I figured, so we talked about Lindsay and Santana, how he was her first non-Commie Hispanic. Oh, and about how Lindsay always closes her eyes when the director is talking, like she's concentrating on the voice of God, and how you wish you could smack her. Anyway, we had this long, really great talk, but there was something left unsaid. I could *sense* it. I mean, Steve, I earn my living by being open to feelings."

"Right," I said encouragingly.

"So I said to her: 'Come on, Kat. Tell me what you heard.' So she makes me swear not to tell a soul. She'd gotten a call from Sy that morning!"

"And?"

"He asked if she would give *Starry Night* an overnight read. *Super*secret. Do you get what I'm saying?"

"He wanted her to look at the part Lindsay was playing?"

"You got it!" Nick said. "I think Sy knew that this was a

potential twenty-million-dollar catastrophe. *And* I think he'd also found himself someone with blonder hair, or *plus grande* boobies. Lindsay had lost her hold on him. You know what, Steve? I think Sy was getting ready to pull the plug on Lindsay."

When Lynne took me on, she knew we had a lot going for us. I wanted what she wanted: love, companionship, a family, plus— since she seemed to average one marriage proposal every two weeks—a chance to stick it to her stick-up-the-ass family. But in taking me on, she knowingly, willingly and of her own free will bought the whole package: recovering alcoholic (to say nothing of a guy with a former fondness for pot, hash, barbiturates and heroin), recovered fuck-arounder, about-to-be-old fart, compulsive runner, workaholic. Her acceptance of me was absolute, unquestioning.

Was she perfect? No. She was a pain in the ass about order, the type who in sixth grade would have won Neatest Three-Ring Binder. I was neat; she was nuts. She had to restrain herself from making the bed the minute I got up to go to the bathroom. She actually inspected her pencils every night to make sure they were all sharpened for the next day. Lynne's idea of wild spontaneity was going out for a nude moonlight swim—after she finished her lesson plan but before the eleven o'clock news. Still, as much as I bitched about it, deep down, her order comforted me. I needed a structured life filled with perfect pencil points and lights out immediately after Johnny Carson's monologue. Her imperfections turned out to be virtues.

So why was I less than wild with happiness? Why couldn't I accept Lynne without reservation, the way she'd accepted me? How come I couldn't say: Sure, she's a little serious, but who gives a shit with that hair, those legs? Why was I wasting time worrying that I wasn't one hundred percent ecstatic? Wasn't ninety-nine percent enough? What was wrong with me? She had five million sterling qualities. Why was I zeroing in on the one she lacked? Why the hell was I waiting for Fun?

It wasn't that Lynne didn't have a sense of humor. She did. But it was a sense of other people's humor. She'd smile whenever I'd say something even mildly clever. She'd laugh at Eddie Murphy and Woody Allen movies, at my friend Marty McCormack's stupid minister-rabbi-priest jokes (where the priest, naturally, always got the punch line) and at any attempt at comedy by any member of grades K through 6 at Holy Spirit Academy, especially her kids, the ones with learning disabilities.

What Lynne lacked was liveliness. I knew it wasn't fair to hold it against her. It was like saying to a woman, I want you to be five foot two and built like a brick shithouse, when she is, in fact, tall and willowy.

Still, I couldn't shake the low feeling that had come over me on the blanket in my backyard the day before. More than disappointment, less than dread. I didn't know what the hell it was. But there I was, taking a phone break, my feet up on the Xerox machine, making it worse—giving her an opening I knew she didn't have the capacity to fill. "Okay, who do you think is sexier? Me or Nicholas Monteleone?"

And as Lynne, predictably, was responding, "You," I found myself ashamed of myself for wanting: "Are you *kidding?* Nicholas Monteleone!"

She asked: "Is he a nice person?"

"Yeah. Friendly; a good talker for someone who speaks other people's lines for a living. When I finished questioning him, I felt: Too damn bad he has to leave; he's great company. But he's *so* terrific that you start wondering whether it's him or it's an act. Like, if he thought that running around the room and imitating an aardvark would put him in a better light with Homicide, would he forget the congeniality bit and start licking up ants?"

"What do you think?"

"Ants," I said. I looked at my watch. It was after five. "Listen, honey, were you counting on lobster?"

"No, but that's what you told me you were counting on."

"Did you melt the butter?"

"No, of course not. And you didn't buy the lobsters. I know you. I know you so well that right now I know I'm going to have a Lean Cuisine and then about ten you'll pop in—just to say hello."

"I'm a very friendly guy."

"Guess what? You won't be able to be too friendly. My room-mates are home tonight."

"Shit. All right, if I get finished by ten, ten-thirty, can I pick you up and take you over to my place?"

Just as Lynne was saying, "Okay, but not too late a night, because I have a huge pile of test results for next year's kids I have to go through," a Southampton Village cop appeared at the door with a surprise guest: Gregory J. Canfield.

Gregory gaped at the room, slack-jawed, trying to register everything, as if the decor—including the brown-stained hot plate of the Mr. Coffee machine and me with my feet up—was going to be the subject of his final in Advance Set Design at NYU film school. Now that there was no corpse to upset his delicate balance, he was Mr. Movie Man.

I said, "People. Speak to you later," to Lynne and "Thanks" to the cop who'd shown Gregory in. Then I hung up, swung my feet off the Xerox machine and told Gregory to sit. But he barely got through the door when he stopped short. You could see his mind moving in for a close-up; he stood before the bulletin board, staring at a yellowing FBI Most Wanted list, at hand-printed signs offering Doberman-mix puppies, an '81 Datsun 280 ZX and a model 12 Winchester pump-action shotgun, probably wishing someone else from NYU was there to share this Moment of Authenticity.

"Okay, now you know what lower middle class looks like, Gregory. Time to sit down." He did. "You're here to help me. Right?"

He nodded. He looked slightly less repulsive than the day before, mainly because instead of baggy shorts, he was wearing baggy slacks. His skeletal white legs, with their bulbous kneecaps, were covered. "I remembered what I couldn't remember last night."

"Great," I replied. I waited. He was staring at my holster, which was clipped onto my belt. "You remembered something?"

"You asked me if there were any threats made to Sy Spencer."

"And?"

"I don't know if you'd classify this as a threat. I mean, a genuine threat." Gregory hesitated. Now he was gazing at me with the same passionate intensity he'd directed at the bulletin board. He'd obviously decided I was the star of this movie. He flushed. He fidgeted. He beamed at me. I was his True Detective.

"Listen, Gregory, anything you think is even remotely threatening—a dirty look—is something I want to hear about."

"Did you know Sy had an ex-wife who lives in Bridgehampton?"

My heart gave a thump. I sat up, alert. Damn it, I'd been right. There was something about her. "Bonnie Spencer," I said. His face fell. "Hey, if by this time I didn't know Sy had an ex in the neighborhood, what the hell kind of detective would I be?" Gregory still looked like he was debating whether or not to be clinically depressed. "Now come on. You're my key man in this investigation. Okay, I gave you a name: Bonnie Spencer. But now it's your job to fill me in."

"Well, Sy married her right at the beginning of his career as producer. She'd written the scenario . . . That's another term for screenplay. It's more common in Britain. In any case, she'd written a movie called *Cowgirl* in the late seventies. Unpretentious film. Her credit was Bonnie Bernstein."

That big Utah jockette didn't strike me as a Bernstein. "Had she ever been married before Sy?" I asked.

"I don't know."

"Okay, go on."

It's funny; as he was talking, I realized that Bonnie had been on my mind since I'd left her that morning. I couldn't shake the images I had of her. One was the real Bonnie as I'd seen her. The other one was even more vivid, and unconnected with reality; she was in some sort of sleeveless thing, a dress or a tank top, that bared part of her broad shoulders. I could see her arms and shoulders: strong, smooth, with the sheen of a deep tan. Incredibly silky skin. It was really, well, an exciting image—and a strange one, because the bare-shouldered Bonnie in my mind's eye was so incredibly desirable, and really had nothing to do with the big girl in the big T-shirt I'd interviewed.

"The marriage broke up," Gregory reported, "and she went into total eclipse as a writer."

"How come?"

"I don't know."

Maybe, I thought, Bonnie Spencer reminded me of someone else, some large, bewitching girl out of my past. That made sense. But my house was no more than four miles from hers; I could have passed her one summer evening on one of my runs and focused in on her best few square inches. Or maybe I'd given her a half second of consideration in my bar-hopping days, before moving on to someone better. Who the hell knew? In all those years of drinking—especially toward the end—there were black holes in my memory. We could have met at a cocktail lounge and discussed Truth and Beauty all night, and it would be a total blank.

"From what I've heard," Gregory went on, "Bonnie is pretty much of a zero. Her only real significance is that she used to be married to Sy. But even then, I probably wouldn't have heard about her if she hadn't come to the set."

Right. Bonnie had mentioned she'd dropped in to see Sy. "What happened?"

Gregory rubbed his palms together as though he was heating them up for a passionate prayer. "One of the other P.A.s came running over to me, saying Sy's ex-wife was there and what should he do. But he couldn't do *anything*, because she was right there behind him. She'd *followed* him. To see her, she's this very plain Jane type, but you could understand how she must have learned a thing or two from Sy, because before I could say a word or go get one of the assistant directors, she walked right past me and knocked on the trailer door. I said, 'Excuse me, miss, but that trailer is *private*. I'll have to ask you to please wait over by the craft services table.' Well, that *second* Sy opened the trailer door. He took one look at her and . . . you would not believe his face!"

"Tell me."

"Beet red, and I mean b-e-e-t. She said something like 'Hiya, Sy!' as if she expected him to give her this major warm welcome, which, of course, he didn't." Gregory drew in his sunken cheeks. He seemed to be waiting for applause.

I didn't clap. "Gregory, you came in to tell me about a threat."

"Oh. Right. Yes, well, Sy gave her this *withering* look and said, 'This is not a Bonnie Bernstein production. You know you do not come onto a set unless you are invited.' And believe me, the way he said it was not exactly *sotto voce*. I mean, Sy could be *heard*."

Shit. Even though I knew there was something wrong about Bonnie, I felt lousy for her. "How did she react?" I asked.

"Jolted. Absolutely jolted. I mean, for whatever reason, she had been expecting a red carpet. She must have thought he'd welcome her with open arms and—"

I cut him off. "The threat, Gregory."

"Right. Well, she stood there for a minute, paralyzed. I mean, you can *imagine* the humiliation. For a second, I thought she might cry. But she didn't. No. Quietly, and I mean *quietly*, like probably I was the only one close enough to hear, do you know what she said to him? She said, 'Sy, you've just been a rotten bastard for the *last time!*' That's what she said. *Days* before he was murdered. And then she just turned her back on him—and walked away!"

CHAPTER 6

Jesus, what a day! Trying to dope out what was under Lindsay's sheet of ice, behind Nicholas Monteleone's cloud of congeniality. Feeling upset that my brother was so upset, wondering if he'd be able to find another job. Seeing Germy again, seeing my past. Lynne.

And Bonnie Spencer. The hardest part of the whole day. Ever since the morning, I'd been fighting her off—the desirable, bare-armed fantasy Bonnie and the real Bonnie, big, plain. Okay, so with fantastic, gold-medal thighs. But I wanted her out of my mind, and she wasn't cooperating.

After Gregory had gone—although not before he'd announced, in front of about ten guys in the squad room, that I was a "fascinating combination" of Scott Glenn and Keith Carradine—I lifted the phone to call Marty McCormack, at home. I wanted to fill him in, ask him if he thought I should bring Bonnie in for questioning, scare her a little. Actually, I just wanted to talk to a friend.

But all of a sudden, I'd started feeling . . . It's hard to describe, but every drunk knows the sensation: a slight tightening in the throat, a fluttering of the heart, and then weariness, edginess. It all happens in that microsecond before your brain says, Hey, I *really* would love a drink. I hung up the phone and drove over to Westhampton Beach.

And at five o'clock, I was sitting on a brown metal folding chair in the basement of the Methodist church in the usual repulsive fog of cigarette smoke at an AA meeting. But I seemed to be doing everything I could to avoid making the old searching and fearless inventory of myself. Instead, I found myself easing into a real hot reverie—reliving my morning meeting with Bonnie, then improving on it. I was in her kitchen again, moving in on her. Her back was pressed against the sink, but now I was rubbing up against her. I kissed her, and she let out a cry of relief and desire and put her arms around me. Her arms felt so incredibly wonderful.

I became aware that I was breathing a little too deeply, crossing, uncrossing my legs. I forced my attention straight ahead.

The smoky basement haze softened the too-lipsticked dark-red mouth of the speaker. Her name was Jennifer. She had wide maroon makeup stripes on her cheeks and dark-brown eye shadow that went up to her eyebrows. But although she looked hard, she didn't sound it; she had that high, silly, sweet voice of a girl who asks you to make a muscle and then squeals "Oooh!" She couldn't have been much older than Lynne.

"See, I used to empty out the saline solution for my contact lenses and put vodka in the bottles!" Jennifer explained. We all laughed, applauded; that was one we hadn't heard. "Anyhow, I kept three bottles in a drawer at work. Two or three times a day I'd start blinking like crazy and rubbing my eye."

Usually I hated meetings in the summer. Somehow, when I wasn't looking (or was too drunk to notice), AA had become a nonalcoholic version of a singles bar. Dingy church basements were packed with yuppies exchanging degradation stories and slipping each other business cards. Despite all warnings, pickups were common. "Hi, babe. Need a sponsor?" AA had turned into the new Hamptons scene, and locals like me felt like . . . well, locals. Jennifer giggled. "I'd grab a bottle of saline solution, toddle down to the bathroom and chug the vodka! And after work, I'd sneak the bottles into my purse, take them home and refill them for the next day!" This meeting wasn't all that bad; along with most of the others, I nodded with recognition at Jennifer's desperation and—despite her lack of anything resembling intelligence—her enormous ingenuity. I thought: We're all so cunning when we're desperate to fuck ourselves over.

I stretched out my legs and leaned back in the chair, forcing myself to relax, to listen, understand, learn. But just as I was thinking an enlightening thought—about how so many drunks have this almost religious belief in the superiority of vodka, its odorless innocence, its purity—Bonnie pushed her way into my head again.

Beneath that straight-shooter veneer, behind the savvy, self-effacing humor, what the hell was she? A *Fatal Attraction* psychopath pursuing Sy, hounding him to produce some hunk of junk she thought was a screenplay—or to get him to love her again? Or was she simply a no-talent loser who had barreled onto the set after pumping up her courage with cocaine or booze or some dopey assertiveness training book?

And what about the threat Gregory had overheard? Look, telling someone it's the last time he's going to be a rotten bastard is, to a homicide cop, somewhat less significant than a vague "I'm gonna get you" or a specific "I'm going to hack your balls off and make them into cuff links." Still, when I'd interviewed her, Bonnie had tossed off her visit to the set in a couple of words, giving the impression that dear old Sy had asked her to drop by just to be friendly: a little cheek-to-cheek air kiss, a little "Oh, Bon, you must meet Johnny, our key grip," a little chat about some dangling participle in her screenplay.

And what about her story about being invited to Sy's house, getting the fifty-cent tour? Why would a smart operator like Sy Spencer risk the Wrath of Lindsay by bringing home his tall-in-

the-saddle ex-wife to have a look around the master bedroom suite
with its king-size closets, its emperor-size bed? Why would he
offer Bonnie a tour of a house that had to have pointed out to her:
Sweetheart, did you get fucked over on alimony! Was he that
insensitive? That much of a prick? Or had Bonnie pushed her way
in there too? And why had she told me about it? Good old honesty?
Or had anyone seen her, maybe making an unseemly fuss? rifling
through drawers? taking something that didn't belong to her? Had
she been smart enough to know we'd be dusting everything—from
the doorknobs to the blade of Marian Robertson's Cuisinart—for
prints and knew hers were there?

Goddamn Bonnie. It ticked me off that all day long I hadn't
been able to get her out of my mind. When I thought about it,
she was the one who'd ruined Lindsay Keefe for me. Here I'd been
expecting at least a cheap thrill, and what happened? I'd actually
gotten turned off because Lindsay, posturing in front of the window,
had seemed so false after Bonnie's "naturalness."

Big deal. She was in great shape and she'd . . . I don't know.
She'd amused me. But I knew, as I sat there, tuning out the AA
meeting, that I was acting nuts, fixating on Bonnie. By any rational
standard, I'd never had it so good. Lynne was great-looking, sweet,
young. But there I was, eyes closed, imagining running my hands
over the flawless satin of Bonnie's arms—even though, for all I
knew, she could have clammy, fish-belly flesh or rough lizard skin,
or her entire body could be dotted with dime-size brown freckles.

I wasn't sure what was going on. Had Bonnie Spencer gotten
to me? Or had I gotten to me? Gregory, after all, had been right
on target about her: a plain Jane. Barely nice eyes—okay, an
interesting color. An ordinary nose. A forgettable mouth, most
likely with chalky, premenopausal lips; I really hadn't noticed. So
what the hell was I doing wanting to . . . I can't even say wanting
to see her again. Just wanting her.

Forget reality. I wanted my fantasy too much to open my eyes:
I had dropped my jacket onto her kitchen floor. My tie was unknotted, my shirt was open, and I was tearing off Bonnie's bra so

I could hold her against me, skin to skin. Applause startled me. I looked up. Jennifer, smiling with lipsticked teeth, was stepping down.

Engaged-guy nerves. That was my problem. Definitely. After more than half a lifetime of drinking—and womanizing—of being a master self-deceiver ("Only three beers tonight") and a consummate liar ("Oh, sweetheart, oh, you're so beautiful, oh, I love you"), it was so hard to keep it simple.

Willie, the leader, a big local guy in a plaid shirt who was a motorcycle mechanic, stepped to the front. Years before, he'd gotten his teeth knocked out in a fight; his dentures looked as if they'd been molded for a giant; they made him lisp. "Thith hath been a great meeting!" he boomed. "Time to clothe now. Would all thothe who feel like it join me in the Therenity Prayer?"

Was it only that I was having the normal alcoholic's trouble of keeping it simple? Or was I in deeper shit, really looking to self-destruct? To throw over Lynne, which equaled throwing over happiness, stability, a chance to be a human being? Was I still drawn to oblivion?

Forty-five of us stood and held hands. I squeezed tight. I felt warm I'm-with-you squeezes back, even from the yuppie jerk in tennis whites on my right. I thought: *This* is what I'm here for. Support. I can't do it myself. I need these people. I need God. I need . . .

I couldn't fight Bonnie. Something is wrong about her, I thought. Plus, objectively, there is absolutely nothing about her to turn me on. And yet now I was imagining kissing her soft, warm skin.

"God grant me the serenity . . ." My voice was embarrassingly loud.

Maybe I could keep it simple: Just admit she was one of those women who, despite the most commonplace looks, had always been an erotic genius, even now, even as she was getting too old for anyone to want. A not-homely, not-pretty woman you'd overlook on the street but who, in close quarters, knows exactly how to get

to you. Or maybe she wasn't devious. Maybe she did it uncon-
sciously: she gave off primitive, subliminal signals or secreted
some subtle female animal smell. Whatever it was, I wasn't going
to let it affect me.

". . . To accept the things I cannot change," I prayed. "Courage to change the things I can; / And wisdom to know the difference."

Amen.

On the basis of its architecture, my mother's house, an old place
with weathered cedar siding and a deep front porch, should have
been charming or quaint or inviting. But it wasn't. There were too
many trees too close: overpowering oaks, dark, drippy maples,
grim spruces; their humid shadows spooked the house. And inside . . . well, it was always dank, especially in the living room,
with its never-quite-dry upholstery; sit there long enough and your
pubic areas felt about to mildew. No wonder I'd gone off to Vietnam, come home for three days and then never gone back. But
my brother had never moved out.

Oh, right, you could say, hearing that: He still lives with
Mommy. But it really wasn't like that. Easton was no mama's boy.
Sure, with his navy-blue blazers and golden color, he might look
like some harebrained heir to a Southampton fortune. But in truth,
he was very unindulged. My father had given him almost nothing,
except an occasional unbankable belch, and in any case had
cleared out soon after Easton's sixth birthday. My mother, although
she clearly preferred him to me, spent every cent she had on
upping her own Quality Quotient, not his; she would never pass
up buying a hundred-dollar ticket to a benefit for hyperkinetic
Maori Anglicans held on some rich socialite's lawn (with shrimp
in sculpted-ice swan boats) in order to do something nice for her
son. Still, Easton had inherited my mother's grand dreams, although unlike her, he had never lost touch with the truth. He was
not the typical Bridgehampton local who falls in with the summer
crowd; he did not get dizzy drinking rich people's champagne. No

matter how much time he spent in their perfect houses, he knew he wasn't one of them, that he was, essentially, poor and, in addition, not blessed with that mysterious personal magnetism that attracts money.

So forget Easton buying his own place, or even renting an apartment. Both assumed a steady income, and my brother understood that long-term job retention—unlike cutting lemon peels into translucent twists—was not one of his fortes. I'm sure he never actually sat down with my mother and said: Listen, I can play golf, tennis and croquet, sail a boat. I know the correct dress shoes to wear from Memorial Day to Labor Day. But for some reason I keep getting canned after six or eight months. So if you don't mind, I'd going to stay put here. Why go through the embarrassment of setting up housekeeping somewhere and then getting evicted? Right, Mom?

Actually, Easton's living at home suited them both. No rent for him, just whatever he could contribute, whenever. And living in the big house set far back from the road, he could pass himself off as a Bridgehampton blueblood. Who among his city slicker acquaintances would get out of their Porsches to inspect the house—and discover we did not own the adjoining farmland? Who, over the course of a lazy summer, would bother to check his credentials, to find out that his father had been not a gentleman farmer but a drunk given to pissing on the floor of the local tavern?

(I call Easton's friends acquaintances. Just like my mother, he lived for the summer people. From the time he got his driver's license, he ignored the kids at high school and hung out with a semi-social Southampton crew: the Daddy-is-on-Wall-Street-and-by-gosh-so-am-I fraternity. It didn't seem to matter who they were individually; they all had boats to invite him on, golf clubs to take him to, wives' college roommates to fix him up with. They were interchangeable: extremely tan, mildly wealthy and slightly stupid.)

Anyway, the domestic arrangement suited Easton. And I guess my mother liked having him around because he could do all the man jobs: mow the lawn, put up the storm windows, check the mousetraps in the cellar. She'd never been much of a farm wife, even when she'd had a farmer.

Living with Easton gave my mother an audience for her compulsive monologue no one else would be willing to listen to. She'd sit at the table, push her food around her plate, light up a cigarette and—puff, puff—talk about the French five-thousand-dollar dress Mrs. Preston Cortwright had tried to return the Monday after her big party; the rumor that Mr. Edward Dudley, husband of size-three Mrs. Edward—puff, puff—had taken up with their Experiment in International Living seventeen-year-old fatso fräulein from Munich. Or—my mother would tap off the ash—how she herself had made all the right diplomatic moves and had *finally* been named deputy associate chairlady of the Southampton-Peconic Museum of Art's annual cocktail party.

My mother's pretentiousness, her coldness—her absolute nothingness—never got to my brother. Unlike me, he could listen to her expound on Quality without wishing she'd choke to death on one of her goddamn Protestant watercress sandwiches.

Not that they spent a lot of time together. My mother used the big back bedroom on the first floor, and Easton took over the second floor. I don't think either of them longed for more companionship. Okay, compared to me, Easton was my mother's pride and joy, but compared to what she had expected of him—the presidency of a major brokerage firm, senior partner of a Wall Street law firm—he was a loser.

But a well-dressed one.

Robby Kurz did a major double take after we rang the doorbell. "Easton Brady," my brother said to Robby, and shook his hand.

Robby stared at Easton. Then he blinked a couple of times, as if expecting his vision to clear. He had probably been imagining me minus two years, and that was sort of true. But he was also face-to-face with a gent in gray flannel slacks, a pale-blue oxford shirt and a sapphire-blue V-neck sweater, a rich-looking Waspy

guy who was combing back his hair off his forehead with his
fingers—hair that was just slightly too long. Not hippy or scruffy
hair, but hair that seemed to be saying: Forgive the length, but I
just got back from sailing home from Bermuda.

Half an hour later, Robby was still sneaking fast, disbelieving
glances from Easton to me. He sat at a folding card table across
from Easton in my brother's sitting room; it had once been my
bedroom. As a kid, Easton had used the table to build his model
ships; now it was covered with a huge, square fringed gold cloth,
like one of those scarves you see on pianos in old movies. It almost
hid the table's skinny metal legs. I sat directly behind my brother,
on a nice old cracked leather couch he must have picked up at
some yard sale; the shrink at South Oaks had had one like it, the
same dark brown.

My deal with Ray Carbone was that I could be at Easton's
interview without being there. But every now and then my brother
would turn his head and glance at me for reassurance as Robby
questioned him about the cast and crew. What the hell: I'd nod,
letting him know he was doing fine. Well, he was.

"What exactly were you doing in New York yesterday?" Robby
was asking.

"I was meeting with our casting director. Going over deal
memos and negotiating a price on some extra work we wanted
done. Sy and Santana felt we had to cast the Colombian drug
kingpin as threatening, but quietly threatening."

"You mean all the parts weren't filled yet, even after they'd
started making the movie?" Robby asked.

"That's right." Easton sounded casual, like someone who'd
been in the business for twenty years instead of a few months. "It
happens fairly often. We knew we could always sign an actor we'd
already read, but we were hoping for someone special. The problem
was where to look." I rested my head on the back of the couch's
cool leather, crossed my arms over my chest and checked out my
brother. I was impressed: no more of his sweaty, eager, fast-talking
bullshit, like when he was selling houses or Jaguars or hand-

knitted boat-neck sweaters. Easton had become a genuine movie guy. "We'd seen just about every over-fifty swarthy actor in New York and California. No luck, but we weren't ready to give up. Well, not yet." He really seemed to know what he was talking about. I was proud all of a sudden.

He kept plucking at the neck of his sweater, probably to realign the V in front. "The casting director wanted to start looking at actors in Chicago, to farm the work out to her associate there. But the price she quoted us seemed out of line. Sy thought it would be better to negotiate with her in person than over the phone, but he couldn't do it. He was busy on the set and getting ready to go to L.A., so he asked me to."

"How long did that meeting last?"

"From before two until—I'm guessing now—three-thirty, four. I'm not sure. You could check with her."

"Did you speak to Sy on the phone at all during that time?"

"No. I was going to drive over to his house after dinner, around nine, and tie up whatever loose ends there were."

"Was he expecting any company for dinner?" I interjected.

"No," Easton said. "Just Lindsay."

"Did you come straight back here after your meeting?" Robby asked.

"No. I went to Sy's shirtmaker to give him a swatch of Egyptian cotton Sy wanted to use and to pick up some other shirts that were ready." I couldn't see my brother's face from the couch, but Easton must have smiled at Robby because, suddenly, Robby had on his supertoothy grin. "Assistant producer," Easton continued, "and swatch-carrier. My whole job was to smooth things out for Sy. I went to meetings, made phone calls, wheeled and dealed in a minor way. And even played errand boy." He fell silent for a minute, then added solemnly: "It was the best job I ever had."

Outside my old bedroom window, the leaves on the oak tree were almost black against the blue-gray twilight. It's usually a down time for ex-drunks, but there I was, all of a sudden, feeling pretty up—about Easton.

My brother, obviously, had always had some inner aberration that had screwed up his chances at a career. But outwardly he'd been Mr. Moderate. Balanced, temperate, neat, controlled. No fires burning in his soul. You couldn't believe he wasn't able to get a grip on his life, because he *seemed* so balanced. He did nothing to excess; when he drank, it was a watered-down Scotch or a couple of glasses of wine. When he drugged, it was one puff of a joint. Even the women he went out with were understated— to the point of invisibility: well-bred, well-dressed, with boobs barely bigger than their tiny noses.

But strangely, the movie business, famous for its bullshit, had managed to make Easton more real. He was much less pompous. Okay, still not the kind of guy you'd ask over for *Monday Night Football,* but friendlier, looser. A decent man instead of Charlotte Easton Brady's finely featured, immaculately groomed, elegantly dressed prig of a son. Maybe, I started thinking, after all these years, we could really be brothers. Lynne would say, Let's have Easton to dinner, and I'd say, Great.

"Why was Mr. Spencer going to Los Angeles?" Robby asked.

"He had four or five different projects he was interested in. He had a lot of meetings lined up."

I broke in. "Isn't it a little unusual for a producer to leave town while his movie is being made?"

Easton turned around, giving me the profile that demonstrated who'd gotten the best of the genes. "Not necessarily. Sy was executive producer. He had what's called a line producer to supervise the whole production, take care of the day-to-day problems. And he had me to put out smaller fires. So he could afford to get away for a couple of days."

"Except things were pretty lousy here."

"What do you mean?"

"The business with Lindsay."

"Lindsay." Easton seemed a little ill at ease, as if by confirming trouble he'd be letting Sy down. "I see you've heard the rumors."

"We heard about the lousy dailies," I told him. "Were they that bad?"

He shrugged. "I can't be a hundred percent sure, Steve. I haven't been in the business long enough to really know. I mean, when Sy asked, I pretended to have an opinion and crossed my fingers and hoped I didn't sound like a complete fool. But whatever reactions I have, they're still pretty much the same as the man who buys a ticket and sits in a multiplex with a box of popcorn: either bored or enjoying himself. As far as I could see, Lindsay was doing all right. And she looked—there's no other word— breathtaking." Robby started his compulsive Lindsay nodding. "But I *think* I understood what Sy was talking about. Whenever Lindsay was on the screen, I wasn't riveted—except by her beauty. I looked, but I didn't really listen. My attention wandered. And to be honest, it probably would have wandered more if I hadn't been involved in the movie."

"But she wasn't a disaster?" I inquired.

"Not her acting per se. But I think from Sy's point of view the movie itself was a disaster-in-progress, because the audience *had* to love this woman. And even I could see you did not love Lindsay in those dailies. Actually, you didn't even like her all that much. You just didn't care."

Robby took over. "Was Sy going to Los Angeles to speak to Katherine Pourelle about taking over Lindsay's part?"

Just before Easton whipped his head around to face Robby, I saw his reaction: absolutely stunned at how far we'd come so fast. "Jesus, who told you that?" Neither of us responded. Finally, Easton spoke. "Well, congratulations! Whoever your source was knew what he was talking about." He turned back to me, really curious. "Who told you?"

"I can't, East."

"Oh, right," he said. "Sorry. I didn't mean to be pushy. . . ." He smiled. "Well, not too pushy. In any case, Sy *was* going to see Katherine Pourelle. But as far as I was concerned, it was just a typical Sy maneuver. You see, he would let word leak out that he was speaking to Pourelle and her agent. That would put the fear of God into Lindsay, make her wake up and start—well, start acting. But I swear to you, Sy *never* would have fired her."

"He told you that?" Robby asked, then cleared his throat. He was getting hoarse. It had been a long day, and he looked like one exhausted Howdy Doody. Even the perky points of the yellow handkerchief in his breast pocket had gone limp.

"No. But you see, I'd gotten to know Sy. He could be objective, tough, even callous about Lindsay the actress. But he was completely vulnerable to Lindsay the woman. She had an enormous hold over him."

"Sex?" I asked.

"Yes," Easton responded.

"Was it just a sex thing, or did love enter into it too?" Robby inquired.

"It must have been both." Easton lowered his head. His shoulders rose and fell with each of his sighs. And all of a sudden it hit me. Easton, like Sy, was being objective about Lindsay's performance—but not about Lindsay herself. He couldn't hide it. He'd actually fallen for her.

"It's not just that she's beautiful, or talented or intelligent," he was explaining, trying to sound detached, "although she's all those things. She has a way of getting to a man." Robby was bobbing his head again: Yes! Yes! Yes! "Sy . . . Sy needed Lindsay too much to fire her." I heard Easton swallow. He seemed to have needed her too. He had one hell of a lump in his throat.

"He needed her even if it cost him twenty million dollars?" Robby asked.

"*Yes.*"

But what about Nick Monteleone's theory that Sy had chilled on the fair Lindsay and was, in fact, getting his toes curled elsewhere after he left the set every morning at eleven? I thought about those long, unblond hairs caught on the headboard in the guest room.

"Were you there for that conversation about if lightning struck Lindsay?" I asked.

Easton's posture went ramrod straight. Once again, he seemed amazed that we actually had been doing what we were supposed to be doing: being detectives. Finally, he said: "God, you two are thorough! And . . . well, yes. I heard Sy say that. But that wishing Lindsay were out of the picture—literally—was just Sy's way of blowing off steam."

"What do you mean?"

"She was a big disappointment, but he wouldn't have fired her. Trust me, Steve. There was no way he would have been able to cut her loose." Easton's tongue came out to moisten his lips. "He was helpless when it came to Lindsay."

Normally, I would have gone after him, half kidding, half zinging it to him, saying: *Him* helpless? What about you, sucker? I'd have given him a lot of shit about falling for a movie star. But I wasn't going to embarrass my brother in front of Robby. Also, I realized that even if this was a hopeless crush, it was important; this was the first time in Easton's life where he was showing some passion. It was not something to laugh about.

"What about the other investors?" Robby asked. "It wasn't just Sy's money, was it? What about Mikey LoTriglio?"

"Mikey!" Easton said. "Yes, of course. He'd slipped my mind. God, you should see him. What a tough act. Makes Marlon Brando in *The Godfather* look like a pussycat." He stopped and considered what he'd been saying. "But maybe that's not fair. He has a thick New York accent. And he looks like such a . . . hood. Maybe that makes him seem tougher than he is."

"Was Sy afraid of him in any way?"

Silence. Easton must have been chewing his lip over that. I peered around. There was a script on the coffee table in front of the couch. I picked it up. My brother turned at the sound of paper. He saw what I was holding. His body sagged; his poise deserted him. He seemed to have forgotten about Robby. "See that script,

Steve?" He sounded like a kid a few seconds from tears. "Sy gave it to me Thursday, the day before . . . He handed it to me and said, 'Our next movie, Easton. It just might make history.' "

"I'm really sorry," I said. "Things were going great with him, weren't they?"

"I finally—" He cut himself off, realizing Robby was there. "My life was tied to his," he said quietly. He took a deep breath, and when he spoke again he was the old Easton, aggressively cheerful. "Well, I guess I'll have to beat the bushes, find something else." He shook his head. "I'd hate like hell to have to move to California, but I may have to. Be closer to the action, to people in the business."

Oh, shit, I thought. Easton had lucked out with Sy. He'd found a patron who liked his Southampton style and who had the rare and good instinct to trust Easton, to allow him to rise to all sorts of occasions, to prove himself. But Sy couldn't give a reference. And what the hell kind of résumé could my brother hand out in Hollywood? Failed car salesman? For years Easton hadn't even been able to sell madras Bermudas to congenital preppies. He lacked something—conviction, balls. What would he do in Los Angeles? How would he maneuver in a city of sharks?

"Uh, where were we?" Robby wondered. He was massaging the bridge of his nose as if it were some newly discovered acupuncture point that would induce bright eyes and a clear mind. Except it didn't work. Christ, he was wiped. I thought: Thirty years old is too young to get that tired that fast. Maybe that was why he was always trying to jump the gun, pushing for an arrest. The guy had no stamina. He couldn't keep it up for a long investigation.

"We were on Mikey," I reminded him.

"Right. Mikey."

"Sy did get . . . on edge when Mikey called," Easton admitted to Robby. "But 'on edge' for you or me might mean losing our temper, biting our nails. For Sy, it was just a slight tightness in his voice. You'd have to know him quite well to pick it up."

"Did he seem afraid?" Robby asked.

"I don't know. There was just that hint of tension. Although that in itself was a bit unusual. I mean, Sy never *got* anxiety. He gave it—to everybody. But every time Mikey would call, Sy would shake his head and mouth: 'I'm out.' "

While my brother talked, I opened the script. It said: "Night of the Matador" and "An original screenplay by Milton J. Mishkin." I turned the page and read a little:

LOW-ANGLE SHOT of MATADOR, huge, commanding, menacing against black BG.

MATADOR

I am Roderigo Diaz de Bivar—El Cid. And I am Francisco Romero, seven hundred years later, piercing the bull with my sword.

SFX: Thunderous animal breathing. Is it the matador? Or the bull?

And I am Manolete, gored to death. And the young El Cordobes.

CAMERA RISES. BG brightens and WE SEE Matador in the center of the bullring, surrounded by PICADORS on horseback and BANDERILLEROS. He brandishes his red muleta.

I am Spain.

CAMERA MOVES IN to Matador's muleta for ECU and as WE HEAR flamenco music:

I am man.

BEGIN OPENING CREDITS against red.

I thought: They couldn't pay me to read this shit, much less see it—which probably means it's a true work of art.

"Did Mikey LoTriglio call Sy a lot?" Robby was asking.

"The last week or so, yes. About two or three times a day."

Robby began playing with the fringe on the scarf that covered the table, running his fingers through it. "What were Mikey's calls about?"

"I gather he'd been hearing rumors that the movie was having problems. Sy kept denying it, of course."

"Do you think this Mikey made any threats?"

"I never heard his part of the conversation," Easton said. "But whatever his message was, Sy found it . . . disturbing." He paused. "Sy's upper lip would get those little beads of sweat. You can't imagine what that was like. Sy was *not* a man to sweat."

Inducing perspiration is not, in the State of New York, grounds for arrest, but you couldn't tell that from Robby's face. Suddenly he was awake, alert. Mikey was his guy. You could see the gleam of handcuffs shining in Robby's eyes.

"Hey, easy, Robby," I said.

"Steve, this is a good lead," Robby responded, ignoring Easton, as if he were another cop—or a member of the family. "Mikey's bad."

"Sure, but he's no moron. Would he shoot Sy over a bad investment?"

"Come on. He's Mafia."

"Yeah," I acknowledged, "but this doesn't look like their kind of hit. They tend to be more personal, more close-up than a couple of long-distance bullets from a .22."

But Sy might have had other enemies, I thought: a pissed-off poet from his old magazine; an old show-biz connection with a grudge; some South Fork local he'd insulted—a gas station attendant, an electrician, a swimming pool contractor—some guy with a snootful of sauce and a pocketful of ammo. And what about Lindsay? Calculating, egotistical, arrogant, maybe ruthless, maybe about to be bounced in her dual role as star and concubine. Could she fire a rifle?

And, damn it: Bonnie. How much research had she done for *Cowgirl?*

"What about the ex-wife?" I asked Easton. "There's some talk that Sy was developing her screenplay."

Easton shook his head. "No. Sy gave me her script fairly soon after I started working for him, before we were in production. Asked me to find some nice things to say about it. My guess is that when he told her no, he wanted to be able to say: 'Oh, but the dialogue was so fresh, so honest.' "

"How was the dialogue?"

"I don't know. Not horrible. But Sy said she was born forty-some-odd years too late, that she wrote 1942 women's B movies."

"Did she ever call him?" Robby asked.

"Yes. A couple of times a week, as a matter of fact. And she dropped in on him on the set, which did *not* amuse him. I know; I was in the trailer with him. You know how cool Sy always was? Well, I thought he was going to have a fit." Easton stopped. He turned around in his chair to face me.

"What are you thinking?" I asked my brother. "Woman Scorned?"

"I don't know," Easton said thoughtfully. "I'm not a cop. I don't know how to weigh these things. But, Steve, I have to tell you: I didn't like the look on Sy's face when he saw her. I had a feeling something wrong was going on."

CHAPTER 7

If I wanted to be on time, I had two minutes to make the ten-minute drive to Lynne's. So what did I do? I drove right to Bonnie Spencer's, parked around the corner and then stood diagonally across the road.

Her house was plain in that no-nonsense, almost severe colonial style—not much more than a large two-story box with a roof and chimney. But a big, soft willow stood in front, and, in the moonlight, the old gray shingles shone silver against the dark sky.

The curtains were drawn, although not so tightly that I couldn't see the blue flicker of a black-and-white TV. Jesus, what had I promised Lynne when I'd called from the Southampton P.D.? That I'd be at her house by ten, ten-thirty? It was ten twenty-eight. I walked across the road and up the stone path toward Bonnie's house.

That Moose was some watchdog! There wasn't even a mild grrr until I rang the bell; then, through the long, skinny windows that framed the front door, I could see her tail going so fast it made her rear end shimmy.

The outside light went on. I stuck my hands in my pockets. I took them out. Finally, Bonnie walked into the front hallway. For a second I thought maybe I'd interrupted something that she and a guy had been doing with the TV on. But as she got nearer to the door I could see there was no guy. She had on baggy cotton sweats and a red sweater. No makeup, but then maybe she never wore makeup. Her hair was loose, down to her shoulders, but it stood up on the back of her head, as though she'd been lying on a couch for a couple of hours.

I tried to read her expression when she saw it was me. Relief that I wasn't some night-crawling creep, maybe mixed with some apprehension about what was I doing there again, and maybe— although it's a lot to read through a skinny window—anticipation. It could be that moving in on her that morning had worked.

Except, I thought, as the door opened, who needed it? I felt like such a jerk. I couldn't believe I had wasted a whole day fantasizing about this woman. "I know it's late," I said, before she could say anything, "but this is a homicide investigation."

"Uh, would you like to come in?" The corners of her mouth wiggled for a second, deciding whether or not to smile; she opted for not. Then she turned and led me toward the right, into the living room. She switched on a couple of lamps, turned off some old movie she'd been watching on her VCR.

I could see the indentation her head had made on a pillow on the couch. I sat down next to it; the cushion was warm. Moose stood by my legs, stretching her thick, hairy black neck, clearly contemplating the possibility of leaping up beside me. Finally, realistically, she lowered her big butt onto the floor, threw me the doggy equivalent of a come-hither look and, once again, lay down over my shoes. The girl may have turned out to be mediocre, I mused, but the dog was as fantastic as I'd remembered. I swiveled my foot back and forth, rubbing her belly.

Bonnie sat across the room from me, on a rocking chair. The room was nice—yellow and peachy pink and white—but not what I would have expected from her. Sure, it was comfortable, but it was a Manhattan interior decorator farmhouse. A room like this should be plain, nice at best, not charming. But it was all there: braided rag rugs on the pegged oak floor, old quilts, pillows made from more old quilts, samplers in frames and a lineup of old white water pitchers on the mantel. Plus, off to the left of the fireplace, a painted bellows big enough to inflate the fucking Goodyear blimp. She saw me eyeing it.

"When we bought the house, Sy got interested in American folk art." To illustrate, she pointed out some shelves: books interspersed with wood decoys. "If it looked like it could quack, he bought it. He even put in a bid on an 1813 hand-carved loom. What did he think he was going to do? Spend his weekends weaving? Anyway, then we had our first party out here. This famous book editor walked into the room, looked around and said, 'Very cute!' The man was so mean! Why did he have to say that? But from that minute on, Sy hated the house." I didn't respond; she filled in the silence, fast: "So here I am—with a lot of ducks. Um, can I get you something? Coffee? A drink?"

"Why did you go to see Sy on the movie set?"

She took an instant too long to answer. "Just being friendly. And I guess I felt some nostalgia for the good old days."

"Between you and him?"

"No. Between me and the movies. Sometimes . . ." Her voice got a little scratchy. ". . . I miss it so much. The writing—writing something better than 'A yummy cloud of almost-silk.' And I miss the people and—"

I cut her off before she could get into an "I'm So Alone Blues" number. I didn't want to hear it. "You went onto the *Starry Night* set. What happened? Was Sy happy to see you?"

"I guess you must already have the answer to that." The lamplight made a patch of brightness on her dark hair, just where it grazed her shoulder.

"I want your answer." I pulled my feet out from under Moose; the dog peered up at me, surprised at the sudden withdrawal of intimacy. "What's the problem? Was he happy to see you or not? This shouldn't be something you have to think about."

"He seemed upset that I came uninvited," she said at last. "Not furious, like he'd want to beat me to a bloody pulp and stomp on my head and—" Suddenly her eyes grew wide with embarrassment. "Oh, God, for a minute I forgot what you did for a living. I'm really sorry. I didn't mean to make fun of . . ."

"It's okay. You were saying he wasn't about to do you permanent damage."

"Right. But he wasn't about to be polite and say: 'Tsk-tsk, you might have called first, Bonnie, dear.' "

"What was his attitude?"

"Something between—let's see—nonchalance and rage."

"Do you want to be a little more specific?"

"He didn't yell." I did a speed-of-light survey; her red sweater was just tight enough to show she had standard, conventional tits. If you took the entire female adult population of the world, Bonnie Spencer's tits would mark the median. "But maybe that's because he was trying so hard not to spit."

"If you were such great friends, why would he act that way?"

"I don't know. Maybe he was in the middle of a tantrum about something else and I just showed up at the wrong time."

"Maybe." I wanted to give myself a swift kick in the ass: to think that over the day I'd built up this Marlboro Man's sister to be an embodiment of sensuality.

And then Bonnie reached up and smoothed back her hair. For just a second, she held it up in a ponytail. The undersides of her forearms were pearly, flawless. I pictured her stretched out on the couch beside me, her head on the pillow, her arms lifted, showing off that soft skin. I'd bend over and kiss it. Run my tongue over it.

I coughed to clear my throat. "Did you drop in on him to ask about your screenplay?"

"No." She let her hair drop. The action was beautiful, grace-ful, like a slow-mo replay of a perfect catch. "We'd gone over all his notes. I was working on the revisions."

"And you say he liked it?"

"Yes."

"Did you ever think he might be saying nice things about your work to lead you on?"

"Why would he do that?"

"The truth?"

"Go ahead."

"Maybe he found you more interesting than your screenplay. Maybe deep down you sensed that and—"

Her face turned a hot pink. "Let me clue you in to something. I am not one of those typical New York neurotic dames, just dying to believe the worst about herself. And Sy wasn't some sleazo who'd say, 'Ooh, baby, love your montage.' My work was good, and Sy liked it. I knew he did."

"Hey, I'm not trying to hurt your feelings. It's just my job to probe. Okay?"

She calmed down. "The fact is, Sy and I were friends. Look, I wasn't his type, not even when he married me, and ten more years didn't do much for me in the lusciousness department. I know what he went for. A Lindsay, someone breathtaking. Or someone wispy and intellectual and twenty-two from Yale. Or a jet-setty type with a French accent who could quote Racine—with hair under her arms and a château. I was his ex-wife; he had no reason to hand me a line. He knew better than anyone what I had to offer—and he'd already said no thank you."

"What about for old times' sake?" She shook her head hard. Her hair swung softly. "Bonnie, were you sleeping with Sy? Is that why you felt so free to drop by? Maybe just a nice, spontaneous gesture?"

"No!"

"Or maybe to let the world know you were back on the map?"

"No!"

"Because if you were, that wouldn't bring you under any suspicion." Bullshit, of course. "Here you were, two adults who knew each other very well, who liked each other . . ."

"Nothing personal, but that's a lot of bull."

"Okay, no more questions," I said, getting up and walking over to her. Moose, the town slut, stayed by my side. "For now." Then I laid it on thick. Smile. Wink. Charm, charm. "I'm sorry if I offended you."

"It's all right," she said, her voice softening. Charm, charm was working. She looked up at me; her eyes actually became a little misty, almost as if she expected to be kissed.

"Good," I said. "Glad you understand." I reached over and ruffled her hair. Too bad: the button on the sleeve of my sports jacket got caught in her hair. "Sorry," I said, really sincerely, and tried to get the button free. Her hair smelled of some spring flower I couldn't identify: lilac, maybe, or hyacinth. I grasped the button and got it away, but unfortunately it yanked on her hair. "Listen, this doesn't count as police brutality."

She smiled. A great, wide-open, western smile. "I know."

"See you around, Bonnie."

When I got back to my car, I slipped four strands of Bonnie Spencer's hair into a small plastic envelope. Three had roots. Enough for a DNA comparison analysis.

I always hated making it with women who couldn't shut up. Listen, no guy minds an encouraging word here and there, a helpful suggestion, a sincere scream of enthusiasm. But for the longest time before Lynne came into my life, nearly every woman I picked up was a Gray Line tour guide of sex.

They'd all memorized the same script. About how the trip was going: Oh, it feels so wonderful. Oh, don't stop. . . . Directions to the driver: A little harder. No, easy, slow. No, up higher, higher. . . . And what tourist treat was just around the corner: I'm going to take you/it in my mouth (an offer I never sneezed at, since it embraced the twin joys of gratification and silence). . . . And of course, they'd always let you know when the tour was over: Oh, it's happening. Oh, yes. Wait, just a second. Oh, this is too much. Please, no, God, Jesus.

Lynne, though, was quiet. What a relief. Of course, she had the self-confidence of the young and the lovely: she knew she didn't have to keep up a monologue to hold a guy's attention. And she was quiet, also, because somewhere—maybe at Manhattanville College—she'd learned that nice young ladies do not shriek "Fuck me harder!" when in the arms of gentlemen.

But that night, her quiet had some measure of the silent treatment. She was angry at me for ringing her doorbell at eleven-fifteen, saying, "Oh, shit, I'm sorry," when I saw she'd given up hope of seeing me that night and had gotten undressed. Plus she was pissed at herself for letting me go to her closet, grab her raincoat, put it over her nightgown and lead her out her door with a tired line like "Please, I just want to be with you tonight." She hadn't said a word in the car.

But she wasn't only getting back at me by being uncommunicative. As I unbelted her raincoat and eased it off, she reached over and turned out the bedroom light. She was denying me the pleasure of seeing her.

"You're really mad," I said. I took my gun off my belt and laid it down on my chest of drawers gently, so she wouldn't be further put off by its offensive clunk. "Why don't you say it?"

"All right. I'm angry."

"Tell me why."

"Because you just assume I'm always available to you, any hour, day or night. I understand that you work crazy hours. But you don't seem to understand that I have to make a life—a structure—for myself. No. You want sex, you want to talk, so you expect me to drop whatever I'm doing. That's not fair."

"I'm sorry." I came up beside her and slid my hands under the feathery cotton of her nightgown, easing it up and off. I pulled her to me. She was softening, but she wasn't yet at the point of offering assistance. I held her with one hand and took off my clothes with the other. "I love you." I waited. There was no "I love you too" response.

Okay, a romantic, sweep-her-off-her-feet gesture was called for. I was so goddamn tired. But I lifted her up, carried her to the bed and laid her down. A little risky in the dark, what with guys my age slipping disks, developing hernias. But Lynne was light, I was desperate and, hey, it worked. She didn't say "All is forgiven." She didn't say anything. But she reached up from the bed, felt for me and pulled me down beside her.

So in the blackness we started making love. Lynne's silent treatment wasn't so bad, I thought. Better, in a way, than her usual quiet, where she might say a couple of words; it enhanced the pleasure. I could concentrate on everything—the sound of her body against the sheet as she started to squirm, her breathing as it grew deeper.

This had potential; it might be more than a routine roll. But just as I was about to call out, "Lynne," I lost all sense of her.

I was no longer making love with my fiancée. I was screwing the way I used to: It didn't matter at all who it was beside me, on top of me, beneath me, just so long as it had all the stock parts. I just wanted to get it in and over with. And then . . .

Big surprise. Well, it was to me.

The faceless female disappeared. Bonnie Spencer was in bed with me. She was wild. The soft, stroking hands may have been Lynne's, but the Bonnie in my mind had her legs wrapped tight around me and was clawing at my back. Then she groaned with pleasure, letting out the same animal sounds I was making. Louder. Her dark hair was spread out all over the pillow; the flower scent was intoxicating. As I entered Bonnie, she let out a sob. Oh, God, I thought, this is the best. I called out, "I love you. Oh, God, how I love you!" and I heard Bonnie cry out, "Help me!" as she started to come, and then, "I love you so much."

It was perfect.

It was over.

Lynne finally spoke. "That was nice."

"Yeah, it was."

"Wake me at six. Okay? I want to get home early. I have a ton of reading I have to do."

"Okay," I said. Then I closed my eyes against the darkness.

I spent Sunday going over the lab and autopsy reports and doing my paperwork. Then, first thing Monday morning, I pushed open the heavy glass-and-brass door at five after nine and strolled right over to Rochelle Schnell, first vice president of South Fork Bank and Trust, Bridgehampton branch.

"I respect your mind," I told her, and sat on the edge of her desk.

"You gave me that line about twenty-five years ago."

"Did it work?"

"No. Of course not. But I liked it that you tried."

Rochelle was forty years old. I knew that because we'd started Sagaponack Elementary School together, in kindergarten, and since we'd been born two days apart, we'd had to share our class birthday party. (Her mother, Mrs. Maziejka, was supposed to bring the cupcakes and mine the Kool-Aid, but since my mother worked, Mrs. Maziejka had always brought both. She'd never bitched about it; in fact, she even wrote "Rochelle!" in pink icing on half the cupcakes and "Steve!" on the other half in blue.)

Rochelle sat behind her immense wood desk in a dark-gray dress-for-success suit. But then—as she strode over to kiss me and say "I haven't seen you around in months. You look fantastic!"—I noticed her skirt was one of those stretchy, midthigh things that look like an overgrown support bandage.

"Yeah? Well, so do you, Ro-chelle, except you've got a real problem. No one is going to hand out their life savings to a banker whose skirt's so tight you can practically see her pudenda."

"Don't bet on it. Now, what can I do for you? Or did you just drop in to check out my skirt?"

I put my hand on her back and guided her to her chair, then

sat down across the desk from her. "Off the record. I want to know if you have a depositor named Bonnie Spencer—"

Rochelle cut me off. "Big no-no. You know I'm an honest woman. I can't even give you a name. I'll verify it with our lawyers, but I'm sure you have to give me a subpoena. Then, if she does have an account, I'll have to call—"

"All I want to know is if she has an account here. No details. Please. A personal favor, Rochelle. It's not like I'm some jerk you don't know."

"No, you're a jerk I do know." She exhaled slowly. Then she swiveled around in her chair, faced the computer terminal on her desk and put her hands on the keyboard. Her giant diamond ring, courtesy of Mr. Schnell, who'd bought the bank to get her attention, sparkled; her long red nails clicked as she typed. "Yes, she's a depositor."

"Thank you."

"You're welcome."

"Tell me how much is in her account."

"No. You're a cop. Comply with the law. And don't think you're going to charm it out of me. I've already told you more than I should. Not one more thing. Just go to the D.A. and get a subpoena."

"But, Rochelle, with all that Bank Privacy Act shit, that means you're going to have to notify her that there's been an inquiry by a law enforcement agency."

"Is that so terrible?"

"Yeah. Just hear me out. It's terrible because Bonnie Spencer is a genuinely nice lady and I don't want her to get hurt in this investigation. Her ex-husband—"

"Oh, that Spencer!"

"Yeah, well, the powers that be are getting a little antsy, and it would help if I could just find out—fast, without waiting for a subpoena and notification—that she really is as okay as she seems to be, that no big money was going in or out of her account. I'd like to see her name out of this. You know what I mean? This woman's a real sweetheart. She had nothing to do with a homicide. She had nothing to do with *him*. All I need are some numbers to back me up, so we can cross off her name. Time's a factor here. I don't want to risk some gung-ho first-year detective calling her employer and saying, 'I'm from Suffolk County Homicide and I'm checking up on Bonnie Spencer.' Please, Rochelle. Help me help her."

Rochelle's nails went click-click again. "She has a hundred and five in her checking account. There's regular activity, so I guess we're her banker." Click. "Six hundred thirty-four in a savings account, that last month had a balance of a little over seven hundred." Click-click. "And her Visa card . . . she hardly ever uses it."

I pointed to the computer screen. "What does all that tell you?"

"That her ex-husband was *very* behind on his alimony payments."

"She wasn't getting alimony."

"In that case, she's just plain poor."

The only thing appealing about Bonnie's next-door neighbor, Wendy Morrell, was her name; it conjured up a dewy virgin gamboling in a field of clover. In fact, in the morning light, Wendy looked less like Snow White and more like the witchy stepmother— in an olive-green jumpsuit. She had a face full of those air bubble things that grow under the skin. There was one large one on her left cheek, and I found my finger reaching up toward my own cheek, maybe trying to perform a symbolic bubblectomy; I put my hand down at my side.

"I mean, naturally I've been reading everything there is to read about the murder," she said, "but in a million years it would never have occurred to me that *Bonnie* Spencer had any connection with *Sy* Spencer."

Wendy Morrell was probably in her early thirties. Manhattan

thin, a body that if seen in the Third World would evoke pity but that probably commanded admiration in the city. Under the wide gold bracelet on her forearm, you could see the outline of her radius and ulna. Wendy's hair was cut in that chopped-off style that only guys just out of basic training (or very, very beautiful women) should wear.

We stood by the front door of her modern house. She had not invited me in. Maybe she was an elitist bitch. Maybe she was embarrassed; houses like hers, million-dollar exercises in solid geometry, had, overnight, become Out on the South Fork. They'd been replaced by postmodern whiz-bangs, country houses so enormous that they seemed to have been built for a race of giants instead of the periodontists and pocketbook designers who lived in them. Wendy had planted herself smack in the middle of her doorway, as though afraid I'd elbow her aside in an attempt to see how rich people lived—or, if I was hip, to get a look at her hopelessly outdated high-tech kitchen and snicker at it.

"That those two Spencers lived on the same planet was a miracle," she went on. "I mean, I don't mean to denigrate her, but it's such a contradiction of style: elegance versus gaucheness. You know? Look, she goes running. I'm the last person in the world to be a spokesperson for jogging suits. Am I going to make a case for pastel sweatpants and matching zip-ups? I know this may not mean a lot to you, but if she's got a house in the Hamptons, not Kalamazoo or wherever she comes from, she should manage to have a little pride in her appearance, not wear clothes that look like she raided the boys' locker room at the end of the school year. I mean, *some* sense of appropriateness must have rubbed off from Sy."

"You knew him?"

"Well, we were never formally introduced. But you know what they say: there are basically three hundred people in the world." She suddenly realized she was talking to a member of the four billion minus three hundred, because she explained: "That's a New York–Hamptons concept: You know there are certain places in SoHo or East Hampton and you'll walk in and there'll be Calvin Klein or Kurt Vonnegut or Sy Spencer. Sy happened to be the friend of a very dear friend. Teddy Unger. Commercial real estate. You know who he is? Well, he owns half of New York. The better half. So even though we never got to meet formally, Sy and my ex-husband and I were all of the same world."

Even if you stretched the definition of the Beautiful People beyond any rational limits, Wendy Morrell would not have fit in.

"So what's with the ex-wife?" she demanded. "Is she under suspicion?"

"No. This is strictly a background check. I'm just trying to get a sense of the sort of person Bonnie Spencer is."

"I can't help you. I am not a neighbor type." Wendy glanced over at Bonnie's, then at her own driveway, where I'd pulled my Jag all the way up, almost to her garage, so Bonnie couldn't see it from her house. She gave my car a suspicious look, as if it represented something nasty, sexual and, above all, unforgivably pushy, since it was not a car a cop should be driving.

"But maybe you might have picked up something, just out of the corner of your eye," I suggested. "Did she entertain guests with any frequency?"

"I wish I could give you a full report, but my days are *very* full. Believe me, I don't spend my time watching Bonnie Spencer." She touched the gold pin that, thank God, held her jumpsuit closed. It was at the point of her body that, on a woman who hadn't starved herself, would have been called a cleavage. "I have a business to run." She said "a business" as if she meant General Motors.

"What do you do?"

"Wendy's Soups. I'm president and CEO." As in: Everyone knows Wendy's Soups. Well, everyone who's anyone, as I clearly wasn't. "There have been major articles about me. *New York Times*, *Vogue*, et cetera. *Elle* . . . You know *Elle?* The piece was called 'Superb Soups!' "

"Do you cook them here?"

She smiled. Big mistake. God had given Wendy Morrell the gift of gums. "No. The plant is in a cute little ethnic neighborhood in Queens. I employ forty-six people."

"So you don't live here all year round?"

"No. East End and Eighty-first. Just long weekends here. It used to be all August too, but then there was that cover story in *New York Woman*." With, I assumed, a photo of a bowl of split pea superimposed over her ugly puss. "We went through the roof. You can imagine!"

"Look, Ms. Morrell, obviously you're a very busy person, but busy people tend to be the most efficient." She obviously agreed. "You're not the nosy neighbor type, but . . ."

"I don't know anything about her. We nod hello. That is all. When I'm out here I'm still plagued. The phone, the fax. My office cannot leave me alone. The pressure *never* stops. I have to *force* myself to relax. I do not do coffee klatches."

"Does Bonnie Spencer have coffee klatches?"

"Not that I've ever seen."

"What I'm getting at is, are there any frequent visitors?" She glanced at my Jag again. "Men in sports cars?"

"Men in sports cars. Men in sedans. Men in all *kinds* of vehicles. Is that news to you?" She paused. "Once . . . I saw a pickup truck. I happened to notice it because it was late at night. Well, let's be generous. Maybe she needed some emergency construction done by a kid who couldn't have been more than twenty-two, in tight jeans and work boots."

"I'm going to be direct, Ms. Morrell, but I feel I can be direct with someone who's a CEO." She acknowledged the tribute with a brief flash of gums. "Is it your impression that Ms. Spencer is promiscuous?"

"Maybe she's just interviewing half the men in Bridgehampton for that happy-news column she writes. She came over once, asked if she could interview me! I was very pleasant. I told her I was horrendously tied up, but I'd love to. Some other time." She stopped. "Are you sure you're with the police?"

I handed her my shield. She brought it up close to her nose, breathing what was probably disgusting, humid, lentil-dill breath on the plastic, and studied it. Then she handed it back.

"Have you seen any one car at Bonnie Spencer's recently? A black sports car?"

"Detective Whatever"—she smiled—"I *know* what a Maserati is. My ex-husband drove a Ferrari 250 GT, '62. Believe me, I had sports cars burned into my brain during *that* marriage." She looked over at mine. "I know an E-type Jaguar roadster when I see one. The English don't say 'convertible,' you know." I hated it that this witch had any sort of intimacy with great cars. "And the answer to your question is yes."

"Yes, what, Ms. Morrell?"

"There was a Maserati in her driveway. Last week. Every morning that I was here. A quarter to twelve. Like clockwork. And a *fabulously* dressed man got out of it. I realize now that it must have been Sy Spencer. But I'm sure there's an innocent explanation. Maybe she just served an early lunch."

"Maybe. When did he leave?"

"Two, three, four."

"Any sounds of fighting?"

She shook her head. "I cannot believe it! He was so fine— and *re*fined. I mean, this man could have any woman he wanted. Why would someone like him waste his time on a nothing like her?"

"Maybe she's nice."

Wendy Morrell cocked her head, drew her eyebrows together, as if she were hearing about a sensational new trend for the first time. *"Nice?"*

CHAPTER 8

Nice Bonnie Spencer.

Well, fuck her and the horse she rode in on. All along I'd known something was wrong. All along I'd known she was lying to me about Sy. Still, somewhere I'd kept a candle burning, a flicker of hope that she was a good person, that whatever ties she had to her ex-husband had to do strictly with making movies. Because if I ever was going to be friends with a woman, Bonnie would have been exactly the kind of woman I would have picked. She seemed so straight that in spite of all my doubts, when Wendy Morrell opened her gummy mouth, I truly believed she was going to say: A black sports car? No! The only car *I* ever saw in her driveway was the Lilco meter reader's—and he was never there for more than ninety seconds.

To hell with Bonnie. I shifted into third.

The trip from Bridgehampton to Headquarters in Yaphank was thirty-nine miles, most of it along straight-arrow, four-lane Route 27. Once it had been my own personal test track. Since sobriety, though, I'd become an old fart and never pushed much beyond seventy-five mph.

But now, going west against beach traffic, I decided I needed speed. I couldn't believe how badly I'd misjudged her. Moose wasn't the town slut; the animal wasn't the animal. The stupid bitch, Bonnie, couldn't keep her legs together. I shifted into fourth, heard the deep, throaty hum of the exhaust, watched the tachometer go into redline. I eased up when I got to a hundred and five. Fuck Bonnie Spencer! This was fantastic! In most sports cars, when you're in last gear, you feel like you're skyrocketing, leaving the pull of earth's gravity. But the XKE kind of squats, fuses with the road. It's the ultimate down-to-earth experience.

There just isn't anything like speed to take you away, especially sober. (Driving drunk, you know in your gut that Death, carrying a scythe, in that hooded bathrobe—sort of like Sy's, although not as good-quality terry cloth—is standing over the next rise.)

So fuck Bonnie. And fuck this case. The minute it was over, I'd say to Lynne: Come on. No waiting till Thanksgiving weekend. Let's find some priest whose dance card isn't all filled up the way your guy's is. We'll get married right away. And forget Saint John. We'll go to London. I'll go to museums with you. To Shakespeare. I'll visit English schools and stand by your side and learn all about the newest methods for combating dyscalculia. I swear to God, I'll even go to the opera.

Sergeant Alvin Miller of the Ogden, Utah, Police Department talked re-e-e-eal slo-o-o-ow, as if each word had to mosey down a long dirt road before it could come out. "Well, now, Detective Brady. One of the boys passed on your message last night. 'Bout ten. I'm not with the department anymore. Re-tired, you know. Have been for eleven years." I transferred the phone to my other ear. "But seeing as you said it wasn't urgent, I wasn't going to call you up there in Noooo Yorrrk, where it was midnight." He said "New York" in the resentful way guys in my company in

Vietnam did, as if ordinary people and ordinary places—suburbs, farms, beaches and forests—were just camouflage for a state whose sole business was mocking the rest of America. "Hope my not calling back right away didn't hold you up."

"No problem." Across the room, Charlie Sanchez sat at his desk holding aloft a cheese Danish from the daily love-me bag of bakery goodies Robby had brought in. Charlie was sticking out his tongue, licking the yellow cheese in the center. The crime-scene photographs on my desk, showing Sy with his two small, neat little wounds, were less revolting than watching Charlie tongue a pastry. "I appreciate your calling back," I said to Sergeant Miller.

"You bet. Now, you wanted to know something about the Bernstein girl. Don't tell me she's in trouble?"

"No, she's okay. Her ex-husband—"

"She got a divorce?"

"Yeah. A few years ago."

"No kiddin'. What was her first name, now?"

"Bonnie."

"That's it, all right. Bonnie Bernstein. She living in New York?"

"No. In Bridgehampton. It's a little town on the East End of Long Island."

"Oh. I heard she went to Hollywood. She made a picture, you know. I forget what they called it, but I saw it. Not bad."

"The detective I spoke to said you might know the family."

"Yup. Knew them. Pretty well, at one time." I wanted to grab this fucker by his string tie and shake him, make the words come out faster.

"Can you tell me about them?"

"Sure." I licked my fingertip and erased a coffee ring while I hung around and waited for his next word. "If memory serves me, the Bernsteins—that would be Bonnie's grandparents— opened the store."

"Uh-huh," I muttered encouragingly.

"Called it Bernstein's."

"Did her parents keep it up?"

"Kept it up real nice."

Out in the anteroom, Ray Carbone was handing one of Homicide's two secretaries a piece of paper. From the pained look in his eyes, it was probably a draft of the next press release, which would say, essentially, that we knew nothing. The secretary glanced around for her glasses, didn't find them, and so stretched out her arm and pulled back her head to read. Hanging above her head was the giant banner that no one could miss when they walked into Suffolk County Homicide: THOU SHALT NOT KILL.

"What kind of a store was Bernstein's?"

"A sporting goods store."

"Bats, balls?"

"Nope. More like guns, fishing gear."

"Handguns?"

"Sure, handguns. This is Utah."

"Rifles?"

"Yup."

"Is the store still around?"

"No. Mrs. Bernstein—that would be Bonnie's mother—died. Dan—that's her father—sold the place and retired. I believe to Arizona, but I won't swear to it. Maybe New Mexico. And the boys—three or four of them—didn't stay in Ogden. One of them is a college professor at U.U., and I don't know what the others did."

"Bonnie was the only girl."

"So far as I can remember, and I remember her because she was friends with the boys and girls in my Eddie's Mutual. I guess you don't know what that is."

"No."

"It's a group for Mormon junior high and high school kids."

"Were the Bernsteins Mormons?"

"Of course not. You're from New York. You should know that."

"Right. Okay now, let me be straight with you, Sergeant Miller."

"Best way to be."

"The incident I'm investigating—"

"I know what kind of an incident. They told me you were on the Homicide Squad. You need a whole department out there on Long Island just for homicide, huh?"

"Yeah. The victim was Bonnie's ex-husband. He was shot with a .22. The perpetrator was a good shot. I'd like to rule out Bonnie."

"What are you asking me?"

"I'm asking you whether you have any idea if she could shoot a .22."

"I don't know."

"Your best guess."

"My best guess is, a girl like Bonnie—a tomboy kind of girl—whose family owned a sporting goods store and whose dad was probably the damn finest shot in Ogden . . . I used to go up to Wyoming with him and a couple other fellas, hunting elk. Well, she was the apple of her father's eye. Possible he or one of her brothers taught her to shoot a .22."

"Thank you."

"Well now, you expect me to say she couldn't have done it, don't you?"

"I wouldn't be surprised if you did."

"Well, I won't say it. She left Ogden. Went to Hollywood, then New York. Can't issue any guarantees under those conditions, right?"

"Right."

"But just between you and me, Detective Brady? You may be from Noooo Yorrrk and think you're pretty wily, saying you're trying to rule out Bonnie Bernstein. Sounds to me like you've got it in your head that she shot her former husband. With malice aforethought. Maybe." He took a long and very slow breath. "But if the girl you suspect is anything like the nice, smiley girl in my boy Eddie's Mutual, you know what I think? I think you got yourself one lousy theory. You get me? I think you're pissing into the wind."

Robby Kurz placed his bet: "Fat Mikey LoTriglio. Okay, never convicted of anything, but his name has been linked with two mob hits. All he has to do is raise his fat finger, and someone dies."

"No way," I said. "Bonnie Spencer. Motive. Opportunity."

Ray Carbone added his twenty to ours. "Who's left? Lindsay Keefe? All right. She may have felt cornered, her job, her reputation on the line. And she probably has a lacuna of the superego. It would be too much like a movie if she did it, but I'll go with her anyway."

Charlie Sanchez was about to retire and didn't care enough anymore to join the pool. He wrote down our bets, folded the money and slipped it into the pocket of his beloved suede vest.

The interrogation room we were in at Headquarters was better than a naked light bulb and a chair, but it wouldn't win any awards for design excellence. Headquarters itself had originally been a county social services agency, and in the heart of the soft green and brown fields of Yaphank, the building rose up, uncompromisingly ugly. Inside, it was full of gray asphalt tile and orange plastic furniture—just to remind the meek that while they might be in line to inherit the earth, their actual lives were shit and likely to remain that way.

Four of us sat around the fake-wood table. Charlie, who'd been with the department for twenty years and was within weeks of becoming head of security for a shopping center in Bay Shore, stroked the vest his girlfriend had given him for his forty-second birthday. He wore it inside and outside, even in ninety-five-degree heat. He loved the vest almost as much as he loved his girlfriend. (His wife had given him a snow-blower for his birthday, probably in response to the electric pencil sharpener he'd given her for hers.)

"We got a missing-one-thousand-bucks situation," Charlie began. He'd been doing background on Sy. "Here's what I found out. At fourteen minutes past eight on Friday morning, Sy was at the cash machine at the Marine Midland Bank over in Southampton."

"His secretary in New York said he told her he'd be getting cash for his trip to L.A.," Ray added.

Charlie went on: "Sy had one of those preferred-customer cards, so he could withdraw up to a thou. Well, that's what he withdrew. Did any of you guys come across a thousand bucks?"

Robby shook his head. "No. There was"—Robby checked his notebook—"a hundred and forty-seven bucks in his wallet."

I closed my eyes, concentrated. Then I said: "Hey! Hold on! Listen to this timetable. Sy went to the bank at eight-fourteen. He got to the set in East Hampton eight thirty-five, eight-forty, which is about what it takes from Southampton to East Hampton if you don't make any stops. When he got there, he stayed pretty much in his trailer, talking to people. Right? That Gregory kid was around a lot, and we talked to everyone else who talked to Sy. Did anyone say anything about any cash changing hands? No. The people he was seeing were mainly technical—a special effects guy who was doing a fire and some gunshots, Nick Monteleone and his makeup lady. Spent a few minutes with Lindsay, but she was being fitted for a dress, so a seamstress and the costume design lady were there the whole time. He wasn't talking to union guys or local cops or politicians—people he might pay off. You with me?" Robby and Ray nodded. Charlie caressed his vest some more. "Okay, assuming he didn't slip anyone a wad of cash, he leaves the set about eleven-fifteen with a thousand bucks in his pocket. Doesn't stop at Bonnie's this time. Instead, he seems to have gone straight home; he was there at ten of twelve. We have the cook's word on that, because he asked for a green salad and bread for lunch, ASAP."

"That's lunch?" Charlie shook his head. "Can you believe

it? A guy has a cook all to himself and he says, 'Give me a salad.' New York faggots, I swear to Christ. Makes me sick."

"What does all this add up to, Steve?" Ray demanded.

"It adds up to that after he got home, Sy saw only one person besides the cook: the person he as a practicing nonfaggot seems to have humped in the guest room. Now, there was Bonnie Spencer–type hair on the pillow in the guest room—okay, we have to wait till Lifecodes finishes the DNA analysis, but I'll bet you anything it's hers."

"Why are you fixating on her?" Ray asked.

"Because this is an intelligent murder, and she's very intelligent. Because he used her—twice—and I don't think this is a broad who allows three strikes. I think she's got a tough streak in her. And because she's been hiding something from me from the minute she opened the door Saturday morning. And because she was *there* Friday, at his house. Motive and opportunity, Ray."

"You know what I can't figure out? He was cheating on Lindsay Keefe with his ex-wife," Charlie said. "What was he? Nuts?"

"Keep your eye on the missing thousand bucks," I reminded them. "Ask yourselves: Where was the wallet we found that *did* have some money in it?"

"In the inside pocket of his blazer," Ray said.

"Where?"

"In his and Lindsay's bedroom, on a hanger outside the closet door. Stuff for his trip was all set out—a packed carry-on, a leather envelope with a couple of scripts."

"Right," I said. "But the pockets of the pants he was wearing that day were empty except for some change and his car keys, and those pants were in the guest room. My guess is, he packs, then has an hour or so, decides he wants to get laid and calls Bonnie to get over. He sneaks her past the cook, upstairs, into the guest room. He throws his pants over a chair, fucks her, then . . ."

"Then what?" Ray asked. "This is the first serious speculation I'm hearing about this person—other than the fact that she was his ex who lived nearby. What do you think went on?"

"My best guess? They had words. He tells her to get dressed and get out. Or he doesn't have to say it; she figures it out for herself. Whatever. But he grabs a robe and leaves her there while he goes for a fast swim before the plane ride. In any case, she feels she's been had. She goes through his pants, takes the thou."

"And then she goes outside, finds a .22 and shoots him?" Charlie asked. "A lady writer is able to score two bull's-eyes from fifty feet?"

"Could you do it, Charlie, if you had the rifle?"

"From fifty feet? Why not?"

"Yeah, well, why not her too?" I said. I told him what I'd learned about Bernstein's inventory from Ogden's finest.

"Well, I can't buy Bonnie as a serious suspect," Robby said. He shifted, and his rayon pants rubbed against the plastic of the chair and gave off a squeaky fart sound. "Even if she has long dark hair, even if she was sleeping with him, even if she can shoot that well, which I seriously doubt, why would she kill him?"

"Lots of reasons." I was starting to like this, the explaining, the persuading, the idea that things were coming together. But most of all, I was liking the realization that I had no trouble making a case against Bonnie, that finally, where she was concerned, my head was harder than my dick. "First of all, she's living hand-to-mouth." I explained. "She got shafted in the divorce. She's gotten a look at Sy's way of life, sees how he's given up the humble Farmer Spencer bit he was doing when he was married to her, the denim overalls and butter-churn crap. Now he's living like an out-and-out multimillionaire, which he is. She sees the richness of his life, compares it to the poorness of hers. Probably has already told him how rough things are, asked him for help. And expects it too, what with her probably giving him a blow job and soup and sandwiches every goddamn day that last week. Except he says no."

"Why didn't she just keep at it?" Ray asked. "Play on his sympathy? Or make him feel guilty?"

"Maybe she's already given it everything she has—which

isn't that much. She fucks and she's nice. What else does someone like her have to offer? And anyway, it wasn't just money. She could have been in love with him and really believed she could get him back. But no matter what she wanted from him, Sy said, No way."

"He just turned off on her, so she kills him?" Robby asked. He didn't sound convinced, but then again, he had his twenty on Mikey LoTriglio.

I pushed harder. "All she's been doing is covering up, lying to us. Why? So we don't think she's a fast girl who lets a man put his thing into her you-know-what? No. Because she has something important to hide. A murder."

Robby turned that over for a minute. Then he asked: "But *why* would she shoot him? Revenge?"

"Revenge. Plus desperation, plus greed."

"Where would she get the .22?" Charlie asked.

"She lives alone. Probably had it for years, a present from Daddy Bernstein. Could be she sensed this was the final fuck and brought it along in her car. Or maybe she left, went home, got it and came back. Come on, guys. Sy was wearing his pants at the movie set, so no one took the thousand off of him there. Then he gets home, sticks it to the as-yet-unknown brunette we *know* has to be Bonnie, goes for a swim and bang. He's gonzo—and so is the money."

"Even if she was there, it could have been someone else who shot him," Carbone said.

"It could have been. But who? Why? We already know about Bonnie."

"So she killed him for a thousand bucks?" Robby asked. "I've got to tell you, Steve, that still doesn't compute. Not with the way you described her. She doesn't sound like a really bad person. Except for the screwing around, and what the hell, she's lonely."

"But *why* is she lonely?" Naturally, I didn't look at Ray Carbone, even though I was playing to him, trying to get the psychology vote. "Ask yourselves, what kind of a normal single woman stays in a town she has no roots in, a town that's deserted three quarters of the year except for locals like me and some antique-dealer types who talk about stuff like the bleak beauty of the winter seascape and shit like that. How come she didn't sell the house, which could bring her big bucks even with real estate being what it is, and move to Manhattan, get a decent job?" Charlie rubbed his chin, Robby looked mildly intrigued and Ray leaned forward. "I'll tell you why not. She's a loser, and she knows it. She had one minute of success that might have been a fluke, and in that minute she lands Sy. You know what that marriage said to her? It said: 'Bonnie, babe, you're terrific.' But then he gets bored and takes a walk. She stays in that isolated house because she knows if she moved to the city, she'd have no excuse for being a loser. This way, she lives hand-to-mouth—but she can keep up her illusions. That Sy will come back. That one of her shitty screenplays will get made into a movie. That she's worth something. And then what happens?"

Despite the fact that Mikey LoTriglio was due any second with his lawyer, Robby was getting hooked. "What happens?" he said, as if waiting for the end of a bedtime story.

I gave it everything I had; I knew it would be a major asset to have Robby on my side, not off after the Mafia. "Sy starts sleeping with Bonnie again, gives her hope. Suddenly she's thinking: I *am* terrific. I can have a life. I'll have my husband back and live in New York, on Fifth Avenue, and in a seven-million-dollar mansion on the beach. And she must have started sharing her dream with Sy, because all of a sudden he blows her off. Maybe nicely. Or maybe he just tells her the truth: 'Bonnie, baby, I was P.O.'d at Lindsay and felt like a grudge fuck, and you were available. It didn't mean anything.' "

Ray was breaking his empty Styrofoam coffee cup into white chips. "All right. His rejection might hurt her. Destroy her. But would it push her over the edge?"

"Yeah, because this time he didn't leave her with any illusions. He didn't want her. He didn't want her screenplay. Don't forget: He humiliated her, treated her like a two-bit whore when she came to visit him on the set. And he didn't value old times' sake enough to help her out of a crappy financial situation. Look, two strikes: he'd used her once, to get a foot in the door of the movie business, and he'd used her again, to get his rocks off when he got mad at Lindsay. And now it was kiss-kiss, sweetie, I'm off to L.A. I'm telling you, he walked out of that guest room leaving her with *nothing*."

"It's just a theory," Robby murmured. But he sounded on the verge of being convinced.

So did Ray. "Okay, Steve and Robby," he said, "keep your other options open, but follow up on this Bonnie. It sounds like she needs a little extra attention."

Fat Mikey LoTriglio looked like a Sicilian version of Humpty-Dumpty. He had no visible neck; his silk tie, a dark blue dangerously close to purple, seemed suspended from one of the chins that rested on his chest. "I grew up wit' Sy," he was explaining to me and Robby. "He was like a brother to me. Let me tell you, you find the guy who took him out, you call me. You tell me, 'Hey, Mikey, we found the guy who blasted Sy,' and I swear to God, I'll—"

"At the time Mr. Spencer was murdered," Fat Mikey's lawyer interrupted, "Mr. LoTriglio was having cocktails with several business associates, who, naturally, can vouch for his whereabouts." The lawyer, a guy around my age, wore round little glasses with wire frames, as though hoping someone would assure him that he didn't look like the sleazy mob lawyer he'd become, that he still looked like John Lennon.

"Hey." Mikey turned to the lawyer. "I don't have cocktails, okay? I have drinks." He looked back at us and explained: "This is a new lawyer. My old one, Terry Connelly. Ever deal with him? Massive stroke. They got him in some hospital in Rhode Island, poor vegetable. Sad, sad. And now this fuckin' murder . . ." He shook his head in disbelief. "It's a knife in my heart, Sy gone."

"What's going to happen to your investment in *Starry Night?*"
I asked.

"Mr. LoTriglio's participation in that venture has not been
established," the lawyer said.

"We know Mikey invested four hundred thousand in the movie
and got his brother-in-law and an uncle to put up another six
hundred thousand," Robby said, but reasonably, not with his usual
I'm-gonna-see-you-fry vengefulness. At some moment between the
time Ray and Charlie left the interrogation room and the time
Mikey and his lawyer walked in, Robby had switched to Bonnie
Spencer. I smiled to myself. I was really happy. I'd won Robby
over. I could stand back; she was his girl now, and he would do
anything to get her.

"How was your investment going, Mikey?" I asked.

Mikey fluttered his eyes, a single flutter: his naive expression.
"What do I know about producin' movies?"

"You must know something if you put up a million bucks."

"Hey, my friend Sy asks me to put up some money, I do it."

"Mr. LoTriglio's accountants were impressed by Mr. Spencer's track record," the lawyer said softly. "They felt *Starry Night*
was an excellent investment—albeit any investment in filmmaking
entails a certain degree of risk, of which they were fully cognizant."

"Did Sy let you know how the movie was coming along?" I
asked. Fat Mikey shook his head; his chins jiggled. "A million
bucks, Mikey. Weren't you curious?"

"Nah. What do I care? Sy says this is gonna be an Oscar
winner. He says, 'Mikey, get your tuxedo cleaned for a year from
March.' That's all I needed to know."

"You didn't hear anything about any problems with the
movie?"

Mikey smiled. Well, the corners of his lips moved upward.
He crossed his arms and rested them on his belly. "What problems?"

"Problems like the movie was looking like a piece of shit."

"Fuck you. I didn't hear *nothin'* like that."

"Problems like the only way to save it was to get rid of Lindsay Keefe, which would have put the producers—that's you—a few million deeper into the hole before they even began again."

"Bullshit," Mikey said.

"You were on the phone a lot with Sy Spencer last week. What were you talking about?" Robby inquired.

Mikey looked at his lawyer, who seemed to be lost in wonder, beholding his shoelace. "You from Harvard!" he bellowed. "Look alive. My memory isn't so good. I need a reminder. Maybe I happened to mention it to you. What was I talkin' to Sy about last week? I think Sy and I *might* have been on the phone a couple of times, but for the life of me I can't remember what we said."

"I think you did mention that you had the most general conversation with Mr. Spencer. Hello, how are you, how are things going—and he assured you all was well."

"That's right," Mikey said. He rotated his head and looked Robby right in the eye. "All was well. And then—a fuckin' bullet. *Two* fuckin' bullets. I gotta tell you, a piece of me died when Sy went. We were like flesh and blood. When we were kids we'd follow his old man and my old man around through one of the processing plants, and while they talked about all the cheap shit they could stuff into one salami, Sy and me talked about . . . Life."

"*Life?*" I repeated.

"Yeah. Life. Like philosophy. *Now* I remember. We were talkin' about philosophy last week, on the phone." His lawyer put a restraining hand on Mikey's huge, sausagelike thigh, but Mikey either didn't feel it or was ignoring it. "There we were, two businessmen, but we're such good friends we don't talk business. We talk . . . Plato!"

"Where were you last Friday night, Mikey?" Robby asked.

"You mean what's my alibi?"

"Mr. LoTriglio was at Rosie's, a bar in the meat district," the lawyer said. "He is widely known there. A good many people saw him, and several engaged him in conversation."

"Talking Plato?" I asked.

"No, you stupid asshole," Mikey answered. "Talkin' fuckin' liverwurst."

One of the guys I sometimes ran with, T.J., a marathoner, owned a couple of video stores on the South Fork. He was in love with my Jag, so I made a deal with him. Whenever I wanted to be inconspicuous, I could take one of his married-man cars—his Honda Accord or Plymouth Voyager—and leave my car in his garage. At a little after four in the afternoon, I parked the Voyager across from Bonnie's house and waited.

Surveillance had always been a snap for me. I'd bring along a bottle of club soda, a Thermos of coffee, and a jar to pee in, sit back and enter into some kind of twilight state. It was like being asleep with my eyes open; I could keep watch, but my mind was someplace else, and I'd be totally unaware of the passage of time. I'd know that I'd sat through a whole night when the sky turned red at sunrise.

But now I was itchy, looking at my watch every couple of minutes, as if to encourage it, wishing that I'd stopped at the luncheonette on the way over for a sundae because I felt like I needed a hit of chocolate. I was annoyed with myself that I hadn't sent one of the younger guys to do this job. Finally, though, it wasn't that long a wait.

She came out at five o'clock, dressed for a run. The weird thing was, she was dressed exactly the way I would dress for running. Shorts and a T-shirt, wool crew socks, with a light sweatshirt tied around her waist, in case it got cool down by the ocean. She was carrying a red ball; Moose was barking with joy at her side. I slid down in the seat. She braced herself against her mailbox, stretched her calf muscles and then her quads. What a pair of legs! They looked like she'd been captain of the girls' soccer team since nursery school. She and Moose started out at a nice clip, picking up more speed as they rounded the corner and headed down toward the beach.

Jesus, I thought, as they disappeared, I really am in love with that dog. Maybe because it was black, it reminded me of a Labrador we'd had at the farm when I was little, Inky, a dumb, sweet-natured bitch who treated me and Easton as if we were her puppies, watching us play, barking if we wandered off too far, growling at anybody who drove up to the house and approached us.

I pulled on a pair of the thin rubber gloves we used for crime-scene work, turned off my beeper and checked out the area. Clear. I crossed the street, studying the house. I could probably sneak in through a basement window; even if I had to break a pane, she might not notice for days. Or I might be able to jimmy open the back door. But, as I suspected, neither was necessary. Bonnie had left the front door unlocked.

Even if she ran like hell and just threw the ball once down at the beach, I had a clear twenty minutes. But I worked the upstairs first, in case I heard her and had to get out the back door.

Bingo! She used one of the bedrooms as an office, and there, under a big framed poster from the movie *Cowgirl*, beside a computer half-covered with stickum notes, in a messy, overstuffed folder marked "Pending," was a Xeroxed real estate listing for her house. It was dated August 4, so she'd decided to put it on the market while there were still summer people around to come, look and oooh: "Oh, Ian, the exposed beams!" Had she taken up with Sy yet? Was she selling it because she was already having dreams of a grand house by the ocean, a screening room, charge accounts, a wedding ring? Or was the real estate listing pre-Sy? Had she been at the end of her rope? I jotted down the broker's number.

I had to work fast—and neat. Neat wasn't too much of a problem since Bonnie's papers were just this side of chaotic. Still, this was not exactly what you could call a legal search, so I couldn't risk leaving any trace.

I went through her bedroom too, finding, mainly, that she kept the local library in business, that although her tangle of bras were what you'd expect from a female jock, utilitarian and uninspiring, her panties weren't: little string bikinis, black, red. I was starting to imagine her, but I cut myself off. Time. Also, there was something about being in her bedroom, its peacefulness, with its tied-back white lace curtains, plain four-poster bed and old-fashioned dresser with a white doilylike thing on top of it, that made me uneasy. I wanted out of there. I was half out the door, on my way downstairs, when I turned back to check out her closet.

Bingo again! Inside the toe of a pair of boots—one of those places women inevitably hide their valuable stuff—I found it: a wad of cash rolled up in a rubber band. Eight hundred and eighty dollars. More than she had in her savings account. Big bucks for a poor girl like Bonnie.

Change from a thousand.

CHAPTER 9

What was so terrible? Sex, even with someone as fabulous as Lynne, can become routine. So big deal: you superimpose another woman over your dearly beloved and suddenly a predictable quickie becomes the Fuck That Shook the World. It can happen, especially if a guy's pattern has always been to step out a lot. Is that so bad? There is no betrayal. Nobody gets hurt.

But it wasn't just that one brief late-night fantasy. My whole life—not just the case—was starting to focus on Bonnie. Like when I'd gone to the bank to speak to Rochelle, I stopped at the cashier's for a couple of rolls of quarters. More than a couple: enough to hit every pay phone on the South Fork. And so once or twice—all right, three or four times—a day I'd drop in a quarter just to hear Bonnie say "Hello." Once, when I heard the tightness in her throat (she must have known it would be another hang-up, because who the hell else would call her?), I stood by the phone outside the East Hampton post office and got this terrible lump in my own throat; I wanted to cry for her.

Maybe I was so overcome with pity because an hour earlier I'd been looking over all the records we'd pulled on her, and discovered on the printout from Motor Vehicles that besides being five foot nine inches, which was not exactly a feminine asset, she was forty-five years old. Forty fucking five! I did the math three times. I couldn't believe it. But what kind of sense did it make for me to be getting all choked up with pity for a put-upon, middle-aged loser if I was the schmuck standing out in the rain, praying she'd give me another "hello" before she slammed down the phone?

Listen, I told myself, this is definitely one of those sexual obsession things. But instead of ignoring it, or figuring it out, I kept borrowing T.J.'s cars, so Bonnie wouldn't spot my Jag. I drove by her house on the way to work and on the way home. Sometimes in between. All I had to do was spot a shadow passing by an upstairs window, or catch the flutter of a white curtain, and I would feel God's grace upon me. One time, Moose was lying on the front lawn, giving her front paw a manicure with her big pink tongue, and I had this dizzying, blood-to-the-head flush of joy.

And when I'd searched her house, I'd looked in her garage right before I left and saw an old Jeep Wrangler. It made me so incredibly, stupidly happy that Bonnie drove a four-wheel-drive recreational vehicle.

But I felt the same degree of happiness when I found the wad of cash in her boot. I thought: Fantastic! I've really nailed the bitch.

So when Carbone and the lieutenant, a guy named Jack Byrne, who was so shy or weird that he whispered instead of talked, called me in and said, Listen, here are a couple of people to see in the city. The first wife and Sy's divorce lawyer. You'll have to go, not Robby. We need someone with a little finesse . . . Well, I should have been relieved. Here it was: a chance to get the hell off the South Fork, shake off the fixation, stop the Bonnie mania, cut the shit.

Except as I drove west on the Long Island Expressway, all I could think about was her dark, shiny, sweet-smelling hair. I wanted to stroke it back off her forehead, play with it, wrap it around my finger after we finished making love. But also, I wanted to see it inside a small plastic envelope: Government Exhibit D.

Goddamn, I wanted to take T.J.'s minivan, park it down the street and watch her house all day, catch a glimpse of her. I didn't want to work. And I definitely didn't want to go to Manhattan.

Imagine a cartoon of a snooty, stick-up-the-ass rich WASP. That's what Felice Tompkins Spencer Vanderventer looked like, except in 3-D. Yes, she'd heard her first husband had been murdered. Sorry.

Not really sorry or terribly sorry; she didn't gush. Everything about Felice was austere, from her face (which was very long and rectangular, like a gift box for a bottle of booze, except instead of a ribbon on top she had a thin figure eight of gray-brown hair tacked down by a couple of bobby pins) to her dress, which looked as if it were made out of a humongous brown Kleenex held together by a narrow brown belt.

She was Sy's age, fifty-three. Maybe when they were twenty-one they'd looked like a couple, but now, had he been alive and had they stayed married, she would have had to handle embarrassing references to her son; they had separated not only into different worlds but into different generations.

Like Felice, her Park Avenue living room was outmoded. But it wasn't austere. First of all, it was so big you could play basketball in there, except you'd break your neck because it was so chock-full of stuff. The place looked as though someone had bought out the entire inventory of a store specializing in dark, ugly antiques. There was no faded, restful old-money homeyness like at Germy's, just a lot of very high, overstuffed, heavy furniture with claw feet. It would have taken five moving men just to lift one of her hideous black carved-wood chairs. The pictures were heavy too, fancy gold-framed oil paintings of fruit and pitchers and dead rabbits.

"When was the last time you spoke with Mr. Spencer?" My left shoe squeaked every time I shifted my weight. She hadn't asked me to sit.

"About ten years ago." Even in the early-afternoon glare, the room was so shadowy it was hard to make out her features—except for her teeth. They were double normal human size; it looked as if she'd had a transplant from a thoroughbred mare. Felice was so aggressively unattractive that, considering her surroundings, you knew it was her, and not Mr. Spencer or Mr. Vanderventer, who owned the sixteen-foot-high ceilings and everything under them.

"Did you ever meet or speak with his second wife, Bonnie Spencer?"

"I saw them together briefly, once, in front of Carnegie Hall. Sy introduced us." Outside Felice's window, the only bright spot in the room, Park Avenue stretched out like a parade ground for the rich. The island in the middle of the street had huge tubs of bright-gold flowers; they gleamed like piles of money. Past the traffic, over at the curb, elderly doormen opened limousine doors and helped out the rich and able-bodied.

"During the time you knew him, did Sy ever mention a man named Mikey LoTriglio?"

"I believe so."

"What did he say about him?"

"I don't know. Something about their fathers having been in the meat business." She said "meat business" with distaste, as if Sy had been in wholesale carrion. "I never paid attention to that aspect of his life."

I gave it another five minutes, but all I could get was that Felice had married Sy because he could quote all of Wordsworth's "Intimations of Immortality from Recollections of Early Childhood." She'd divorced him because she finally found out he was more interested in "social advancement" than in poetry. And all right, yes, since I'd asked (her upper lip curled, covering about half of her giant teeth), because she caught him cheating. Who with? With her first cousin Claudia Giddings, a trustee of the New

York Philharmonic. He told her he'd fallen in love with Claudia, that he wanted to marry her, but of course he never did.

The trip to Manhattan looked like a waste. What had I gotten? Corroboration that Sy couldn't keep his pants on, especially when there was someone screwable who could boost either his status or his career. And that Germy had been right on the money: Sy was a chameleon. A refined poetry-spouter to Felice. An "I care" Down-to-Earth Human Being to Bonnie. A cool, masterful mogul to Lindsay. And not just to women: somehow, he became whatever anyone wanted him to be. A remote God of Cinema to Gregory J. Canfield. A congenial producer-pal to Nicholas Monteleone. A blood brother to Mikey. A savior to Easton.

I walked down Park Avenue to stretch my legs and let my shoe desqueak, twenty-five blocks from Felice's brown fortress of an apartment house to a silvery glass-and-granite office building. Nature had given up on this part of Manhattan and was hiding out in Central Park. On Park Avenue, there were only too-flawless horticulturist's gold flowers, and a thin, bleached-out strip of sky. Jesus, I hated New York.

Well, maybe not hated. When I was a kid I'd gone on a class trip to the top of the Empire State Building and to see the Christmas tree in Rockefeller Center, and I'd let out an "Oooh!" of honest delight. But after that, I could never figure out what to do with myself in the city, except that I always felt I should do *something*— like take advantage of Culture. Once I'd been down at NYPD Headquarters on a case and then had taken a couple of subways uptown and wound up at the Metropolitan Museum of Art. But it was so big. And I'd had to check my gun with security. The guy there had treated me with a combination of suspicion and contempt, like I was some Bible Belt anti-smut loony who was going to shoot the dicks off the Greek statues. Finally, I'd found myself in a room full of Egyptian mummies, and when I'd asked where the pictures were, a guard, who I'd actually smiled at because he looked like an older Dave Winfield, had said, " 'Pictures'? Do you mean 'paintings'?" That had been it for Culture.

And just walking through the streets, either I'd see nothing but the homeless, and sick whores, and drug deals going down, or—today, as I pushed open the heavy door of the office building— swanky, Sy-like people saying, throatily, "Hiiii" to each other. I always felt like a rube. All dressed up with no place to go. And no matter what jacket I put on in Bridgehampton, when I got to Manhattan my shirt cuffs were too short.

Jonathan Tullius Esq.'s cuffs were, of course, just the right length. He'd been Sy's divorce lawyer, both times. It looked like business was good. His office, filled with soft-looking leather furniture, smelled like the inside of an expensive loafer. "Sit down, Detective Brady." He had a deep, melodic voice and the barrel chest of an opera singer. He said: "I called your offices immediately after I heard about the murder, and spoke with a Sergeant Carbone. And I see now I was right to do so. You people must have some interest in Bonnie Spencer, since you are, in fact, responding to my call." He was crazy about the sound of his own voice. "To get to the point, Detective Brady: Sergeant Carbone agreed this conversation would be strictly off the record and disclosed *only* on a need-to-know basis."

"Right."

"You see, on one hand the attorney-client privilege survives death."

"Yeah."

"Therefore, I should not be talking to you." He swiveled around in his throne of a leather chair and then rested his elbows on his desk. "On the other hand, Sy was a dear friend as well as a client. He called me last Thursday. The day before he was killed. He was quite, quite concerned." Tullius had one of those soft, pampered, self-satisfied faces you see at Republican National Conventions.

"What was he concerned about, Mr. Tullius?"

"Money." I waited. "And his former wife. Bonnie Spencer."

I thought: Oh, fuck it! "Was she holding him up for money?"

"No. But Sy was concerned that she might. You see, he'd

run into her out in the Hamptons. She lives there full-time. Got their old summer house. He had nothing to do with her after the divorce, but then she'd dropped him a note about some screenplay she'd written. . . ." He paused. "You do know that she had been a screenwriter at one time."

"Yeah," I told him. "I'm the squad's Bonnie Spencer expert."

"They had one or two telephone conversations about it. He was trying to be nice, encourage her. And then he was out there almost the entire summer, filming *Starry Night*. Well, just on a whim, he dropped by her house. One thing led to another." The lawyer cleared his throat.

"Sexual congress," I suggested.

"Yes. He called me about it. Apparently, she's in a bad way financially, and Sy—*post hoc ergo propter hoc*—was worried that she might attempt to make some sort of a case for alimony because they had resumed sexual intimacy. I assured him she could not. The marriage was over, as was his responsibility toward her."

"He said they only slept together once?"

"Oh, yes. Absolutely. You see, he was living with Lindsay Keefe. Why, under that circumstance, he chose a dalliance with Bonnie is one of those conundrums only the Higher Powers can unravel, but there you have it."

"Did Bonnie make any threats?"

"No, but Sy seemed unduly concerned over her. Disquieted, guilty. And over a single lapse. It didn't 'play,' as they say in the film world. That's why I decided to phone your office. There was *something* about Bonnie. I met her during the divorce proceedings and, quite frankly, did not care for her. That rampant good nature; there was something so false. I simply did not trust her. My guess is, Sy finally smelled something fishy too. He might have been worrying about the possibility of extortion: Pay me or I'll tell Lindsay. Or he might have been thinking she would seek revenge against him, against his property. You see, he was quite taken aback by Bonnie's poverty. He said he'd seen holes in one of her pillowcases. Just a symbol, naturally, but he *did* say about his little tryst with her, his little one-afternoon stand: 'I wonder what this is going to cost me?' What's been bothering me ever since his murder is . . . did he have any intimation that the cost would be his life?"

What a toad-load, I thought, as I walked up Park Avenue again, back to my car. I couldn't believe Carbone and Byrne had insisted I piss away a day on these two fuckheads. The entire bureaucracy of the County of Suffolk was losing its grip, peeing in its collective pants over the media exposure the case was getting. CBS, NBC, CNN and ABC were showing helicopter shots of Sandy Court, and some photographer in a boat had taken long-distance shots of Lindsay walking on the beach. Plus there seemed to be thousands of close-ups of Captain Shea in front of a bouquet of microphones, saying, "We are at the present time investigating a variety of possibilities." Neither Peter Jennings nor Bryant Gumbel sounded hopeful of an immediate solution. The *New York Times* came right out and said that the Suffolk County P.D. "appeared stymied." And *Newsweek* agreed: "The police seem not to have a clue. . . ." The department only wanted to look good and to protect itself, and that meant following up every single lead, even the most idiotic. So a whole day shot to shit. A hundred miles to New York and a hundred miles back, to find out that Sy Spencer liked to fuck rich and/or famous women and that some supercilious lawyer was sure Sy had foreseen his doom in a threadbare pillow-case.

I turned up a side street, went into a drugstore, got out a couple of bucks' worth of quarters. I stared at the colossal condom display, wondered what kind of a moron would buy blue, ribbed rubbers and dialed 1-516, the area code for Long Island. But instead of dialing Headquarters, I dialed Bonnie's house. She answered. "Hello." Her tone was cautious, weary, as though she expected another hang-up. I didn't say anything. *"Hello?"* she repeated. I hung up and called Robby. No DNA report yet. No nothing. To kill time, so I wouldn't have to drive back during rush hour, I had Robby give me the names, addresses and phone numbers for Mikey LoTriglio's known associates that he'd gotten from the FBI and the NYPD.

Three of Robby's names were the guys who had sworn and deposed that Fat Mikey had sat with them in a booth at Rosie's Bar in the meat district on Friday, August 18, from approximately three in the afternoon to—at least—six or seven. A couple of the other known associates were unavailable, currently residing in Allenwood federal correctional facility in Pennsylvania. Mrs. Fat, Loretta LoTriglio, had checked into Mount Sinai Hospital two days before the murder and was still there, recovering from a new silicon breast implant because the old one had slipped and her tit had wound up in her armpit or something.

So for lack of anything better to do, I decided to check out Mikey's girlfriend, Terri Noonan, a part-time receptionist for an optician, who lived ten minutes from the Triborough Bridge in Jackson Heights, Queens.

I had an image of a gun moll with blond, teased hair and a wad of chewing gum. Terri Noonan had plain curly brown hair and no makeup. She wore a starched white blouse with a little round collar and a pale-blue cardigan sweater buttoned at the top. No jewelry. She looked like she belonged to an order of nuns that had given up the habit but not the vows. Except when you looked twice—and you had to because she didn't show it off—you could see she had an absolutely spectacular, long-legged, big-boobed showgirl body. My guess was that Mikey had gotten it mixed up: he'd married the bimbo and kept the sweetie pie on the side.

Terri tried a whispery "Mikey Who?" but gave up after I said "Come on, Terri." She asked me in and made me a cup of tea. The apartment, like the woman, was comfortable, simple, although as I'd passed the bedroom, I'd spotted a round bed with a quilted violet cover. But the living room had a green-and-white-striped plaid couch, green tweedy club chairs, a couple of trees in giant pots and green wall-to-wall carpet. Nice, comfortable. The kind of stuff a cop's wife who had good taste would buy. She poured the tea from a pot with flowers, then went back to the kitchen and returned with a plate of bakery cookies; she probably bought them fresh every day in case Mikey dropped by. I couldn't help staring; instead of the nun cardigan and the plain navy skirt, she should be wearing tassels and a G-string. She said, "God, Mikey was so upset about Sy. No kidding." She pointed to a Linzer torte. "Raspberry jelly inside that one."

"You mean Mikey was upset because they were fighting about the way the movie was going?" I didn't think Terri was trying to look dumb; Mikey probably hadn't told her a thing. "You know," I said. "The movie Sy was making, *Starry Night*. The movie Mikey invested in."

"I swear to God, Officer, he never said anything about any movie or any investment."

"And he never said he and Sy had words?"

She crossed her heart, held her hand up and said, "Cross my heart, my mother's life to die. Not a word. I mean, I knew about Sy because he was kind of famous, and one time when Loretta—Mikey's wife—was out at La Costa we went to a premiere and a big party after for one of Sy's movies. But they was friends from the old days, and Mikey didn't talk about him all that much, except, like, to reminisce. But when he died, Mikey came right over." Terri blinked. "He was in tears, and Mikey's not one of these phony guys who cries all the time. I never, ever saw him like that before."

"When was that, Terri?"

"Uh, let me think. Saturday morning. That's when I make him my cheese omelet."

"You know Sy was killed late Friday afternoon. About four-twenty."

"I didn't know the exact time," she said, and broke off a tiny end of a chocolate chip cookie and put it in her mouth.

I put down the teacup and looked straight at her. "Terri, this is important. Where was Mikey at the time of the murder?"

"Friday?"

"Friday."

"Why is it important?"

"Do I have to draw you a picture?"

Terri readjusted the stiff little collar of her blouse so it lay flat over the cardigan. "Mikey was here. In this apartment."

"With you?"

"Yes."

"What was he doing?"

She glanced down at her flat-heeled shoes. "It was personal."

"You and Mikey were having relations at or about four P.M. last Friday?"

She raised her right hand. "From three till six," she swore.

"Mikey must be quite a guy."

"He's a little on the large side, but he's in very good health."

"Will you sign a statement to the effect that he was here with you?"

"In blood," she said. Instead, I handed her my Bic and watched as she began writing "I, Theresa Kathleen Noonan, do swear . . ." "See," she said, after she signed her name, "Mikey couldn't have been out in the Hamptons when Sy was killed, because he was here with me!"

But now Mikey had two alibis—which was as good as none at all.

So I should have felt better about Bonnie, right? It ought to be comforting to know that your sicko obsession may, in fact, be a nice, nonhomicidal girl.

Driving home on the Northern State, somewhere around the middle of Nassau County, I started having this fantasy about knocking at Bonnie's door and saying, Thank me. She asks why, and I say, Because I blew Mikey LoTriglio's alibi out of the water. And then, We put a tap on his phone and guess what? He got a call from some two-bit, piece-of-shit wise guy who, it turns out, pulled the trigger of the .22—on Mikey's orders. You're home free, Bonnie.

Then I had an alternate fantasy where she's back from a hard run, her face rosy, her breath coming in gulps, and I pull up, get out of the car and tell her, Listen, everything's okay. We did a routine check, and it turns out that Victor Santana, the director, was renting a house that had a gun rack—and the owner confirmed a .22 was missing! Oh, no—not Santana. Lindsay! She knew Sy was going to California to replace her, and she just snapped. Can you believe, she went to a sporting goods store five minutes from the *Starry Night* set and bought ammo. She was wearing dark sunglasses—like the guy at the store had never seen a movie and wouldn't recognize her! Listen, I tell Bonnie, I know it's been hell for you. I'm sorry. And Bonnie says, Thank God, and she's so grateful she puts her arms around me and I say, It's okay, but then I rub my face against the softness of her skin and one thing leads to another and we're inside, in her bedroom, having incredible, sweaty sex that lasts the whole night.

The daydream lasted all the way to Southampton, to the point where I was crying out Bonnie, baby! and about to come for the fourth time, when, out of the corner of my eye, I spotted the turnoff to Lynne's. That's when I cooled down enough for my brain to start functioning again.

And it told me that no matter how many phony alibis he had, it wasn't Mikey or Lindsay who killed Sy Spencer. In my heart I knew it was Bonnie.

It was confirmed. It was confirmed by Bonnie's real estate agent that Bonnie had been expecting big things from Sy. I finally reached the agent at home. She answered her phone with a hearty "Hi! Regina!" She sounded like one of those fervently friendly divorcées, women abandoned by rich men, stuck on the South Fork, who con other women with rich husbands into houses so expensive that the husbands will feel fucked over and so, after an exorbitant season or two, leave, thus creating still more real estate agents.

She was saying: "I told Bonnie, 'Hon, this is *not* a seller's market. Hold on to your house. Wait.' " It was after nine at night, but the agent's voice was still horribly hearty, although a little mushy around the edges, probably from two or three gimlets. "But she said she really needed the money and to try."

"Did she say what she was going to do if she sold it?" I asked.

"Let me think." I waited. "Something about going back to wherever it was she came from, even though I told her, 'Bonnie, you can't go home again.' Right?"

"Any interest in the house?"

"One or two offers, but very low-ball, and she was holding out for the asking price, which was very unrealistic, and believe me, I told her so."

"And then?"

"I called to ask if I could come over and show the house to people, and all of a sudden she was saying, Sorry, I have guests. This happened two or three times. Well, finally I said, Bonnie, they're not beating down the door to buy an upper-midrange listing, because you literally have hundreds of them from Quogue to Montauk, so the next time I call maybe you can take your guests to the beach or into town for a half hour. And then she laughed— she's got a sense of humor—and said it wasn't guests, it was a man. And the next day she called me to put the deal on hold, because things were really looking up. I asked her if that was French for man, and she said yes. Like, he was a very high-powered type, but he was still managing to see her *every single day* for the last few days, and so she wasn't about to have people looking at the house with that kind of interest. So I said, Marriage-type interest? And she said she'd settle for someone's hand to hold on New Year's Eve. Sweet. Right? But the thing of it was, she was staying put. To me, that meant she was thinking about more than a New Year's Eve date; it had a certain ring of seriousness. You know? I remember, I kidded her and asked if her man had a friend, and we had a good laugh about two old dames like us— not really *old*, we're in our forties—having a double wedding."

So Bonnie had expected something from Sy. Well, why not?

She was putting out plenty. That, too, confirmed: the DNA report was on Carbone's desk first thing the next morning. The hair I had gotten off Bonnie's head was a genetic match to the hair on the headboard in Sy's guest room. She had been in the house with Sy the afternoon of his murder.

Motive? Yeah. And now, definitively, opportunity.

CHAPTER 10

I'd gotten Bonnie out of the tub. She was wearing a blue-and-white-striped bathrobe, and the bottom of her ponytail was wet. Her wrists glowed from too-hot water. I guess she'd been trying to soak out the tension. Maybe she'd succeeded, although her eyes were puffy, probably from sleeplessness, possibly from crying. She had to know she was on our Hit Parade. Maybe she even knew she was Number One.

But she wasn't doing any wounded-petunia number. She crossed her arms and stood up straight, an I'm-not-taking-any-shit stance. "I'd be grateful if you could come by during normal business hours," she said. Her crossed arms pushed her breasts up. She saw me staring and, slowly, trying to look casual, lowered her arms and slipped her hands into her pockets. I pictured myself standing behind her, kissing her sweet-smelling hair, the nape of her neck, then slipping my hands into her pockets and feeling her.

It was one of those she-knows-that-I-know-that-she-knows

176

moments. We both knew she wasn't wearing anything under the robe. We both knew I was aware of it. And we both knew if I tugged at the sash, the robe would open. We'd do it standing up in that front hallway of her house because we were so wild for each other we couldn't wait.

I said: "I understand you don't like being disturbed this late. But these are my normal business hours."

She said: "All right. Excuse me for a minute. I'll put something on." She walked upstairs. I closed my eyes, leaned against the wall and began to imagine I had pulled the sash. The robe opens and I pull her up against me—she's still hot from the bath— but before I can ease the robe off, she goes for my pants, unzips them, takes it out, holds it in her hands and . . .

I heard her on the landing and opened my eyes fast, in time to watch her walk downstairs. She'd put on jeans and a white T-shirt, a man's V-neck undershirt of washed-out cotton, only hers was tucked in tight, so you could see every stitch of the white lace of her bra. I hadn't seen this one on my illegal search; it was one of those tiny bras women wear not for support but for men. I thought: Over-the-hill bitch. Except she looked fantastic. I caught myself rubbing the pads of my fingers together, in anticipation.

"Uh," I said. Oh, was I one cool cop.

"Beg your pardon?"

"Where's your dog?" That was the only thing I could think of to say.

"My *dog?*" She started to relax. Even to get playful. "Why? Do you want to question her?"

"Yeah. I want to know about her relationship with the deceased."

"I got her at Bide-A-Wee about two years ago, so I don't think she ever really got to know Sy. I mean, beyond the usual social superficialities. 'Hi, angel. *Fabulous* haircut.' "

I started to smile. "I just asked where your dog was."

Bonnie's tone stayed teasing, light. "I shot her."

"Stop it."

"Ha!" she exclaimed, like a TV lawyer who's just elicited a damaging admission in front of a jury that will help his client. "See? Deep down, you don't think I'm capable of murder."

"No. I don't think you're capable of murdering your dog." Bonnie laughed a little too hard. She took a step back; this was too real, and suddenly she was comprehending how terrified she was. But she made herself take a deep, deliberate breath. Easy, she was telling herself. Relax. She stuck her thumbs into the belt loops on her jeans, cowgirl style, as in, Get off my ranch, mister. "Where is she?" I hated to keep asking the same stupid question, but having made a fool of myself asking about the dog, I now had to treat it like it was a key to the investigation.

"She likes to go out at night." A cool, matter-of-fact response. No, cold. "Sometimes around ten I open the back door and yell for her. She's back inside in two minutes." Bonnie turned away from me, probably to hide her fear. Despite her laid-back, home-on-the-range posture, it was stealing over her face—jaw a little rigid, eyes too wide. She strode into the kitchen, opened the door and yelled: "Moose! Milk-Bone!" While we waited, she went to the refrigerator and took out an Amstel Light. She did not offer me one, so I wasn't able to say "No, thanks." By the time she popped off the cap, Moose came barreling up to the screen door. I opened it. She let out a blissful bark and started licking my hand.

But Bonnie was hardly blissed out. She was busy being tough. She pulled the dog away from me, patted its head, then took a doggy bone out of a cookie jar and put it in Moose's mouth. For that instant, Bonnie forgot herself and was tender, a mother offering her child a lollipop. Moose, meanwhile, glanced up. She may have been nuts about me, but I wasn't part of her nightly ritual; she decided I might want to grab her treasure, so she hightailed it out of the kitchen, bone in mouth. I grinned. Bonnie didn't.

"What do you want to know?" she demanded. She tilted back her head and took a swig of beer. I stared at the arch of her throat, the rise of her breasts. I wanted her so much. "Well?"

All right. She wanted it, I'd give it to her. "Can you shoot a .22 rifle?"

In a movie, Bonnie would have shown her shock by spritzing out the beer. Real life lacks grand gestures, or even spectacularly messy ones. She just swallowed a little harder than normal. "That's not funny."

"I'm not being funny. You're the funny one. I'm the cop. And I'm very, very serious. I want to know whether you can shoot a .22."

"I don't have to answer that."

"You already have. You didn't say no."

"I didn't say yes, either." Suddenly her fear turned to anger. She slammed the beer bottle down on the counter. "Just let me tell you something. I've been watching detective movies since I've been eight or nine years old. I know hard-boiled and soft-boiled. I know you're supposed to frighten me so much that I spill whatever beans there are to be spilled. Or you're supposed to charm me, so I'll get giddy and babble all my girlish secrets. Well, guess what, buster? You're no Humphrey Bogart. And guess what again? I didn't do anything wrong. I have nothing to confess. You're wasting your time."

"Yeah?" I shouldered an invisible rifle. I sighted. I pulled the trigger. "Bonnie Bernstein Spencer. Her family owned Bernstein's Sporting Goods in Ogden, Utah, a store which did not sell junior lacrosse sticks. No: rifles, handguns. Ms. Bernstein-Spencer grew up with several older brothers and was reputed to be a tomboy. Her father was known as a fine shot; he even used to go up to Wyoming to shoot elk. Tell me, Bonnie, is Ogden a nice place to visit? Because if you don't answer my question now, I'll be on the next plane out, spend half a day in town, and I guarantee you, I'll come home with whatever's left of the rabbit you shot between the eyes in 1965, plus affidavits from ten witnesses who saw you shoot it."

She started to cry, those round, silent tears that drift down cheeks and leave trails. "Please," she whispered, "don't do this to me."

"I just have to get to the truth." I realized I was whispering too. "Bonnie, can you shoot?"

"Yes." I could barely hear her. "But I swear to God, I didn't kill Sy."

Jesus, I thought, I almost have her. Almost. "You have to understand," I told her gently, "people swear to God all the time. 'I swear to God, I'm innocent.' "

"But I am."

"Prove it to me."

"How?"

All I had to do was pull her in very slowly, lovingly, as though seducing the most reluctant of women. "We can rule you out with a simple little test. Come with me. I'll drive you down to Head-quarters, stay with you the whole time. You just give a small sample of saliva and blood—a pinprick, nothing more. And then you're in the clear."

For a long moment there was silence. I heard the deep hum of the refrigerator and then the click of Moose's paws as she toddled back into the kitchen, across the tile, to look up at us. She didn't understand why we weren't having fun.

"Come on, Bonnie."

I imagined her beside me in the Jag on the way to Head-quarters, our arms and shoulders touching when I took a curve; I thought about the heat that instant of friction would give off. Shit, I don't want this fantasy.

But then, at Headquarters, my bewitchment would finally be over. In that hard fluorescent light, I'd see Bonnie Spencer for what she was: a killer. Of course, she hadn't meant to do it. Of course, if she could live the moment all over again, Sy would still be alive. And of course, she was, without a doubt, honestly and profoundly sorry. But still, a killer. And seeing her in that mer-ciless light, I would no longer be able to desire the thing I most hated. Murderer.

I would no longer spend every goddamn obsessed minute creating different scenarios of kissing her, caressing her, fucking her: in beds, in chairs, on tables, in showers, on floors, in cars, on the beach, in the ocean, in the woods. I would be relieved of my madness. I would save thousands staying away from pay phones. I would go to my wedding with a peaceful mind and a loving heart.

All of a sudden, I felt sick, awful—the opposite of dizzy: heavy-headed. Despair settled on me. In that terrible moment, I wondered, How the hell am I going to live out the rest of my life without this woman? For a minute I truly could not speak. Then, I don't know how, I got it together: "Let's go, Bonnie."

"No."

"Come on. You've got everything to gain, nothing to lose. Let it be over."

"I want you out of here."

"Bonnie—"

"Don't come back. I won't speak to you again."

"Honey, I'm sorry, but you'll have to."

"No. And I'm not your honey. Not by a long shot, you son of a bitch. If you have any more questions, you can speak to my lawyer. Now *out*."

Robby Kurz came swishing over to my desk, licked his pinkie and ran it over his eyebrow. I told him: "Hey, you're not telling me anything about yourself I don't already know."

"Gideon is outside," Robby simpered, in an exaggeratedly faggy way. Well, what do you expect from a cop? A gay rights button? "He's simply *dying* to see you."

"Gideon who?"

"Are you ready for this?" He waved a business card. "Gideon Isaiah Friedman, Esquire. Of East Hampton, sweetie. Attorney for Bonnie Spencer."

Gideon Friedman walked toward me. He didn't take little mincing steps. And he didn't lisp or wave a limp wrist. Still, you

knew what he was. Maybe it was that his getup was impeccable
country lawyer, English style: awesomely casual, perfectly cut
brown tweed suit with a tattersall shirt, green knit tie and shoes
that looked like wing tips, except they were brown suede. Or maybe
it was the flawless haircut, where every single strand of brown
hair lay smooth against his head, as if his skull were magnetized.
Or maybe it was that he was too boyishly handsome for a guy in
his late thirties, with that innocent, round-eyed, ultra upper-class
queer look male models have, the ones who always have very long
scarves tossed around their necks in interesting ways. Forget his
name; he had the look of one of those guys with a wood racquet
who leap over the net at the Meadow Club.

Or maybe it was just the way he checked me out when I stood
up to shake his hand. "Hi," he said.

"Hi," I responded.

"I'm here representing Bonnie Spencer." He had a breathy
voice, like a waiter in one of those trendy, expensive seafood
restaurants, Fish Hampton or whatever, that open and close every
summer because nobody, not even the most pretentious schmuck
from New York, would voluntarily eat rare scallops more than
once. I looked at him and thought: Oh, Christ, Bonnie's going to
sit in Bedford for twenty-five to life.

"Why don't you sit down?" I suggested. He sat in the plastic
chair next to my desk and glanced around the squad room. I figured
he'd murmur, Oooh, how butch! or at least cross his legs at the
knees. "Well, Mr. Friedman, what can I do for you?"

"Well . . ." And suddenly he stopped being a homo. He
became a lawyer. "Why not start by telling me what this bullshit
is about Bonnie coming in and taking blood and saliva tests to
'rule her out' as a suspect."

"I meant that. Sincerely."

"Give me a break. You were referring to that DNA testing,
right?" I shrugged. "What's the story here? Sy Spencer was shot
from a distance. Are we talking about some perspiration that

dripped onto the murder weapon? A little saliva? Did the perpetrator drool?" It was weird, the hard-edge-lawyer sarcasm pre-
sented in that whispery waiter's voice. "Or was there some kind
of a fight, and you have blood—or skin cells from under Sy's
nails?" For a lawyer with no leverage, who had no idea what we
had or where we were going, he was pretty good.

"I'm not prepared to discuss the evidence at this time."

"Why not?"

"You should know why not. There's no percentage in it."

"Okay," he said. "Then I suppose there's no percentage in
anyone taking any blood tests." He stood, regretfully, as if he
hadn't been able to save me from making the most grievous mis-
judgment of my career. "I'm going to have to advise my client to
stand on her Fifth Amendment privilege against self-incrimination
and not take the test."

It was only then that it hit me that Gideon probably represented dress designers. "You're not a criminal lawyer, are you?"
I asked.

I waited for him to get pissed or, minimally, petulant, but to
his credit he stayed composed; serene, even. He sat back down
and examined the nap of the suede on his English shoe. "Why do
you ask?"

"Because a criminal lawyer would know that a suspect in a
murder case can't refuse a blood test."

"Why not?"

"Because blood tests and other medical tests are fact, not
testimony. They aren't covered by the Fifth Amendment."

"Says who?"

"Says the U.S. Supreme Court."

"Really? Recently?"

"Within the last five or ten years."

"It must have happened after law school. I'll check it out."

All right, so maybe he represented a hairdressers' lobbying
group. But he wasn't that bad a guy. Not full of shit. And not full

of himself. Except what the hell would he do when he got to court? Go fancy dress, show up in a black robe and white wig? And what would he do when the chief of the Homicide Bureau of the D.A.'s office cross-examined Bonnie? Take smelling salts?

"What kind of lawyer are you?" I asked.

He smiled. Perfect, even white teeth, like Chiclets. "I specialize in real estate."

"Real estate," I repeated. "Must be busy, over in East Hampton."

"Let me tell you what you're thinking," Gideon said. "Okay?" I shrugged. "You're thinking: Oh, goody! I can send Bonnie Spencer up the river for life and that land-use faggot lawyer who represents her won't be able to do a thing except wave bye-bye as she goes." I sat back in my seat, trying to look astounded at such a ridiculous—no, prejudiced—notion. It was not all that easy since, basically, that was what had been going through my mind. "Well, that's not the way it's going to be, Brady. Let me tell you how it's going to be. If you're just toying with her, I would hope you'd be smart enough to stop right now. Before I make a scene in front of your superiors."

"You think I give a shit? Go ahead. Make a scene. The captain's in that office off the reception area."

"You should give a shit, don't you think?"

"No."

He paused for a second. "All right. If you sincerely think you have any kind of a case, I'd appreciate it if you'd let me know. Because then I'd have to step out—and bring in Bill Paterno." I picked up a pen and twirled it between my palms; Paterno was the best criminal lawyer in Suffolk County.

"Do you think Bonnie Spencer can afford Bill Paterno?" I asked, trying to sound casual, as though I didn't know how broke she was.

"No. But I can." Gideon put on a little-old-man Jewish accent. "I make a very nice living, tanks God, and have some vonderful inwestments." Then he added: "Bonnie is one of my dearest friends."

Well, it figured. I could see them. Giddie and Bonnie. He'd have her over to his place in East Hampton for Mexican beer and guacamole or whatever nouvelle hors d'oeuvre had replaced it, and they'd giggle and gossip and talk about James Stewart and Henry Fonda—or Share Deep Feelings.

"You can hire Paterno, Mr. Friedman. You can resurrect Clarence fucking Darrow. Bonnie's still going to have to take the tests. And then we've got her."

"Why? Because she told you she could shoot? *Please*. Girls in Utah do that sort of thing."

"They hand out a .22 with every box of Kotex?"

"Where's the rifle?" he inquired. I said nothing. "Bonnie doesn't own a rifle. She doesn't have access to one." Gideon waited. "You don't have the murder weapon, do you?" I kept silent. "Why Bonnie? Why not Lindsay?"

"Lindsay?"

"Lindsay can shoot. You don't believe me? Go rent *Transvaal*. Bombastic dreck, but you'll see her with a rifle."

"She's an actress. Holding a rifle doesn't mean she can shoot it."

"Why not find out?"

"Mr. Friedman, we know where Lindsay Keefe was at the time of the murder."

"And?" he asked, lifting a nonexistent speck of lint off his tweedy sleeve. "Are you implying my client was anywhere *near* Sy Spencer's house?"

"Possibly."

"I don't believe you." I shrugged again. "Stop that shrugging!" he said. "It's very irritating. Now let's get serious. You don't want to torment this woman, do you? You just want to get her a little agitated. Well, you've done it. She is agitated to the extreme. Now why don't you let me know *why* you want the tests. Be big about it. Maybe I can recommend taking them—if it's not unreasonable, or damaging to her interests."

I thought about it. The only reason to let a suspect know what evidence you have is when you decide to short-circuit an investigation and go for a confession. I wasn't in that much of a rush; I could wait another twenty-four hours. I sensed there were still more leads to follow. And I had to cover my ass on the illegal search of Bonnie's house by getting a warrant and then "finding" the real estate listing and the money in her boot. Those two items would give the D.A.'s office more rope to hang her.

"You know," I said to Gideon, "the perpetrator was a very intelligent person. But not that intelligent. He or she"—Gideon made a sour face—"left so many loose ends we're still tripping all over them. The evidence box on this one is going to be so heavy the court clerk will need a goddamned moving van to bring it in. So what's the point of telling you what we have, when by this afternoon we'd have to give you a major update."

"You're playing poker," Gideon commented.

"Do me a favor, Mr. Friedman. Give your client a message for me. Tell her that if she did it, she should come in now. Maybe we can bring the matter to a conclusion that's mutually advantageous."

"Why won't you be decent? She's a truly good person. Why won't you give her the benefit of the doubt?"

"Let me continue. If she lets this thing play out, if she doesn't come forward with a confession, it's going to be harder for her."

"Tell me something," Gideon said. "Do you honestly think you can be objective about my client?" I didn't like the way he was eyeing me; I got a quick, bad, pukey feeling. Had he picked up something from me? Had Bonnie told him anything? But what could she tell him? That once I stood a little too close to her? That a couple of times she'd sensed a bulge under my clothes that wasn't my gun?

"Yeah, I can be objective. She's a lovely lady. Good sense

of humor. Friendly. Personally, I think she's a sweetheart." Gideon listened, alert. "But she's a sweetheart with a mean streak."

"You're wrong."

"Hate to say it, but I'm right. You see, I think Bonnie got— what's the word?—piqued at Sy. She was lonely, divorced, poor, unsuccessful. And along came her ex. He winked, then fucked her a few times. . . . Hey, we know about that, even though she swears she didn't. She lies all the time. Anyhow, he fucked her. And then he told her goodbye. No companionship, no marriage, no money. Oh, and no movie. No nothing. So she blew him away."

"You don't really believe that."

"I do."

"You have no evidence."

"We've got plenty of evidence." I put my feet up on the desk. "I've got to tell you, I find homicidal behavior not worthy of a sweetheart. But what I think isn't important. The lady's going away. So be prepared. Maybe make her a nice bon voyage party."

Marian Robertson, Sy's cook, was being paid by the movie production company to remain on her job until Lindsay finished *Starry Night*. "Cook?" she sneered. "Lindsay Keefe needs a cook? Do you know what she eats? Fruit. All right, an occasional nut. No wonder she looks like a glass of milk. I sit here all day so that maybe, when she gets home, I can make her seven Crenshaw melon balls. What kind of person can live on melon balls?"

For a second I couldn't answer because my mouth was full. She'd insisted on making me bacon and eggs, to say nothing of a tower of English muffins and coffee. "You don't like her," I managed to say.

"There are worse."

"Who?"

"Oh, the pushy ones. The braggarts. And the ones who come in two minutes before a dinner party for twenty and tell me they're on Pritikin. The ones who have to explain to a colored woman what *milles feuilles* is."

The marmalade was in a tiny white crock, like a soufflé dish for midgets. I spooned some onto another muffin. "What about someone like Bonnie Spencer?" I asked. Marian Robertson started to gnaw on the inside of her cheek. "Remember Bonnie? Sy's ex-wife."

"Oh, of course! Nice girl."

"Mrs. Robertson, this is very difficult for me. I've known you since I was a kid. I look up to you. I would hate to see you in trouble."

"Me?"

"Yes. We have physical evidence that Bonnie Spencer was in the house the afternoon of Sy's murder. Now, you can tell me you didn't know she was here, but sooner or later we're going to confront Bonnie with our evidence. And she may say something like: '. . . and that nice Mrs. Robertson, who knew me so well when I was married to Sy. She always made me my favorite . . . whatever. Kumquat pudding. Well, Mrs. Robertson and I had a nice chat that afternoon.' And then you'd have a legal problem, because in your statement you said no one was here."

"More coffee?"

"Mrs. Robertson, withholding evidence, lying to the police—it's a crime."

Finally, she said: "You're barking up the wrong tree, Steve. Bonnie's as good as they come."

"If she's that good, why did you lie to protect her? Don't you think it would be better to let her goodness shine through?"

"If she wanted to tell you she was here, it was her business, not mine." She cleared the cream and the marmalade off the table. I was no longer a welcome guest.

"Was she here last Friday afternoon?" She took away the sugar bowl.

"Yes." Clipped. No, Steve, you're looking fine. No, You were the best shortstop the Bridgies ever had.

"Did you speak with her?"

"Just hello, how are you, and just a couple of minutes of catching up."

"Was it friendly? Did she kiss you hello? Did you make a fuss? 'Good to see you, Mrs. Spencer!' "

"I call her Bonnie. And I was glad to see her and she was glad to see me. I gave her a big hug. What are you going to do about that? Put me in the electric chair?"

"Mrs. Robertson, I'm just trying to get the feeling of the afternoon."

"The feeling was, Mr. Spencer must have gotten tired of Madame Melon Balls, because he actually brought Bonnie into the house. And he was smiling, happy to be with her—like the old days. And they didn't stay in the kitchen to chat. My guess is they had other fish to fry upstairs. But that was all right, because I got the feeling Bonnie would be back. Then we could catch up. I know her; Mr. Spencer would get busy on the phone, and she'd wander down to the kitchen and we'd have ourselves a good gabfest."

"I'd like the truth now. Were there any sounds of fighting coming from upstairs?"

"No."

"Any sounds of anything?"

"No. Listen to me. He wouldn't have gone out to the pool to relax and make his last-minute phone calls if Bonnie was still upstairs. Say what you will about him, his manners were perfect. It wasn't in his nature not to drive a lady home, or if she'd come on her own, escort her to her car. Believe me, after Bonnie and before Lindsay, there was quite a parade of women going upstairs to see his ocean view or whatever. He *always* said a proper good-bye."

"Then how come you didn't hear him escort her out?"

"I don't know. Maybe I was beating egg whites. Maybe I was powdering my nose."

"Did you hear Mr. Spencer come down and go out to the

pool?" She did a cheek chew before she nodded. "And what about Bonnie? Did you hear her leave after he went outside?" She didn't answer. "Okay, between the time Bonnie went upstairs with Sy and the time you heard the shot, what precisely did you hear? Her voice? Her footsteps? The sound of her car?"

"She didn't kill him."

"What did you hear, Mrs. Robertson?"

"I didn't hear anything." She took away the muffins and my plate. "Does that make you happy, Steve?"

I knew the old saying was true: You don't remember pain. Physical pain, like in Vietnam, when some new kid from North Carolina heard enemy fire, aimed his M-60, and blasted me through the shoulder. The medic shot me up with a ton of shit, but they had to stuff a gag into my mouth so I wouldn't scream and give away our position when they cut open my shirt. Me, who'd always looked at wounded, screaming guys and thought: Sure, it must hurt like hell, but can't he just bite the bullet, control himself? I kept moaning so loud that they kept the gag in, and they took it out only when I puked and almost choked to death on my own vomit.

I can recall thinking, when they joggled my shoulder as they put me on the stretcher to get me to the helicopter: I will not live through this flight because the pain will kill me. I truly cannot take it. I kept howling, "I want a priest!" Me, whose last confession pretty much coincided with my first communion. But I don't remember the pain itself.

And you don't remember emotional pain either.

Like being a seven-year-old kid playing ball and my father drives onto the field in some farmer's tractor he's doing day work for, and he cuts the engine, stopping between the pitcher's mound and first base, practically breaks his neck getting down and then grabs a bat out of the hands of one of my friends and insists on hitting a few.

More pain? Being a thirty-five-year-old and seeing my pal, my confidant, the only person I ever really spoke to outside work, the one person I thought to buy a Christmas card for—the guy who owned the liquor store—flash his wife a look of revulsion when I walked through the door.

You know all that pain and more occurred. Recalling it, you might feel sad or even cringe. But you do not remember the pain itself.

So when I rang Bonnie's bell and got no answer, and then ran to her garage to see if her car was missing, and then, finally, spotted her in her chicken-wired garden, picking vegetables, I almost laughed at the panic I'd felt, the horror, the stab in the gut—the pain—when I thought she'd gone. So what if she had? You do get over these things.

And when Moose barked a welcome and Bonnie looked up and saw me and shuddered—a violent, uncontrollable shiver of fear—I wanted to disappear, or die, it hurt so much. But I said to myself: I'll get over it.

She was squatting over a basket of eggplants. "What are you going to do with all those things?" I asked.

"Get out of here." Her voice was a hoarse whisper. She braced her hands on her knees and slowly, as if it were too much of an effort, pushed herself up. All her energy, all her fire, all her humor was gone.

"Look, I just want you to understand . . ." What was I going to say? Nothing personal. "You lied, Bonnie."

She walked out of the garden, leaving the eggplants, a plastic bucket full of tomatoes, Moose—everything—behind. She headed toward the house, awkwardly, without any of her great jock grace, as if she'd lost her center of gravity. I followed her. "We have a neighbor who can not only identify Sy's car as being here every day the week he died, but who can identify Sy himself. I mean, we can place you with him enough times . . . Why did you lie about a thing like that?"

She didn't answer me, didn't acknowledge that I'd grabbed onto her arm, trying to steady her or just hold on to her. "And why did you lie about your screenplay? Didn't you bother to think that he'd tell the people he worked with that it was a piece of shit?"

She tripped over a tree root. I lost my grip on her, and she fell on her hands and knees. "Are you okay?" I asked. She couldn't get up. She sat back on the ground, breathless, and looked down at the pebbles and grass embedded in her hands, at the little rivulet of blood that ran toward her wrist, but she didn't wince or weep. "Bonnie," I said. Her spirit was gone.

Moose wandered over, wagged her tail and licked Bonnie's hand, but Bonnie didn't acknowledge her. "Please," I said. I pulled her up. She didn't stop me. When she was on her feet again, she continued her unsteady journey toward the house. "Listen, your lawyer friend . . . He's going to pay for the best criminal lawyer around."

I felt sick. Empty. But I'd lived through too much. I knew. Part of me understood that in two weeks, I'd be hoisting an alcohol-free beer, eating potato chips, and Lynne would be saying: "Forget that you're going to get the fattest gut in Bridgehampton. Do you *know* what those chips look like on your insides?"

You forget pain. You really do.

Bonnie opened the screen door to her kitchen. "Congratulations," she said softly.

"I don't want congratulations. Believe me, I'm sorry."

"No. You did what you set out to do. You got me. That's it. My life is over. What you did isn't homicide, but the effect is pretty much the same: a dead person."

There was so much grief in her voice, as if she was mourning someone she had loved very much.

"It has to be," I said.

"Why?"

"Because you killed someone." She walked inside and closed the screen door. I looked at her, blurred, distant, through the mesh. "Don't try and leave. There'll be a twenty-four-hour watch—"

"Where could I go that you wouldn't find me?"

"That's right."

"It's so sad."

"It is," I agreed.

"No. It's sad because I didn't do it. You know I didn't." It was about sixty-five degrees. I began to shake. I knew: This would be pain I would never forget. "Don't worry," Bonnie said, just before she closed the kitchen door. "You'll get over it."

CHAPTER 11

e got to Bonnie's house before eight the next morning. Less than thirty seconds later, she looked up from the fine print on the search warrant, swallowed and said: "I'll have to call my lawyer."

"Feel free," Robby said magnanimously, a second before he and the other detective, a short bodybuilder type in his late twenties, tried to push past her, into the house. The kid's thighs were so overdeveloped that he couldn't get his legs together. He walked like a chimpanzee.

"You can't do this!" Bonnie shouted, trying to block us. I was the one who finally shoved her aside.

"Reasonable force," I said. "Call your Civil Liberties Union."

At first I'd expected hysteria. Then—especially when I noticed she was wearing those tight turquoise bicycle shorts and a T-shirt—I did a fast fantasy number. She'd faint. I'd grab her, lead her over to her couch and mumble something calming, like "Easy, Bonnie," as, slowly, I let her out of my arms. Easy, Bonnie:

I liked the idea of saying her name out loud.

But she'd just stood near the staircase, completely still. She was there, but she wasn't there. The world she was living in was so awful that she withdrew and entered some other, kinder universe. At last, she drifted past me, into the kitchen to call Gideon. I could have been a ghost, just air and vapor. Moose picked up Bonnie's mood, staying right beside her, concerned, not giving me so much as a wag of the tail.

I followed them into the kitchen and started going through her cabinets as if assuming I'd find a cupful of .22 bullets behind the Down Home Gourmet barbecue sauce. For someone who was close to broke, Bonnie was spending too much money on mustard: honey mustard, tarragon mustard, green peppercorn mustard. I looked over at her. Maybe I'd try a little mustard humor, clear the air. But her back was toward me, and she was speaking quietly into the phone.

I shook a jar of popcorn hard and loud, like some maracas-playing fool in a Latin American band. I wanted attention. Maybe if she acknowledged I was alive I would be able to feel alive. I was so goddamn down.

Fuck this sadness shit, I told myself. Your obsession's dead. Be glad. But I couldn't let it rest in peace. And I couldn't stop trying to get a rise out of Bonnie.

I made a big production out of going through her pocketbook. Obnoxious. Intrusive. A deliberate invasion of privacy. I examined each key, flattened out a couple of linty tissues, studied a supermarket cash register tape. In slow motion, I took apart her wallet, laying out her seventeen bucks in bills, her forty-four cents in change, her driver's license, her Visa card, her library card, her video store membership card. And the pictures: father in a plaid shirt holding up a prizewinner of a trout. Father and mother—tall and broad-shouldered like Bonnie—all dressed up, like for a wedding, smiling, but starched, stiff. You just knew they'd rather be in their plaid shirts. Brothers and sisters-in-law on skis. Nieces with horses. Nephews with dogs. All the Bernstein pictures had mountains in the background.

I waited for her to show some spirit: run, try and punch me, scream out something like "I hate you!" Nothing. So I made a big deal of opening a purple plastic case that held a couple of Tampax. I held each one—Super—up to the light, as if anticipating a fuse instead of a string. Zero response. Should I taunt her? Say, No shit. You still have a period? and then deny it if her lawyer bitched about my being insulting? But I kept quiet. Thighs, the kid detective, was around; I didn't want him to think I was anything other than neutral.

Bonnie hung up the phone. I went back to the pocketbook. There was some powder on the bottom of her purse, red, obviously the blushing stuff women put on with those big fluff brushes. But I did a major number, sifting it into a plastic envelope, like it was a new, killer form of cocaine that made crack look like aspirin. She made no snide remarks. Clutching the warrant in her hand, she simply walked out on me. I stood there, a complete jerk, helpless, yearning, watching her turquoise ass until it disappeared into the hall.

I was like a husband whose wife has just walked out on him. I sank into the same chair where I'd sat that first day, having coffee. I was still holding her pocketbook.

About ten minutes later, when I finished the kitchen and found absolute squat, I went looking for her. She was sitting on the brick ledge in front of her fireplace, the search warrant beside her. She was hugging herself, as if waiting for logs to blaze up and thaw her out. Of course, there was no fire. Outside, it was already over seventy. The sky was too bright, an almost painful blue, the brilliant morning light of the end of August. The sun poured through Bonnie's living room window, making shining squares on a dozing Moose and on the dark wood floor beneath her.

Bonnie's head was down, so she didn't notice Thighs rush over and hand me a heavy shopping bag. Since all he'd turned up so far was one of Moose's half-chewed rawhide bones under the couch, he was clearly longing for some significant sign of Bonnie's guilt.

I emptied the shopping bag onto the coffee table. Bonnie glanced over. There were two unopened boxes: a coffee grinder and one of those expensive espresso-cappuccino machines. In the bottom of the bag was an American Express receipt: Sy Spencer, card member since 1960, had paid for them.

I walked over to her, sat down on the other side of the search warrant and fluttered the receipt in front of her. "Sy like a cup of espresso afterwards?" I inquired. "Or before? Some guys need a little stimulant." She didn't answer, but then I hadn't expected her to. I didn't exist. Plus Gideon had obviously warned her not to say anything, and she was taking him literally. "Is your lawyer coming over?" I asked. She picked up the warrant. She looked for a pocket for it, but since she was wearing the shorts and T-shirt, she didn't have any. She just held on to it. I shifted so I could at least look at her. Her T-shirt was from some film festival, probably a feminist thing. Across her breasts it said WOMEN MAKE MOVIES in red and green and yellow and blue.

I rested the receipt on top of the warrant she was holding and pointed to Sy's name. "Three hundred and fifty-five bucks for a cup of coffee," I said. Across the room, Thighs sniggered; he probably thought the sound was a manly detective laugh. Bonnie brushed away the receipt with the back of her hand. It floated onto the floor.

It was so quiet. The only sound was the dog's snoring and then the clunk, clunk of Robby walking around upstairs. I'd wanted him to be the one to find the money in her boot, the real estate listing. I told him: I'll stay downstairs, keep an eye on her.

But she wasn't going anywhere, and I couldn't move anymore. I just sat there beside her. We could have been a heartbroken

couple waiting for some sad appointment together, cancer spe-
cialist, marriage counselor. I kept sneaking glances at her; instead
of wearing her hair loose, tucked behind her ears, or in a ponytail,
she'd put it into a braid. I had the urge to reach over and, with
the tip of my index finger, stroke each one of the shiny intertwin-
ings. I'd say, It'll be all right.

What I actually said was: "Where'd you hide the rifle?" She
didn't move. "Bonnie, your window of opportunity is closing. You
make it tough on us, we'll make it tough on you."

Just then, Gideon Friedman came striding in. Ninja Lawyer:
baggy, rolled-at-the-cuff black cotton slacks, a black sweater, hair
combed back with slickum. I stood up. "Hey, Counselor Friedman," I said. "Good to see you."

He walked past me and hunkered down in front of Bonnie.
"Did you say anything to him?" he asked her. "Anything at all?"
She shook her head. "Good girl." He picked up the search warrant,
stood, and read it over. He saw it was okay. He wanted it out of
sight, but since he didn't have any pockets either, he held on to
it and, with his other hand, pulled Bonnie up and steered her into
the kitchen.

They must have been talking softly in there. I couldn't hear
anything, not even the hum of muted conversation. I walked over
to her bookshelves. Most of them were paperbacks: hundreds of
mysteries and novels. There were books about movies—biogra-
phies of actors and directors, *Cinematographer's Handbook*, *Farce
in Film*—and about nature stuff. *Flowering Plants of Beach and
Dune*. *Hiking Long Island*. There were no sex books tucked behind
Birds of North America, no *Memoirs of a Victorian Serving Wench*,
and no *Stop Being a Compliant Cunt and Get Him to Marry You*,
one of those books single women always seem to have.

Just then Robby clomped down the stairs. His beige loafers
had thick black heels with what sounded like metal taps. He was
grinning, brandishing a plastic evidence bag with the wad of bills
that had been in Bonnie's boot. I walked over to him. "Eight
hundred eighty!" he announced.

"In tens or twenties?" I tried to look amazed, thrilled. "Like from a cash machine?"

"You got it."

"Anything else?"

"Not really." Robby seemed a little disappointed. He'd probably been hoping for a smoking rifle.

"No vibrator in the night table?" Robby shook his head. "No interesting papers?"

"Nothing." Shit, I'd have to go up to have a casual look-through and then find the real estate listing. Unless she'd thrown it out. "Just a lot of movie script stuff in her office," he said. "Rejection letters in a file. But listen, we have enough! This money is the stake in her heart. And once we get her blood samples, it's all over."

"Any rejection letters from Sy?"

"No, but we don't need any. Where is she?"

"In the kitchen with her lawyer."

"Think we should stick it to her now?" He was like a leashed, drooling Doberman; he couldn't wait.

"Yeah," I said. "Might as well get it over with."

My throat felt swollen. My chest rose, but I couldn't get enough air.

We walked into the kitchen. Robby waved the bag of money in front of Bonnie's face. "Eight hundred eighty dollars in twenties," he said to her.

"If you have any comments, please address them to me," Gideon responded.

"Oh, *sorry*," Robby said, giving him a big, shit-eating grin. "We found this hidden in your client's boot. All I want to know is where this money came from. Maybe she could tell us."

"Oh," Bonnie began, "it's—"

"Quiet," Gideon snapped at her.

"But, Gideon, it doesn't have anything to do with Sy."

Gideon did not look thrilled with her. "Would you please leave us alone for a minute?" he asked. We walked into the hall outside the kitchen, heard whispers. I took deep breaths, but I just made myself dizzy. Then Gideon called, "All right. You can come back in." When we did, he nodded at Bonnie.

She spoke to Robby, as if there was only one cop in the room. "The money you found is what's left of twenty-five hundred dollars I got last December. I do a lot of work for a catalog company, and the owner pays me once a year. In cash." Then she added, "Off the books."

"So there's no record of your having received the payment," I said. Bonnie made herself look at me, except her eyes did not meet mine.

"That's the point of being paid off the books," she explained, too patiently, as if talking to someone with an IQ in the minus column. "There isn't supposed to be any record."

"So we just have your word that that's where the money came from?"

"Where else would I get eight hundred and eighty dollars?"

"On the morning of his death, Sy Spencer withdrew a thousand bucks from a cash machine. It was gone when we found him."

Gideon broke in. "Do you call this police work? You don't investigate. You just drop whatever you can't explain at Bonnie Spencer's front door. Obviously Sy gave it to someone. Or he bought something."

"No," Robby said.

"Don't say no. I knew the man. He had a great eye, and he loved to indulge himself. If he saw a hundred-dollar tie he liked, he'd buy one in every color."

"Believe me, we checked," Robby continued. "There was no time for him to buy anything. And he didn't give anything to anyone. Whoever was with Sy Spencer last took the money. And we know that person was Mrs. Spencer here."

"You *know* that? How do you *know?*" Gideon asked, as if he couldn't believe our stupidity. But I could tell; he knew too.

"Because they were in bed together in the guest room of his house that afternoon."

"Really?" There's nothing like watching a desperate lawyer trying to do an amused act.

"Yeah, really," I broke in. "There was some hair in the bed that wasn't Sy's. We're betting that when we get a sample of Ms. Spencer's blood, it'll be a perfect DNA match."

Bonnie's hand flew up to touch the top of her head. She remembered. She understood. She looked at me with a terrible mixture of fury and grief.

"Now, you want to know what happened the afternoon Sy was killed?" I could only talk to Gideon. I didn't have the courage to look at Bonnie anymore. "Your client had relations with Sy Spencer. They had a disagreement. He left the bedroom. She took the thousand bucks from his pants pocket. When he went for a swim, she put on a pair of rubber thongs—"

"I don't have rubber thongs," she said to Gideon.

"—and went downstairs. At some point, she walked to a spot right by the back porch, where she—"

I could feel Bonnie staring straight at me. Her eyes were huge. "*No.* I did not do it. That money . . . I got it—"

"Okay," I cut her off. "Give me the number of the guy at the catalog company."

Bonnie looked over at Gideon but didn't wait for a signal. Just as he started to shake his head no, she said, "The man's name is Vincent Kelleher. He lives in Flagstaff, Arizona. I do three catalogs for him. *Country Cookin'*, *Juno*—that's for heavy women—and . . . God, I'm going blank on the other one right now. Oh, *Handy Dandy*. Hardware, gadgets."

Before I could say anything, she hurried out of the kitchen, upstairs, to her office. I followed. Her hands were shaking as she leafed through her address book. "Here."

I dialed the number. The place wasn't open yet. Gideon came upstairs, into the office, followed by Robby. Finally, I got Kelleher's home phone from Information and woke him up. Yes, he was Vincent Kelleher. Thighs must have sensed something going on, because he came upstairs too, but the small office was too crowded for him to fit in; he stood outside the door, staring at Bonnie's *Cowgirl* poster. Yes, Vincent Kelleher affirmed, he owned several mail-order catalog companies. Yes, Detective Brady, a Bonnie Spencer had done some work for him. Off the books? I demanded. In cash? No! Did you pay Ms. Spencer two thousand five hundred dollars in cash last December? No! At any other time? No! She'd done some work for him a couple of years ago, and he'd paid her . . . by check. Was she in some sort of trouble, Detective Brady?

I hung up the phone. I turned to Robby. "He never made a cash payment to her."

"That's what I figured," he said.

Bonnie grabbed onto the lapel of my jacket. "I swear to you—" It was the first time she'd touched me. I pushed her hand away.

"Out of curiosity," I continued, "Mr. Kelleher wants to know if the lady's in some sort of trouble."

"I'll say she is," Robby said. "Big trouble." He looked at Gideon and smiled. "In fact, by tomorrow, I think the lady could find herself under arrest."

"I think you and I should talk," Gideon said to me.

"I think it's too late," I said.

"The man's right," Robby told Gideon. "It's too late. Deal time is over."

"There are not going to be any deals," Gideon said.

"You're right," Robby told him. "No deals. You know why? Because your client is dead meat—and all of us know it."

Oh, right. Vietnam vet with Purple Heart and Bronze Star. Big, brave cop with brass balls so big they clang. Except when the cars lined up in front of Bonnie's house like a cortege—Bonnie and Gideon in Gideon's BMW 735i, Robby and Thighs in Robby's silver Olds Cutlass, which was actually gray, and me—to take Bonnie to Headquarters for a blood test. I couldn't force myself to go along for the ride; I didn't have the guts to watch Bonnie being driven to her own funeral. As soon as we passed the two-block-long run of stores that was downtown Bridgehampton, I cut north off the main street and tore along the back roads until I got to the highway. Then I floored it. A hundred and ten.

Big stud in a Jaguar. When I got to Headquarters, way ahead of them, I couldn't even make myself go into Homicide. I went into a stall in the men's room and sat down on the can.

I was afraid to face Bonnie.

No, I was afraid to face what I had done. I sat there, heart hammering, realizing I was the butt of some Almighty joke: This woman who somehow had come to mean a lot—no, everything—to me, this woman who I couldn't imagine living without, was, due to my sharp investigatory skills, my crafty persuasiveness, my flawless logic, going to go to jail and would come out an old lady. I would never see this woman, this enchantress, again.

Whatever the hell her magic was, this woman was able to do what no one else had ever done before: bring me to life. But before I could solve the mystery of what her power was, I solved the mystery of Sy Spencer's murder. Oh, I was one shrewd dude. I'd broken her spell.

So now I was totally, wholly and entirely without her, without any hope of touching her or talking to her, for the rest of what will be, at best, thirty or forty years of my lifeless life. I would move through marriage, kids, more homicides, grandchildren, retirement, as though moving through a thick and dirty fog.

There I was, a real man. A homicide detective, sitting on a toilet because I was afraid to face some killer with a shining braid who makes good coffee and has a wonderful dog.

But I got myself under control, except for one or two trembling breaths. Still, I couldn't leave for another five minutes because some guy from Sex Crimes or Robbery could come in to take a leak and when I passed him, I might suddenly get the shakes, or even burst into tears. He would realize then that, somehow, I was not the tough guy he and I and everybody else were so convinced I was.

So I just hid out in the toilet until I could become a man again.

Bonnie and Gideon, while not true locals, had probably lived on the South Fork long enough to know how to get to the Long Island Expressway without having to wait in the summer traffic caused by Yorkers, who, while normally the world's pushiest people, were totally feeble when it came to driving: sitting passively in their overheating cars, moving at the speed of a slug, on their way to buy a bottle of balsamic vinegar for thirty dollars. Their city brains could not comprehend the concept of turning off main roads. Naturally, all this would change the second *New York* magazine published an "Insiders Tell Their Secret Hamptons Shortcuts" article.

But Bonnie and Gideon wouldn't take a shortcut. What was waiting for them that would make them want to rush over to Headquarters? And Robby and Thighs weren't going to push them; they knew just enough about the South Fork of Suffolk to know that a road on a map did not necessarily mean a road in reality. Why risk a wrong turn, wind up in the middle of a field of cauliflower and have Gideon reconsider and decide to spend a few days fighting the blood test, litigating the unlitigable? So they'd creep along with all the other cars. They could be another thirty, forty minutes. An hour even.

I left the men's room and dragged myself into Homicide. Since we work on shifts, two or three guys share a desk. Hugo the Sour Kraut was at mine. I waved at him to stay put and sat down at Robby's. Two minutes later, Ray Carbone stuck his head into the room. He was wearing his congenial expression, like he wanted to talk about the exit wound in Sy's skull, or the Jungian theory of personality, so I picked up the phone, dialed the number for time and made a show of holding on, expectant, like I was waiting to speak to some Ultimate Witness. "Eastern Daylight Time, ten-fourteen . . . and twenty seconds," the computer voice said. Carbone saluted goodbye and left. I was too exhausted to even hang up the phone, so I just sat there, listening to time passing. "Eastern Daylight Time, ten-sixteen . . . and thirty seconds."

I opened Robby's drawer, searching for a pen so I could look like I was taking notes. No pens, but there were a couple of near-empty bottles of breath freshener drops, a business card from Mikey LoTriglio's lawyer and, toward the back, Robby's file on Mikey. I took it out: Michael Francis LoTriglio, aka Mikey Lo-Triglio, aka Fat Mikey, aka Mickey Lopkowitz, aka Mr. Piggy, aka Michael Trillingham. Faxed forms and computer printouts from NYPD and the FBI showing his arrest record: extortion, loan-sharking, conspiracy to sell stolen securities, tax evasion. And homicide, twice. Richie Garmendia of the Retail Butchers Union had been found floating under a West Side pier with his skull battered in. And Al Jacobson, an accountant for a carting company, was missing and presumed dead, death reportedly caused by being dropped in a cement mixer and thereby becoming part of Battery Park City in Lower Manhattan.

With all his arrests, Mikey had been brought to trial only once, on tax evasion. Well, twice. Two hung juries, and the government had severed him from their case.

"Eastern Daylight Time, ten-eighteen . . . and ten seconds." I closed my eyes and pictured Bonnie as I'd last seen her; she had changed clothes to come to Headquarters. I'd watched her walk downstairs in a black cotton sweater tucked into a straight white skirt, and black-and-white high heels. She must have put on some makeup, because her eyelids had turned bronze and her lips looked like she'd been eating raspberries. It wasn't Bonnie; it was a tall and very tasteful tragic figure. She wore long gold earrings and looked heartsick.

I opened my eyes but couldn't shake the vision of her, so I made myself look down at the file again. Robby had made lots of notes in his rounded fourth-grade penmanship: about Mikey's mob associations, including known hit men, about his use of his family's business as a front for Family business, about his friendship with

Sy and his investment in *Starry Night*. Detailed notes, pages and pages. I could see how he'd prepared for Monday's Homicide meeting, for making his case that Mikey was our guy.

But at the meeting I'd convinced him our guy was Bonnie. And starting after the meeting, the pages had become paragraphs, the paragraphs, phrases. "8/22. 4:10." That was about a half hour after Mikey and his lawyer had been in, not that Robby or I had cared all that much. We both knew by then who'd killed Sy. "Spoke to Nancy Hales, bookkeeper for Starry Night Productions, Inc.," he'd written. "Finally admitted Mikey tried bribe for info re movie $$."

I turned to the next page, but it wasn't there. I hung up on "Daylight . . ." Something wasn't sitting right. No more notes? Even if Robby had a videotape of Bonnie pulling the trigger, he should have asked some more questions. Like what did "Finally admitted" mean? Like how much was the bribe? Like how had it been offered to the bookkeeper? On the phone? In person? Like had this bookkeeper known what a bad guy Mikey was? How had she said no? Or hadn't she? I put the file back in the drawer, leaned back and closed my eyes. Relax. Not my problem.

But then I opened my eyes, leaned forward and called Nancy Hales in the *Starry Night* production office at a film studio in Astoria, Queens. I gave her a song and dance about Robby being assigned to another case; I was just checking up on his notes.

"How many times did you speak with Detective Kurz?" I asked casually.

"That once in person."

"In your office?"

"Yes. And two times on the phone." Her voice was husky and overly slow. She was dull-witted or southern, or maybe she was into phone sex.

"Tell me about Mikey LoTriglio."

"I told—"

"I know, but I want to hear it in your own words, not rely on his notes." Then I added: "Believe me, it'll be better for you."

"He said . . ." She was nervous. "The detective said I wouldn't be in any trouble if I cooperated."

"You won't be. Now tell me what happened."

"Mr. LoTriglio came up to the office one day looking for Mr. Spencer, but I think he knew Mr. Spencer wouldn't be there. Do you know what I mean?"

"Yeah."

"He asked for the bookkeeper, and someone brought him over to my desk. He pulled over a chair and asked if anything funny was going on. I said, 'Funny?' "

"What did he say?"

"He said, 'Don't shit me.' So I told him I couldn't discuss business with him and he told me he was a major investor and I said I knew that but he'd still have to get Mr. Spencer's okay." She paused. "He was . . . I kind of knew he was a gangster. Not like *Scarface*, but still, I was scared. That's why I did it."

"Took his money?" I asked.

"Uh-huh."

"How did he give it to you?"

"He sort of slipped it under my telephone."

"I mean, in what denominations?"

"Fifties."

"How many fifties?"

"Didn't the other detective tell you how much it was?"

"I thought you were cooperating," I said.

"Ten fifties."

"And what did he get for his five hundred dollars?"

"The Lindsay Keefe business."

"Do me a favor, Nancy. I'm making my own notes. Let's start fresh. Spell out the Lindsay business for me."

"That the extra location scout and the two extra trailers and Teamster drivers and Nicholas Monteleone's bonus on signing and four interior sets we built . . . well, all that didn't exist. Sy just had me put in some invoices and . . . kind of move some money around."

"Move some money to Lindsay?"

"Yes."

"How much did it come to?"

She whispered: "Half."

"Half a million?"

"Uh-huh."

"Why did Lindsay Keefe get an extra half million?"

Her whisper became even softer. "I don't know. I guess she was threatening to quit."

I didn't get it. Sy had wanted to get rid of her. "When was this?"

"Three days before the start of principal photography."

I took a deep breath. "Nancy, why would he give her a half million more? She had a contract, didn't she?"

"Yes."

"So?"

"So he was crazy about her. I mean *crazy*. Like he would have done *anything* to keep her happy."

Or, at that point, to keep her in his bed. No big deal. He was Sy Spencer. He could get creative with the budget, and when *Starry Night* made ninety mil, who'd miss a few hundred thousand? And so, for a million plus another half million, Sy had bought himself a truly superior lay—and a lemon of an actress who was killing his movie. That must have been some kick in his arrogant ass. "Did you get the sense that Mikey LoTriglio had heard any of the negative talk about Lindsay's acting that was going around?"

"I think . . . There *were* a lot of rumors. I'm pretty sure he heard about them."

"How?"

"Probably by paying off someone in the crew."

"Like who?"

"I don't know."

"And then he found out from you that Sy had diddled the books to give Lindsay a five-hundred-thousand-dollar bonus."

"Yes."

"And how did Mikey react?" Silence. "Didn't Detective Kurz talk to you about this?"

"No. I would have told him, but he didn't ask."

"And you didn't volunteer."

"No. I was scared."

"Tell me what Mr. LoTriglio said."

"He said . . . when he heard the exact figure on what Lindsay had gotten, he said, 'My friend Sy is goin' to get his nuts chopped for this.' And then he walked out."

CHAPTER 12

What the hell was wrong with Robby? Jesus, if I'd been the one assigned to Mikey LoTriglio, I'd have been kicking chairs, screaming at the cop who kept insisting the perpetrator was the ex-wife. So what if Bonnie slept with Sy, I'd yell. There's a law against that? She humped him, kissed him goodbye, told him to call when he got back from L.A., and then went home. Period. Oh, your she-can-shoot theory? Is that your problem, jerk? Well, what about Mikey—or one of his boys? And what about that Lindsay? Turn on your VCR and watch her toting a rifle, in living color.

And even if the ex-wife had, in fact, slept with a .22 between her legs all the years when she was a kid in Utah, could she still bag Sy? Could such a nice, warm lady plan such a mean, cold killing? This is life we're talking about here, not goddamn Agatha Christie, where Lord Smedley-Bedley's black-sheep cousin gets murdered after crumpets with the vicar on a rainy afternoon.

And listen, jerk, I'd bellow, and maybe jab my pen toward

him, like it was a dart, *listen!* What about the criminal personality? Who is more likely to shoot when betrayed? A kissed-off screenwriter who's slept with every other guy on the South Fork, who's so used to hearing guys tell her goodbye that she could write their rejection speeches for them? Or a Known Bad Guy who's just discovered his alleged good friend is screwing him out of half a million bucks?

If I were Robby I'd have fought. I'd have built up a terrific case against Fat Mikey. Against Lindsay, come to think of it. She was a movie star, a professional egomaniac, and Sy was about to blow her out of the water.

So what the hell was wrong? When I'd sat at the meeting, stacking up the cards against Bonnie, why hadn't Robby knocked down a few of them? It would have been so easy.

I had a fast thought: Oh, Jesus, could I have destroyed an innocent life?

But then I told myself: Asshole, look what she's done to you! Miss All-Natural is a brilliant con artist. First she looks up from the warrant, gives you that look of pain, then that disbelieving how-can-you-hurt-me? stare. And then the cold shoulder. She's got great ESP, that Bonnie. You thought you were so cool, but she's known all along you've had a major thing for her. So she sits and shivers by the fireplace on a hot day. Lets her mouth quiver. Swears she didn't do it. Why shouldn't she swear? She knows how the conned want so desperately to keep being conned. But then she sees she can't get to you. . . . Well then, okay, too bad; she gave it her best shot. So she goes upstairs and puts on a sexy skirt and gold earrings.

But what if she's telling the truth?

Then why did she lie so much?

Well, what if she lied through her teeth . . . but still didn't kill him?

Didn't kill him? Take Bonnie Spencer, Mikey LoTriglio and Lindsay Keefe. Which one of the three is most likely—

Robby came in just then and hurried over. He didn't like my

feet up on his desk, near his pen set, but he was too excited to waste time in a protest. "Bonnie's in the lab!" Only his nervousness that the side of my shoe would smear the "Detective Robert Leo Kurz" brass plate kept him from positively gurgling with delight. "She's down there now. With the lawyer." I didn't budge. "What's wrong? Don't you want to go?"

"What about Mikey's payoff?" I asked him. He gave me a village idiot look that was so completely moronic I knew it was fake. "His payoff to the bookkeeper at the *Starry Night* office."

"Who cares?"

"I care. We know Mikey's alibi sucks shit. So he had opportunity. And now, from what the bookkeeper says, motive. Why the hell didn't you pursue that line of questioning and—"

Robby held up his hand, swift, full-palm. Stop! Aggressive, angry, like one of the neo-Nazi cretins in the police academy who demonstrate how to direct traffic. "Wait just one second here, Steve." Huffy. Definitely huffy. "We *have* our perpetrator, who we all agree is our perpetrator, over in the lab, as we speak." He did an about-face, marched out of Homicide, down toward the lab.

I kept up with him. What a born dork Robby was, with his white Tums crust at the edges of his mouth. He radiated hairspray scent. His suit matched his pale-beige loafers. A fucking dork suit: the fabric was supposed to look luxurious, like nubby linen, but instead it looked as if it was cut from a bolt of cloth that was having an allergic reaction to its own ugliness. You could see its unhealthy sheen; it was covered with minuscule bumps.

"Hey, I want to talk to you for a second," I called out. He didn't stop.

We got to the door of the lab just as Bonnie and Gideon were leaving. She was pressing a gauze pad against the bend in her arm where they'd drawn blood, so she didn't see me until I said "How'd it go?" She glanced up, startled, terrified, the nice girl in a horror movie who had just seen the monster.

I might as well have been one. She tried to get away so fast that she wound up stepping on her own high-heel shoe and would have fallen if Gideon hadn't grabbed her arm. She slumped against him for just a second, until she regained her balance.

For that one second, though, Bonnie's eyes were on my face. Finally, there it was: absolute fear. Eyes floating in the whites, unfocused, in terror of the monster who was stalking her. And then she was rushing away, down the hall. Her long, fast strides were restrained only by the knee-hobbling hem of her skirt, so Gideon was able to keep up.

After they disappeared around a corner, Robby said: "I'll go over to court, get the arrest warrant." He started to go.

I grabbed the sleeve of his repulsive suit. "Not yet."

"What do you mean, not yet?"

"I mean, we'd be making a mistake to push it."

"No, we wouldn't!"

"Yes, we would."

"No!"

"Robby, how many man-hours have you put in looking for that .22? Not enough. We've got to give it a better shot."

His upper lip drew up, so he was almost snarling. His bared teeth were the same color as his beige suit and shoes. "What the hell's the matter with you?" he demanded. "You going soft? You going to risk letting her run?"

"Where is she going to run to?"

"Anyplace. Listen, I was in her closet. She has hiking boots! A backpack!"

"For crissakes, she's a Jewish broad. What the hell is she going to do? Go to ground in the wetlands?" I didn't tell him that was precisely it: the waking nightmare that had stolen five hours off my sleep the night before. Bonnie *could* get away. I'd almost choked myself with my sweaty, twisted rope of a sheet as I tossed around. She could disappear, live off the land, gradually make her way north, steal a boat, get off Long Island. "Or you think the fag lawyer's going to hide her in his wine cellar?"

"She could go back to Utah!"

"And do what? We've got the addresses of all her brothers,

and her old man in Arizona. There's no place for her to hide."

"If we bring her in now, before the weekend, we're heroes. Damn it, don't you care about your career?"

"Blow it out your ass, Robby."

Robby banged the wall with his fist. It made a dull, undramatic thud. But his voice made up for it, blaring, amplified by the narrow corridor so the whole floor could hear him. "You're gonna fuck up this case!"

"No! I'm going to do my job, follow up *all* the leads. I'm not going to be some ass-kisser who cuts corners because he can't wait to pucker up." I made a wet, kissy sound in the air. " 'Yoo-hoo, Captain Shea. Here is the solution to the heinous murder that has so captured the attention of the national media. Please, *you* take all the credit. I only want the satisfaction of a job well done—' " Robby brought up his fists and bounced on the balls of his feet. His keys jingled in his pants pocket. "Holy shit! Don't hit me, Robby!"

"Shut your fucking mouth, Brady."

"Don't hurt me! I'm forty years old."

"Listen, you loser, son-of-a-bitch drunk, I'm going to court to get a warrant. Now."

"Good. Get the hell out of here. And while you're on your way, I'm going in to Shea and telling him what a lazy bastard you've been, and how you're jumping the gun and handing him a case that could fall apart five seconds after it gets to the grand jury."

It was more like a movie than life, almost a freeze-frame. I didn't move. Robby kept his fists up, but finally, slowly, opened them. His fingers spread out; it looked as though he'd decided to throttle me. Finally, I said: "Calm down."

"Fuck you, you dipso."

"Listen to me. Don't rush this. You're gonna push Shea, and then the D.A. will find fifty loose ends—like Mikey LoTriglio. Like Lindsay."

"Lindsay," he sneered.

"Don't you get it? Some rag newspaper in the supermarket is going to print a picture of her from *Transvaal* holding a rifle. 'Is Lindsay Keefe Trained to Kill?' Don't you get that the *Daily News* is going to do a big piece on Sy's mob connections? And don't you get that unless we can respond to every single question that could come up with one single answer—Bonnie Spencer—the department could be made to look like it's trying to pin it on some poverty-stricken sweetie pie of an ex-wife, and you and I are the ones who'll get creamed for it?"

Robby didn't answer. And he didn't choke me. He just lowered his hands, turned and, in his clunk-heeled beige loafers, stomped back to Homicide.

"Don't ask me about the case, Germy," I said into the phone.

"I am not asking you about the case," he honked in his hundred-thousand-dollars'-worth-of-New-England-schools voice. "I am a film critic, not a gossip columnist. And I didn't ask what was wrong with your case. I asked what was wrong with you. You sound—it's hard to describe—flat. Tired."

"I'm too old for this shit." Having bounced the Sour Kraut from our mutual desk, I had my files fanned out in front of me, all unopened. "Tell me about Lindsay Keefe."

"I love it. Classic film noir. The uncouth cop falls for the ice-blond sophisticate."

He did it; he made me smile for a second. "I just want to know about *Transvaal*."

"Why?"

I hesitated, but then I said: "I know you long enough to know you'll keep your mouth shut, Jeremy."

"That's right, Steve."

I saw I'd been doodling on the cover of Bonnie's file. Shaded 3-D boxes. Her initials: I realized they were mine, backwards. "Okay, I heard Lindsay was shown shooting a rifle in the movie." Germy made that upper-class exhaling sound that comes out between Ah! and Oh! "What I'm asking is if—without raising bicoastal eyebrows—you can get me the name of someone who knows what went on while they were making that movie."

"Someone who knows whether Lindsay could actually shoot or if she just pulled the trigger and the sound editor went 'Bang!' "

"Yeah."

"Call me back in an hour." He paused. "And listen, from an old friend . . . You sound something less than yourself. Take it easy. All right?"

"Sure," I said. "I'll be fine."

I called Lynne, hoping I'd get her machine. But she picked up. "Hello!" Cheery, welcoming. I had nothing to say to her. I hung up the phone and dialed my brother.

"Easton, come on. *Listen*. Remember you told me Sy would never have fired Lindsay?" I asked.

"Um, he would have let her think it, but he never would have." Easton sounded thick-tongued, slightly dopey.

I'd obviously woken him from one of his ritual marathon sleeps: striped pajamas on, phone on a pillow on the floor to muffle the ring, curtains safety-pinned to ensure unending darkness. His sleeps were escapes that would last for weeks, except for shuffling excursions in flapping leather slippers down to the kitchen, where he'd spoon soft food—ice cream, canned fruit cocktail—into his mouth listlessly, as though feeding a baby who wasn't hungry. Occasionally, he'd offer a thin excuse: The doctor says it's probably mono, and then give a feeble cough. Easton's sleeps came whenever he realized he wasn't going to be superstar insurance agent, or hero of men's wear. He'd start going in to work late, coming home early—sometimes after lunch. A boss would call, first to lecture, finally to fire him, and Easton would simply mumble, If that's how you want it, and hang up the phone and go back to sleep.

Well, what did he have to stay awake for now that Sy was dead? "East, come on. Focus for a second."

Irritable. "I *am* focused."

"Do you think there was any chance Lindsay knew that Katherine Pourelle had been sent the *Starry Night* script, or that Sy was going to see her out in L.A.?"

Easton tried to rise to the occasion. You could almost see him shaking his head, clearing out the fog. "Did she know?" he repeated. Suddenly he sounded alert, interested, protective. "Why do you want to know about Lindsay?"

"Look, I know you're—you know—kind of attracted to her, but try to be objective, East. This is a homicide."

"And you think if Lindsay had found out somehow . . . Steve, that's idiotic."

"Probably. But I can't leave any loose ends untied."

"Give me a second," he said. "I must have dozed off for a couple of minutes. I'm still a little groggy." I reached into my drawer and retrieved a combo key ring–nail clipper I'd gotten at a grand opening of a car wash and gave myself something resembling a manicure. It seemed I'd have time to take off my shoes and socks and do my toes, but finally Easton spoke, although hesitantly. "Lindsay had . . . a certain curiosity about Sy's business."

"What does that mean in real life? She was nosy?"

"If you want to look at it superficially."

"Give me a for-instance." He didn't reply. "Stop the chivalry shit. I'm not looking to arrest her. I'm just looking to finish the paperwork on this case."

"Is Lindsay a real suspect?"

"No."

"Who is?"

"Not for public consumption, okay?"

"Of course not."

"The ex-wife, Bonnie. But Lindsay shot a rifle in a movie called *Transvaal,* so I've got to check her out some more. Now, how was she nosy?"

"The word I used was 'curious.' You see, Sy usually swam his laps after she did hers. So when she came back into the house, supposedly to take a shower, she'd actually go into his study."

"And?"

"And pretend to be looking for a stamp or a paper clip, but actually go through whatever papers were lying on the desk. Oh, I just remembered. Sy had one of those pocket computer calendars. One time, I saw her pressing some buttons on it. My guess was she was reading off all his entries. I know this makes her sound like a sneak. She really wasn't. Sy was more than her lover; he was her employer. She knew as well as anyone how brutal he could be with anyone he wasn't pleased with, and he definitely wasn't pleased with her. So she was protecting her own interests, so to speak."

"Bottom line, Easton. Do you think she knew why he was going to L.A.?"

"Bottom line?" He gave it real thought. I waited. "She *was* getting curiouser and curiouser. Extra visits to his study. Checking out the fax machine early in the morning, before Sy was up, before she went to the set."

"How do you know what went on so early?"

"I liked to get in early. This is . . . embarrassing."

"Listen, do you think you're the first guy in human history to get stupid over a girl? I'm your brother. You can tell me. You went in early because you wanted to see her?"

"Yes. But she never really tried to hide her curiosity from me. Either she thought I was so much a part of the household that I was like wallpaper—there, no threat—or she sensed how I felt about her, and felt safe." Easton sighed. "I think that must have been it. But in any case, what you want to know is if I think Lindsay knew Sy was going to take some action. And the answer is yes. I do."

Germy called back a half hour later. He'd spoken to the producer of *Transvaal*. They had hired some South African game warden as a technical adviser, and he'd given Lindsay a couple of hours of lessons with a rifle. The producer had no idea what kind of a shot she was, but he'd added she'd had a quickie affair with the game warden but then switched over to a black actor who was playing an anti-apartheid activist.

Gideon called around noon. He was back in his office. He'd hired Bill Paterno for Bonnie, but wanted one last talk with me. In person. Man to man. He said that without self-consciousness. Could he come back to my office? I glanced over at Robby. He was hunched over his desk, going over all the DNA and lab reports, index finger inching down the pages, lips moving, calling on the God of Science to bless his crusade against Bonnie Spencer. He looked pasty and intense and a little nuts, so I gave Gideon quick directions to the nearest diner, told him to meet me there at one-thirty, that he could have as long as it took me to finish a chicken salad and bacon sandwich and a vanilla malted—which, when I was minding my manners, took approximately four minutes.

The Blue Sky had once been a regular greasy spoon, but the Greek guy who'd bought it had done it over, so now the spoon was hardly greasy at all. The walls were paneled in fake oak, the ceilings dripped with fat-globed chandeliers and hanging plastic plants. The menu, a listing of every food product capable of being microwaved, was almost as thick as the Bible. The owner hovered over us, pad open, ready to transcribe whatever we happened to say.

I looked at Gideon. "The cook usually washes his hands after he takes a dump, so you can have the chicken salad or tuna fish and not die. The hamburgers taste like snow tires. They nuke everything else."

"Don' listen to him," said the owner. "He's a stupid cop. All my food's good. Today the special is nice flounder on a bed of spinach wit' feta cheese."

Gideon said no thank you, he'd already eaten. Just an iced coffee. I ordered, and the owner strolled off, toward the kitchen.

"Go ahead," I said. "Make your pitch."

Gideon adjusted his knife, fork and spoon and took a minute to make sure the edge of his napkin was absolutely parallel with the edge of the table. Once that was accomplished, he immediately opened the napkin and put it on his lap. I noticed that for all his clean-cut, square-jawed handsomeness, the bridge of his nose appeared to have gotten squished in the birth canal or in a fight and never popped back into place. "I was hoping this conversation wouldn't be necessary," he said quietly.

"It's not. You could have saved yourself the trip—and acid indigestion from the iced coffee. All we're doing now is neatening up a few loose ends. Probably by tomorrow we'll be arresting your client."

"Her name is Bonnie."

"I know that." My cheeks began to ache; I could feel the pressure of tears someplace way behind my eyes. I wasn't going to lose it, but if I was, it wouldn't be in front of this guy. "Let's get on with it."

"Why are you out to get her?"

"Mr. Friedman, with all due respect, you're her friend. And this is not your field. You're personalizing a criminal investigation. And you're wasting my time and not doing your client any good. Do everybody a favor: wait till tomorrow. Let Paterno handle it. He's used to dealing with us and the D.A."

The owner came back with the iced coffee and a little bowl of teaspoon-size containers of half-and-half. Gideon waited until he was gone. "You're the one who's been personalizing it," he said.

"What are you getting at?"

"I'm getting at that it is morally and ethically wrong to in-vestigate someone you've—"

Put up the umbrella, I thought, because here it comes: a shower of shit. "I've *what?*"

"Slept with."

Heat rises. Blood rushed up to my forehead, my ears. I was so fucking furious. Disappointed too: I couldn't believe she'd resort to something that cheesy—which shows the state I was in. I'd had no trouble believing that, with evil intent, she could plan and execute a homicide. But tell a tacky lie? Not my Bonnie! "That's total and complete crap," I said.

"No, it's not crap." He was calm, at peace. Whatever shit he was dropping on me, it was shit the bitch Bonnie had made him believe.

"Your friend has a little problem in the truth department, counselor. I never laid a hand on her. I never made a suggestive remark. Nothing."

"Now, *that's* crap."

"Look, you don't really want that iced coffee. Go back to East Hampton, practice some real estate law, forget this conversation." He stayed put. "Okay, the head of Homicide's a guy named Shea. Go ahead. Talk to him. Or file a formal complaint with the department."

"What happened between the two of you that makes you want to get her so badly?"

I looked up and saw the guy coming back with my sandwich and the malted. The food looked pale, puffed-up, dead—like something pulled out of the water, something that, before you can stop yourself, makes you gag. "Look," I said to Gideon, "obviously she has you believing something went on. I'm not going to try and talk you out of it." A piece of bacon hung out of the roll, dark, curled, wormy. "But I'm not going to ruin my lunch and sit here listening to you tell me I copped a feel when I was questioning her, or showed her my shield and said, 'Fuck me or go to jail.' Okay? So take a walk, Mr. Friedman."

I could hardly hear him. "I'm not talking about the investigation. I'm talking about what went on five years ago."

"What?"

"Five years ago. You . . . I wouldn't call it an affair. But it wasn't just a typical one-night stand."

"Wrong guy," I snapped.

"She called me about it the next day. I remember. She sounded elated. She said, 'Gideon, I met this wonderful man!' "

"She's lying. Or maybe she's just . . . Maybe this whole experience has made her a little crazy, if she wasn't that way to begin with."

"Bonnie's as uncrazy as they come."

"So maybe it's an honest mistake, and she just thought she saw me under her covers. Look, I'm sure you know it isn't any secret that a lot of guys have rolled around in that bed."

Gideon had put a lightweight olive-green blazer over his ninja outfit. Silk probably. He rolled down a sleeve, then recuffed it. "Bonnie told me, 'He grew up here in Bridgehampton. On a farm. About two minutes from here.' " I didn't say anything. I shook my head. "I remember this conversation, Mr. Brady. I'd never heard her so high. She said, 'He's a cop, of all things. A detective. Very bright. And a wonderful sense of humor. I had *fun*.' "

"Not with me she didn't." He started working on his other sleeve. "I'm sorry. I know you believe what you're saying, but it wasn't me."

Gideon peeled the top off a little container and dumped cream into his glass. "She said—"

"Please. There's really no point to this."

"Let me finish. She said, 'His name is Stephen Brady.' " I sat across from him in the booth, still shaking my head no. "I remember your name, because we had this long . . . well, amusing discussion about whether Brady is a WASP or an Irish name and about the . . . sexual proclivities of each group. Bonnie said she'd ask you what you were the next time she saw you." Gideon took a packet of Equal and sprinkled a dusting of the powder into his coffee. "She had no doubt that she'd see you again. That was the funny part: her absolute certainty that the night had been special. She'd been around a long time, knew the ropes. She was never given to self-deception. She knew what happens when you ask someone you meet in a bar—"

"What bar?"

"The Gin Mill. Over on—"

"I know where it is. Go on."

"What else is there to say? Bonnie knew that when you invite a man you meet in a bar to come back to your house, you don't expect him to send flowers the next day."

"She said I sent flowers?"

"No. A metaphor for romance. But she felt something had happened between the two of you. Something out of the ordinary." I rested my forehead in the palm of my hand and rubbed, back and forth. "You can't have forgotten. Or even if she had been just another pickup to you, seeing her, seeing the house—"

"I'm telling you, I have no memory."

Gideon's young, handsome, squished-nosed face looked more uncomprehending than angry. "Why the vendetta if you have no memory?"

"There's no vendetta. She's guilty."

His spoon clanged against the glass as he stirred, but his voice was very gentle. "Why didn't you ask one of your colleagues to take over the Bonnie aspect of the investigation?"

"There was no reason to have someone else step in. I never met her before."

"But you did. It happened."

It took a very long time, but at last I said: "Look, I'm an alcoholic. I've been sober for almost four years. But there are blanks in my life. Days, maybe weeks I'll never be able to recall. Maybe . . . There were a lot of women. For all I know, she might have been one of them. I had this feeling almost from the beginning that she looked familiar. I figured I'd seen her around town."

"You don't deny it, then."

"No. But I don't admit it either. Maybe I spent the night with her. Maybe I told her she was a terrific person. It was one of the things I always said: 'It's not just the sex, babe. It's *you*. You're a terrific person.' But if I did spend some time with her, I'll never know what I did or what I said."

"For the record, you told her you loved her."

"But I never saw her again, did I?"

Gideon sat back in the booth and crossed his arms over his chest. Relaxed, conversational. "She said you were heavier then."

I'd dropped twenty pounds after I'd stopped drinking and started running. "And you had a mustache. Thick, droopy." Yes. "That's why it took her a minute to realize it was you at her door. And do you know what went through her mind then? She thought: Who cares why he never called? He's back!"

"Mr. Friedman, don't you get it? Either she did a little research on me in town and made this whole thing up—or it actually happened. But it doesn't matter. They can take me off the case, put someone else in my place, and the outcome will still be the same. Bonnie Spencer will be brought to trial on—yeah, sure— circumstantial evidence. But *strong* circumstantial evidence. Most likely she will be found guilty. And she will go to jail. And whether I slept with her or gave her a line about loving her or never met her before I rang her front doorbell won't matter one goddamn bit."

"Bonnie was right. You are very, very bright."

"Thanks."

"Hear me out. You've constructed an intelligent, imaginative theory about how Sy was killed. All I ask now is that you look back at your data, put that same creativity to work again."

I shook my head.

"Try it. Build another case. A real one this time, not a myth."

"I can't."

"You have to."

CHAPTER 13

I left the diner, my lunch untouched. The afternoon had turned from plain August hot to sweltering. I thought about finding an AA meeting but instead drove north, aimlessly, farther from Headquarters. I pulled into the parking lot of a shopping center. Suburban heaven, with its open-twenty-four-hours Grand Union, its nail salon, its frozen-yogurt store and its card shop featuring Charlie Brown paper tablecloths, plates, cups and guest towels.

I put the top up, locked away my gun and changed into the shorts and sneakers I kept behind the two front seats, on the parcel shelf of the car—my gym locker on wheels. I hooked my pager onto the elastic waistband of the shorts. I had used my running shirt with the Clorox-eaten sleeve to clean the dipstick, so I had to run shirtless.

The humidity was suffocating. I would gladly have taken one of those blue bandannas I'd been laughing at all summer, the kind New York runners were twirling and wrapping around their foreheads, trying to look like construction workers instead of rich idiots. And I'd even take one of their ass packs too, with its plastic bottle of mineral water.

For the first couple of miles through central Suffolk—past tract houses sided with cheap, already-pitted aluminum, where nobody, apparently, had enough home-owning pride to stick a mailbox with a painted "The McCarthy's" up on a post, or plant a crab apple or a rosebush or anything beyond the token scraggly juniper the builder had stuck in the front lawn, past about ten acres of open grassland with a For Sale sign—I didn't think about Bonnie at all. I didn't think about anything.

I ran past a small farm, just like any on the South Fork, although here there was no sweet ocean tang in the air to obscure the harsh perfume of fertilizer and pesticides. Pretty, though: a brown field of russet potatoes, almost ready for harvest. It was edged by a border of dark-pink clover and white trumpet vines. The potatoes look good, I was thinking. A lot of Long Island farmers don't like russets because they can get all knobby, but there'd been just enough rain—

Bonnie! Not a fantasy this time. A true recollection.

Labor Day, about four in the afternoon. Inside the bar— yeah, Gideon, the Gin Mill—it was murky, and packed, like the Friday night of Memorial Day weekend. But the season was over, and the too-old-to-be-yuppies were no longer cruising loose, happy, expectant. The same hot-shit Yorkers now jammed against the bar, pushing each other. They were overtanned and overdesperate, with stiff, extended, sun-dried arms, hands grasping for their margaritas ("No salt!"), drinking too hard to hide their despair that another summer had passed without their falling in love, or at least finding someone who wouldn't humiliate them by guffawing—Har! Har! Har!—in a movie on the Upper East Side, or by being fat in TriBeCa, or by wearing brown suede Hush Puppies on Central Park South.

It was the perfect time for a local like me, bored with a June, July and August of receptionists and nurses, who wanted (for one night) a grown-up, dressed-for-success lay. Easy pickings: By that first Monday in September, I knew the thirty-five-year-old lady corporate vice presidents would have stopped playing the Geography Game, with an automatic You're Out for Hamptons hicks. I also knew all those frosted-haired, lip-glossed, scrawny-necked financiers would no longer be muttering "Really?" and then two seconds later going to the ladies' room when they heard I was a cop. These women at the Gin Mill hadn't caught themselves a banker or a doctor or even an accountant without his CPA. So now it would be: "I envy you, living here year round" and "A *homicide* detective! Tell me, how can you stand looking at . . . what's the best way to express it? Looking at the dark side of the human condition day after day?"

Except instead of hitting on one of those, I spotted Bonnie. If I had to say why I chose her, it could have been because it was the Summer of the Perm, and she was the only woman without cascades of frizzles. Or because she wasn't wearing an outfit, one of those things with plaids and stripes and flowers, where nothing matches on purpose.

Bonnie leaned against the bar, foot up on the rail, standing tall among the other women. She was working her way through tissues and keys in the side pocket of a short red-and-yellow-plaid skirt, on her way to money to pay for a beer. She wore a red tank top. As I maneuvered toward her, I could see the sheen of her broad, tanned shoulders. Silky skin, I thought, not leathery. I put my hand on her shoulder. It was silky. I said: "I'll buy," and gave the bartender three bucks for her beer. She smiled. "Thanks."

But that was all that would come: an image. I kept on running, sweat dripping down onto the blacktop, for another two miles, all around the farm, then back past the grassland, into that pathetic stretch of aluminum-sided Long Island. I'd been hoping to clear my head. But all I could recollect in that killing heat was Bonnie Spencer in the crisp, conditioned air of the Gin Mill, holding her beer in front of her with two hands, the way a bride would hold her bouquet. Her hair was short then, a little choppy; maybe she'd tried to give herself a sophisticated haircut, but she'd wound up looking like a wood nymph's older sister instead. The recessed lights over the bar made her arms and shoulders gleam.

I walked around the parking lot a few times to cool down, except the air was so thick and humid all I was able to do was stop wheezing. I hung around for another five minutes, hoping for a breeze, but none came, so I got into the car and used the oil-streaked T-shirt as a towel. The pager had rubbed against my skin, and there was a dark-red bruised spot on my right side.

I got into the Jag, sprayed a little Right Guard under my arms and then contorted myself to get back into my shirt, tie and suit fast, before some housewife could peer down and catch me humping the steering wheel as I pulled up my zipper. I kept replaying the scene in my mind.

"I'll buy." Putting down my drink—vodka with a wedge of lime—and handing three folded singles to the bartender.

Bonnie's smile, so radiant that for a second I felt light-headed. "Thanks."

I went into the supermarket and bought a big bottle of club soda. My face must have been close to purple, because the express-line cashier said, "Y'oughta watch it, hon. This heat and all."

"I'll buy," I said to Bonnie.

"Thanks."

I sat in the car again, glugging down the soda, trying to re-create what happened next. Logically I would have said "Steve Brady" and she would have said "Bonnie Spencer," and a couple of minutes later maybe we would have chuckled about two Bridge-hampton rubes having to meet in East Hampton, in a phony "genuine" gin joint with a bullshit ceiling fan and bartenders who deliberately didn't shave because scruffy was a Great Look, surrounded by city slickers in two-hundred-dollar sandals.

Except I couldn't remember anything more. Maybe nothing more had happened. Maybe, for some reason, she had just recalled what turned out to be an aborted pickup attempt. Being a screenwriter, she'd whipped up a little love story around it and, casting herself in the leading role, said to her lawyer: Here, maybe you

can use this. Except Gideon had remembered her euphoria, remembered hearing my name. Whatever else he was, he was a
smart man, and a savvy, probably even an ethical, lawyer. I didn't
think he would lie to a cop during a homicide investigation, not
even to help a friend.

Well, whatever had happened with Bonnie, it was lost to me.
Too bad. I would have liked to know what it had been like, screwing
her. I drove back toward the farm, put the top down again, took
a leak by the side of the road and got back into the car to drive
to Headquarters. I put my hand on the stick.

God almighty, it began to come back.

We took a sip of our drinks and then exchanged names and
discovered we both lived in Bridgehampton, although on different
sides of the tracks. "You weren't born here," I said.

"Which means you must have been."

"Right. Where are you from?"

She must have said the West, or Utah, because somehow—
and this came back so vividly—we got to talking about trout
fishing. It turned out that she could tie her own flies. I said, I'm
not much of a fisherman. I've only gone for fluke and blues a
couple of times, but maybe we could go together one day. And
she said, Night's better for trout, and smiled and added, Tell you
what. Give me a call when you can tie at least three leader knots
as easy as you tie your shoelaces, and I'll take you to the perfect
mountain stream. I said, Can't I give you a call before that? and
she flashed me a beautiful smile.

Just as I was thinking to myself, This is one incredible woman,
somebody pushed to get closer to the bar, knocking me into Bonnie.
Oh my God!

Electricity. Magnetism. Whatever the hell it was, I couldn't
believe it was happening. We stood there, body against body,
unable to pull apart, like victims of an uncontrollable mob, crushed
together. Except we could have parted, without too much trouble.
We were just being jostled by a crowd of ordinary, pushy New
Yorkers. But I was so aroused, and the pressure felt so good.

And clean-cut Bonnie—courteous ("Nice of you to pay for my beer"), amiable, humorous, lover of mountains and fisher for golden trout—was as hot and irrational as I was. Her hand slid between my legs. Jesus! In the dim, smoky light of the bar, in the press of bodies, in the dehumidified, perfume- and aftershave- and mouthwash-scented air, in the noise of raised voices and clanking glasses, she was tuning out everything—and going for it. Not just to provoke me, but for her own pleasure, which, of course, became my pleasure. She let out a small, low sound. She was going to be a noisy one, a wild one.

"Let's get out of here," we both said at the exact same time. Normally, when that happens, you laugh, but we had crossed some boundary and gone where there was no kidding around.

What happened next? We took my car to her house. I must have been in a white heat, because I couldn't remember any conversation or anything about her street, or the downstairs of her house—only following her ass up to the bedroom and pulling off her clothes the minute we passed through the doorway.

We were just starting, but both of us were so inflamed we tore at each other, groaning, the way people do in that moment right before the end. We parted for a second; Bonnie's hands were trembling, and she couldn't manage my buttons, so I undressed myself. She watched me, spellbound, and I became so excited by her intensity I couldn't finish the slow strip I'd begun. I threw off my khakis, my undershorts, my shoes.

Bonnie moved close to me and touched me for a second, to verify that what I had wasn't going to go away. Then she moved in even closer. She raised her hips, straddled me. No teasing, no foreplay; we were way past that. I pushed in right away and we stood, her back against the bedpost, screwing our brains out.

She came first. I lowered her onto the bed. I wanted to finish on top. Her arms and legs wrapped around me, and we became the two halves of a greater person.

I'd never had sex like that before. It wasn't that I was vol- untarily letting go; it was that I had no control. Just when I thought that I'd ridden out the last wave, that I could catch my breath, slow things down, speed them up, subdue her, another, bigger wave knocked me senseless.

At last, her whimpers and moans turned to shrieks of pleasure. I joined her. I heard myself screaming so loud it scared me.

We lay there on top of the white popcorn bedspread, not knowing what to say to one another. It was that moment where my foot or my hand would inevitably begin to drift along the floor, searching for a sock or my shorts. Except I couldn't move. And I didn't want to go. Finally, Bonnie said: "Think of a way we can get over the awkward silence."

"Tell me more about fly-fishing."

"You need an eight-foot glass rod," she murmured. "Don't let them talk you into bamboo."

I held her lightly, running my hand up and down her back. Her skin was like velvet. A breeze that had a hint of autumn in it fluttered the white lace curtains.

"This is wonderful," I said.

"I know."

"I meant the breeze."

Suddenly she noticed the window was open. She sat up. "Oh, God."

"What?"

"We were kind of loud. Just watch. One of my neighbors will think I was being murdered and call the police—after she serves the carpaccio." I started to laugh. I hadn't told her what I did for a living. "You won't think it's so funny when you hear the sirens."

"Want to bet?" I pulled her back down, so she was lying facing me. "I'm a cop. A detective on the Homicide Squad."

"No. That would be too interesting. You're not."

"Of course I am." She shook her head. "Okay, what am I?"

"I don't know. You sort of have a macho style, but you probably do something adorable. Sell children's shoes. Teeny size-two Mary Janes, with a free balloon." She bit her lip. "God, I'm going to die if that's what you really do."

I forced myself out of bed and retrieved my pants from where I'd tossed them, between a little stool and one of those old-fashioned makeup tables with a skirt. Bonnie looked bewildered, then hurt; she combed her short hair with her fingers, as if preparing for a dignified goodbye. But I tossed her my shield. She caught it, too, and it had been a lousy throw. Her left hand shot out.

"Good reflexes," I said.

"I need them. You're not exactly Sandy Koufax."

We stared at each other across the room, she amazed that I was a cop, me, that she knew baseball. For some crazy reason, after all that had transpired, this was too intimate. Real fast, we began to talk over each other, she saying something pointless about loving whodunits, me asking if she had anything to drink. She offered iced tea or Diet Coke, but then I said "*drink* drink." All she had was light beer and a bottle of one-step-up-from-rotgut red wine she'd bought to use for sangria, for a picnic, but it had rained. I settled for the wine. She threw on a bathrobe and went downstairs.

The minute she was gone, I got claustrophobic; I wanted out. It wasn't the room. I knew that much. It was sizable, appealing, all white except for the old wood beams and the painted blue-green chair rail. It definitely wasn't overstuffed; there was a four-poster bed with plain wood nightstands on either side, the little stool and vanity table with its ladylike yellow-and-white-striped skirt, and a clumsy, cozy-looking club chair, covered in a shiny cotton—big yellow flowers with blue-green leaves—a stand-up lamp beside it.

But even though there was that cool breath of air coming through the open windows, I wanted to get outside. Go home, have a couple of drinks, maybe drive up to the bay afterwards, watch the sunset. I put on my shorts.

I heard her coming upstairs, so I picked up the phone. I'd say "Damn. Yeah. Right away" when she walked in, and then tell her a fast-but-grisly homicide story: maybe a stabbing followed by

arson. Something nice and graphic, full of gaping tracheas, mu-
tilated genitals. Run while she was still gagging.

Except she came in carrying a can of Diet Coke, a wineglass,
the bottle, and holding a corkscrew between her teeth. She looked
so goofy. I hung up the phone and took the corkscrew. "Calling
your office?" she asked, and handed me the wine.

"Yeah. No emergencies that can't wait." I opened the bottle,
poured, drank. The pressure to escape eased a little. I'm sure we
must have talked for a while, because if I had taken her in my
arms again, I would have been lost. I remember stretching out on
my side, letting my fingers graze over her fabulous skin, but not
getting too close. It was perfection, lying there like that, feeling
the warmth of her, the coolness of the breeze. The sky had lost
its daytime glare and had become softer, finer: blue tinged with
pink and gold.

I whispered, not to disturb the beauty: "I love this time of
day."

Bonnie glanced at the window. "Magic hour." She kissed me
on the mouth, but sweetly, almost daintily. "It's a term in cine-
matography. The time after dawn or before dusk. Enough light for
shooting, but there's a fineness, a tranquillity to it—magical light.
You have to work fast, because before you know it, the enchant-
ment is over, but while it's there . . . you can get something beautiful."

I drank some more wine. I must have fallen asleep for a
couple of minutes. When I woke up I caught Bonnie studying my
face. She averted her eyes and said too fast: "I was just wondering
how you'd look without the mustache."

"No. You were thinking: This is one hell of a man."

"Yes."

I let my fingers glide down, over her throat and breasts. I
caressed her stomach and felt her muscles contract. Two or three
good, deep kisses. And then we were at it again, this time with
a lust that made the last go-round seem a lighthearted tease. We
were biting and clawing at each other. I heard myself growl.

Bonnie pulled back. The wildness disturbed her. She wanted to be civilized again, a sexy woman, not an animal. She got cool and urbane on me, did a couple of cute maneuvers with the tip of her tongue. Then she got to her knees to climb on top. I knew what would happen: She'd arch her back, toss her head, let her breasts bounce. Then she'd bend over and do some more tongue tricks. She wanted what I wanted: mastery.

But I didn't want well-bred sex games. I pushed her down, onto her back. We were animals, and I was the male. I wanted her to know that. I pinned down her arms, pried open her legs with my knee and started giving it to her. She was strong, and she struggled to get free, but at the same time, she was sobbing one word over and over: More.

After it was over she turned away from me. She wasn't making any noise, but I could feel her back shaking as she cried. I was kind of shaky too. I hadn't been in control at all. What if she hadn't cried for more? What if she'd wanted me to stop? Would I have?

I rested my cheek against the nape of her neck. "Bonnie, it's okay." She didn't say anything. "Too rough?"

"No."

"Too what?"

"Too much."

"Too much what?"

"I don't know."

I rolled her over onto her back and kissed her. Her cheeks were wet. "Next time I'll be real suave. Okay? You'll think: Jesus, what technique!" Bonnie's face softened as she smiled; I knew she wasn't pretty, but for that second, she was so beautiful. "I'll come up with some position where I'm all twisted up, with my head coming out of my ass and my dick pointing east. You'll have to slide on sideways."

She wiped away the last tear with the tip of her index finger, a lovely ethereal gesture from such a big, hearty girl. "When you were holding me down . . ."

"Tell me."

"What if you'd been a bad person?"

"But I'm not. I'm a great person. Now let's talk about something else. Are your eyes blue-gray or gray-blue?"

"Please. I'm serious."

I turned the pillow over to the cool side. "Well, if you are serious, maybe you should think twice before inviting guys you've just met to come into your house." Until I said it, I hadn't realized how much it bothered me. Angered me. Goddamn it, she had been so easy. I hadn't wanted her to reach out and touch me, a stranger. Play with me. In a public place, for crissakes. Here she was, tall and clean and fine, and she tied her own flies: a wonderful woman. But instead of a light kiss, a smile to turn down the thermostat after we'd been pushed together, she'd cupped my balls, stroked my dick; her hand was still cold from holding the beer. "You knew absolutely zilch about me, and you said, 'Let's get out of here.' "

Bonnie didn't get that guilty, You-think-I'm-a-whore look I'd expected, maybe wanted. "I thought you were better than this."

"Hey, I'm not talking about morals. I'm talking as a cop who's seen some nice girls get hurt when things got out of hand."

"I can take care of myself."

"You're strong. Mountain woman, right? If someone you meet at a bar gets out of hand, you'll just use some self-defense shit you read in *Ms*. magazine. Let me tell you something, sister. Before you can stick your finger into his eyeball or crash down on his instep or knee him in the nuts, you could be raped—or dead."

"I'm a good judge of character."

"You think all those nice, dead girls said to themselves: 'This guy's a psychopath, but he's got cute dimples'? No, they said: 'I'm a good judge of character.' "

For a minute she didn't say anything. Then she propped herself up on her elbow and said: "Aren't you *starved?*"

"Yeah, come to think of it."

"Scrambled eggs? An omelet and toast?"

I took a fast shower while she went downstairs to make supper.

I put my clothes back on but went downstairs barefoot. Sitting in the kitchen and watching her in her bathrobe, flipping an omelet, I felt snug; I thought: This is what husbands must feel like. But it was strange: the homebody with the spatula didn't seem to have any connection with the wild woman I'd been fucking upstairs. Then she turned around, and I saw her mouth was swollen from all the kissing.

Bonnie handed me a blue-and-white plate with the omelet and the toast, buttered and cut in triangles. I went to the refrigerator and took out a couple of her crappy light beers. I remember we sat there in the kitchen talking for an hour or more, but I don't remember what we said.

Later, I remember thinking, as I followed her back upstairs, that Bonnie had grace. Physical grace that born athletes have. The surefooted walk, the upright, easy posture. And commonsense grace. When to kid around and when to be serious, when to talk, when to shut up.

And sexual grace. She loved having sex—and having it with me—and every kiss, every touch, every thrust was something she wanted. She didn't posture: didn't stick her ass out for admiration, even though it was admirable, didn't offer her tits up like they were twin trophies in some erotic contest. It was all natural. Graceful. No strings attached.

We must have been too exhausted to fuck, so we made love. Afterwards, I lay on my back, stared at the beams in the ceiling and thought: I did more than satisfy her. I'm important to her.

"Can I go to sleep now?" she asked.

"Sure."

"I hope you'll stay till morning."

"Of course I will." I got mad, though. Did she think I was some goddamn one-night stand who was going to tiptoe out at three A.M.?

"Don't be angry," she said. "It's not you. It's me. I needed a little reassurance."

"Be reassured," I whispered.

At about three A.M. I woke up for a minute. She was sound asleep. "Bonnie."

Her head was resting on my arm. I could feel the flutter of her lashes as she opened her eyes. "Hi."

"Hi. Listen," I said. "I want to tell you something."

"What?"

"I love you."

"I love you too." Then she asked me: "Aren't we too old for this?"

"No. Go back to sleep."

I got up about six-thirty. She made me coffee. I said it again: I love you. I promised I'd call her from work or, if things got crazy, the second I got off.

I got into the Jag. It had been out all night, and the leather seats were wet with dew. I drove home, wet, limp, but filled with what I suppose was joy.

I got home. Yawned. Wished I was back in bed, wrapped in Bonnie's arms. Really tired. Needed a pick-me-up. Made a double screwdriver. Drank it, then another. Called work and coughed. Said I had some lousy virus. A hundred and three. Ray Carbone said, You sound terrible. Yeah, I said. I feel like hell.

I went on a five-day bender. By the end of it, Bonnie was just a vague, irritating memory.

By the end of the following year, when I was forced to check into South Oaks for treatment for alcohol abuse—plus pancreatic insufficiency and malnutrition caused by my drinking—I had managed to wipe out her memory completely.

Bonnie Spencer never existed.

CHAPTER 14

I got back to Headquarters a little before four o'clock. Even before I saw Ray Carbone, flushed an ominous crimson, I saw Julie, the receptionist, pick up a pen and draw it across her throat. So I knew I was about to be declared dead. But since noncompliance with official department guidelines was standard operating procedure with me, I had no idea what I was going to get killed for this time. Then Carbone jerked his thumb toward the captain's office; I knew it had to do with the Spencer case—and I knew it was not going to be a routine reprimand.

And seeing Frank Shea, Captain Shea, tie knotted tight, jacket buttoned, jabbing his index finger toward a chair was not exactly reassuring. Despite the American and Suffolk County flags in back of him, Shea usually looked more like a lounge singer than a cop: a lock of Brylcreemed hair trailing over his forehead, his tie hanging unknotted, his shirt half unbuttoned, displaying a huge gold Saint Michael's medal, a crucifix, a long, curvy tooth from what must have been some large, pissed-off animal, plus three chest hairs. He put on his jacket only to see the commissioner and for funerals.

Carbone took a chair and put it beside Shea's desk, so they were both arrayed against me. "What's up?" I asked.

"I warned you, Brady," Shea responded.

"About what?"

"You know! Look at you!" Okay, I'd been running, then sitting in the car with the top down, thinking about Bonnie. So maybe I was on the verge of sunstroke; I'd glanced in the rearview mirror just a couple of minutes before, in the parking lot outside Head-quarters, and noticed that under the sunburn, my skin was gray. And I had a headache and couldn't stop sweating. But I didn't look *that* bad. "Look at you!" Shea bellowed.

"What? The department has some new good-grooming direc-tive?"

"Fuck you and die, Brady!"

I peered over at Carbone. "Do you want to tell me what's going on?"

"Steve." Now that Shea was playing bad cop, Carbone could get compassionate. He sounded like a cross between shrink and priest. "Robby told us."

"Told you what?"

Shea picked up a paperweight and slammed it down on his desk. "That you wouldn't get a warrant!"

"Yeah? Well, goddamn right. I'm not ready to arrest yet."

"Who the hell do you think you are?" Shea demanded. "We've got enough evidence to send her away for life. She knows it! She's gonna flee!"

"Where?"

"Shut up! She's gonna flee while you're babbling theories about Lindsay Keefe!"

"Listen, we've been . . . a little hasty. My fault, probably more than anybody else's. But we've got to think about Lindsay. And Fat Mikey too. Shea, just cool it a second and—"

"You bastard, I listened to you once."

"What are you talking about?"

"Remember? You told me how you were going to stay sober."

"Well, fuck you. I am sober."

"Robby Kurz says you're not."

"I'm drinking? Bullshit."

"Robby was genuinely upset. It killed him to tell me." Shea paused for a second. "He *swore* it was true! Robby saw how I kept shaking my head, not wanting to believe it, and he swore. Vodka. Drunks think there's no odor, but believe me, there's an odor. I've smelled it on people, and he said the smell was rising off your skin."

"Robby can take a goddamn fifth of Smirnoff's and shove it up his lying ass. Listen, we had a few words. Maybe I flew off the handle. But to say I was drinking is such slander—"

"He *smelled* it. You were weaving when you walked, and—"

"No!"

"He realized it two days ago. His only mistake was holding out, trying to protect you."

I really thought I was going to be sick. I felt the acid burn of vomit in my throat. I got very quiet. "You think I'm drunk now?"

Carbone looked sad for me. Shea said, "Stinko."

"I want one of you to walk over to the lab with me. I want a Breathalyzer test." They shot a glance at each other; they knew you could only get accurate readings for about two hours after drinking. So I added: "Blood, urine too. Right now. I want you both to understand: I've been sober for almost four years."

"You're all red!" Shea accused. "You're sweating like a pig."

"Why the hell didn't you ask me how come? Don't you think you owe me that? You want to know why I look like I'm going to get sick?" I thought fast. "I've been out at Old Town Pond in Southampton—less than a quarter of a mile from Sy's house—walking over every goddamn inch of marshland. You know and I know that we need the weapon, and that rat-ass Robby Kurz—

who's been in charge of finding it—has been sitting on his behind, shoving Danish into his mouth, writing his acceptance speech for his commendation, instead of looking for the goddamn .22. Excuse me: writing his speech and making up lies."

"You're accusing *him* of lying?" Shea asked, with a nasty, unamused chuckle.

"Yeah."

"Why would he lie, Brady?"

"Because he's a fanatical, ambitious, self-righteous turd. You *know* what he's like when he goes after somebody. He wears blinders; he refuses to see reality. And he's lying because he knows if he can put the lid on this fast, he can make sergeant by next month—and be first on line for your chair when you retire. Plus he's a sneaky ass-kisser who doesn't like the way I operate and wants me out of the way. He wants me out of the way so I won't stop him from arresting her. Because I've got to tell you, Frank, I might stop him. I have real doubts, and if we false-arrest her, she can make trouble. She has a big mouth." Shea and Carbone glanced at each other. I went on: "And Robby wants me out of the way because Bonnie was my idea to begin with—as Ray can attest—and he doesn't want me to get any credit." All Shea did was sneer. Carbone hung his head. He really liked me. He wanted to believe me. But he'd had too much Psychology 205; he knew alcoholics are infantile, egocentric, that they lie as naturally as most people tell the truth. "Come on, Ray. Walk me down to the lab."

"Brady," Shea said, "you know what this bravado shit—'Take me to the lab!'—is gonna get you?"

"Yeah. Exonerated."

"No. Because I am going to call your bluff, you son of a bitch. I want you in the lab *now*. You hear me? You built a great case, and all of a sudden, when the commissioner, the county exec, the goddamn national media is at my throat, you're sabotaging it. What are we gonna look like when the press finds out we had her and we let her slip through our fingers?"

"Frank, ask yourself: Why would I let a thing like that happen?"

"Because you've been on a binge and you've lost all sense of judgment, of decency . . ." His voice got louder, more theatrical. He grabbed the paperweight, held it in his fist and shook it at me. ". . . of obligation to the department. And to me! I stuck my neck out for you."

I stood and turned to Ray. "You're the psychology genius. Why would I . . . Even if I'd fallen off the wagon and went on the biggest bender of my life, what motive would I have for screwing up a case? If I thought Bonnie Spencer killed Sy, why wouldn't I drink four or five toasts to justice and arrest the bitch?"

Shea didn't give Carbone time to answer. "Because Robby saw you with her in her house when you went in with the search warrant. He saw how you got rid of him, sent him upstairs. And he saw you nosing around after her, following her from room to room. And then, when you asked her about where she got the money in the boot, you put on kid gloves. *So* gentlemanly. Wimping out: You called that catalog guy like it was killing you. Like the *truth* was killing you."

"Shea, this is nuts."

"And then all of a sudden, you're onto Lindsay theories, Mikey theories. Onto *anything* that will keep Robby off Bonnie Spencer. So to answer your question: Why wouldn't you arrest the bitch? Because for some stupid, drunken reason, you've fallen for her."

I passed the Breathalyzer test, of course. Then I walked a painted line, from heel to toe, picked up a nickel, a dime and a quarter without fumbling, recited the alphabet. It took a couple of minutes more to pee into a cup and get blood drawn. Ray stood by while the tech stuck the needle in. He said, "Shea will be glad to hear about the breath test, and if the others come out all right—"

"You believe that feeling in love shit?"

"I don't know."

"You know Lynne, Ray. I'm asking you, do you think when I have someone like her I'd go for an old broad that every guy in town has had a piece of?"

"I saw her when she came in for the test. She's not bad."

"She's no Lynne."

"Look, all I know is you have a beautiful, well-constructed case against her—I heard you present it—and suddenly you're throwing it away. *Why?*"

"Because I don't think she did it."

Carbone shook his head. "I can't buy that, Steve."

"Where's Robby?"

"Why?"

"Because I want to know why he didn't have the balls to face me."

"He would have."

"Except?"

"Except he's down at Southampton Town Court getting a warrant. And then he's going to arrest Bonnie Spencer."

Bonnie opened the back door a crack. "Do you have a warrant?"

"No. Listen, Bonnie—"

She shut the door hard, just short of a slam. I rang the bell. Nothing, except Moose right by the door, barking, trying to sound like a watchdog but giving away the game by the ecstatic wagging of her tail. I squinted, trying to see past the lace kitchen curtains. Bonnie had disappeared into the house.

I love the way cops in movies whip out a credit card, diddle a cylinder and the door springs open. I wasted about five minutes with a card, my Swiss Army knife and every key I had on my key ring. It was a bitch, because I had to do it quietly, so she wouldn't call Headquarters and claim I was harassing her. Finally, the lock clicked open and I was in.

I didn't have to do a room-to-room; Moose led me to an open door, then downstairs, to the basement. Bonnie stood by the dryer, folding a dish towel. When she looked up to greet Moose, she saw me. Jesus, did she scream!

"Bonnie, please, listen to me. I'm not here to hurt you." Her head swiveled in a frantic search for something to protect herself with, but you can't fight off an armed and dangerous psychopathic cop with a plastic bottle of Downy. I took a step toward her, I suppose wanting to touch her, reassure her I was there to help, but she drew back, as if trying to disappear into the narrow gap between the washer and the dryer. So I kept my distance. "I know you think I'm insane or something, but just listen, because there's not much time." Shit. "Not much time" was the wrong thing to say. Bonnie's eyes clouded, as if she comprehended she had only a few minutes more to live. "Bonnie, pay attention. The guy I'm working with on this case, Kurz, the asshole with the hairspray. He left Headquarters before I did. He's going to court to get a warrant for your arrest. So time is a factor here. If he knocks on your door in the next couple of minutes, I can't . . . I can't help you. Understand?" She didn't say anything, but she was listening. She looked straight into my eyes. It was such a probing gaze I felt she could absorb all my thoughts, understand precisely what I was there for. But she just waited for me to go on. "I have doubts. I mean, I don't think you should be arrested yet. There are still too many questions about Sy's death for us to be saying, The case is closed. I want those questions answered. I want the case to stay open. But it's your call. You can stay here, go with Kurz when he comes here for you."

"Or?"

"Get the hell out of here. With me. Now."

Smart girl. She thought to toss all the folded laundry back into the dryer, so it wouldn't look as if she'd run on a moment's notice. We raced out her back door, and I led her through her yard, across an open field to a small wooded area where I'd hidden the Jag, in case Robby showed. Moose sprinted after us, if something with that big a butt can be said to sprint. Bonnie got into the car, and while the door was still open, the dog leapt in, over her lap and into the driver's seat.

"Get her *out*," I said, at the same moment as I opened the driver's door and grabbed her collar.

"When will I get back?"

"How the hell should I know. Two minutes, if you don't convince me."

"What if I do?"

"I don't know."

Suddenly she brightened. "If you put the top down, I could hold her in my lap and there'd be room for the three of us."

"If I put the top down, you idiot, there'd be a hundred witnesses who could say, 'Oh, I saw Bonnie and her dog. They were tooling over to Steve Brady's, in his car. A hundred witnesses to my hindering prosecution. A Class D felony."

"You mean this isn't legal?" But before she'd finished the question, she knew the answer. "I can't let you do this."

She put her hand on the door handle. "Don't move," I ordered.

She shook her head. "No. I'm getting out of here."

I drew my gun. "You move, Bonnie, and I'll shoot you between the fucking eyes."

"Oh, stop it."

Jesus Christ. My head was pounding, I was nauseous from dehydration, I was standing there holding a gun on a murder suspect I was helping escape, and there was a hundred-pound black, hairy mongrel with its tongue hanging out sitting upright, its claws gripped nice and tight into the leather, gazing out the front window, as if waiting for a traffic light to change. "I'm not going to talk about this now! Your goddamn life is on the line, so get that mutt out of here and let's move."

Bonnie's voice was so low I could hardly hear her. "The back door is closed. She can't get to her water, and if I'm not there . . ."

I stuck my gun back in my holster, hauled Moose out of the car and climbed into the driver's seat. Which of course was the cue for Bonnie to open her door and get out. "Get back in!" I

shouted. She shook her head. I started the engine. "Goodbye."
Bonnie whistled, two high, quick notes. Moose raced around to
her side and Bonnie pushed her in.

And that's how we came to drive to my house with Bonnie
in the passenger seat, me in the driver's seat, and fatso Moose
stretched over both our laps, barking with pleasure at this wonderful game.

Migrant workers' shacks not being known for expansive rooms or
cathedral ceilings, the architect-entrepreneur-loser I'd bought my
house from hadn't had much space to work with, so he'd made
most of the place into a "family area," one main room that served
as kitchen, den, dining and living room. Then he hacked off a
little at each end, so that when he was taking potential buyers
around, he could make one of those *Voilà!* gestures with his hand
and say, "To sleep . . . ," then wait for the Yorkers to say,
". . . perchance to dream," and they could all be good friends
and bask in the radiance of each other's culture, plus make a nice,
civilized deal. Except I'd rather have gotten strung up by the nuts
than say ". . . perchance to dream," and the architect had gotten
real nervous because he knew I was a cop and therefore I might
think the "To sleep . . ." meant he was making a pass, because
he wore a ponytail, and this could queer the deal in every sense.
So he'd just added, "The bedroom," real fast and left it at that.

The master bedroom, like the rest of the house, had come
furnished—since this was to be the model for the hundreds of
migrant-worker shacks he had dreamed of renovating. But the bed
he'd put in was just large enough for midgets to do it in the
missionary position, so I'd gotten rid of it and put in a king-size
bed. Once I did that, there was just enough space to get to the
closets and the bathroom.

On the opposite side of the house, he'd taken the same amount
of square footage and stuck in two guest rooms, connected by a
bathroom. I led Bonnie into the first, which wasn't much different
from the second, except instead of scallops and conch shells sten-

ciled on the floors and around the top of the walls, it had pine-
apples. Since I hardly ever went near this part of the house, I'd
forgotten about them, and about the hideous lamp with a green
shade and a base of some fat sticks tied together with rawhide the
architect had told me was a rustic touch I might conceivably wish
to change. The poor guy was such a basket case because he couldn't
sell his house; I wound up putting in a bid that same day.

I pulled down the shades. "Don't get the wrong idea," I said,
my back to Bonnie. "This is to make sure you're not seen."

"I won't get the wrong idea." Her voice had a tremor. That
was the only sign she was as terrified as I sensed she was.

"Not that I get a lot of company, but just in case." When I
turned back to her, she was sitting, primly, on a small ladder-
back chair. I sat on the edge of the bed, but because the room
was so small, our knees were about four inches apart. "Now, I
want to hear what actually happened, right from the beginning.
Every detail, from the minute you first spoke to Sy or laid eyes
on him again. Unless you'd been in touch with him all the years
since the divorce."

"No."

"Okay, but first, I want to clear up something."

"You mean about—"

"No."

But she couldn't let it be. "Gideon called. He told me you
have no recollection that you and I . . . that you and I had met."

"Look, I don't have time for that now." I was detached.
Professional. "What I want to clear up is your last lie."

"You make it sound like it's the last of a hundred thousand."

"It is, give or take a few."

"If I'm such a liar, why would I tell the truth now, when the
police are closing in on me?"

"Because you're desperate."

"Well," she said, in that trembling voice, "I guess I am."
She dropped her head and stared down at her hands, folded on
her lap. She had beautiful, long-fingered hands, with nice, no-

polish oval nails, hands you would see in commercials for hand lotion.

"Okay, why did you make up the story about the eight hundred eighty bucks we found in your boot?"

"That *was* the truth."

"Bonnie, understand one thing. You shit me, you're out of here."

"Please, call him again." I shook my head. "Try to understand," she pleaded. "Vincent Kelleher is a very nervous, not-too-successful businessman who sells pot holders that look like armadillos, and size fifty-four sweatsuits in pink, aqua or lilac with appliqués. All of a sudden, this nebbish gets a long-distance phone call from a detective asking him about money he slipped me off the books. An illegal payment. He was always nervous about doing it, and when you called, he must have been convinced Eliot Ness and the tax squad would swoop down and arrest him."

"You're good, Bonnie. Really good."

"No. If I were that good, you would have believed the lies I did tell. I wouldn't be in this mess now. Please, call Vincent Kelleher."

But just then my pager squeaked: "Brady call Carbone ASAP." I told her not to move, and I hurried across the house, into my bedroom, and closed the door.

Carbone asked where I was, and I told him I'd gone home after sixty hours of being on, because I was wiped, and sick of the shit he and Shea had handed me, but did he want me in for another Breathalyzer test, to make sure I wasn't sitting around with a bottle of Canadian Club and a straw? He said, Look, maybe we were too hasty, and Robby, not being a drinking man, might have misread some of the signs and . . . And *what?* I demanded. There's no sign of Bonnie Spencer, he said. Is Robby hysterical? I asked. Yes, and so is Shea, and if you think the commissioner isn't shitting a brick, then you're not thinking. Hey, Ray, everybody should calm down. It's six-thirty. The cool of the evening is upon us. Maybe she's down at the beach. Maybe she's having dinner with a friend. Tell everybody to relax. Have a drink—on me. Look, you want me to check around? He said, Maybe that would be a good idea. Okay, I said, I'll surveil her place until you can get someone else over there, then I'll check around, make a few calls. Just do me a favor. Page Robby. Get him the hell away from her house, because if I see him, I swear to God I'll kill him. Carbone said all right. He was about to hang up when I inquired: They finish my pee and blood workup yet? You're okay, Steve. Thanks. Be reasonable, he said. We've got an anxiety-provoking situation here. A lot of pressure. Sometimes people make errors in judgment. I asked him if Shea realized he had made an error in judgment, or would I have to piss into a Dixie cup every day? Carbone, being patient, said, Shea knows the results of the tests, and he's not a stupid man. But let's face it: the two of you don't have a natural affinity. He let you back on the squad because he needed you, not because he liked you or trusted you, which I guess isn't news. Not by a long shot, I said. Carbone said, So do yourself a favor, Detective Brady. Earn a gold star. Bring in Bonnie Spencer.

The engine on Robby's car was running as I drove up to Bonnie's, and when I pulled over beside him, he flung the arrest warrant into my car and peeled out—as fast as an Olds Cutlass can peel— before he had to look me in the eye or hear what I had to say. He knew what it was, though: I was going to get him. And I knew what his response would be: Not if I get you first.

A few minutes later, two Southampton Town P.D. squad cars pulled up. They were supposed to hang around until someone from Suffolk County Homicide came to relieve them, so I handed them the warrant to pass along and told them I was just going to check out the house one more time. I slipped on a pair of rubber gloves carefully, ostentatiously, as if getting ready to perform neurosurgery, and went in. Five minutes later I came out with some of Bonnie's underwear and a T-shirt folded flat in one pocket, along with her toothbrush, and a Ziploc with Purina Dog Chow in the other. I swung two evidence bags with a pair of sneakers and a hairbrush as I walked down the front path, then gave a mock salute to the Southampton cops before I drove off.

Some blithe spirit. My hands were clammy, my stomach churning. Not for any rational reason, like I knew I was destroying my entire professional and personal life, to say nothing of risking two years in the can for hindering prosecution by rendering criminal assistance to a person who has committed a Class A felony— like second-degree murder. I was actually very clear about the consequences of the devastation I was bringing on myself. I remember I contemplated what a felony conviction could do to my pension rights, wondered whether they had AA meetings at the Green Haven Correctional Facility and decided that because I had a couple of good friends in the Suffolk County D.A.'s, maybe they'd only go for a misdemeanor. But the drippy palms, the twisting gut, had nothing to do with these objective considerations.

No, I drove back to my house with an unswallowable lump in my throat because I was afraid Bonnie would be gone. She'd think fast, as she had the week before, at Sy's, when she'd killed him, and do what she thought she had to do: run. *No.* She hadn't killed him. I did believe her. But she'd have visions of the jury nodding, convinced, as the People summed up its circumstantial case against Spencer, and she'd run. Or just be frightened, and want someone to hold her, comfort her, kiss the top of her head, like her friend Gideon, and she'd run. Or knowing Bonnie, be a good, chin-up American, face the music, trust in God and the Constitution, and she'd run, find a phone, call Homicide and ask, Is Detective Kurz in?

Oh, Jesus. What would I do if she wasn't there?

It was Thursday night, but weekenders were already pouring in. Traffic had gotten even heavier than when I'd left for Bonnie's a half hour earlier; it was like one endless, metallic reptile snaking its way east. And every person in those thousands of cars was an important person, with important things to do. They *had* to hear what last-minute truly fun invitations were on their answering machines so they could break the dates they'd already made. They *had* to change into the three-hundred-dollar black gauze shirt. They *had* to refresh their potpourri before their houseguests arrived. There was fresh mozzarella oozing in the shopping bag on the back seat, wetting their baguettes, an intolerable situation that *had* to be stopped.

Not a single car would defer and let me cross Montauk Highway. I honked and flicked my brights at a new 560SL, made eye contact with the driver and then didn't look back at the road; I kept staring at him—and driving. It unnerved him enough that at the last possible second, he slammed on his brakes. Hatred disfigured his jowly face, but he knew I looked demented enough to actually hit a Mercedes.

Then I floored it back to my house. Except I had to stop when the guardrail went down at the train tracks. It was the longest fucking train in the history of the Long Island Rail Road.

I rushed into the house and tripped over Moose, who was running to greet me. I said, "Get out of my way, you goddamn bag of shit." She wagged her tail. I patted her head. Okay, I thought, Bonnie left the dog. Clever: she knew I'd take care of it. The house was absolutely silent. I trudged toward the pineapple room and called out "Hi" against the emptiness. Still a little hope. "Hello?" Not a sound. "Bonnie!" I yelled.

"Hi," Bonnie called back. Did I jump! "It's you! I heard you say 'Hi,' and I thought it was your voice, but I couldn't be sure. I thought: What if it's one of his friends, or a burglar?"

My whole body was flooded with relief, and it left me so empty, that sudden decrease in tension, that I had to lean against the wall for a minute to get my equilibrium back. Then I went into the pineapple room.

She was curled up on the bed reading *This Date in New York Yankees History*, the only book that had been in there. She put it down on the floor, then sat up on the bed, Indian style. "Who is the all-time leader for career grand slams?" she asked.

"Gehrig," I mumbled.

"It said Henry Gehrig. Is that the same as Lou?"

I nodded and said, "Here." I handed her the sneakers and hairbrush and took the underwear and toothbrush out of my pocket. I was still too emotional. I couldn't make conversation.

"Thanks."

I jiggled the bag with the dog chow. She smiled and waited for me to say something, so I told her I'd give it to Moose, take a quick shower and be back. I was amazed; I sounded so matter-of-fact. Like a normal person. Did she want something? I had a bunch of TV dinners. She said, No, thanks, she wasn't hungry.

I shoved two Hungry Man dinners in the oven, figuring when push came to shove she wouldn't be able to resist an aluminum-foil tray of greasy, breaded chicken, or worst case, I'd eat it. I got into the shower. Water, a lot of soap, the nice pine smell of shampoo. This was better. A cool, clean man instead of a sweaty, feverish, overwrought wreck. I reached out for the towel, a little disappointed Bonnie hadn't sneaked in to hand it to me; in the back of my mind, I'd been imagining getting out of the shower and having her there. I'd say, Get the hell out of here, and she'd say, Let me do your back. But then, resting her body against me, she'd reach around to the front, stroke me, murmur, Oh, Stephen.

I got dressed, took out my notebook and called Vincent Kelleher, the catalog king. "Detective Brady again."

"Yes, sir?"

"Mr. Kelleher, I don't know you, but somehow I get the feeling that you weren't being straight with me, and that makes me very upset." Silence. "Now listen, I'm not interested in your tax situation. You want to pay off the books, on the books, I don't give a damn. But I do give a damn if you lie in response to a simple question."

"Why do you think I lied?" he whispered in Flagstaff, Arizona.

"Because I'm a cop. I *know*. You want to tell me about your financial arrangements with Bonnie Spencer?" Silence. "If you're straightforward with me, we'll both hang up and that will be the end of it. If you dick me around, I'll pass on my suspicions to a buddy of mine in the IRS in Washington."

"I paid her . . ." His voice faded. This guy had an Irish name; I couldn't believe he could be such a wimp. Fucking assimilation.

"How did you pay her?"

"In cash."

"How much?"

"Twenty-five hundred dollars. She was the one who asked to be paid in cash. I swear to you, I never offered it."

"How did you get it to her?"

"Her father lives outside of Scottsdale. She visits him once a year, then drives over, sees the mock-ups for new catalogs. We talk and . . ." If this guy went through a red light, he'd probably handcuff himself, turn himself in and beg the judge for the max.

"You talk and what? You hand her the money?"

"Yes, in an envelope. But I promise you, it won't happen again." All right! I thought, as I hung up. Score one for the good guys.

I searched around and finally found a couple of paperbacks, Stephen King and Clancy, and brought them into her room. I didn't want her to hate it, being stuck in there, and I didn't want her to think I was a semiliterate jerk who, when he read at all, read statistics—although that was more true than not. She was a writer; she had full bookshelves. What was I going to say? Hey, Bonnie, I may not read books much, but I read three papers a day and watch all the historical documentaries on cable. You want to know about the Battle of Midway? Metternich's life story? Just ask me.

"These are for later," I said. "Now it's time to talk." I pulled back the shade and looked outside. The last of the soft, magic daylight was fading.

"Okay, but . . . I'm not telling you how to do your job . . . maybe you could give Vincent Kelleher a call."

"Why?"

"Because he wasn't telling you the truth. And *I'm* going to tell you the truth. I know how badly I've messed things up for myself, and now you're giving me another chance. Well, I want to be worthy of your confidence. And I want you to believe me about everything."

This time, the cop beat out the man. She shouldn't think she had me on her side; she should convince me. I said: "Maybe I'll call him later. For now, tell me how you hooked up with Sy again."

CHAPTER 15

W hen you and Sy split, was there a lot of bad feeling?"

"No." Bonnie leaned back against the headboard, one of those cheapo woven wood jobs that squeak every time you inhale. She was wearing what she'd worn when I found her folding laundry: red nylon running shorts and a black tank top. The white socks she'd had on had gotten filthy on the run through the field, so she'd taken them off. She hadn't been wearing shoes.

She drew her knees up together, folded her arms over them, then rested her head on the arms. Jesus, was she flexible; it was the kind of position that normally only an eight-year-old can be comfortable in. "The day I signed the separation agreement, he took me out to lunch. Le Cirque. Soft lights, soft linen napkins. Soft food, so you wouldn't crunch when you chew. We were sitting on the same side on the banquette. He held my hand under the table and said, 'It's my fault that I wasn't able to love you enough. But I'll always be there for you, Bonnie.' "

So, obviously, would Moose. The dog rested her face on the blanket until Bonnie patted her. Then she lay down on my feet.

"Did you throw up when he said that?"

"No, it was before the appetizer. But see, in his own way, Sy was sincere. He truly believed what he was saying, even though twenty seconds after he dropped me off at Penn Station so I could get the train back to Bridgehampton, I ceased to exist. But since I hadn't given him a hard time about splitting up . . . I mean, I cried a lot and asked him to go to a marriage counselor, but that was all. I didn't want alimony. So he felt kindly toward me. If someone had asked, 'Sy, what was your second wife like?' he'd have said, 'Hmmm, second wife. Oh, yes. Bonnie. So *sweet*. Down-to-earth.' It was funny: If you crossed him, he'd never forget you, but niceness made no impression on him."

"Why didn't you fight harder to stay together?"

"Because . . ." She put her hands together, prayer fashion, and touched her forefingers to her lips. Finally, she said: "Because I knew he didn't love me anymore—if he ever had. Sy could fall in love, but it was like an actor immersing himself in a character. The week I met him, in L.A., he must have just come back from a John Ford retrospective—so I became his cowgirl. He walked around wearing a denim jacket, squinting, smoking; this was before his decaffeinated days. He broke off the filters and lit his cigarettes with those matches you'd strike on the bottom of your boot; he actually took to wearing an old pair of shit-kickers, which wasn't so terrible because he was three inches shorter than me. God knows where he got them—probably in some Madison Avenue antique-boot boutique. We'd go riding a lot. Western saddle. He said, 'The English saddle is so effete.' But after three weeks back in New York—six weeks into our marriage—he got tired of being Hopalong Cassidy. And he got tired of loving me. I knew it." She turned away from me for a minute and got busy folding over the pillow, so it made a better support for the small of her back. "There was no percentage in fighting him on the divorce. He'd tried to be a decent husband, and it got to be too much of a burden."

"How was he a decent husband? I thought you said he cheated on you—with some socialite."

"Decent for Sy. He held doors open. He remembered birthdays, anniversaries. He had great style; one Valentine's Day he bought me a new tackle box, and when I opened it, there was a beautiful long strand of fourteen-millimeter pearls."

"What are fourteen-millimeter pearls?"

"*Big* pearls." Her hands described a sphere that was about the size of the average classroom globe. It annoyed me that she liked such an expensive gift. I wanted her to say, I told Sy to take back the pearls; I only wanted the tackle box. But she didn't. "You have to understand Sy," she went on. "He couldn't be faithful. He couldn't be straight. He *had* to be . . . I don't know if 'crooked' is the word. He had to manipulate every situation. Some of it was money. He was always afraid someone was cheating him, so he played one stockbroker, one lawyer, one accountant, against another. But *he* cheated people all the time. He hid personal expenses in movie budgets. I'm not just talking about a sweatsuit and a set of barbells; his second movie paid for a gym and a hot tub in our apartment in the city. And you couldn't use words like 'illegal' or 'immoral' with him, because in a weird way, he took them as compliments. He saw his finagling as an adventure and himself as a kind of swanky Robin Hood. But all he was doing was robbing from the rich to give to the rich."

"You didn't see any of this when you agreed to marry him?"

"No. I just saw this charming, cultured man with crinkles around his eyes who was crazy about *Cowgirl* and who knew all about westerns. Not just a superficial knowledge: I remember him describing one of Tom Mix's silent movies—*Cactus Jim's Shop Girl*. Actually, he seemed to know about everything: Cambodian architecture, the Big Bang theory, the linguistic connection between Finnish and Hungarian. But I think what got me most about

Sy was that he *appreciated* me. My work. My eyes. My hair. My . . . All the usual stuff. This man was such a connoisseur, I thought: Lord, am I something!"

She concentrated on massaging her knee, a slow back-and-forth motion, the way you do to ease an old injury. Suddenly she glanced up at me, then, quickly, back down to her knee. I knew what she was thinking: despite our very different résumés, I was like Sy. Oh, how I had appreciated her that night: I swear to God, I've never met anyone like you, Bonnie. Bonnie, your skin is like warm velvet. You know what, Bonnie? Your eyes are the color of the ocean. Not a summer ocean. Like on a bright winter day—so beautiful. I could talk to you for hours, Bonnie. Bonnie, I love you.

"But Sy's enthusiasms never lasted. He had a closet with equipment from sports he'd tried a few times and given up: golf, racquetball, scuba diving, polo, cross-country skiing. And if he could have put women in a closet, he would have; he was on to other enthusiasms by our two-month anniversary."

"I'm sorry."

"Don't be. Actually, it got to be amusing." She lifted her chin and gave a little closed-lipped smile, a superior city-slicker expression that overflowed with savoir faire. It was fake as hell. "I could tell who he was having an affair with by the way he dressed. One day he put away his nipped-in-waist Italian suit and took out a torn T-shirt and bleached jeans, and I knew he'd stopped with the production designer with the surrealist jewelry and taken up with the third-string *Village Voice* movie critic, this girl with a lot of hair who was about ten minutes past her Sweet Sixteen. You couldn't help but laugh."

"Don't bullshit me."

The blanket on the bed, which the architect had probably decided was a grand bucolic design statement, was a pukey green plaid. Bonnie traced a thin, dark-green line with her finger. "All right," she said quietly, "what he did to me stank. More than that. It broke my heart. I'm not the kind of woman men fall for. Then, finally, one did. I was so happy. But before I could even finish the love poem I was writing to him, a sonnet—fourteen lousy lines—he stopped loving me."

"So the marriage was over before it was officially over."

She nodded. "We still had sex, but there was no love, and not much companionship. On the nights he was home, he'd hole up in his study and read scripts or make phone calls. After the separation, I went on with my life. It wasn't hard to do; we hadn't really been a couple."

"But your economic situation, your social status, changed. What was your life like?"

"What do you mean?" She got very engrossed in following another, thicker line in the plaid.

"Happy, sad, wonderful, terrible?"

"It was okay." She didn't look up at me.

"Come on, Bonnie."

"Why is this necessary?"

"Because I want to know the circumstances surrounding your taking up with Sy again."

"The circumstances were that I was—am—an independent woman. No ties. My mom died when I was seventeen: a brain tumor. My dad remarried—to a woman from Salt Lake who gets pedicures. He sold his store and they moved to Arizona, to a retirement community; they play bridge. My brothers are all married, with families of their own."

She got quiet, thoughtful. She stopped with the blanket and reached back and played with the end of her braid. Absentmindedly, she unwound the rubber band. She unplaited her hair, and, as she began to talk again, stroked it, as if comforting herself. In the light of the green-shaded lamp, it gave off soft copper glints.

"My life: I live in a lovely town by the ocean in a part of the country I don't belong in. I have Gideon and his lover, two women friends, and a lot of pleasant acquaintances. Summers are a little better; I kept a couple of friends from my Sy days—a film editor, a *Wall Street Journal* entertainment industry reporter—and they have houses around here. We have some good times. I do volunteer work with illiterate adults and for every environmental cause that comes down the pike. That's how I met Gideon. He was representing a land rapist, and we started out screaming at each other because roseate terns have become an endangered species, but we wound up great friends. You want more? I make eighteen thousand dollars a year writing pap for catalogs and the local paper and industrial publications like *Auto Glass News*. What else do you want to know? Sex? Until AIDS, I slept with any man who appealed to me. Now I read and watch two movies a night and run five miles a day. I had an abortion when I was married to Sy because he said he wasn't ready to have children. I wanted to have a baby more than anything. From the time I was thirty-eight, when it dawned on me that I'd never get married again because no one would ever ask, I stopped using birth control. I was never able to conceive; I found out my fallopian tubes were scarred closed from a dose of gonorrhea I'd gotten from my husband about six months after the abortion. Well, that's it." Bonnie clasped her hands on her knees. "I guess you expected something a little more upbeat."

"A little." I had to be professional. What was the alternative? Taking her in my arms, hugging her, whispering tender words of condolence? I asked: "We found two condom wrappers in a wastebasket in Sy's guest room. If you couldn't get pregnant—"

"AIDS, chlamydia, gonorrhea again. If I could have found a way of slipping a Trojan over his head before I kissed him, I would have, but it would have lacked a certain subtlety."

"Tell me more about your life."

"What's there to tell? I had such a happy childhood. And then my screenplay became a movie and got wonderful reviews, and then Sy came along and married me. Sure, I knew there'd be bumps. Tragedy even, like losing my mom. But it didn't occur to me that life wouldn't basically be wonderful. Well, it's not. It isn't terrible, but I never thought I would be so lonely."

"But now you have to deal with something a little more serious than personal happiness," I reminded her.

"I know."

"Like the possibility of a murder conviction." My voice was grim, deep and low, like a 45 record playing at 33. The small bedroom suddenly felt tight, airless, like a cell.

Bonnie seemed determined not to succumb to the gloom. She flashed one of her great grins. "So worse comes to worse, I get convicted for murder. After twenty, thirty years in jail, think of the script I could write. None of those *Blondes in Chains* clichés for me. You know: the dyke matron, the ripped uniforms so breasts peekaboo out. No, I'll write a socially significant screenplay and maybe get on *Entertainment Tonight.*"

"Tell me about the screenplay you were working on with Sy."

"Oh, right. *A Sea Change.* It's based on a real incident during World War II. A German submarine surfaced off the coast of Long Island, and a couple of saboteurs slipped in. In my story, two women spot them down by the beach: a middle-class housewife and a bargirl who turns tricks on weekends. Anyway, it's about their helping catch the Nazis, but also about the friendship that develops."

"You sent it to Sy when you got finished with it?"

"I called him."

"What happened?"

"Well, first I spoke to his secretary, asked that he call me back, which he did a couple of days later. Kind of wary, to tell you the truth: I guess he was nervous I might be asking for money. But when I told him what it was, he was nice: You sound fan*ta*stic. Send it Fed Ex. Can't *wait* to read it."

It wasn't only that she didn't wear makeup, or that she did have incredible calf muscles; Bonnie was simply like no other woman I'd ever met. She seemed to be incapable of womanly wiles in any form. I looked her straight in the eye and she made no defensive feminine gestures. Her hand didn't fly up to touch her nose to check if it was oily, or up to her head to smooth down or fluff up her hair. She didn't make cow eyes or wounded-doe eyes, spread her legs an intriguing inch, thrust out her pelvis. No, she just looked straight back at me. I thought: Maybe it came from growing up with all those older brothers and that elk-shooting father and that rangy, broad-shouldered mother. Maybe she'd even tried batting her eyelashes or giggling, and nobody noticed. Maybe she'd acted wide-eyed and inept around all those Brownings and Remmingtons and Winchesters in the store, or gazed upon the engine of the family Buick and said, "Oooh, what's all that?" and got a swift kick in the butt, real or symbolic. She wasn't feminine. She was female.

"You say Sy liked your screenplay?"

"Yup."

I thought about what Easton had said about it. "Then why would he have told one of his people to find something nice to say about it, so he could get you off his back? And why would he have told Lindsay . . ." I tried to think of a way to say Sy thought the script was a piece of crap without actually having to say it.

"I can't say for sure. With Lindsay, I think it was natural he'd try and cover up any relationship with me." Bonnie rotated her ankles, making circles with her feet. "I mean, Lindsay has perpetually twitching, supersensitive antennae that can pick up any other woman within a fifty-mile radius. Sy was so careful; he did everything except wear sunglasses and a false nose when he came over." She stopped twirling her feet and started to do toe touches, flexing her calves as she bent over. She could have been stretching for a marathon; she was ready to run. She was not someone who could tolerate being confined.

"Why would he ask his assistant to find something nice to say?"

"Busywork, maybe."

"No."

"When did he ask his assistant to read it?"

"A couple of months ago."

"I'd just handed in my second draft then. Sy *said* he liked it a lot but that he wouldn't have time to really go over it until *Starry Night* wrapped."

"This was the rewriting you did based on his suggestions?"

"Yes."

"Knowing Sy, was it possible he didn't like it, even though he told you he did?"

She considered the question. "Knowing Sy, yes. Maybe he—I don't know—wanted me back in his life for a while." She looked disheartened, as if she'd just gotten a brusque rejection letter in the mail. "But he did write me this nice note. Something like: 'Skimmed it. Adore it. Can't wait to *really* read it.' "

This could be another one for the good guys; if Sy had liked the screenplay, and if she had written proof, she'd have every motive for wanting him alive; a dead executive producer can't make a movie. "He wrote you a note?" I demanded.

"Yes. He has little three-by-five note cards with his name. He used one of them."

"Typed or in his own handwriting?"

"I think he wrote it."

"Did you save it?"

"It should be in my *Sea Change* file. In my office." She stopped cold. "Oh, wait a second. You want proof that he liked it originally too. Right? Fine. Look in that same file. There's his original memo, the one he wrote after he read the first draft. Typical Sy. Eight pages, single-spaced, multisyllabic. Talking about everything from character arc to how I misused the subjunctive mood. But filled with 'brilliant' and 'trenchant' and 'poignant.' "

"What does 'trenchant' mean?"

She chewed her lip for a second. "I don't know, to tell you the truth. It's one of those words that nobody in human history has ever said out loud, and you don't see it written that often. He also wrote it was 'au courant.' *That* must have been a shock to him. Sy had always told me I was born too late, that I belonged under contract to RKO—if there still was an RKO—because my writing talent was for great 1941 movies. He couldn't get over that I'd finally written a screenplay that would appeal to someone besides my Aunt Shirley, and a perverse USC film professor. An eastern, not a western." She got off the bed and began to pace, which isn't easy when you can only pace three steps forward and three steps back. "You know, you had a search warrant. How come you didn't read that file?"

"Robby Kurz probably looked at it and decided it wasn't important." I took out my notebook and jotted down: "Bon's Sea file."

"Not important? You're hearing from people that Sy hated my work, that he rejected me—which would give me a motive to kill him if I was a homicidal maniac, which I'm not. And you say it's not important?"

"It's not our job to dig up exculpatory evidence."

"No. It's your job to railroad people."

"Sit down."

"I don't want to sit down," she snapped. "God, I feel so cooped up in here."

I was pissed. I wanted her to like being with me. "Want to try a jail cell?"

"Do you? Maybe you can have the one next door. You know, when you go up the river for your Class D felony." Bonnie's pacing got faster, more desperate. Suddenly she stopped short. Smiled. That phony, movie-biz smile, falsely warm, fraudulently agreeable. "Listen, I have a great idea. We can share a cell! Have a hot affair after lights-out. Not just your conventional hot affair. I mean, a *love* affair. We'll actually talk! Tell each other our life stories. The true ones, even when they hurt. Not the slick ones we make up to entertain people. And sex! We'll do it standing up, sitting down, frontways, sideways—"

"Bonnie, stop it!"

"Why? I'm telling you, it could be magic. Like we were creating something the world had never known before. And then the next day—"

"I asked you to stop it."

"—the next day you'd be free. You could forget it happened.

You could forget it meant something." She hoisted an imaginary glass. "Hey, I'll drink to that!"

"I'm sorry if I hurt you," I began. "That time of my life, I was a mess."

I got up and walked into the bathroom. Moose followed. No tissues, so I brought her a wad of toilet paper, knowing she was going to cry. I came back and put my arm around her shoulders, ready to absorb her sobs. But she pulled away and turned from me; she wasn't crying, and she didn't want me comforting her.

"Bonnie," I said to her back, "in AA, one of the things we do is to make a list of all the people we've harmed. Then we've got to be willing to make amends. I know I harmed you. I'm not going to make excuses—"

"Gideon said you didn't remember what happened."

"I didn't. But later, after he left . . . I remembered some of it. I know I'll never be able to know what really went on between us—what we talked about. But let me just say how sorry—"

She turned back and gazed at me so straight I looked away. "No amends, okay? I don't want any magnanimous Twelve Step gestures that will make you Feel Good About Yourself. Yes, you hurt me. But I let myself get hurt. I was playing a raunchy sex scene, and I tried to score it with violins. Well, I was the dope."

"You know it wasn't any scene."

"I know it's history." She sat down on the bed again, feet on the floor this time, hands in her lap. Mormon schoolmarm posture, not Bonnie posture. There was a long silence. It was broken by the screech of a gull flying toward the water. Bonnie finally said: "I apologize for the outburst."

"No problem."

"I don't want to be a bitter person. I lost control for a second. I'm exhausted. I haven't been sleeping, not since Sy was killed. Not since you rang my bell. I'm scared. I wake up and the sun is shining and I yawn and stretch—and suddenly I'm overwhelmed with terror. I'm trapped inside a nightmare, and the sunshine doesn't give me any light. And you: I can't resolve my memory of you and my fear of you. It's very hard being here in your house."

"I understand, and I just want to say how sorry—"

"Let's drop it now."

"Can't I—"

"Please, don't."

It was getting dark. I knew I had to call Lynne. I walked into the kitchen, but instead of picking up the phone, I put Moose's dog chow in a bowl and got her some water. Then I took the dinners out of the oven and brought them back into Bonnie's room on plates, with forks and napkins. I thought she'd say, No, thanks, I'm much too upset to eat, but by the time I got back again with Cokes, she'd woofed down a drumstick and half the mashed potatoes and corn.

I sat there holding a wing, like I couldn't figure out what to do about it, thinking that there were approximately a million subjects I wanted to talk to this woman about: what teams she liked, although I had a dread suspicion she would be a Mets fan; what Mormons were all about; whether she read about stuff like Eastern Europe and the national debt in the paper or just articles about movies and saving marsh grasses; what was her favorite running route; how had she hurt her knee; did she only like the John Wayne and Katharine Hepburn stuff or did she ever watch a good horror movie; did she believe in God and did she feel guilty or only regretful about her abortion; had it simply been the sex— amazing, all-star sex—or had she fallen in love with me in the course of that night.

What I asked her was: "When did you begin sleeping with Sy again?"

"That last week."

"Why?"

" 'Why?' "

"What was it, a casting couch kind of thing? You thought if you slept with him, he'd make your movie?"

"You know," she said, and reached for another napkin,

"there's an old show-business joke: A gorgeous, talented actress walks into a producer's office and says, 'I want that part. I'll do anything, and I mean *anything*, for that part.' She gets down on her knees and says, 'I'm going to give you the world's most incredible blow job.' And the producer looks down at her and says, 'Yeah, but what's in it for me?' " Bonnie wiped the bread crumbs from the chicken off her hands. "So what was in it for Sy? Nothing. There was nothing I could do for him that would entice him into doing anything he didn't want to do."

"But how could you sleep with such a bastard? Okay, he let you have the house, but other than that, he left you broke. He made you get an abortion—"

She cut me off. "No one held a gun to my head."

"Maybe he didn't, but he gave you the clap, didn't he? Forget that it's proof positive of adultery. It took away the chance for you to have the one thing you wanted more than anything in the world."

I'd just hit her most painful spot. She didn't wince; she just stood, holding out her plate. "Why don't I bring this into the kitchen?" Her voice was artificially high, as if she were being stretched too tight.

"No. I don't have curtains or anything on the windows. I can't risk having you seen. I'll take it in later." I took the plate from her and put it down on the floor. "You're going stir-crazy, aren't you?"

"And this isn't even stir," she said softly.

"Put on your sneakers." When she did, I turned off the lamp, took her arm and steered her out of the bedroom, through the dark main room and out the back door. It was nearly night; the sky, already dotted with stars, was a uniform blue. Dark, indigo, like my Jag. I sat her down on the back step and murmured, "Keep your voice down."

"You're worried about nocturnal farmers, plowing out there, right past those bushes, listening in?"

"I always worry about nocturnal farmers. Or a friend could drop over. So what do you want? To sit out here or go back inside?"

In response, she leaned against the doorframe and took a deep breath. Whatever she'd had in mountains, this had to be better. The bracing salt of the sea, the fragrance of pine, the deep, musky smell of the earth. "More questions, Bonnie."

"Okay."

"Why did you sleep with Sy after what he did to you?" She didn't answer; I think she was still with that lost baby. "Come on," I pushed her. "You don't strike me as one of those masochistic broads who lets herself be used. You seem to play more by men's rules than women's rules. You have a good time, you say thank you and that's it. You don't wake up the next morning feeling like a piece of shit; you wake up and say to yourself, 'Hey, I got laid. It was good. Cleared my sinuses.' And that's that."

"That is never that."

"But it's not that far from the truth, is it? You're not saying, 'Sweet Jesus, help me. I hate myself.' "

"People of my persuasion generally don't say 'Sweet Jesus.' "

"You know what I mean."

"Am I one of those women who sleeps around to degrade herself? No. I sleep around—or slept around—for sex. Sometimes to be held."

"So answer my question."

"I slept with Sy because he was there, a real, live person who *knew* me. He came to the house to go over his memo on my screenplay, and we wound up talking about my brother Jim's wife, who Sy had always had a little crush on, and about his Uncle Charlie's bypass surgery, and about all the movies he wanted to make after *Starry Night*."

Talk about stars. The night was so clear that the stars were not cold, distant lights but twinkling points of warmth: Hi! Welcome! Nice universe we've got here!

Bonnie went on: "When Sy saw the pitchers on the mantel, he reminisced about the trip we'd taken to Maine, where we bought a couple of them. It was so nice—a shared memory. What else? He said my script looked like hell and he couldn't believe I was still using a typewriter, and he picked up the phone and called his assistant and had him order a computer and printer for me." I made a mental note to ask Easton about that. "Let's see. He brought me flowers. So I guess you're wondering, was I had for an IBM-compatible and a bunch of day lilies? Partly. Sy swoops into your life, takes over everything. Let me tell you, it's very seductive, having someone come and care for you: buy you electronic toys, brush your hair, ask you how your day was. So that was part of it. And the other part was, I slept with him because I was so unloved. I couldn't stand it anymore." Before I could say anything, she added: "And don't ask if I really think he loved me, because we both know what the answer to that one is."

"Why you? Look, I'm not putting you down, but he was living with Lindsay Keefe."

"I'm sexier than Lindsay Keefe." She wasn't being falsely immodest. She was being matter-of-fact. She meant it. Then she stretched out her legs and got busy doing toe touches again. She couldn't sit still; she had too much energy. I wondered how she sat for two hours to see a movie. It was such a dark, sedentary passion for someone who seemed all daylight and outdoors. "It wasn't just sex for Sy," she was explaining. "He was screwing me literally to screw Lindsay figuratively. He was always so much happier when he was cheating. Somehow, his women always suspected, and he liked their scrambling to hold on to him. He liked their anguish too. And he *loved* the logistics of sneaking around. But with Lindsay, it was more than his usual infidelity. He was *furious* at her."

"Why? Because she wasn't good in the movie?"

"Because she wasn't good—and she wasn't trying. See, Sy had his own money, the bank's money and some of his friends' money invested. It was a real risk. He knew this kind of sophisticated adventure-romance doesn't do fabulous business unless there's something very special about it. But he felt he had that in the *Starry Night* script. For all Sy's baloney, he truly believed in what he did."

I remembered that Germy had liked the screenplay. "Did you read it?"

"Yes. It was terrific. But Sy needed box office clout *and* ecstatic reviews: 'An American classic! See it!' And Lindsay Keefe was his ticket. She's a star. Men, especially, love her. But more important, she's made quality movies. The critics take her seriously. Also, Sy knew that with the wrong stars, actors with a limited emotional range, *Starry Night* would be just another one of those 1950s Eastman Color—style rich-adventurers-on-the-Riviera movies, except set in the Hamptons and New York. But with actors who could show innocence, sweetness, under elegance, who could really deliver lines—because the dialogue is *so* good—he'd have a major commercial and critical hit. He was on his way; from what he said, Nick Monteleone was born to play this role. He was debonair without being too Cary Grant; he was manly, exciting. But Lindsay just ruined it. She walked through the part as though it was beneath her, and that was showing contempt for Sy's judgment, and for Sy. You didn't do that to him, not if you had any brains. It was a major no-no."

"Why didn't he kick her out of his house? Fire her?"

"Well, he wasn't going to fire her until he had a replacement, which was going to be terribly expensive. Lindsay had a pay-or-play contract: she got paid in full whether she made the movie or not. But he was looking for someone else. That's why he was going to L.A. As far as kicking her out of his house, he was first and foremost a smart operator. If for any reason he couldn't make a deal with another actress, he'd be stuck with Lindsay, and while she was living with him and having sex with him and getting little ten-thousand-dollar trinkets from him, she'd at least be semi-manageable. If he gave her the heave-ho, she'd be blatantly hostile."

"Do you think Lindsay knew Sy was seeing you?"

"Me specifically? No. Seeing someone? Definitely. Not that Sy told me, but he'd call her trailer from my house; they have those portable phones. She'd come to the phone and obviously ask where he was, and he'd take a long beat and then say, 'Oh, I'm, uh, having lunch with an old friend from college, uh, Bob, just ran into him. We're at this little hole-in-the-wall.' And she asked him where, and he took another beat and said, 'Uh, uh, Water Mill.' He was lying but letting her know he was lying."

"Did you get any sense from Sy that Lindsay might have someone on the side?" Bonnie smiled and shook her head, as if the possibility was too ridiculous to even consider. "Why not? Was he that terrific in the sack that she wouldn't want anyone else?" I confess: this was not strictly a police question. I wanted to know.

Maybe she knew I wanted to know. But she didn't want to tell me. "That's really not relevant."

"Yes, it is. I've got to know everything about him. I've got to know how he behaved toward people, toward women. It's important that I know what kind of number he was doing with Lindsay Keefe. Why are you so sure she wasn't stepping out?"

"Because Sy could satisfy anyone." She sat up, eyes right on me, trying to act detached, trying for a clinical look, like a woman in a white coat on TV selling April Showers douche. If she'd worn glasses she would have taken them off and looked sincere. "Sy was extremely adaptable with women. He could be whatever they wanted. Well, he couldn't be six three, with a thing that went from here to Philadelphia. But he could talk dirty or romantically. He could be an animal, or he could be Fred Astaire to your Ginger Rogers. Forget real passion, or real warmth—he wasn't capable of either. But he could be a sensational animal, a fantastic Fred Astaire. Or whatever it was you wanted."

Moose came to the door and started barking. She wanted to join the conversation. I couldn't risk letting her run out and setting off my neighbors' dogs in the dark. So we went back inside, back to the pineapple room. I switched on the lamp, and we took up our previously staked-out positions. But since we were getting along better, I decided it was safe to put my feet up on the bed. "What if I told you Lindsay was having a go at Victor Santana?" I inquired.

"No!"

"Well?"

"I'd say . . ." Bonnie gave it about five seconds' thought. The fresh air had brightened her eyes, cleared her head. "She probably could have gotten away with it. You know why? Sy would never believe it." She pulled up her legs, hugged her knees. "But if he did, that would have been it for her. He was *so* vindictive. If anyone—an agent, a studio executive—crossed him, he'd go on Sy's list. Seriously, he had this mental list, including a top ten, that kept changing. Whenever he could zing it to someone on his list, no matter what number, he would. And once you were on, you never dropped off."

I kept thinking Sy's vengefulness had to mean something. Maybe he'd confronted Lindsay, worked her over about her crummy acting. Or he'd found out about Santana. Maybe she sensed he was about to do damage to her: not just fire her but try and destroy her career, let everyone know she'd lost it as an actress. Would she have gone after him then? It added up, I thought. No. But almost.

Bonnie said: "I honestly don't think Sy knew. He wasn't in one of his I'll-rip-out-her-heart-with-my-teeth moods. He was very optimistic about his trip to L.A. Very relaxed too. He'd planned on taking the ten-fifteen morning flight, but instead he decided to go over to the set, to make nice to everybody because he knew morale wasn't all that high. Then he called me to meet him at his place. I'd never seen it before. He gave me the grand tour. Wanted to hear me say 'Gosh! Gee! My God!' "

"Did you?"

"Sure. If you're going to make a fuss over a house, this was the one to do it with."

"He was relatively relaxed?"

"He wasn't tense. He said he'd done everything but wave pom-poms and cheer on the set, and when he'd left, he could feel the change in atmosphere. Much more positive. And as far as the L.A. trip, he'd gotten copies of the screenplay to three different actresses, and he was going to take the seven o'clock evening flight, get a decent night's sleep, and the next day he was going to have breakfast, lunch and dinner with them. He was going to make one of them an offer that same night. He told me, 'I'm a little in the hole right now with *Starry*, but watch. I'm going to pull it out. It's going to be my biggest. My best.' "

I put my feet down and pulled the chair closer to the bed: straight talk time. I didn't like being so charmed by her. "Tell me why you threatened Sy."

"What are you talking about?"

"Bonnie, come on. You went to see him at the *Starry Night* set. We have witnesses. You said: 'Sy, you've just been a rotten bastard for the last time.' "

"You call this an interrogation?" Too cute. Like a snotty Upper East Side bitch.

"Fuck off, Bonnie."

"No, you eff off. Don't you know *anything* about people? Here's Sy Spencer, my former husband who's been coming to my house every day, having sex with me, telling me how he's missed me, how wonderfully *human* I am, how there's been an emptiness in his life since I've been gone despite all the other women and he's beginning to think he made a ghastly mistake. 'Ghastly' was his word. Sure, I knew it was almost all bull, but he said, I want you to come down to the set one day soon; I want you to see what I'm doing firsthand. So I went. Okay, it might have been better to wait for an engraved invitation: big deal. But when I got there, he told me to leave—so everyone could hear. I wasn't hurt. I was furious. And that *was* going to be the last time he was a rotten bastard. He came over to my house later and I wouldn't let him in. Over. Goodbye."

"Except it wasn't over."

"He called about two seconds later from his car phone. He said he felt *terrible*. He explained that if he had invited me on the set, it would look like we had something going, because he never took anyone to the set except big banker types. And he couldn't afford to have Lindsay focus on me; it would give the game away, and he wasn't ready for that yet. So he had to disavow me publicly. Naturally, he apologized all over himself and swore he was getting rid of her. As soon as she was gone, I'd have carte blanche to visit anytime I wanted. He said he was proud of me. I'd created *Cowgirl*. He wanted to parade me around, show me off to the crew." I didn't say anything. I didn't have to. She acknowledged: "Even if you were dying to believe him, you couldn't. For a sophisticated man, he could be such an ass."

The day's heat was finally rising off the land. The first night breeze blew through the window. The shade flapped, and Bonnie shivered. "Let me get you a sweatshirt or something."

"No, thanks. I'm fine."

Okay, I would have liked to see her in my old SUNY Albany sweatshirt. I would have liked to take her hands between my hands and rub them. The fact was, I liked having Bonnie in my house. Despite the insane circumstances, despite the occasional angry sparks that flared up between us, it was so comfortable. So much about her pleased me, from her not making cholesterol remarks when I handed her the TV dinner to her courage to her wonderful, glossy hair. But the great thing was, I realized, that in spite of the pleasure of her company, I had recovered from my obsession with her.

Maybe by allowing myself to remember what had gone on between us, I had broken her hold over me. Here I was, able to sit in a box of a room, inches away from her, question her, behave like a real cop. Her power was gone. I could relax, not fantasize about kissing her. Or about licking her lips, putting my tongue in her mouth. I was past that hump of desire. Hey, I thought, about time.

In that instant of self-congratulation, I glanced away from her mouth. If the shade hadn't been pulled down, I might have looked out the window, leaned back and watched the moon on the rise. But since there was no night sky to admire, no stars, I looked elsewhere and noticed the tautness of the nylon shorts stretched between her legs.

If we'd been characters in some porno cartoon, the God of Passion would, at that moment, have hurled down a bolt of lightning; it would have slashed across the sky, forked into two jagged spears and, at the exact same moment, zapped each of us, right in the pubes.

Just as my breathing deepened, Bonnie reached behind her, took the pillow and placed it in her lap. It was one of those unconscious gestures of self-defense. But without realizing it, she began fondling the edge of the pillow, rubbing the protruding corner with her thumb. Oh, God, I thought, she could be doing that to me. I got more and more excited. I could almost feel the soft pressure of her thumb.

I tried to picture Lynne, use her as a magic charm against what was happening: auburn hair, I said to myself, and big brown eyes, peaches-and-cream complexion. The waist, the gorgeous long legs. But I couldn't get the parts to add up to anything. I couldn't break Bonnie's spell.

But she could. Either she suddenly realized what she was doing or she simply sensed the change of climate in the room, because she tucked the pillow behind her again. "What else would you like to know?" she asked, all perky, cheerleadery, like she was going for the Miss Teenage Ogden title.

"Why did you lie to me?"

"You mean, when you first came to my house?"

"I came in, asked a simple question: When was the last time you saw Sy? You said you weren't sure, but you thought a few days before, at the set. I asked when you'd seen him before that, and you were kind of vague, but you thought it was about a week before, when he gave you the fifty-cent tour of his house. You said you hadn't spent much time with him."

"For someone who can't remember, you have a great memory."

If I looked at her, I'd see her crotch, or her breasts, or the hollow of her collarbone where the neck of her stretched-out T-shirt drooped. So I looked right past her and concentrated on the weave of the crappy wood headboard. "I asked if Sy had visited you at your house. Again, vague, but then you said maybe he had dropped by. Real casual. Just two old pals working on a movie script together. So what I want to know is, did you construct an alibi before I showed up? Or were you winging it?"

"Aren't you going to give me one of your warnings? You know: 'If you don't tell me the truth, I'll bust your head open.' "

"No. It's 'I'll bust your fucking head open.' Now, can we get on with it?"

"What's wrong?"

Just because I was making major eye contact with a headboard, she thought something was wrong? "Nothing's wrong. I asked you a question. I'm waiting for an answer."

"I had an alibi, but I was winging it too." She took a deep breath. "After Sy called, I drove over. He showed me the house, and—big surprise—we ended up in bed."

"Yeah, big surprise." I could picture him, his arm around her, leading her from room to beautiful room, the 'This could be yours again' unspoken. I could see his hand on her ass, guiding her into the guest room, closing the door. "When did you start screwing and when did you finish?"

She snapped: "Why don't you just come right out and ask me exactly what we did and how it was?"

"Why don't you shut your mouth? Understand something: you're here to work. I didn't bring you over for the pleasure of your company or to get off on hearing about your sex life." Thwarted desire is great for the disposition. "Now, from when to when?"

"From about one until two-thirty. Do you want to know if it was good for me?"

"I'm sure it's always good for you, sweetheart. Otherwise you wouldn't do it so often."

Well, I'd said it to hurt her. And it worked. Nothing like a deep, wounding insult to snap a woman out of enticing you, put her on the verge of tears. Works like magic. "It wasn't necessary to say that." Her voice quavered; it was costing her to fight back.

"Did anyone see you while you were at Sy's?"

"Mrs. Robertson. She's the cook." She spoke to the green blanket.

"Did you have any conversation with her?"

"Yes. Sy went to call California for a minute, to make sure all his meetings were in place. She and I talked."

"What about?"

"About our families, Sy's family. She'd begun working for us the second summer we were married. I hadn't seen her since the divorce."

"Was that before or after you got laid?"

"Don't talk to me like that."

"Before or after? Hurry up, Bonnie. There's a time bomb ticking. Robby Kurz is out there looking for you."

"Before."

"So you talked with Mrs. Robertson, went upstairs, had sexual intercourse . . . Is that better?" She didn't answer. Just then I got another picture of Sy, with his tight cap of short gray hair, climbing all over her, petting, fondling, squeezing, feeling her skin. "And then what? Come *on*. Any conversation?"

"Only about the three actresses he was seeing. Who I thought would be best for the part, and why. He said he'd call me from L.A. and give me a report."

"That's it?"

"Pretty near."

"What else?"

"He said he loved me."

"Did you believe him?"

"I believed he believed it for that second."

"Did you believe him?"

"No."

"Any signs he was under pressure?"

"Not really."

"So you kissed goodbye, and what?"

"He went to shower and pack, I guess. I went down to say goodbye to Mrs. Robertson, but she wasn't in the kitchen. So I went home."

"Did you speak to Sy again?"

"No. Never again. The next thing I know, I was out in the backyard, cutting some dahlias. The phone rang and it was Mrs. Robertson, telling me what had happened, that the police were there. I was just . . . I don't know what I was. What she was saying wasn't making any impact: it was like dialogue that doesn't ring true. Then Mrs. Robertson said, 'They asked me if he had anyone with him, and I told them no. What they don't know won't hurt them, so keep your lip zipped.' And I thanked her."

"That was some favor."

"She meant it to be. Please, don't hold it against her."

Like I'd really arrest Mark Robertson's mom, impound her rolling pin, throw her into a cage with a bunch of hookers and crack dealers. But I just said to Bonnie: "Go on."

"I was too upset to cry. I put on the news. And then I began to think: What if the cops question me? I read police procedurals. I'm a natural: the ex-wife. I didn't sit down and plan anything, but during the night—I couldn't sleep—I realized my fingerprints would be in his house and his in mine, so I shouldn't lie about that. And also to say I'd been to the set—although I didn't realize anyone had heard me mouth off to him."

"So you decided to tell the truth and just fudge a little on the details."

"Yes. That's right. I thought I'd be smart, not mention that I'd been sleeping with him, avoid a lot of embarrassing questions. But I wasn't sure about saying I hadn't been in his house that afternoon. There was no reason *not* to admit it: I certainly had no motive to kill him; I wouldn't be a suspect. But Marian Robertson had already said I wasn't there, so I thought: Well, if worst comes to worst, I'll tell the truth, but if not, I'll keep quiet—for her sake and mine."

"But worst came to worst, and you didn't tell the truth."

Bonnie stood, pulled the shade back about an inch so she could see out into the night. "I opened the door the next morning and . . ." She turned, leaned against the wall, faced me. "Please don't interrupt now. It's going to be hard for me to say what I have to say." I nodded. "I only spent that one night with you, but it was significant. Well, significant is an understatement. I fell in love with you. When you didn't call, I tried to call you. Your home phone is unlisted. And at your office, I left my name four times. I assumed the Homicide Squad is geared up so that its detectives get phone messages and either they answer them or . . . they don't.

"I was in pain beyond anything I want to talk about. And so ashamed. It took me a long time to get over it. But I did.

"And then there you were, five years later, on my doorstep. I didn't recognize you for a second, or maybe I just couldn't believe it, and then . . . I was so happy! I mean, Sy had been murdered the night before, a shocking, horrible thing. I'd lost a good friend, or at least an ex-husband, a lover, a producer. But all I could think was: Stephen is back! But instead of showing any . . . affection, you showed me your badge. It suddenly hit me why you were there. And you were so correct. So I got myself together. I figured this must be as awkward for you as it was for me. But the odd thing was, you didn't *seem* awkward. You were businesslike but nice. Every once in a while I saw a flash of the man I'd known that night. You have a wonderful smile, which you use to great effect. And I . . ."

Again she turned to the window. I kept quiet, because she'd asked me to and because I didn't know what to say. "I wanted you to want me again. I wanted your good opinion; I didn't want to be a tramp."

"You're not." I wished she would turn back again, but she just stood there, facing the drawn shade.

"It's my turn. You agreed. Fact: You picked me up in a bar. I came on to you; to put it mildly, I wasn't subtle. Fact: I brought you back to my house and, to use your terminology, got laid before I knew what you did for a living. Fact: I didn't even know what your last name was. I didn't know that until later, when you showed me your police ID. But all that didn't matter. I *knew* you were right. This was a miracle—and it was happening to me. So I just let go. I gave everything I had. Why hold back? It never occurred to me that you wouldn't understand completely, approve of me, rejoice in what we were doing, because we had this magic. You understood that.

"But five years after the fact, I was just some woman who felt you up in a bar, who couldn't wait to get you home. Then you asked me when was the last time I saw Sy. I wasn't going to say, Oh, yesterday afternoon, in his bed. Because I didn't want you to know I was still easy, that I'd dropped my drawers less then twenty-four hours before, for a man who was living with another woman: Lindsay Keefe, a world-famous beauty. You'd think that all I could possibly be was a quickie; I knew you'd assume that I had about as much value to Sy as I had to you, to any man: zero.

"I guess I wanted retroactive chastity. I wanted your respect. I wanted you to appreciate that my openness with you was exceptional, that you brought it out, that I wasn't a bimbo who'd do it for anybody. I never was like that. Well, maybe I'm not being totally honest. I don't know how many men I've been with: thirty, forty, maybe more." I remember telling the shrink at South Oaks that the women I'd had were into triple digits, but I didn't know whether it was two hundred or five hundred. Summers in the seventies and most of the eighties, I'd fucked my way from Hampton Bays to Montauk. Bonnie said: "You knew I was easy, promiscuous, whatever. You knew I had a past. But I thought: I have another chance now. Maybe he can come to understand that what happened between us was unique."

At last, she turned back. She was so tired; her face was puffy with fatigue. I thought: She's old and now she looks it. Lynne is so young.

"You know," Bonnie went on, "you never asked me what I did. The morning you came to question me and it came out that I was working with Sy, I was so glad. Because I wanted you to be impressed. I wanted you to think, Gee, she's a screenwriter. She's not a slut; she's an interesting woman. A good woman. She has worth." Bonnie stood tall and straight. "I wanted to be a woman you would be able to love. And that's why I lied to you."

A sharp breeze billowed the shade. It banged it against the windowsill. Bonnie jumped as if it had been the crack of a gun. I stood up and told her: "I know I've contributed to your unhappiness. I'm sorry."

She moved away from the window, until she was standing near the wood cube of a nightstand with its lamp, just inches from me. "How about this?" she proposed. "Instead of apologizing, why don't you just act with a little more decency? Stop talking about my fucking and screwing and getting laid as if I'm the Whore of Bridgehampton and you're a dumb, pig redneck in line for a gang bang. I'm a human being, and I'm in terrible trouble. If you're going to help me, why not be generous? Do it with a little kindness."

"All right," I said. The breeze was changing to a chilly late-August wind. I felt cold. "Sorry."

"Thank you."

Bonnie had goose bumps on her arms and legs. I went into my bedroom to get a sweater and some stuff for her. Moose trotted beside me. I tried to put a pair of socks in her mouth so she could bring them in to Bonnie, like a retriever. It would be funny. But Moose didn't get it; she let the socks drop out of her mouth and threw me an injured look, like I'd been leading her on to think she was getting a Big Mac.

When I turned out the light to leave, I noticed the red light flashing on the answering machine. Two messages. Loud ones: I lowered the volume. One was Germy, saying he had a good source for Yankee tickets. They were on the road, playing Detroit, but did I want to go when they got back? And Lynne: "Hi. I love you and I'm thinking about you. Honey, I *know* how busy you are, but could you call for just a second? I have to tell my mother if we want breast of chicken stuffed with wild rice or roast beef for the reception. You'll say it's up to me, but please, I want you to feel a part of this."

I called Headquarters and got Carbone. No trace of Bonnie yet, he reported. I haven't found her either, I said. But I'd checked her house and it didn't look as though she'd left in a hurry or taken stuff with her. My guess was she'd gone out for the evening and would be back later. Meanwhile, I had my list of her friends and acquaintances and was going house to house, checking them all out. So far, no luck. I asked if Robby had gone home, and Carbone said no, he was still in the office, reading over the files.

I went back inside and gave Bonnie a set of sweats and some socks. Women usually look adorable when they put on your clothes, with the sleeves all floppy, but she just looked normal in mine; they fit. She tucked the socks into the elastic of the pants. I said: "There were a couple of calls on my answering machine. Did they come in when I was over at your house?"

She reached for the sneakers I'd brought from her house. "One did."

"Were you able to hear it?" She nodded. I recalled Lynne's sunny "Hi, I love you . . ." I felt blue, for Bonnie's sake. "So you know I have someone."

"Yes."

"I'm getting married."

"Congratulations." Direct. No bitchiness.

"Thanks. She's really a find. Teaches learning-disabled kids. Wants all the things I want, you know? Stability. A family. And she's Catholic. That's important to me." Bonnie double-knotted her sneakers. "Lately—I guess since AA—I've been feeling this need to return to the Church. To have a place to pray. And for the ritual too, I suppose."

I was really going on. But I wanted to tell her that the last time I'd been to church, I was eight, and the Mass had been in Latin. I was wondering what it would be like if you understood it, whether you'd wonder, This is what the big deal was all about? and lose your faith. I was a little worried about that.

And I wanted to tell her about how when my mother had married my father, she'd agreed to raise any children Catholic. She knew her obligations. She dropped me off once a week for confraternity class, but after I made my First Communion she'd said: Steve, dear, you're a big boy. If you want to go to Queen of Whatever, you'll have to go on your bike. I would take you, but I'm on my feet all week. Sunday is *my* day of rest. I'd gone every single Sunday from that May until right after Christmas, when it began to snow. It was such a cold winter; the roads became a solid sheet of ice. After the spring thaw I never went back.

I started to smile then; I'd gotten to know Bonnie so well I could almost hear her: You're forty years old. Stop blaming your mother.

But I wanted to tell her how my mother hadn't sent Easton at all. She'd protected him from the killer Roman virus. Years later, when he was hanging out with the Southampton summer crowd, I'd heard him on the phone, going on about how his great-great-grandfather had been the Episcopal bishop of Long Island. I had no idea if my mother had told him that or if he'd made it up, but I knew it was a lie. What kind of person would lie about a God thing?

I was jabbering again. "Listen, I know I'm going to feel ridiculous when I go in and say, 'Bless me, Father, for I have sinned. It's been thirty-two years since my last confession.' But it's something I want to do, and Lynne's so supportive. Okay, I don't need someone to hold my hand and drag me over to the priest. But it's nice that the Church will be part of our life together."

Bonnie turned away from me, braced herself against the wall with both hands and leaned forward to stretch out her calf muscles. I felt so dumb. I was babbling like a silly woman trying to make an impression on a man fast, before he could bolt, and I couldn't stop. "Lynne's young for me. Twenty-four. But she's a really solid person. And great-looking. Long dark-red hair—"

"Calm down," Bonnie said, taking one last stretch. "I'm not going to make a pass at you."

"I am calm," I said, trying to sound it. "I just thought it wouldn't hurt if you knew what the score was."

"The score was, and is, that you're not looking for a sterile, forty-five-year-old Jew. Believe me, I know I'm not a hot ticket. But since you're going back in the prayer biz, which is admirable, you might want to check out your conscience with your Big Three. Would you have told me the score if you hadn't thought there was a good chance I'd heard your machine?"

"I don't know the answer to that."

"If I hadn't found out the score, would you have made a pass?"

"I don't know that either. I think there's still a certain attraction between us."

"It's more than a certain attraction."

"Okay, it is more. A lot more. All I can say is I hope I would have had the strength to fight it. But now that it's out in the open about Lynne, I feel a lot better. A lot safer, to tell you the truth. Don't you?"

Bonnie laughed, a delighted, spirited laugh. I would have loved it, except it was at my expense. She said: "Well, I wasn't worrying about my safety. But I'm glad it's out in the open. I'm glad for you. I wish you well. "And I wish myself well too," she added. "I want to try to get out of this mess, if that's possible. I want a future."

"I hope you have one."

"Well, you're the detective. What's the next step?"

"I want to check Lindsay's alibi. It sounds as if she was over in East Hampton, glued to the camera, the whole time, but I want to make sure. There's supposed to be a lot of dead time making a movie, right?" She nodded. "Tell me how that works."

"Whenever they change the setup to get another angle, they have to move the lights, the tracks, the camera. It depends on how complicated the shot is: If the crew hustles, it can take twenty minutes, especially if all they're doing is moving in a little for a close-up. But if they're turning around, reversing the angle com-pletely, all the lights that were in the background need to get put into the foreground. And crew members had been standing behind where the lights and camera had been, so the grips and prop men have to get in and hang pictures, put back furniture, that sort of thing. Then the script supervisor has to check the continuity; if a chair had an afghan draped over the left arm in the last scene, it has to have the afghan draped in the exact same way again. It can take an hour. Sometimes more."

"I want to find out if there was about forty minutes of dead time. Twenty minutes between the set and Sandy Court, twenty minutes back. Now, who would be most likely to know her where-abouts? Her agent? Ever hear of a guy named Eddie Pomerantz?"

Bonnie knew the name. "He's probably been around since D. W. Griffith. I doubt if he'd be on the set with her. He's a businessman, a deal-maker, not a hand-holder. More likely it would be a manager, or a personal assistant, if she had one of her own people."

"No. I don't think so."

"She might have spent time with other actors."

"No. From what I saw and from what Monteleone told me, no one could stand her. She's cold. Nasty. Like someone told her: Okay, Lindsay, you're absolved from all the normal rules of be-havior that everybody else has to live by."

"But she is absolved. When you're a big success in the movie business, you have license to behave badly. You know that. But even though Lindsay is a perfectly awful human being, she can act—when she wants to. She's beautiful, and she has the best breasts in the world. And the most important thing—people feel compelled to watch her. They can't take their eyes off her. She is a true star. So it makes sense that she wasn't hanging out with anyone from the cast. They're just plain actors, not stars. And Santana: even if he is her boyfriend, by late afternoon he'd be too involved in problems on the set to take care of her."

I thought back to the reports I'd read and all the interviews I'd done. "From what I can remember, Santana was doing whatever it is directors do the whole afternoon. There's not even an indication he took time out to go to the john; he was out there the whole time. So who else could have been with her?"

"A lot of stars get close with their makeup and hair people. Like regular ladies do with their hairdressers; it's a natural, easy intimacy. They might have been working on her."

"The idea is to break down Lindsay's alibi, not reinforce it."

"The idea is to find the truth. Anyway, the makeup person would at least know if Lindsay had any good friends on the set. As for off the set, if she went anywhere or needed an errand, there'd be a Teamster driver. But I can't imagine her saying, 'Jack, drive me over to Sandy Court so I can knock off Sy.' "

"How can I get the names of all these different crew people, fast?"

"Everybody gets a crew list. There should be one at Sy's house."

"When Sy was killed, he was on his portable phone with Eddie Pomerantz. Do you think there's a chance that word had gotten back to Pomerantz that Sy was going to see other actresses in L.A.?"

"Sure."

"How?"

"Because this is a gossipy business. More than that: a public business. *Everything*—contracts, food, cars, sex, lawsuits, flatulence—is talked about. My guess is, if Lindsay hadn't figured it out for herself, Eddie Pomerantz would know what was going on, probably from two or three different sources, and was trying to convince Sy to call off his trip."

"He claims they were arguing about some photo approval problems."

"To quote you," Bonnie said, " 'bullshit.' "

"Okay. I'm going out to see if I can dig anything up. I want you to stay right where you are."

Bonnie shook her head. "No, I have to get back."

"You're in a hurry to get arrested?"

"No. But I can't let you ruin your career by harboring a known fugitive. I mean that." She did.

"You may read mysteries, but you don't know shit about the law. You're not a fugitive. Not yet. You're just my houseguest. Relax. Read a book. Go to sleep."

"I can't sleep."

"So write a screenplay about a producer who gets killed, and figure out whodunit." She glanced past me, out into the house, toward the front door. "You're thinking of taking a nice little run after I go. Right, Bonnie? Maybe a nice ten-mile sprint over to Gideon's? Ask yourself: Do you want to put your best friend in the position of either protecting you or turning you in?"

"No."

"Then stay here. Promise me. I don't want my gut in a knot, wondering where you are, what you're doing, when I'm out there."

She reached out and took my hand. "Will you promise me that if you decide you can't help me, you won't arrest me?"

"Jesus, give me a little credit." She squeezed my hand, then let it go. "If I can't help you, I'll let you know. And you'll be on your own."

She said, "On my word of honor: No matter how it turns out, I'll never tell anyone you did this."

"I know." We stood together for a minute. Finally, I said: "I have to go now." But then I couldn't leave. "Bonnie?"

"What?"

"Want to kiss me goodbye?"

"I tried that once. It didn't work out so well."

"Yes, it did."

"No, it didn't. Anyway, you have bigger things to do besides kissing."

"Like what?"

"Like going inside and calling your fiancée and telling her chicken breasts or roast beef. And then going out to try to save my life."

CHAPTER 16

Easton had taken to his bed and hadn't gotten out, but at least he wasn't sleeping with his blankie pulled over his head anymore; he was lying on his side, his cheek propped up by his hand, and he was absorbed in a script. I was mature, big-brotherly. I yelled "Boo!"

He screamed, but he was so startled it sounded more like the squawk of an oversize bird. "Don't ever do that again!" he roared. "Don't you dare!" Two seconds later, he calmed down enough to ask, "What did you do, you dimwit? Sneak up the stairs so you wouldn't have to say hello to Mother?"

"Yeah. You know, I remember when you used to call her 'Mom'—before you decided to be born upper-class."

"At least I can get away with it. If you tried it . . ."

I liked it. Easton appeared to be coming out of his big sleep. Not exactly tear-assing around town—he was still in his striped pajamas—but to be fair, where did he have to go that needed a pair of pants? "You sound a lot better. When I spoke to you on the phone, it was like listening to a Quaalude commercial."

"I feel better. I've had some good news!"

"What?"

"I'd been planning on making a few calls, to see if I could find something resembling work. Never got around to it. Too upset. Well, a friend of Sy's whom I'd met, Philip Scholes, the director . . . He'd been renting over in Quogue in July and needed some Xeroxing done fast and called Sy to find out where to go. Sy wasn't in, but I offered to help and got it done for him in less than an hour. Well, he called me today! He's been needing an aide-de-camp, and when he heard about Sy, he started thinking about me. Bottom line is, he's paying for a round-trip ticket so I can go out to California and discuss the job with him!"

"Hey, terrific!" Easton smoothed down the top of his pajamas as if about to begin the job interview. "I'm really glad for you. It was such a rotten break with Sy. You'd come into your own, working for him; I'd never seen you so happy." My brother gave a fast, sad nod of assent, but I could see his allegiance was already transferring to Philip Scholes. "You can do something for me."

"What?"

"Get me a copy of the crew list. You have one?"

Easton got out bed, slipped into his backless leather slippers and padded into the next room, the study, the slippers flapping against his heels. "Why do you need it?" he asked.

"Checking out if certain people were where they claimed they were last Friday."

"Like who?"

"Like everyone who gave a statement. Routine shit."

But Easton shook his head, stubborn, not buying it. "Lindsay?"

"Lindsay."

"Steve, believe me, you're way off base."

"East, believe me, you've got such a hard-on for her you can't see straight."

"Well, maybe I do. But so did Sy. He never would have

gotten rid of her." He got a little petulant. "I *told* you that." He opened a drawer of his desk, drew out a manila folder with an orange tab, leafed through the neat stack of papers. He knew precisely what he was looking for and where. It was amazing; we were so alike in that regard. Everything had to have a place, be under control. For most of my drinking days, when I'd come off a bender, I'd find bottles and cans neatly lined up against the splashboard of the sink; in that last year before sobriety, when I started finding beer cans on the floor by my TV chair and, once, an empty bottle of wine cooler on the bathroom sink, I began to understand how lost I was.

Easton handed me the crew list. "I know what you told me about Lindsay, but we've got a lot of evidence that says you're wrong, that Sy was getting ready to bounce her." Easton looked unconvinced, and a little shaken by the threat to Lindsay. I tried to cheer him up. "Look, I'm sure she was in her trailer from four to seven, with a dozen unimpeachable witnesses. It's just that we found out that there was bad blood between her and Sy. Plus she was screwing around with"—my brother drew back his head, as though somehow he could avoid hearing—"Victor Santana." No expression, not even surprise, crossed his face. "And it turns out she may have known how to shoot a rifle. She had some firearms instruction for a movie she did. *Transvaal*."

Easton smacked the folder onto the desk hard, as if swatting a big, obnoxious insect. "But what about Sy's ex-wife? Damn it all. I thought you had her dead to rights."

"We're having doubts. Oh, by the way, did Sy ask you to buy a computer and a printer for her?"

Easton looked blank for a second. Then he stared up at the ceiling, as if searching out the answer there. I was getting a little scared. What if she was still lying? Finally, he said: "Right. I remember now. A bargain-basement computer and printer. Sy said forget IBM; too expensive. He'd heard the Korean ones were all right, and not to go above a thousand for the whole package."

"Did he say why he was sending it to her?"

"No. I assumed it was a consolation prize for rejecting her screenplay."

"Do you have a copy of the screenplay? *A Sea Change*."

"No." He paused. "Steve, I'm not telling you your business, but she had every reason to kill him."

"Why?"

"He passed on her script."

"Did you read any memos, any letters he sent her, that said 'I pass'?"

"No. That sort of thing he'd dictate to his secretary in the New York office over the phone; unless she faxed it back for him to proofread, she'd have signed his name. It wouldn't have come back to the house."

"So you don't actually know that he turned down her script."

"He couldn't have been trying to cement a relationship, for God's sake. He ordered her off the set. Very harshly. She must have been humiliated."

"Even if she was, it may not be motive for murder—unless she's crazy, and she just doesn't seem crazy."

"So you need a suspect, and now you're going to pick on Lindsay?" My brother, Mr. Moderate, wasn't acting so moderate. His neck and ears were flushed bright red. He was really working himself up, defending his damsel in distress. "*Why?* Give me one good reason why Homicide would go after her. The publicity?"

"Don't be a jerk."

"I think what you're doing is out-and-out disgraceful!" I shrugged. Easton stomped over to the leather couch and plopped down on it. He put his face in his hands and shook his head back and forth. I was about to break in, when he looked up.

Easton's mood had changed. He was quiet, thoughtful, no longer outraged; he seemed like a man beginning to acknowledge doubt. "I don't know; maybe I can't see straight when it comes to Lindsay—my adolescent crush. Maybe you're right."

"Right about what?"

"About Lindsay being less than the loving . . . well, not wife.

Less than the loving lover. It's possible she *could* have been stepping out. I can't swear to it. You see, no one would talk in front of me because I was Sy's boy, so to speak. But I did hear a few whispers about her and Santana."

"Was there any chance Sy knew about the two of them?" Easton gave it a lot of thought. Too much; it was getting late. I glanced at the crew list, then at my watch. Most of the *Starry Night* company was staying at a motel in the Three Mile Harbor section of East Hampton. Maybe I could catch them; some of them might have left town for a long weekend, but I didn't think many would voluntarily walk away from what was probably the most renowned vacation spot in America for three days on West Ninety-fifth Street or in Hoboken. "East, I've got to go."

"Sy played it very close to the vest," he said thoughtfully, not hearing me. "But I remember one thing. Maybe it's significant. Every Saturday, the week before, and the first two weeks of shooting, he gave Lindsay a present. Left it at her place at the table so when she came down for coffee, she'd find it. I don't mean a box of chocolates. I mean Art Deco diamond ear clips. Five-hundred-dollar cashmere shawls in a rainbow of colors: I think he gave her seven or eight of them at once. They were spilling over her chair; it was an incredible sight. A Piaget watch. Nothing he gave her cost less than two or three thousand, and the average was closer to five. But that last Saturday he was alive, all he left was a note: 'In tennis tournament. See you tonight.' "

"You saw the note?"

"Yes. It was just lying there. Not in an envelope, or even folded. And all right, maybe I'm not the gentleman I pretend to be. I guess you know that better than anyone. I have no qualms about reading other people's mail, especially not a note to Lindsay."

"Was he actually playing in a tennis tournament?"

"I would seriously doubt it. He wasn't a particularly good player. Limp forehand; he would have been eliminated long before lunch. And, Steve, this is the thing: I was in the house when

Lindsay came down. I saw her. She looked at her place setting. Nothing there. At her chair, under the table. Nothing. Then she read the note. And she *stormed* out of the room."

The only time I went into a bar anymore was when I was on a case; otherwise it was a risk I figured I didn't need to take. Still, even though it was business, the first thing I did when I walked into the Harbor Room at the Summerview Motel was to grab a glass of club soda, grip it hard and sip like crazy.

The Teamster drivers, a group of six, were big-bellied and Irish, beardless Santa Clauses who could hold their liquor. They were guys who had brothers or sons who were cops and who respected the shield. We got to be pals fast. Lindsay's driver was a two-hundred-fifty-pound, apple-cheeked guy named Pete Dooley.

"She doesn't get a chauffeured limo?" I asked.

"Uh-uh." Classic Brooklyn. "Maybe, you know, Stallone, somebody like that. Lindsay gets me and a station wagon." He glanced at my glass. "Want something stronger?"

"Can't." He understood. "What's she like, Pete?"

"I've had worse. She's a bitch. Big deal. Doesn't feel she has to say things like hello or please or thank you. But on the other hand, she don't snort coke, or mess herself, or cry and ask me to hook up a hose to the tail pipe."

"She ever talk to you?"

"Uh-uh. Just says where she wants to go, what she wants."

"What did she want on the day Sy Spencer was shot?"

"Nothing much. I picked her up at six in the morning. Didn't drive her home. Her agent came to break the bad news, and he took her back."

"Did you see her at all during that day?"

"Just, you know, around. Before lunch, she sent a P.A. over to me with a note. I should pick up a package at an underwear store on Hill Street back in Southampton. Pay them, get a receipt— and make sure to count the change. What a bitch! So I waited till after lunch, did it, came back."

"The package was already wrapped?" He nodded. "Did it feel light like underwear, or could it have been something heavier?"

"Underwear. Four hundred sixty-three bucks and eighteen cents' worth of underwear, and this is for someone who lets 'em bounce all the time. Never wears a bra. What the hell could cost over four hundred bucks?"

"Beats me. Fancy lace shit, maybe. She gave you the money in cash, Pete?"

"Yeah. Twenties."

I got another club soda. He and the other drivers went over the crew list with me. They said Barbara, her makeup lady, had gone back to the city for the weekend, but to try the hair guy and the costume lady. They pointed out their names and said they were probably somewhere around the motel.

Except for the fact that he had four or five superblond, Lindsay-color wigs in his room, on faceless Styrofoam heads, the hair guy could have passed for a cabdriver, or a steamfitter. He was about as stylish as the pizza sauce, cheese and pepperoni that had plopped down onto his shirt. He and a couple of other guys—he said they were grips—were watching one of those soft-core horny-airline-stewardess movies that motels pipe into rooms. All he could tell me was that in the party scene they'd been shooting, Lindsay, trying to show how wild and carefree she was even though she was hurting inside, ran into the ocean, fully dressed. On the TV, a stewardess with no underwear in a tiny skirt was bending over to serve a passenger a drink, and the hairstylist kept turning back to watch her, like he'd never seen a bare ass before and couldn't get over how wondrous it was. Lindsay, I reminded him. We're talking about Lindsay. Right, he said.

Lindsay's own hair had been under a wig cap, and they'd put on dry wigs for when she ran and a wet wig for when she came up out of the water; he'd stood there in the surf, styling it for her. When they'd called her for a scene, she'd always been ready. Where was she when she wasn't acting? In wardrobe or her trailer.

Yes, it was possible for her to have gone out and come back. Sometime late afternoon, there had been a turnaround that took over an hour. There was no big deal with the lights, but the Steadicam operator was having trouble with his harness. No one saw her during that time; she always liked her privacy. Nobody knew what she did: probably read magazines, because the trailer was filled with every magazine ever printed—she was probably looking for her name or her picture; they all did that. But maybe she slept, or meditated. Who knew? Who cared?

I thought that Lindsay would have been taking a big chance if she'd tried to slip away unnoticed, because of the time factor. Besides, as the hair guy explained, there could always be a wardrobe or script crisis that required her presence. Also, she was just too noticeable.

I asked if there were any other wigs around. Not white-blond ones. He said there were a couple of dark-brown ones in the makeup trailer, but they were for Nick Monteleone.

On the TV, one of the airline stewardesses was starting to play with another one's nipples; they were standing in the galley with their blouses off. I yawned. I was so wiped out. The grips gazed at the screen, nudged each other. I lost the hair guy's attention. I was too tired to care. I left the room.

The Summerview was standard motel, an elongated two-story rectangle with a balcony running the length of the upper floor. It was not for the socially ambitious visitor to East Hampton: no famous newspaper columnists or politicians or fashion designers would be found rubbing shoulders over the toaster waffles in the King of the Sea Coffee Shop. It was a place for normal people who wanted to sit on a perfect beach by day and get a little glamour by night: browse in shops they couldn't afford, or squint into passing Rolls-Royces to see if Steven Spielberg was inside.

The *Starry Night* production company had taken over the whole second floor of the Summerview. I walked along the balcony. From the sounds coming from room 237, either that TV was on, too, and one of the stewardesses had found a guy—or a couple was making it in a major way. I yawned again and waited about thirty seconds for them to come, but they didn't sound like that was on the agenda for a while, so I knocked, hard. About a minute later, the costume designer, Myrna Fisher, opened the chained door about two inches and peered out at me. She was a woman in her fifties, in an inside-out negligee. I showed her my shield and said I was sorry if I'd woken her, but I had some questions, and could I come in. She said she had a . . . a guest. I said I wouldn't keep them long. Just a few questions.

She unchained the door and let me in. In the bed, with the sheet pulled up to the top of his neck so just his skeleton head showed, was Gregory J. Canfield, Sy's production assistant—all one hundred and ten pounds and twenty years of him. "Hi, Gregory," I said.

"Hi," he peeped.

I wanted to tell him it was okay, I wouldn't call his mother, but instead I motioned to Myrna to take a seat at the round Formica table that stood in front of the tightly closed drapes. I sat on the chair across from her. "Tell me about Lindsay Keefe last Friday. How was she behaving? Did she see Sy Spencer when he came to the set? Anything you can think of."

For a minute, Myrna kept feeling for the buttons of her negligee, but since it was inside out, she finally settled for holding it closed. I couldn't believe she was a costume designer; with her dumpy figure, gray hair and blotchy skin, she looked like a Suffolk County payroll clerk. "It's the big party scene under a tent. Originally I was going to put her in a canary-yellow Scaasi—halter top, pouffy skirt—but then they changed the script and she had to run into the ocean, so she was in saffron silk pants and blouse. Cheapies: we had six of them. Elizabeth Gage jewelry. Charles Jourdan mules, but she loses them in the sand."

Gregory chimed in from the bed. "Mules are shoes. Backless, with heels." I nodded thanks. Myrna beamed at him before she turned back to me.

"Sy came into the wardrobe trailer sometime around eleven.

We'd just gotten Lindsay out of her wet clothes, wrapped her in a bath sheet. They said hello."

"Did they kiss or show any signs of affection?"

Myrna considered the question. "I think—I won't swear to it—he kissed her on the neck or shoulder. But I didn't believe it. They'd lost it."

"Lost what?"

"Their thing for each other. Well, his thing. It was always his. I've worked on three films with her, and I don't think she *really* . . ." She gave me a Know-what-I-mean? look; I gave her a Gotcha nod. "But Sy Spencer was crazy for her."

"What was the attraction, other than her looks?" I liked Myrna. She was a shrewdie. "That she was such an intellectual?"

"Sleeping with brainy men doesn't make you an intellectual. Lindsay's not really all that smart. But Sy was wild for her—and not for her mind. He was wild because she was so cold. I'd never worked on one of his projects before, but my guess is that women fell all over themselves trying to impress him. Lindsay couldn't have cared less. He wasn't one of her left-wing passion pots. He was just a rich sucker who could buy her things. She didn't care what he thought, or what he had to say. It made him *crazy* about her."

"But that stopped."

"Yes."

"Why?"

"Well, I don't know what went on in their bedroom." She snatched a quick, happy eyeful of Gregory. "But you must have heard there was a problem with her performance. I'm sure that didn't sit well with him. And also, she's very boring. She talks about her approach to a character—for hours. Or she gives you a speech on racism or on world hunger. She acts like she's the only person in the whole world with a conscience—except her boyfriends with *Viva Zapata!* mustaches. That's ridiculous. Most of us care. Some of us are charitable. But that's not how real people talk when they're getting a seam pinned. Lindsay does, though. She can't talk about normal things, real life, because she's dead inside. And in the long run, Sy Spencer was no necrophiliac."

"That means—" Gregory began.

"I know what it means, Gregory." I turned back to Myrna. She was smiling, charmed by Gregory's earnestness. "What happened after Sy kissed her?"

"Not much. He said he was off to L.A., that he hated to go and he'd miss her terribly. I didn't believe a word of it."

"Anything else?" Then I added: "Anything about money?"

"Yes. Right. She said she needed some cash, and he said all he had was the money he needed for the trip, but by that time she was going through his pockets—patting them, like police do—and she took out a wad of bills."

"What did he say?"

"Nothing. He let her have it. My guess is, it had happened before."

"And then?"

"They both said, 'I love you, darling,' 'I'll miss you, angel,' and he left."

"Did she seem sad? Upset?"

"Actually? Angry. She held that wad of cash like it was his balls. She squeezed as hard as she could."

I sat in the office of the Summerview. The night manager had been more than cooperative. She'd stopped just short of curtsying when I'd asked to use the phone, and she'd begged to be allowed to bring me coffee. Either she was a cop groupie or she was running numbers out of there. Probably numbers.

I called Carbone at home and told him that since I'd been in East Hampton anyway, checking out Bonnie's friends, I'd dropped over at the Summerview on a hunch; I explained how I'd gotten the catalog creep to admit he'd paid Bonnie off the books, and now I had a witness who'd seen Lindsay dredging in Sy's pocket and coming up with a bundle of cash, and another who'd taken five hundreds' worth of twenties she gave him to pay for underwear.

"The case against Bonnie is starting to look feeble," I remarked. He didn't respond, which I took as agreement.

I asked if he'd left Robby at the office, still reading files. Carbone said no, that he'd gone into the squad room right before he'd left and Robby hadn't been there. One of the other guys had told him Robby had rushed out, as if something was up. Like what, I wanted to know. Carbone hadn't a clue, but knowing how Robby lacked stamina, maybe he'd just had to hurry and get home and hit the sack.

I hung up feeling edgy. Robby was on a rampage; he'd been enraged enough to lie about my drinking. A guy that crazed doesn't just go to sleep.

I drove west, toward Bridgehampton, then dipped south of the highway, past Bonnie's house. No sign of Robby: Thighs had just come on duty and was parked across the street from her place. He was devouring a bologna-and-American-cheese hero; the mayonnaise on his chin glistened in the moonlight. I asked, She turn up yet? He shook his head.

I had him come inside with me, up to her office. Bonnie had loads of files, but I couldn't believe it. For a writer, she had no sense of letters; it looked as though she'd never figured out how to alphabetize. Most of her papers were in folders or manila envelopes, but these were stuffed, randomly, into drawers or piled on an old-fashioned wooden in/out box. Eventually I found her *Sea Change* file. My heart started to hammer. I opened the folder as if half expecting it would blow up in my face. But there were Sy's memo and his note: "Adore it!"

I had Thighs read over my shoulder. I told him the case against Bonnie was falling apart, and he might as well pick up a few points by helping it collapse, bringing in the file showing that although Sy hadn't written, Sure I'll make your movie, he hadn't rejected her screenplay either, not by a long shot. You're sure you don't want the points? Thighs asked. You found this. Hey, I told him, it's okay, buddy. You'll be doing me a favor. I don't need points anymore; I've gone as high as I can go in the squad. And all I've been doing lately is sabotaging the case against Bonnie. Carbone and Shea already think I'm on some crazy crusade to clear her, and since she's going to get cleared anyway, you might as well be the hero. I sensed Thighs was no great fan of Robby's, so I added: I guess you've heard Kurz is nipping at my ass on this one. He wants to nail her. I'd appreciate it if you could help me out. Thighs said, My pleasure.

Good: I wanted a witness that the memo and Sy's note really existed. I couldn't believe that if Robby came back he would actually destroy them. But I wouldn't have put it past him to lose them for a few days.

I figured any guy who could eat bologna, American cheese and mayo was my kind of guy, a human septic tank, so after I left, I stopped at the deli, got a six-pack of Yoo-Hoo and some Ring-Dings and Devil Dogs, and brought them back to Thighs. That sealed the deal. Jeez, he said, Steve, thanks a hell of a lot. Let me pay you for all this. You sure? Oh, hey.

He was mine.

Moose began to bark as I pulled into my driveway, and I had such a surge of gladness that I forgot I was stupid with fatigue. I pictured walking in to the dog's delirious tail-wagging, hand-licking greeting, then rushing into the pineapple room, sitting on the edge of the bed and having Bonnie put her arms around me, draw me close, press her cheek against mine and whisper, Please, just hold me. The homeyness of it made it such a enticing vision.

I squared my shoulders, stood up straight and braced myself. I knew from AA how fatigue can make you vulnerable; you cannot stand firm when all you want is comfort. The mood I was in, it wouldn't be the consolation of booze that would seduce me. It wouldn't be wild sex. It would be sweetness, and soft conversation.

I strolled inside, gave Moose an indifferent, platonic pat and checked my answering machine. Just Lynne: "I guess you must be *very* busy. Good night, Steve. I love you and I'm thinking about you. Speak to you tomorrow."

I was wiped; maybe that was why Lynne's understanding irritated the hell out of me. Why, for once, couldn't she say, You self-centered fuck, why can't you take two minutes and pick up the phone? But then I thought: No. You had to appreciate how serene she was, how adult, how truly superior. Only then, fortified, did I go in to see Bonnie.

She put the Stephen King book she'd been reading on the nightstand. She'd taken a shower, washed her hair; it was shiny and wet, pulled back tight, braided. She'd changed into the clean pink T-shirt I'd brought from her house. The plaid blanket was pulled up high, prim, almost to her neck, as if she'd decided to become the definitive old maid. Except she gave me her wonderful, welcoming beacon of a smile.

"Hi!"

"How's it going?" Hey, forewarned is forearmed. I was on alert. I could afford to be slightly friendly.

"It's going okay," Bonnie said. "I had a couple of minutes of panic. I mean, I've been making jail jokes, but when I actually think about it—"

"Then take it easy on yourself. It's been a rough time. Don't think about it."

Hearing Lynne's message had really cleared my head. Bonnie was the next couple of days; Lynne was the rest of my life. The only thing that made me edgy was sleeping in the same house with her. I'd be okay. I was so knocked out I'd probably be asleep as soon as I took off my shoes. But I was troubled by a picture of Bonnie tiptoeing through the dark house and slipping into my bed and murmuring, Please, just hold me. Any touch—her fingers grazing my chest, her legs brushing against mine—might make me lose all sense. I couldn't afford to be faced with that. My palms started to sweat. I pretended to be kneading sore muscles and wiped them on my pants. I decided I would just lock the door of my bedroom.

Then I sat, but I maneuvered the chair so it was farther from her bed. Okay, this was better. The situation was under control. "Let me give you the Lindsay Keefe story," I said. I told her, in detail, everything I'd learned in the course of the investigation.

She sat with her arms hugging her knees, like a kid at a campfire listening to a riveting ghost story. I waited for her to say, Wow! Good work!

Except she just shook her head and said: "Get a good night's sleep. You need it."

"What do you mean?"

"I mean, you'll think better in the morning."

"Stop that patronizing crap. It irritates the hell out of me."

"You call this a case against Lindsay?" Bonnie demanded.

"She had motive. He was going to fire her."

"So she'd hire a lawyer and fight it. Or hire a publicist and leak word about what a disaster *Starry Night* is and how she couldn't compromise her standards of excellence by working on such a consummate piece of schlock."

"Come on. Word was around the movie business about what a disaster she was. If Sy fired her, it could ruin her." Bonnie gave me a fast roll of the eyes, a supercilious you're-not-an-insider look. "I want you to stop being so fucking condescending, Bonnie."

"Who do you think Sy was? A 1939 mogul with a big cigar, a Louis B. Mayer who could say, 'You'll never work in this town again'? No. Sy was a first-class producer, which is a good thing to be. But Lindsay's a star. One crummy performance wouldn't do her in."

"You're the one who said her agent was probably begging Sy not to fire her."

"That's his job. But what if Sy *had* told him to stuff it and did fire her? Lindsay would survive. Listen, she's as cold and calculating as they come. I'm sure she knew getting the ax wasn't going to help her career, but she also knew it wouldn't hurt it, not that much. Certainly not enough to kill for."

"You're assuming she's rational," I said.

"Do you have any evidence that she's not?"

I edged forward in the chair. I wanted to convince her, get her over to my side. "I have to trust my gut in this business, and I'm telling you, she's flawed. Beautiful, yeah, but something major is missing. A realization that she's human. And when Sy withdrew from her, first as her number one fan, then as her boyfriend or fiancé or whatever the hell he was, it was a sign she wasn't perfect. And she couldn't take it."

"I hate to say it, but you have a better case against me."

"You know, you can read all the stupid mysteries you want, but you're still a total ignoramus when it comes to homicide."

"How did she get from the set in East Hampton—without being seen—to Sandy Court?"

"I'll figure it out."

"How?"

"What are you, her goddamn defense lawyer?"

"And even assuming she knows something about a rifle, beyond holding it right so she looks like she knows how to shoot, where would she have gotten the weapon?"

"In a gun store, you jerk."

"You have to register in New York State, don't you?"

"They have to record the sale of rifles. But she'd give a false name."

"And the gun store owner wouldn't recognize her and be overjoyed that Lindsay Keefe had bought a .22 from him? He wouldn't tell the world? Tell the police?"

"She's an actress," I insisted. "Do you think she'd walk in with blond hair and tits, or would she disguise herself—maybe in one of Nick Monteleone's wigs?"

"Where would she have hidden a rifle? Under the bed she was sharing with Sy? In Mrs. Robertson's cookie jar?"

I got up. "Anything else?"

"Don't get angry just because I don't agree with you. Listen: I used to be a pretty good shot. My dad gave me a Marlin for my twelfth birthday, and I went hunting with him and my brothers on and off for the next six years. If I had to shoot someone through the head from what . . . fifty feet?"

"Yeah."

"Okay, if I decided on the spur of the moment to blast Sy, could I get him in the first round? Maybe. If I'd planned a murder, took target practice, I'd say I'd have had a good chance. But to think someone like Lindsay—who had a couple of hours of instruction with some sex-crazed white hunter she'd been sleeping with—is going to be able to fire two bullets into Sy and score bull's-eyes both times, then you should hang up that gut you trust and go into another business."

I didn't say good night. I didn't say anything. I just stalked out of the room.

CHAPTER 17

This is why I knew I wouldn't be able to sleep:

The gallon of coffee I'd drunk during the day.

My fears about Bonnie. Fear one: The case against her was unraveling, but the sideburnless, crew-cut, pink-faced assistant D.A., who looked like a cross between a pig and a Ku Klux Klan grand kleagle, might still be able to get an indictment and then a conviction. Fear two: Bonnie, knowing her own innocence (or her own guilt), would steal out of the house during the night, and none of us would ever see her again. Fear three: She'd slip into my bedroom, and I'd have to reject her. Fear four: Knowing I'd never be able to reject her, Bonnie would slip into my bedroom, keep me at it the whole night, then use her hold over me, get me to build a case against someone—anyone—else. Fear five: Bonnie Bernstein Spencer was a killer, whose rage was surpassed only by her coolheadedness and coldbloodedness. The girl with the great smile was a criminal genius, who would always be one step ahead of the smartest cop. Fear six: Bonnie was what she seemed to be, a good and smart and thoroughly decent human being. If I did manage to prove her innocent, she would spend the rest of her life alone, without ever having had someone to love her.

Also, I couldn't sleep because of the dry tickle in the back of my throat, and I couldn't shake the memory of how an icy, malty beer could soothe it.

And I couldn't sleep because I sensed this case was crucial, a turning point in my life. Was it that the crime had been perpetrated on home ground, the South Fork? Was it the coincidence that the victim and I, two men of the world, had used (or been used by) the same woman? Was it some cockeyed sense of Brady family honor, that this case couldn't wind up in an Open Investigation file drawer; I had to come through for Sy because he had come through for my brother? Or was I wide awake simply because this would be my last homicide investigation as a free man, unencumbered by husbandly obligations? Soon I would have to be someplace at five-thirty. To choose among swatches for our upholstery. To install our energy-efficient room air conditioner–dehumidifier. To set up the barbecue for the swordfish steaks we'd serve when Sister Marie, the principal of Lynne's school, came to dinner. To umpire our Little Leaguer's Little League game.

Forget sleep. I couldn't even rest. The coffee sloshed around in my stomach, and I felt sick, disoriented, frightened, the way a kid feels in a small boat on a rough sea when he loses sight of land. I lay in bed, worrying whether I should leave my bedroom door the way it was, half open, so I could hear if Bonnie made a move to escape, or whether to close it, lock out the possibility of a silhouetted figure whispering "Are you asleep?"

I kept flipping from my side to my back around to my other side, trying to get my stomach to calm down. But all that happened was I wound up so mummified in the sheet I had to get up and unwrap myself. Then I lay back down and stared at the dark rectangle of ceiling. I couldn't get my motor to stop racing.

Another reason for insomnia: Somewhere along the way, as

I'd been following the Spencer case, had there been a signal I'd missed, a sign I should have read?

In the stillness, I heard my breathing, shallow, rapid. God, did I feel lousy. My neck and left shoulder were horribly sore, as though I had been punched again and again. The left side of my head began to throb. I tried to recall the relaxation technique they'd taught us at South Oaks, but I forgot whether you inhaled through your nose and exhaled through your mouth, or vice versa.

A stab of pain shot down my arm. My heart raced. I put my hand against my chest; my skin was clammy. The nausea wouldn't go away. A coronary? No, exhaustion.

No, a stroke. I kneaded my upper arm. The pain was receding, but the triceps felt almost numb. God, could this actually be a stroke? I thought: By the time I get up the courage to cry out for Bonnie, it'll be too late. All I'll be able to do is dribble and make mewing-kitten noises.

Just then, instead of falling into a coma, I fell sound asleep. It was such a deep, dreamless sleep that when I woke up and it was still dark, I thought: Holy shit, I slept the clock around. But then I propped myself up on my elbow and looked at the green gleam of the clock: three forty-six.

I performed my customary back-to-sleep ritual. I turned my pillow over and puffed it up into a mountain, fluffed out the sheet, turned the clock facedown to hide its garish, Emerald City glow. No good. I was wide awake.

I knew what had woken me. I wanted Bonnie.

Moonlight slipped past the curled edges of the shades, and the white walls of the pineapple room gleamed. I heard a rhythmic thumping, but it was only Moose's big tail slapping against the wood floor, applauding the prospect of unexpected fellowship. Bonnie stirred for a second, but the happy tail thump was obviously a familiar, comforting night sound. She curled back up, fast asleep.

I could have walked away right then. It would have been

easy. Nothing to tempt me: no languorous arm draped across the narrow single bed, no naked leg or bare hip to tantalize. The only part of her not covered by the plaid blanket was her head.

But on the chair were the sweats I'd lent her, neatly folded, and dropped on the floor near the bed, less neatly, her own T-shirt. And the thin band of sheer white that was her underpants. That did it.

I sat on the edge of the bed, kissed her hair, whispered her name. She raised her head, opened her eyes. No fluttery eyelashes and pseudo-dopey where-am-I? looks. Bonnie knew.

"What do you want?"

"To visit." I flashed what I hoped was a devil-may-care smile. Charm wasn't doing it, though. There was no smile back. I drew aside the blanket. She was naked. "See? You knew I was coming. You got all dressed up for me." I lay down on the bed beside her. In the moonlight, the slender strips of white where a two-piece bathing suit had prevented a tan shone with a pearly luster, like the inside of a seashell. "A host has an obligation to entertain his guest." I kissed her cheek, her mouth, the demarcation line between her dark chest and white breasts. I was soft and gentle, demonstrating: I'm not just out for nooky. See? I've got finesse. Style. Technique.

Bonnie didn't arch her neck, or murmur a sophisticated That feels marvelous. No, she smoothed my hair off my forehead, away from my temples. It was such a loving gesture, and so soothing, that it caught me off guard. I stopped the casual kissing. I reached for her hand, but she kept it to herself.

"Tell me," she whispered. "Does this visit mean something?" Direct words, forthright gaze. Give me the truth, they said. Total bullshit: I knew I could tell her whatever I wanted to tell her. She was so goddamn gullible. "Or are you here . . . is it just for tonight?"

She made it so much harder on herself. Why couldn't she simply pretend it didn't matter to her? She all but walked through

life wearing a sandwich board that said BIG MOUTH BUT COM-
PLETELY VULNERABLE in huge red letters. What can you say to
someone like that?

"Just for tonight, Bonnie." We lay side by side, barely apart.
If either of us had taken a deep breath, skin would have grazed
skin.

"Another one-night stand? That's all you want for us?"

I closed my eyes because I felt tears. "Yeah."

"Can't offer me anything better?"

"No."

"Does it make any difference that I love you?"

"No, it doesn't." Before I could tell her how sorry I was, she
pressed her fingers against my lips.

"Let me cut you off at the pass," she said. "Don't say 'I'm
sorry.' Not that you would. Apologizing for not being able to love
me . . . Well, that would be cheap, and you're not cheap."

"Neither are you."

"I know."

She shifted that fraction of an inch so we were touching. I
ran my hands over the whole length of her body. She was silky,
sleep-warmed. I couldn't believe the softness of her.

"Wait. Listen to me," she said. "Here are my one-night-stand
rules. You can't say 'You're beautiful.' You can't say 'You're a
truly fine person.' " She paused. "And you can't say 'I love you.'
Other than that, anything goes."

She put her arms around me and guided me on top of her.
Slowly, as if we had weeks, years, all the time in the world, she
let her fingers drift down my back, over my ass, and then between
my legs. I was so overwhelmed by finally being able to touch her
again, kiss her, that I felt I was going to lose it.

I did. Suddenly tears were drenching my face.

"Stephen, are you okay?"

"Yeah. Just over-something. Overtired. Overstimulated."
Bonnie wiped my cheeks with the sheet. It didn't help that she

was so tender. I patted her hand, then pushed it away. "I'm okay. And listen, nobody calls me Stephen."

"You don't have to have sex with me if you don't want to, Stephen."

"Does it feel like I don't want to?"

"No, it feels downright enthusiastic. But it and you may be two distinct entities."

"Well, it and I want to make love to you."

So we did.

Afterwards, I brought her into my bedroom, and before we slept, we made love again. My memory of our other night, five summers before, did not begin to do her justice. I had remembered the passion; I had forgotten the sweetness.

Except this time there were rules: Bonnie's Rules of Play for the One-Night Stand. No You're beautiful. No You're a truly fine person. No I love you. The whole time we were making love, and after, just lying there, talking softly about nothing much, I wanted more than moans, cries, animal grunts, sighs, inane sweet nothings. But all I could think of to say were the no-nos, words of love and admiration. I thought: Well, she's certainly mastered the fine points of the game; only an ace at one-night stands could anticipate the need for such rules.

I had to play fair. I didn't want her to think I was cheap. So I didn't call out, I love you. But I tried to show her.

When we finally fell asleep, my head was resting against hers on the pillow. I held both her hands tight in mine, close against my heart.

Magic hour.

Bonnie had made the bed while I took Moose for a run, but she'd folded the sheet over the top of the blanket, and there was too much sheet showing, so when she went into the shower, I fixed it. She spotted it right away. "You remade the bed."

"It wasn't right."

"You're not supposed to care about order. It's not masculine."
She was sitting on the bed in her shorts and one of my undershirts.
She gripped the mug of coffee the way a guy does; she didn't use
the handle the way a woman is supposed to. "Order is feminine,"
she announced. "Chaos is masculine."

"After last night you're telling me I'm not masculine?"

"Don't you ever go to movies?" She held up her hands and
positioned her thumbs at right angles to her outstretched fingers,
like a director framing a shot. " 'CAMERA TRACKS INTO COP'S
BEDROOM. Total chaos. Suspiciously gray sheet half-off mattress.
CLOSE ON night table, where WE SEE gun, empty whiskey bottle,
crumpled papers, remains of last week's Chinese takeout and
overflowing ashtray.' So how come you're neat?"

"Good cops are organized. I like things under control. The
real question is: Why are you such a slob?"

"What are you talking about? I'm not a slob."

I laughed. "Give me a break, Bonnie. I executed a search
warrant. You don't pair your socks. You just throw them into a
drawer, along with your bras, which look like a pile of spaghetti.
Your teaspoons and tablespoons are all mixed up. Oh, and your
papers aren't in alphabetical order; they don't make any sense."

"Neatness doesn't count. Cleanness counts."

"You haven't thrown out a magazine or a paperback in ten
years. What kind of person keeps a *TV Guide* from 1982?"

"Obviously not your kind of person."

Well, there it was. Ever since we'd woken up, a little before
six, Bonnie had been withdrawing from me. Not the injured-female
bit, with cold, clipped responses to my questions. No, Bonnie was
all thumbs-in-the-belt-loops, howdy-partner friendly: Gee, OJ and
raisin bran would be terrific. Thanks. Of course she understood
she had to stay in the bedroom once I went out, that the windows
in the main room weren't covered and on the off chance someone
dropped by . . . And sure she'd be glad to tell me anything more
I wanted to know about Sy. Discuss the whole case? You bet!

She could have been anyone I'd put up for the night—a

visiting cop, someone grateful for bed and breakfast, a cheerful, outgoing kind of guy. When she'd finished the last spoonful of milk and put the cereal bowl back on the storm window I'd used as a tray because I didn't have a tray, she'd smiled and said, real chipper: You know what's good about you? Your cereal is crisp. I can never keep things from sogging up out here. Back in Ogden, you can keep Cheerios for *decades*.

"Bonnie, let's clear the air."

She smiled a TV weathergirl smile: much too many teeth. "The air's clear." She reached over and picked up my clock; it was still facedown. "Look, it's almost seven. The night's over. The sun's shining." Her smile faded. Her lips pursed together, serious, prim. "It's time to work."

But I kept at it. "I'm not much of a bargain, you know."

"I know."

"Something's missing. I'm defective." No argument, no agreement. She sat silently, with too-perfect posture. "The thing is, with Lynne I have a chance of coming closer to having a normal life than I ever thought I could." I waited for Bonnie to cry out: But do you love her? What about me? She said: "Let's talk about motive."

"It's not that I don't care about you. You know I do."

"I'm sure every single person in the *Starry Night* crew had some grudge against Sy."

"Bonnie, if we talk, it'll make it easier for you."

"Sy cheated people on money, he lied to them about opening credits, he humiliated them in front of fifty people. So there are seventy, eighty people right there in East Hampton who you'd think had a motive to kill him. And another five or six hundred people he'd hurt or insulted over the years. What do you do in a case like this, where the murder victim is an SOB?"

I'd only been trying to help her. But if she wanted to work, I'd work. "You look for real injury," I explained. "Was there anyone Sy really harmed, or was about to harm? Not just hurt feelings, where someone might say, 'I hope Sy Spencer dies.' I'm talking damage that could destroy someone's life. So that's the main thing; you look for serious grievances. You rule out people who are just pissed. Pissed doesn't count. With one exception. Nut jobs. Maybe Sy promised some actor star billing three movies ago and the guy wound up with his name at the tail end of the movie, next to something like best boy. A normal guy would forget it. A nut job could have spent two, three years plotting revenge."

"How often does that happen?"

"Not often. Even nuts get bored. They find new villains. So unless we get bogged down—I'm talking completely, totally stumped—we wouldn't do anything more than a routine check on a victim's distant past. See, nuts usually don't suffer in silence. They send hate mail, make threatening phone calls. And a guy like Sy would be smart; he's seen too many celebrities hit by psychos to ignore those kind of threats. Right?"

"Definitely. If Sy had thought someone crazy was out to get him, he'd have probably gone the whole route. Hired bodyguards, even. Sy had no physical courage."

That surprised me. He was so smooth. "Give me a for-instance."

Bonnie thought, rubbing her forehead to help herself along. "Like one time, we were riding, up in the Grand Tetons. Sy got thrown. Nothing happened; he wound up with a sore behind. You couldn't blame the horse; it saw a bear and got spooked. But he wouldn't get back on that horse for anything, even when I kidded him about being a scaredy-cat—which, okay, I admit might have not been my most sensitive moment in my career as wife.

"But it didn't take an actual event to frighten him. Sy could get scared by nothing. We'd be walking in the theater district and if a couple of black guys who didn't look like they were headed for an NAACP fund-raiser at the Pierre walked by, he'd stiffen. Just a little, but you knew in the back of his mind he was seeing headlines: 'Producer Castrated by Rampaging Youth Gang.' What I'm getting at is, if someone from his past had been gunning for Sy, he'd have gotten protection. You'd have heard about it."

"Good." I went into the kitchen for another cup of coffee. When I came back I started telling her: "You know, talk about riding, my family had a farm when I was little. We kept a horse. Prancer. I haven't ridden for years, but—"

"What do you want from me?" Bonnie asked softly.

"I don't know," I answered, just as softly.

"Whatever we had ended an hour and a half ago. Just remember that. And no matter what happens today, what you find or don't find, I'm out of here by five o'clock. So I don't want to know that you rode horsies when you were a little boy. I don't want to hear about your first Yankee game. I don't want you to tell me how you got the monkey off your back after Vietnam."

"I told you about that? My drug problem?"

"Your heroin problem. You told me. I don't care about it. And I don't care about your alcoholism—which obviously made you forget you told me about your heroin addiction."

"What did I say about heroin?"

"Not much. It was when you were telling me about Vietnam."

"I told you about Vietnam?"

Bonnie said coldly: "It must have been one heck of a night for you, that you remember so much of it."

"I remember enough to know it was one hell of a night."

"Do you remember talking about why you became a cop?"

"No. I didn't think I ever really gave it much thought, much less talked about it."

"You told me how terrified you'd been after you got back from the war. Walking down a street, if there was a crumpled-up Burger King bag on the sidewalk, you'd stop short, almost panic. Remember telling me that?" I didn't say anything, but I couldn't believe I'd told anyone about that time; my heart would bang in my chest and I'd want to scream out, Clear the area! Clear out! Watch that crumpled Burger King bag! We can all get killed! "We were talking about how come you chose something potentially dangerous like being a cop instead of something safe, and you said, 'This will show you how irrational I was—I thought of being a cop as safe, maybe because I'd be armed. I was so goddamn frightened all the time.' "

"I didn't realize how I opened up to you, how I—"

Bonnie cut me off. "Well, it doesn't matter now. I want you to understand: I don't give a damn about what you did in Vietnam, or what Vietnam did to you. I don't give a damn about your drugs or your alcohol or your recurring nightmares. I don't give a damn about *you*. And while we're at it, I don't give a damn about your fiancée's long auburn tresses or her commitment to the learning disabled. In another ten hours—unless, God forbid, I happen to wind up in court and you're a witness for the prosecution—we'll never see each other again."

I got up and walked out of the room. I remember nothing about what I thought or felt. I do remember rinsing the breakfast dishes and sticking them in the dishwasher and pouring what was left of the milk into the container. Then I went back in. Bonnie was the same; maybe even more remote.

If she had been in a movie, they'd have had some lens that would make her look as if she was moving back, farther and farther. Eventually she would become just a point of light. And then she'd vanish.

"Tell me who had a real motive to kill Sy," she said.

"You."

"Who else?"

"Lindsay."

"You know what I think of that theory."

"I don't give a flying fuck what you think," I said. "She's on the list."

"Anyone else?"

"Some guy who invested in *Starry Night*, a guy from Sy's days in the meat industry."

"Who?"

"Mikey LoTriglio."

"Fat Mikey?" Bonnie's face got all pink and glowy; just hear-

ing his name seemed to make her happy. She forgot to be remote.
"I love Fat Mikey!"

"You love him? He's a bad guy. Mafia."

"I know. But for a bad guy, he was *so* wonderful. Well,
wonderful to me."

"What do you mean?"

"He knew I was a writer, so he was convinced I didn't have
the foggiest notion about how the real world worked. He became
very protective. Asking, 'Sy treatin' you good?' I was always taking
these ten-mile-long hikes through the city, and he didn't like it.
Not one bit. He told Sy a husband shouldn't let a wife do things
like that. But when he decided Sy couldn't stop me, he bought
me a map. He marked all the neighborhoods he thought were
dangerous in red. Oh, he called me Bonita. For some reason, he'd
decided I was a classy dame, and he couldn't accept that I didn't
have a more dignified name. When he heard we were splitting,
that I wasn't asking for alimony, he called me up and gave me
advice. I was so surprised to hear from him."

"What did he say?"

"He told me he admired what I was doing but that this wasn't
a movie. It was real life, 'and in real life, Bonita, ladies whose
husbands take a walk got to get lawyers.' See, Mikey was Sy's
friend. His loyalty should have been to Sy. That's the way people
in his world operate. But he went out on a limb for me, tried to
get me to go to a matrimonial lawyer he recommended. And the
reason he did it was because he liked me a lot. And I liked him.
I mean, he was a *man*. The men I met in New York, Sy's
friends . . . they could get destroyed by a four-foot-two maître d'
with bad breath and nose hair who sat them at a wrong table. Not
Mikey. He was bad, but he was real."

"Have you seen him or spoken to him since the divorce?"

"No."

"Did Sy tell you he'd invested in *Starry Night?*"

"Yup." Casual, relaxed, as if I'd asked if she wanted ketchup
on her hamburger.

Except I'd asked her about Sy's investors before, and she'd given me some crap about his being edgy about "the boys." But she'd denied any knowledge of who they were. I blew up. "I asked you about Sy's meat buddies before, goddamn it, and you told me—"

"Stop yelling."

"I'm not yelling!" I banged my fist on the dresser. I hit my loose-change dish, and a dime jumped onto the floor. "I'm talking loud." I stopped, until I could regulate my voice. "Tell me, Bonita, is there anything you don't lie about?"

"I didn't tell you about Mikey because he'd had a lot of trouble with the police in the past."

"Do you think there may have been a reason for the trouble?"

"Oh, stuff it. Of course there was a reason for the trouble. He's a criminal. Just because he wears zoot suits and sounds like Sheldon Leonard in *Guys and Dolls* doesn't mean I don't know what he is. He's morally reprehensible—but he's not guilty of Sy's murder. If I'd told you about his investment it could have meant big trouble for him, and I *know* he didn't kill Sy."

"Why? Because you did?"

"Yup."

"Listen, honey, why don't you do Mikey a favor? Confess. Say: 'Sy made me get rid of my baby, cheated on me, gave me the clap, burned out my tubes . . .' " No reaction. I could have been reciting my multiplication tables. " '. . . and dropped me like a hot potato. Then he came back into my life and turned it upside down. He didn't love me, never has. He just *used* me. Over and over. And here I am: not getting any younger, lonely, broke. So I got out my .22 I brought back East from Daddy's store and shot the bastard.' That would give Mikey a real alibi."

"Stop babbling," she ordered. "Start thinking. Does Sy's murder sound like any kind of Mafia hit you've ever heard of?" It didn't, but all I did was shrug. "It *couldn't* have been Mikey LoTriglio. There was no way Sy would have let things get to the point of offending Il Tubbo; he was afraid of him."

"I thought he and Mikey were friends."

"They were. Sort of. See, part of Sy, the cosmopolitan part, loved knowing someone who was connected, who could tell stories about how Jimmy the Nunz put Tony Tomato and his Lincoln Continental in the East River to see if they would float. And the ruthless part of Sy . . . well, having a boyhood friend like Fat Mikey was a potential business asset. But Sy's New York nervous-Nellie part was afraid of being with a man who carried a gun, someone who could order men hurt or killed. Sy was as afraid of potential violence as of real violence. He was the ultimate urban neurotic; he couldn't distinguish between a threat and an act. So no matter what it was, Sy *always* deferred to Mikey. I mean, we'd go out to dinner with Mikey and his wife or Mikey and his girlfriend, and Sy, who was the world's biggest, pickiest pain in a restaurant, would let Mikey order for him. He'd wind up eating what must have been fried goldfish or lard in marinara sauce because Mikey said, 'You'll love this, Sy.' So trust me on this one: If Mikey was upset that his investment was going sour, Sy would have taken out his wallet and paid Mikey back right then and there. Double."

"We're talking a million-buck investment."

"That wouldn't be a problem for Sy. He was probably worth ten or fifteen million."

I shook my head. "Forty-five big ones." Bonnie looked astonished. "You could have had a nice chunk."

But she didn't seem interested in history. "Who inherits his money?" she asked. "His parents both died."

"No one. He has some sort of charitable foundation set up. For the arts."

Bonnie got up off the bed and lay facedown on the floor. She started doing push-ups, counting softly to herself. "I don't like your list of suspects," she said after forty-five. She wasn't at all winded.

"Why should you? You're on it."

Maybe she and I were doing business, but I still wanted to keep my business private. Plus she'd passed sixty push-ups, which was more than I could do, and showed no signs of stopping; I figured I didn't have to be around to watch her hit a hundred.

I went into the kitchen and called Thighs, told him to track down Mikey; I had a couple more questions.

Then I woke up Germy on Beekman Place and asked him to get me the names of the cast and crew of Lindsay's rifle-toting African movie, *Transvaal*, ASAP. He told me I sounded better. I told him I was. He said he was driving out to Bridgehampton around noon, and to drop by over the weekend if I could. Bring my girl. I said I'd try. He'd just gotten a copy of a beautifully edited video about DiMaggio that hadn't been released yet. He'd bring it out.

I called Robby. According to Freckled Cleavage, he'd left for work *hours* ago. Which probably meant he'd just lifted the garage door. I called back Thighs; he said he'd been in since six-thirty and hadn't seen or heard from Robby.

Then I called Lindsay's agent, Eddie Pomerantz, who had a house in East Hampton. I told him I'd be over in an hour. He said, Today isn't good, and in fact my whole weekend is booked solid, and I said, Have your attorney call me within the next ten minutes and he said, Awright, see you in an hour.

I called Lynne. She said she'd been thinking about me, and I said I'd been thinking about her. She was going to be home most of the day, going over the psychological evaluations of her kids for next year. I said I'd try and drop over, but not to hold her breath until I got there. She said she wouldn't, but it would be lovely if I could find a few minutes.

I thought, I'll have a wife and kids. I'll be happy. And I'm going to spend the rest of my life longing for what Bonnie gave me.

When I went back into the bedroom, Bonnie was sitting on the bed again, cross-legged, seemingly communing with her feet. She didn't look up. "Listen," I said, "about before. I'm sorry when I was ribbing you about killing Sy that I brought up . . ."

"My sterility."

"Yeah. You know I go for the jugular. It was in bad taste."

"Actually, it was beyond bad taste. It was cruel."

"I apologize."

"Fine," she said to her nicely arched soles. "Okay, let's get back to work. Any other theories? Random thoughts?"

"Like what?"

"I've been thinking about Sy. I know I told you he didn't seem worried, upset, anything like that. But on the other hand: he wasn't a hundred percent himself." She paused. "I feel uncomfortable talking about sex, but the last time we did it . . . he wasn't there. I mean, he was okay in the performance department, although that in itself doesn't mean a lot; Sy's equipment wasn't wired to his brain. But he wasn't concentrating on me. And that was such a critical thing for him, tuning in on precisely what a woman wanted and fulfilling that want. It was much more important than the physical act itself. But all of a sudden, it was strictly mechanical. Like he had some extra time because he'd changed his plane reservation, so he called and had me come over. But when I got there, he was an actor walking through a part that didn't interest him. He did what he had to do, but his mind was someplace else."

"He was never preoccupied like that before?"

She shook her head. "No. But see, it's nothing concrete. It's just a sense that a wife—or an ex-wife—gets about a man. That he wasn't really with me."

"I don't want to hurt your feelings, but could he have been cooling down on you?"

"No, because then he wouldn't have had me come over. If he'd just wanted sex and gorgeousness, he could have spent some time with Lindsay in her trailer. Or found someone else. Don't forget; Sy was an unmarried heterosexual multimillionaire movie producer. With a hundred forty IQ and a thirty-two-inch waist. Women tend to find that attractive. But he wanted me that afternoon."

"What for? I'm not being a shit now. I know why I would want you. Why would he want you?"

"Comfort. He could be himself with me. Well, as close to himself as Sy could ever get. I can't say he wanted me for fun, because he took himself too seriously to really let loose and laugh. But he seemed to have a good time bird-watching, walking with me; it was such a change from the rest of his life. And he loved sitting out in back—he called it his ex-yard—drinking lemonade and gossiping. And the sex was good." I waited for her to say, Not anything approaching the way it was with you, Stephen. Ah, Stephen: what a beautiful name. She said: "Sy and I knew how to please each other."

"It's nice that you had that." Tramp, I thought. I was so steamed. I went to my closet and picked out a tie, one that Easton had gotten me four or five Christmases earlier. Naturally, it was tasteful: red and blue and pale-yellow stripes.

Bonnie didn't seem to notice. "I know you have to get going, but just think for a minute. From your professional point of view: Did anyone say anything that would back up the feeling I got of Sy's being preoccupied? Was there any kind of a change in him?"

I sat on the edge of the bed and started doing my collar buttons. She did not lean over to help. "That's not an easy call to make," I explained. "Sy had a talent—a genius—for being what people wanted him to be. Not just what you've told me about, in the sack. He could be tough with a Mikey, be intellectual with a film critic, be Mr. Chicken Soup with an old Jewish reporter. He didn't seem to have any center. You knew him better than anyone. Who was the real Sy Spencer?"

"I don't know if there was one."

"Right. So it's almost impossible for me to find out if Sy wasn't himself, because no one can tell me who 'himself' is. Except that he always kept the lid on; I mean, his normal behavior was not screaming and kicking the crap out of production assistants and spitting on actors. And there was nothing in his behavior before his murder to show anything different. He was acting like a reasonable, rational man. No sudden blowups, no fits of melancholy."

"So you don't see anything."

"Shut up and let me finish."

"Don't tell me to shut up. Ask me to please be quiet."

"Please be quiet and go fuck yourself."

"That's better."

"Good. Now, two things strike me, but they're so petty they may not mean anything. But like you have a wife's sense, I have a cop's sense."

"What are they?" She caught me staring at the inner part of her thighs again. Taut, no baggy skin. Paler than the tanned tops of her legs. She pushed herself back, so she was leaning against the headboard, stretched her legs straight out and clasped her hands over that indefinite region south of her vulva and north of her thighs. "Come on," she urged. "You said two things struck you. Tell me. Function."

"I am functioning. Okay, Sy could definitely indulge himself with material things, indulge women if he was in the mood. But basically he was a real cheapo. Always trying to get a better deal, always afraid that people were trying to cheat him. And you told me one of the reasons you didn't ask for alimony is that you wanted to stay in his good graces, and you knew he had a bug up his ass about women wanting him for his money. Am I right?"

"Yup."

"Okay, so knowing all that, how come he paid Lindsay Keefe a half-million bucks more than her contract called for?" Bonnie looked astounded. "Does that sound like him?"

"No. Not at all. It sounds like a schnook who never made a movie before."

"Right. Some guy who's letting a movie star lead him around by the dick. I mean, so thrilled she's letting him in her pants, so scared she'll change her mind, that he throws in another five hundred thou."

Bonnie brought up her clasped hands and rested her chin on

them. She was intrigued. "You're on to something. I don't know what. But Sy wouldn't let go of a nickel without a reason."

"So what was the reason? Is it possible he made an off-the-books deal with her agent?"

She began to gnaw her knuckles while she considered the question. "I doubt it," she said finally. "Lindsay and Nick were getting a million each. Normally, they're in the two-to-three-million range, but they were getting it on the back end."

"A percentage of the profits?"

"Yup. The first-dollar gross. And Lindsay's agent . . . Why would he go for an off-the-books deal? He's not going to trust an actress. He, his agency, is going to want the protection of a written contract to collect his ten percent."

"So if a deal was struck, it would have been a private one between Sy and Lindsay."

"It would have been. I just can't see him doing it. Except . . ."

"Except what?"

"Except she *was* living with him, had been for months. Sy took women out, had sex with them, maybe had an occasional sleep-over in Southampton for a weekend. But nobody besides me and Lindsay ever kept a toothbrush in his house; he didn't operate that way. So maybe he had fallen in love with her. Maybe he *was* going to marry her."

"But it went sour."

"Well, you have to ask whose fault that was. If it was hers, she was in trouble. Sy was vengeful."

"How would he get his vengeance?"

"Just for starters, he'd stop having sex with her—but not tell her why. And he did that."

"You don't know that for a fact."

"I do know that's what he told me: He'd stopped sleeping with her. And I know him well enough sexually to know that you could stand on your head and whistle 'Dixie' stark naked, and he still wouldn't—couldn't, probably—do it more than once a day. God, I hate getting clinical."

"Get clinical."

"Well, he could keep going for what seemed like forever, but once he . . . you know . . ." She got all flustered.

"Bonnie, you're forty-five years old."

"Thank you. Well, once he came, that was it. And so if he was keeping company with me every single day, he would have had to put on a splint to do anything for her."

"He saw you every day?"

"Every day. And he was so *angry* at her. He always got hostile during production, that quiet, nasty seething; I mean, if a fly would land on a wall, he'd want five grips with bazookas to go after it. But with Lindsay it was more. He was venomous. He called her terrible things, and that was so out of character for him."

"Like what?"

"Well, maybe you won't think it's so terrible, because you have a filthy mouth. But Sy liked to think of himself as the epitome of refinement. And also as a clearheaded man of enlightenment. That meant buying politically correct ice cream and being pro-environment, anti-fur and ultra-pro-feminist. All of a sudden, though, he was calling her 'cunt.' You have no idea how out of character that was for him. Sure, he could be a miserable, heartless, vindictive rat, but always a genteel rat. He'd eat your face and tell you how profoundly he valued your friendship. So my guess is, Sy did love her. But then he turned on her. And just from his language, I'd say he'd lost control. In his mind, she'd betrayed him in some fundamental way."

"Well, she'd betrayed him by screwing up her acting," I suggested.

"Right. But for the first week or so, that didn't seem to stop his attraction. I mean, dailies were horrible, but you said people saw him around her on the set with steam coming out of his ears."

"Okay. So what do we have? He was upset with her, angry

with her, but he was still hot for her despite her lousy performance. But then she seeks out Santana as an ally—and Lindsay's way of forming an alliance is to fuck somebody. Then, within a day or two, Sy is looking to replace her. With other actresses for *Starry Night*. And with you for sex. So I'm asking: What's your gut? Doesn't it look like Sy knew?"

"It sure looks like it. I can't say definitely, because he had an enormous ego, and it would have been hard for him to accept that a woman would prefer anyone else to him. But on the other hand, he was very, very astute. And he *had* crossed her off his list. Now, you could call it a business decision, maybe a smart one; I don't know enough about the economics of moviemaking to say. But it was personal too. This was Lindsay's first soft, romantic role, and he was letting it leak to everyone in the business that she—his lover, girlfriend, fiancée, whatever—didn't have the versatility, the charm, the comedic talent, to handle the light stuff. He knew what the gossip would be: 'If Sy has to replace Lindsay, she must be doing a *horrendous* job.' "

"Was he trying to ruin her?"

"If he could have, he probably would have. But I told you: no producer today has the power to ruin a star. Still, Sy was out to do Lindsay as much damage as he could."

"At the dailies, a few people were talking about lightning special effects. Sy said if Lindsay got hit by lightning, it would be the answer to his prayers. Obviously he was kidding about the completion guarantee business, but the impression was that for all he cared, she could be dead, and in fact, if she *had* been dead he probably would have thrown a party."

Bonnie was doing a great job chewing her knuckles. "Okay, Sy had fallen in love and had been cuckolded and was out to get even."

I nodded. "Right. Now all we've got to figure out is whether his Lindsay passion was a temporary lapse for such a dispassionate man, or if he was starting to lose his marbles." I went and unlocked the strongbox on the top of my closet, got out my service revolver, then got my suit jacket. "I have this feeling he was really losing his marbles."

"Why?" She watched me putting on the holster and the jacket. I could see she didn't want me to leave. I could also see that, unlike every other woman I'd ever slept with (except for girl cops), she didn't blink or recoil or raise eyebrows or in any way show discomfort in the presence of a .38.

"Sy had this assistant or associate producer," I said. "A new guy he hired for *Starry Night*. A guy from around here."

"Super WASP?"

"My brother. His name's Easton."

"He's your *brother?* Oh. Sy told me about him."

"What did he say?" Bonnie didn't want to tell me. "Go on. I know what he is."

"Sy said he was very good-looking, personable, but a little . . ."

"A loser."

"Someone who hadn't had much success in life. But he turned out to be terrific. Sy liked him a lot. It was a perfect match. Sy needed someone who'd be on call twenty-four hours a day, who'd jump to do anything he wanted done. It sounded as though your brother was thrilled to do that. And more important, it sounded like he didn't have—forgive me, but I'm just repeating what Sy said—much ambition. Sy saw him as someone for the long haul."

"A glorified valet."

"Why don't we just say a lifetime retainer?"

"That's my brother. Anyway, I was over at Easton's, with Robby Kurz. Department ethics: I couldn't question my own brother. So I'm sitting there, and I pick up a script. Easton says Sy told him it was their next movie."

"Was it mine?"

"No. Okay, now; in all fairness, I just glanced at it. And I never read a screenplay before. But I'm telling you, Bonnie, what I read was such complete, unmitigated shit I couldn't believe it. He was losing his marbles."

"Do you remember the title?"

"Yeah. *Night of the Matador,* by—"

"Mishkin! Milton or Murray."

"You read it?"

"Years ago. Look, Sy wasn't going to make *Night of the Matador.* Not in a million years. It was a joke. Well, the writer hadn't written it as a joke, but Sy had gotten it about a year after we were married, and it was so terrible it was funny. It was one of his Hideous Scripts collection. He treasured it. He used to give readings from it: 'I kill the beast to kill the beast in my heart, Carlotta.' Now, I'll grant you, Sy did get a little goofy over Lindsay. But he *never* would have gotten goofy enough to make that movie."

"Then why would he tell my brother that was the movie they were going to do together?"

"Kidding around."

"I don't buy that."

"Knowing Sy, maybe he wanted to see if your brother had the guts to stand up to him, tell him it was the worst hundred and twenty pages in the world. And God forbid if he said he liked it; Sy would torture him about it for the next twenty years."

"Easton was positive this was Sy's next project."

"Well, it could all be a mistake. Maybe you just looked at the wrong screenplay."

"Maybe," I said. "I'll give my brother a call." I walked to the door. "We have a deal," I reminded her. "You won't leave till I get back."

"I know."

"I said five, but if it's six, just hang on. I know it's rough on you. What can I tell you?"

"Tell me, 'Bonnie, you're beautiful. You're a truly fine person. And I love you.' "

"Bye," I said.

"See you around, big boy."

CHAPTER 18

onnie had wanted to call Gideon to reassure him that she was
all right, and I'd wanted to call him before he decided her
absence had something to do with me. I could picture him
gazing at his phone, wondering, Is it possible? Could this
Brady be one of those congenial psychopaths, someone who smiles,
chats and tortures? Slowly, he would lift the receiver, call Homicide, demand Shea, tell him I'd once slept with Bonnie and I
might be obsessed. Dangerous.

But I couldn't risk a call from my house. Someone on the
squad—Robby—could already have put an illegal tap on Gideon's
phone, hoping she'd call him. So before I went to Pomerantz's, I
stopped at one of those self-serve gas stations/snack food stores,
called something like Thrif-T Gas, a place where only locals went,
since to New Yorkers, concepts like fuel supplied by a company
not traded on the New York Stock Exchange, thrift, and sour-
cream-and-onion-flavored corn chips were too degrading to the

human spirit to even consider. The place was on one of the more obscure north roads. I used the pay phone.

Gideon's boyfriend answered. He had one of those powerful, honeyed, southern Do-you-believe-in-Jesus-Christ-as-yo'-Savior? voices. When I said I was calling about Bonnie Spencer, Gideon got on right away.

"Your friend Bonnie is fine," I said, disguising my voice so it sounded like a cross between Casey Stengel and a frog. "She just didn't think it was time to get arrested yet."

Gideon didn't bother to ask who I was. He knew. "I'm concerned about her," he said slowly. "I would feel better if I knew—"

"—that she's okay? She said to tell you Gary Cooper was at his most beautiful in *The Westerner*." I couldn't believe that I'd agreed to deliver such a goddamn stupid message. "End of conversation. She'll call you tonight."

An orange shirt, with its itsy-bitsy polo player, stretched across Eddie Pomerantz's belly, while a pair of half-glasses dangled from a darker-orange cord. The shirt hung over a pair of khaki bermuda shorts.

We were standing in his living room; the entire back wall was glass. The house itself stood on top of a bluff overlooking the bright, white-capped water and bobbing sailboats of Northwest Harbor. It was an incredible, expensive view.

"I went through this whole thing with you the night Sy got killed," he said. "Remember? We'd been discussing a picture of Lindsay that turned up in *USA Today* that she hadn't approved." To show me he was keeping his temper, he filled up his cheeks with air and let it leak out. I was trying not to lose my cool, even though he was lying through his shiny false teeth. "I had to cancel a breakfast meeting because of this," he complained. "I don't know what you want from me." He looked down at the giant face of his gold-and-stainless-steel watch.

I took out my stainless-steel handcuffs and swung them before his eyes. "I don't want anything from you, Mr. Pomerantz. I'm here to arrest you. Section four ninety-two of the New York State Penal Code." I made that up. "Impeding a criminal investigation. And section eleven thirty-eight, Sub A: Aiding and abetting—"

I didn't have to finish. He tottered backward to a long couch and dropped onto it. He seemed mesmerized by the swinging cuffs. I put them back in my pocket. He wheezed: "If I tell you something now that's different than what I told you last week . . ." His mouth kept working, but he couldn't finish his sentence.

I didn't want him to drop dead of a coronary. Seeing him in daylight, I realized he was well into his seventies. My guess was, if I'd caught him when he was younger, he would have been tough enough to give me a hard time. But he was old, tired, probably not in the best of health. I felt kind of bad for scaring him. "If you cooperate, nothing will happen."

"I'll cooperate." The couch was covered in something like sailcloth, broad red and white stripes; his orange shirt looked particularly hideous against it.

"Tell me about the phone call," I said. "Did you call Sy or did he call you?"

"I called him."

"What about?"

"He was having trouble with some aspects of Lindsay's performance."

"I'd appreciate it if you didn't try to jerk me off, Mr. Pomerantz."

"Sy was going to California to take meetings with other actresses to discuss Lindsay's role. He seemed to be willing to throw three weeks of film into the garbage and reshoot with a new star."

"And what were you trying to do?"

"Trying to stop him."

"Any success?"

"I don't know. He wanted Lindsay out. He seemed to have made up his mind." Pomerantz fiddled with his eyeglass cord. "I was working on getting him to at least agree to call me after he met with the others, for one last talk. That's when he was shot."

"Two shots?"

"Yes."

"You're positive?"

"Yes. I know what a gunshot sounds like. I was in the army. Battle of the Bulge." I nodded, respectfully. "Wounded. You should've seen me then. A skinny kid. Three quarters of an inch lower, it would have gone straight through my heart. So I know from guns. And I heard two shots."

"You do a lot of your business on the phone?"

"Sure. Most of it."

"You must have a good ear."

"A great ear."

"If someone was having an off day, or had a sudden change of mood, you could pick that up?"

Pomerantz understood what I was saying. "Yes. And there was nothing that made me think Sy saw anyone—with or without a rifle. Or that he felt something was wrong. But wasn't he shot from behind?"

"Yeah, but if the killer was someone he knew, he might have spotted him out of the corner of his eye, acknowledged him in some way and then turned away. What I'm looking for is a 'Hi, Joe' or 'Hello, Mary' that you might have picked up early in the conversation."

"Nothing like that," Pomerantz said.

"No pause at any point? No sudden intake of breath right before?"

"Nothing. Bang, bang, and then absolute silence.' He lifted his shirtfront and used it to clean his glasses.

"Let's talk about Lindsay. Straight talk. Did she know how bad things were with Sy, that he was getting ready to pop her?"

"Yes."

"Did you know she was sleeping with Victor Santana?"

"Yes." Tight lips. "Fifty-two years in the business, and you know what I finally realize? I hate the ones who make it. Even the smartest of them are stupid. Stupid and arrogant. They think they can do anything they want, no consequences."

"You can't do anything you want with a guy like Sy Spencer, can you?" I observed.

"No."

"Do you think Sy had a clue that she was cheating on him?"

"Yes."

"What makes you think so?"

"He told me. I was making my big pitch to keep her on *Starry Night,* and he said, 'I can't do it, Eddie. You've seen the dailies. She's not putting out.' He gave that cold laugh of his. It's like being stabbed to death with an icicle. And then he said, 'Excuse me. She is putting out—in Santana's trailer.' "

"In your mind, if any of those actresses in L.A. would have fit the bill, would it have been all over for Lindsay?"

"Bottom line?"

"Bottom line."

"Sure it would have been all over—except for the fact that it would have cost too much. Even if Sy could have hired a not-so-hot star for less money, it still would have cost him almost three million in salary and reshooting to start from scratch. He couldn't have raised it outside; he'd already maxed out on financing. So unless it was worth it to him to ante up two-point-seven-five million of his own money to get rid of Lindsay, she would have stayed."

"Would it have been worth it to him?"

"I think he was considering it. But I'd been doing deals with Sy for ten years. I knew him. I knew what a tightwad he was. Look, it would have gotten real ugly, but in the long run the names above the title would have been Nicholas Monteleone—and Lindsay Keefe."

"Did Lindsay know that too?"

"I told her."

"Did she believe you?"

"I don't know. She was scared."

"Of what?"

"Of Sy Spencer."

I can't say Lynne was overcome with ecstasy when she answered her door, but she did look pleased. She stood in the doorway. Her beautiful dark-red hair fell over her shoulders. She wore a crisp white blouse and a polka-dot miniskirt. It took me a minute to grasp that she was waiting for me to kiss her. I did. Then she led me inside.

The house had a Sunday hush. Judy and Maddy, her two roommates, were at work, and Lynne had spread her folders over the living room coffee table. Well, not spread. I marveled at how they were in flawlessly symmetrical piles. Her pens and colored highlighters were parallel and equidistant from each other and just the perfect distance from the curved edges of the light wood table so that, should one decide to roll, she could reach it before it fell to the floor. "You're my kind of girl." I smiled at her. "In 2013, when I'm looking for my 1996 New York State tax return, you'll be able to find it in three seconds."

"You don't think I'm compulsive?" Lynne asked. I sat down in a club chair. She squeezed in beside me. "Judy is always saying I'm compulsive. Just because I always put away my shoes with the toes facing out. She says if I could just throw my shoes on my closet floor I'd be more creative."

"Look at it this way. Neither of us will probably ever write Hamlet, but we'll never misplace a bank statement or a kid. That's reassuring."

"It is." She smiled. "Tell me, how is your case going?"

"We're getting there," I said.

"Good. There must be a lot of pressure, with all the publicity."

"There is." I glanced around the living room. Nothing really went with anything else. The leatherette chairs and the striped chairs, the 1950s Danish-modern coffee table, the massive brass floor lamp, the poster of a bowl of flowers from the Boston Museum of Fine Arts, were castoffs from the families of three pretty, marriageable girls in their mid-twenties, all of whom would have husbands—and nice furniture that coordinated with tasteful rugs—long before they were thirty. "How is your class for September?"

"I think it's really going to be a challenge. I'm excited. Do you have time for me to go through the student list?"

"Can you do it in two minutes?"

Lynne snuggled against me. "That's all you have?"

"Sorry."

"Did you think about stuffed chicken breasts?"

I slipped my hand under the neckline of her blouse, around her bra. "These aren't chicken breasts."

"You know what I mean!"

I smiled, eased my hand out.

I had no desire for her.

"Going to the beach today?" I asked.

"Well, I'd like to, but I have to get my hair trimmed." She seemed to think the news would upset me, so she added, "Just a little bit off the ends."

"The ends look all right to me." I was so bored, and so ashamed of myself for being bored.

I thought: I could be having this same exchange with Bonnie, about chicken breasts and hair ends, and okay, it wouldn't be the world's most enthralling conversation, or the most amusing, but I'd hang on every word.

Even if I'd had two months' vacation, I wouldn't want to hear about Lynne's dyslexics and dysgraphics. And it wasn't that I couldn't get interested in that sort of stuff; it was that I couldn't get interested in Lynne.

How could someone have the perfect résumé and not be right for the job? She was precisely what I should want. Why didn't I want her? Other men did. We'd walk down the street, and heads—local guys, city guys—would turn. Turn? Spin. Half the time her phone was ringing with old boyfriends, or guys she barely knew, none of them willing to believe she could actually consider marrying someone else before she listened to their fantastic, incredible lifetime offer.

Lynne played with the veins in the back of my hand. I suddenly realized that no matter how hard I tried, I couldn't make myself love her. There was nothing more about Lynne I cared to know. Not about her job, her family, her pastimes, her feelings.

But I wanted to know every single course Bonnie had taken at the University of Utah. I wanted to know her brothers' names, who she'd voted for in 1980 and why, what her first sex experience had been like. I wanted her to tell me how a bunch of Jews wound up in Ogden, Utah. I wanted to see *Cowgirl*. I wanted to read her new screenplay and her descriptions of bathing suits for the fatlady catalog. I wanted to meet her old man, haul him away from the new wife and the bridge games and go hunting with him. I even wanted to bird-watch with Bonnie—or at least watch her watch birds. I wanted to go running with her. Camp out. Fish for trout. Take her on a whale watch off Montauk. I wanted to tell her all about my work, my entire life. Watch the Yankees and her 1940s movies with her. Make love to her.

"You're quiet," Lynne said.

"Yeah. I've got a lot on my mind." I thought: Maybe all this is camouflage, and what I really want is custody of Moose.

"What are you smiling about?" Lynne demanded.

"Nothing much."

"Tell me what else is new."

I shifted, trying to sit up straighter, but she was wedged in so close to me I couldn't move. "Oh, Lynne, I'm so sorry."

She knew, but she asked, as if expecting a passionate denial: "Is something wrong?"

"I don't know where to begin. I don't know what to say."

"Oh, God." She got up out of the chair, stood before me. So fabulous-looking. Such a nice person. Responsible. Solid values. Hardworking. "What is it?" It would make so much sense to marry her. "Are you drinking again?"

"No." I don't have to say anything at all, I thought. I can let it ride. Close the Spencer case, sort things out. It made sense to take my time. Lynne was so right for me; there must be a way it could work.

"Is there someone else?"

I should stand up, take her in my arms. Say, Someone else? With you around? Of course not! I sat, paralyzed. "Yes," I said at last.

"Who is she?"

"Someone I knew a few years ago."

"Have you been seeing her?"

"No. It's nothing like that. I just ran into her again recently and realized."

Lynne started to cry. "Realized what?"

"I don't know."

"Realized *what*, Steve?"

"That I want to be with her all the time."

At last, I was able to make myself move. I got up and put my arms around her. I wish I could say I was filled with grief. But I didn't feel anything except sadness that I was hurting her. She was such a decent person and she loved me, or at least loved the man she thought was me, and loved the idea of loving someone who needed her help in getting through life.

She pulled away and gazed up at me. Everything she did was so pretty, even her crying. Two lovely, parallel tears coursed down her cheeks. She swallowed and regained some control. "You don't love me?" she asked.

I took her back into my arms. "Lynne," I said, into her glorious hair, "you're a wonderful person. You're beautiful, kind, patient—"

"You don't love me."

"I thought I did. I truly thought I did."

"Are you going to marry her?"

"No. I don't know. I don't know a lot. I don't feel in control anymore, that I understand anything that's going on. It's all just happening. When I came here, I was only thinking I'd spend a few minutes with you, touch base. In my wildest dreams, it didn't occur to me that we'd be having this conversation. I wish I'd been better prepared. . . ." She started to cry again. "I wish I could have made it less painful for you."

She pulled out of my embrace. "My mother ordered the invitations."

"I'm sorry." What was I going to do? Tell her that her parents, Saint Babs and the Scourge of Godless Communism, would be breaking out the champagne, tearing the invitations into confetti, throwing it into the air in jubilation?

"Is she prettier than I am?" Lynne wiped her cheeks.

"No."

"Younger?"

"No. Older." Then I added: "Older than me." Her beautiful brown eyes grew big with disbelief, as though beholding a Medicare card in a liver-spotted hand. "Not too much older," I added.

"Does she have a good personality?"

"Yes." It was gutless, but at that moment I wished more than anything that I hadn't told her there was someone else, only that it wasn't working out and the blame was all mine. I was a too-old sad case, simply not the marrying kind. But Lynne would be tolerant, compassionate, like a nurse with an invalid who has a long convalescence before him. She'd wait, helping me recuperate, helping me become a better person.

"What does she do?"

"She's a writer."

"Is she from the city?"

"No."

"Is she rich?"

"No."

"What is it? Sex?" I didn't respond. "Is that it?"

"It's a factor."

"It was fine with us. It *was*."

"Yes, it was."

"You owe me an explanation, Steve."

"I know. I know I do. Forgive me." What the hell could I tell her? The truth. Not the whole truth, but at least no lies. "You're everything I admire. When we first started going out, I couldn't believe you were for real, because I thought: No one can be this decent; it's some sort of an act. But it wasn't. I came to understand that you're everything any man could want in a woman."

"Then why don't you want me?"

"Because you *are* so wonderful. Because I'm a messed-up guy and I can't live up to your high standards."

"But I'm not telling you to be anything except what you are."

"But see, Lynne, what I am doesn't necessarily want what you want. I can't live the life that would be right for you. I thought I could. I thought: If I have a good and beautiful wife and nice kids and a comfortable house, I'll be at peace. That's all I ever wanted. But I've got too much damage, and too many needs. Putting a white picket fence around me won't make me into a whole person."

"What will?"

"She will."

"Why?" Lynne asked.

And I finally answered: "Because . . . we have fun."

Carbone had me beeped three times in two minutes. I pulled off at a too-cute lobster restaurant and used the pay phone. "What's so urgent, Ray?"

"Robby's got her nailed."

"Her?" Lindsay. He'd say Lindsay.

"Bonnie."

I knew I couldn't sound the way I felt: crazy with terror. I had to sound solid, sensible, the tough, experienced cop weary of Kid Robby's asshole antics. "Jesus, is he still pulling stupid shit? I've been killing myself. I've got great stuff on Lindsay. We've got to start concentrating our resources—"

"Steve, listen to me. He went back to Sy's house late yesterday. To that area underneath the porch where we found the footprints from the thongs."

"And?"

"He found another dark hair."

"Stop it!"

"Like the ones on the pillow, Steve. It was caught in one of those crisscrosses of the latticework that covers the crawl space under the porch. She must have leaned against it for a minute. He drove it up to the lab in Westchester personally this morning. He's waiting for the test results, but you know and I know: It's got to be Bonnie. Now we've got her in bed with him *and* at the exact location where the shot came from."

She lied, I thought. I stared at the phone, at its idiot instruction card for placing phone calls. That I'd believed Bonnie's explanations wasn't the worst part. The worst part was that I could go back to the house, kick furniture, throw things, pound walls, roar at her, You goddamn lying bitch, and she'd touch my arm, look me straight in the eye and say, Stephen, I wasn't there. I *swear* to you I wasn't there. Then how did your hair get there? She'd say, Someone put it there. That detective who's after me. You *said* he was out to get me, and he is. I'd say, You expect me to believe that, bitch? And she'd say, Yes, I do.

And against all reason, I would.

"Ray," I said, "you're not having any trouble with this?"

"What do you mean?"

"You don't think there's a chance that Robby got a little too enthusiastic?"

"Come off it. He wouldn't go that far. You know he wouldn't plant evidence. Face facts. Face what she is." For a second it got so quiet I could hear water bubbling in the lobster tanks. "Steve? You there?"

"I'm here."

"What are you going to do now?"

"What do you think I should do?" I asked.

"Go find her."

*　　　*　　　*

I happened to glance down toward the shelf in that dingy corner by the pay phone, with its ancient American Express application forms curled from the humidity, and the ashtray with someone's fat, ugly cigar ash. And all of a sudden, in that stinky, dreary corner, I got a gift—a flash of memory from that night five years before.

We'd finished eating and moved into the living room. It was sunset, and Bonnie left the lights off so we could see the horizon, royal blue, deep orange. Then she lit a couple of candles and we sat back in the flickering light. She told me how she'd come to love the South Fork, the vast and beautiful sky, the ocean, the marshes, the birds—she said she was one of those creeps who clomped around with boots and binoculars—but that she missed the mountains. Not just for fishing, hiking, skiing. Growing up in Utah, she'd look out the window in school, bike to the store to pick up a quart of milk for her mother, lie in her bed staring at the stars—and the mountains were always there.

"You sound a little homesick," I said.

"Yes."

"You ever think of going back?"

"None of my family's there anymore. It would just be me and the mountains and the Mormons."

"You didn't answer my question."

"I wish I could go home," she said, very quietly.

And I whispered: "I'll teach you to love it here, Bonnie."

I threw in another quarter and called my pal in the D.A.'s office, Sally-Jo Watkins. From the name, you'd expect one of those exhausted Appalachian women with fourteen children you see on Malnutrition U.S.A. documentaries. But Sally-Jo was strictly Canarsie and unexhausted. She came from a very old but extremely undistinguished Brooklyn family. She always walked double-time and barked rather than talked. She was a career prosecutor, Chief Assistant D.A. for Suffolk County.

"What do you want? I'm busy. This about the Spencer case? Ralph's doing that. Talk to Ralph."

"I have to talk to you."

"Why? We got channels here, same as you guys. I'm drowning in a sea of motions, Brady, you stupid, insensitive mick cop moron. Whatever you want, I can't do it. Call Ralph."

"He's too inflexible. I can't talk to him."

"Well, I can't talk to you."

"Sally-Jo, I saved your ass at least three times when you were in the Homicide Bureau. You fucking owe me."

"I bought you a steak dinner. Remember? When you got sprung from the bin? I had to wait till you dried out, otherwise it would have cost me a year's salary, the way you drank."

"Yeah, well, I put at least twenty thousand calories of cheeseburgers into you over the years, so let's say you still owe me the equivalent of one more extremely large lunch."

"Shoot, schmuck. And shoot fast."

"Hypothetically, say I did everything right: preserved a crime scene till after the autopsy, had my men go over everything with a fine-tooth comb. No rain, no high winds. Nothing to dirty the samples we took, nothing to make our job difficult. Ideal conditions."

"Keep going."

"Not much stuff except some circumstantial evidence good for making a DNA case. Hair. The victim's lover's hair in the bed where they'd been making it. Okay. Then a week later, four days after we take down the tape, I find another hair. Looks like the lover's. Let's say the lab says it is."

"Where do you find said strand of hair?"

"Caught between two crossing slats of wood. If the lover had been firing the murder weapon, that crisscross would be exactly where this lover of unspecified sex's head would have been. Now, as a prosecutor, would you buy this suddenly appearing new piece of evidence? Would you use it?"

"Okay. Generally, all relevant evidence is admissible at a

trial. But the circumstances under which the evidence was found are admissible too. In a case like this, the defense would argue that since you did such a bang-up job under ideal conditions the first time, it's passing strange that you didn't find that extra hair when you were so busy being meticulous."

"They'd argue it was planted."

"Right."

"A lawyer like Paterno would argue that."

"A lawyer like Paterno would cream us on that. We'd claim it was an oversight. Human error. Cops are human, and what in the world would be our motive for trying to frame this lover? Because we believe with all our hearts and souls that the lover is guilty? Ridiculous!"

"If you were prosecuting a case like this, what would you do?"

"I'd spend a couple of days scaring the shit out of the cop who says he found the hair, telling him that if he's not a hundred percent sure that one of his colleagues didn't plant it—I wouldn't accuse him directly—he should forget about it because it could jeopardize our case, give the defense something to fight about. Then I'd sit back and think about it. Chances are, I wouldn't risk introducing it unless the rest of our case was very, very flimsy— but then I'd question the whole proceeding. But if our case was semi-solid, I'd still avoid using it. Look, that one hair makes the DNA testing an issue, and that would put our good evidence— the hair from the bed—into question. And who needs a lawyer like Paterno making the jury wonder how come a miracle happened after a week? From the D.A.'s point of view, a wondering jury is a dangerous jury. Reasonable doubt is a terrible thing."

"Thanks, Sally-Jo."

"So, imbecile, is it your hypothesis that Bonnie Spencer shot Sy Spencer or not?"

"Not."

"That isn't what I hear."

*　　　*　　　*

It was touch and go whether Bonnie would let go of the phone or I'd break her wrist trying to get it out of her hand. She finally let go, but the next thing I knew, she was making a dash for the door, frantic to get to the cops, turn herself in.

"Stop it!" I shouted. I had her in an armlock, but it was like trying to restrain a powerful guy, and her natural strength was reinforced by hysteria. "You didn't do it, so what the hell are you—" She said something, but her words were swallowed up by huge, loud gasps and gulps of air. I held her, waiting for tears, followed by her fervent plea: Stephen, *please* believe me. Instead, I got an elbow to the solar plexus. It knocked the wind out of me so badly that I let her loose. I bent over, hugging myself, trying to catch my breath. Jesus, did it hurt.

At which point Bonnie asked, "Did I hurt you? I'm sorry." Except I couldn't speak. "Stephen? Are you okay? Where does it hurt? Oh, God." Actually, the shock of sudden pain—and pain inflicted by the woman you've just declared to your now ex-fiancée is the woman you love—just lasted for a second. But I didn't reassure Bonnie. I let her lead me to my bed, step by compassionate step, and ease me down. "Take it slow," she warned. By the time I was flat on my back, she was under control again. "Can you breathe all right?" She peered into my eyes, maybe checking to see if the pupils were dilating. "Stephen?"

"No," I muttered, "it's over." She had to bend down to catch my words. "You broke my rib and there's a huge splinter of bone that's piercing my heart. I'm a dead man, Bonnie. Goodbye." I reached out, grabbed her hand and pulled her so she was sitting beside me on the bed. "One last kiss." She threw me a dirty look. "All right," I told her. "Get hysterical again. Run. I'm not going to fight you. You're too big."

"Listen to me. I *have* to turn myself in. That Robby—I guess it's Robby—is out to get me. If I stay here, he'll pull something else." Her voice started to rise again. "Let me go in now, while my lawyer still has a chance to make some sort of a decent case."

"Get a grip on it!" She took a deep but tremulous breath. "You can do it. I need you a little while longer. Once you're arrested, there may be a problem with bail. Second-degree murder, and your roots in the community aren't all that deep. You'll probably wind up in jail. Understand that?"

"Yes."

"It's not a nice place. It doesn't get a fun crowd, and they don't show Bette Davis movies. You won't like it. So if I can, I want to spare you that. But even more, selfishly, I need you a little while longer for consultation. Just till five. Five o'clock, you can call your friend Gideon, have him alert Bill Paterno, and you can set the whole process in motion. But let me just warn you, if you're in the slammer, I may not be able to contact you. Your lawyer is going to say, No cops."

"But I could explain that you're helping."

"Bonnie, do you think a criminal lawyer is going to believe that a detective on the Homicide Squad has a soft spot for his client and will act in her best interests?"

"He might." It disturbed me how naive she was, how God Bless America. She wanted to turn herself in, put her faith in the System. She'd be walking into a hellhole. Jail to her was movies about exploited women with pitiful stories and one twisted prison matron. To her, ugliness was a set designer's vision. She didn't know the lunatic screams, the rage, the violence, the stink. Her crack addicts were on NBC News; she had no idea.

"Now, you told me you were going to be very busy today, solving the case. How far did you get?"

"I don't know. You tell me."

I took her hand. She pulled it away. I'd forgotten I hadn't mentioned that I loved her, or that I wasn't marrying Lynne, so I reached out for her again. But she stood up and went over to my leather recliner. There was a pad and pen on the table next to it, and as she sat back, she picked up the pad, held it to her heart as if it were the ultimate mash note. "I read too many mysteries, see too many detective movies," she explained. "When I thought about the whole case, everything you told me, I wound up suspecting Victor Santana and Mrs. Robertson."

"Why, for Christ's sake?"

"Because he was jealous of Sy and knew Sy thought he was weak—and if Lindsay was going to be fired, he'd be next."

"And Marian Robertson?"

"Who knows? Because Sy went strolling into the kitchen once too often and lifted a lid off a pot and stuck his pinkie into her béarnaise sauce and sniffed it and put a dab on his tongue and suggested a soupçon more chervil."

"Too bad you're over the hill. You'd be some great cop."

"You're not impressed by my deductive powers?"

"No."

"I didn't think you'd be. That's why I gave up looking at the big picture—because I keep trying to turn it into a movie. I decided to concentrate on Sy. Analyze my last few days with him, factor in everything you told me."

"Go ahead."

She pushed back so the recliner was practically horizontal. She glanced from me to the pad and back again. "Think of Sy's behavior. What was out of character for him?"

"Not concentrating when he was humping you."

"Let's just call it distracted behavior," she suggested.

"Distracted behavior. Third-rate fucking. Whatever you want."

"It was second-rate," she said. "With you it was third-rate."

"No. You never had it so good. You know it. Admit it."

"Nope. Anyway, Sy was distracted. That could have meant something big was happening—or about to happen. Now, what else?" I thought she was going to answer her own question, but she was waiting for me.

I thought about it. What in the last few days of Sy Spencer's life had in any way been atypical? Love. "He'd fallen in love with Lindsay," I began. "And she hurt him. All of a sudden, the ultimate victimizer was a victim. It must have come as a real blow to him."

"Right. And so what was going on? Under the best of circumstances, Sy was a vengeful man if someone crossed him. And here was the object of his affection or obsession, his love, cheating on him. He was going to get even."

"But ultimately, he couldn't get even." I told her what Eddie Pomerantz had said, that because of money, Sy would wind up keeping her on the picture.

Bonnie's eyes got huge. "That's even better!" She jumped out of the recliner, came right over to me. "Think!" she ordered.

"Think about what?"

"Vengeance is one thing. That's what I was concentrating on. But how could he get vengeance *and* money?"

I bolted up. "Jesus! The completion insurance!"

Bonnie grabbed onto my jacket sleeve. "If lightning struck Lindsay, he'd get his money, he'd get his new actress."

"And he'd get his revenge," I said slowly. "Okay, but let's slow down. The theory's good, but the truth of the matter is, Lindsay *wasn't* struck by lightning. Sy was. How does that figure?"

"Stephen, ask yourself: Who was killed? Sy?"

"Of course Sy."

"Or someone in a white, hooded bathrobe who was standing at the edge of the pool, the way Lindsay Keefe did when she came home from the set and did her laps?"

"Someone small," I said.

And Bonnie said: "Yup. Small, just like Sy."

CHAPTER 19

onnie was all juiced up, talking too fast, bopping in a U-shaped path around the bed, stopping each time at the shaded window to bounce on the balls of her bare feet and peek out. She was not at her best, excited in a confined space. "Okay," she said. "We've got to figure out if this really is a possibility, and then—"

"Stop. I'm running this show, not you. I'm the lead detective. You're zero."

"Be quiet. I know what I'm doing." She perched on the dresser and swung her leg back and forth fast, like a pendulum running amok.

"With all due respect, you may be semi-smart, but when it comes to police procedure you don't know your ass from a hole in the ground, and we don't have time to debate hierarchy, so I'm in charge." She put her fingers up to her mouth, as though hiding a yawn induced by being too, too bored by such childish jockeying for position. "Don't give me that yawn crap, Bonnie."

"I'm not giving you yawn crap."

"Now think; don't just shoot off your mouth. In the time you knew him, did Sy ever make threats against anyone, or wish a person dead in a way that made you fear for their lives? Beyond the 'I hope he dies' we talked about."

She swung her leg some more and finally shook her head. "But that's not to say he wasn't spiteful. He had his hate list. If thirty years after the fact he could hurt someone who called him Peewee in junior high school, he definitely would. But he didn't think of revenge in terms of death. He didn't want to cause physical pain; he wanted to inflict maximum emotional pain on anyone who ever got in his way."

I added another item to Bonnie's asset column, which now had about five million items: She didn't sway with each trendy breeze. The way things were looking, it would have been easy for her to portray Sy as a Man with Murderous Instincts, but she was too fair to do that.

"All right," I said. "So what it boils down to is that Sy was just your average, malicious guy."

"Except his malice got more intense as he got older—or as he got more successful and powerful. Look, maybe the man I married was no cute little cuddle bunny, but the Sy I got to know again after I gave him the *Sea Change* script was much harder; he was so full of himself, so disdainful of other people. Anyone who crossed him was bad, selfish, stupid and ipso facto deserved whatever damage Sy decided to inflict. In his mind, when he got back at someone, he was only making sure justice was done."

"All right, think about this: Did he have any morals at all?"

Bonnie gave the question some serious, leg-swinging consideration. "He took decent political positions: apartheid is bad, rain forests are good. But no, I never saw any evidence of morals, not in a personal sense."

"So we could call him amoral." She nodded. "And we can say, *maybe*, that he'd have no reservations about murder; it just was unnecessary or dangerous."

"Or unseemly. Dartmouth men don't kill."

"But what if Sy had gotten past unseemly? Look, he was on a nine-year roll, making good movies, big money. He could do no wrong. Is it possible he got so conceited that he finally thought everything he did was by definition seemly?"

Bonnie wriggled farther back on the dresser and sat cross-legged. She grew reflective, staring past me into space. "Sure. It's possible. He believed his own publicity; Sy Spencer was superior, creative, refined. He could never be crass like the West Coast producers he was always going on about, screeching into their car phones or building bowling alleys in their houses. And he was so exquisitely sensitive he couldn't possibly be cruel. But forget Sy's idealized vision of Sy. I think all we've been talking about, all of what was going on in his life—thwarted love, his need for revenge, his need for money—played a part in pushing him toward the edge. What finally made him jump was that he got scared."

"Of what?"

"Failure. The studios hadn't gone for *Starry Night*, but he believed in it and so he went out and got the financing himself. Give Sy credit. He told me *Starry* would be the best kind of American movie, where characters grow and finally come to deserve each other. But Lindsay was ruining everything. Not only making a fool out of him with Santana, really wounding him, but destroying what he really cared about most: his movie, which was his reputation, his immortality."

"So she was costing him an extra half mil, plus future profits. And cutting off his balls and breaking his heart with Santana."

"More than that. She was making him lose status in the business. Sy told me this much: People were starting to say, See? We were right. *Starry Night* was a dog from day one. And the way Lindsay's performance was going—so lifeless—the critics and all his fancy friends would get into the elevator after a screening and say, Was that *thing* we just saw a Sy Spencer film?"

"But you know about those old guys out in Hollywood—those Goldwyn guys," I countered. "They made movies the critics said were lousy, and all their so-called friends laughed at them, and they just went on."

"But they were tough. They could take it."

"You're telling me Sy couldn't?"

"Stephen, remember how we were talking about Sy being different things to different people, that he didn't seem to have any core? Well, it wasn't just something he chose to do when it amused him. Sy always let himself be defined by whoever he was with, and if those people were laughing at him—for being cuckolded by a fancy-pants like Victor Santana, or for making an adventure-romance that wasn't adventurous or romantic—he would allow himself to be transformed into precisely what they were laughing at: a failure, a nothing, a jackass."

"So he wanted her dead for making him a laughingstock. But he wouldn't have killed her himself?"

"No. I can't see him injecting strychnine into her melon balls. Sy was much too squeamish to commit a violent act. And he wouldn't have dirtied his hands in the metaphorical sense. He was a gentleman; he never did anything nasty himself."

"Somebody was there to do it for him."

"Always."

"So who did he know who would do that kind of dirty work?" I asked. She knew, but she didn't want to say it. "How about Mikey LoTriglio?"

"No."

"Why not?"

"Because if Mikey or one of his boys did it, Lindsay Keefe would be on the cover of *People* this week, with a '1957–1989' over her bazooms, and Sy would be rolling with *Starry Night* starring Nicholas Monteleone and Katherine Pourelle."

I told her she was wrong, that La Cosa Nostra boys' invincible reputation was a myth, and in fact, half the time they were such a bunch of screwups they made the FBI look good.

She said she'd read *Wiseguy* and knew all about sociopathic Mafia morons who couldn't make it in the legitimate world, but

Mikey was as clever as they come, and with a different background, he could have been CEO of Merrill Lynch.

I told her she was a fucking dunce, and she smiled at me and said she wasn't.

I had to go into the kitchen to call Thighs at Headquarters, but I didn't feel like leaving Bonnie because I liked looking at her, especially in my undershirt, which was a washed-out cotton you could sort of see through. Also, if I left her alone she'd probably wind up lying on the floor, bench-pressing my stereo, so I picked up the phone on my nightstand. No word from Robby at the Life-codes lab up in Westchester. And no leads at all to Mikey's whereabouts: he wasn't at home in his fifteen-room Tudor in Glen Cove, in Nassau County, or at Terri Noonan's apartment in Queens, or at the Sons of Palermo social club in Little Italy. I asked, What about that bar in the meat district where he hangs out, Rosie's? Thighs said, I asked the bartender if Mikey LoTriglio was there, and he said: Mikey *who?*

"Rosie's?" Bonnie repeated when I hung up. "I remember hearing about Rosie's." She picked up the phone, got Manhattan information and asked for the number of Rosie's Bar and Grill on Ninth Avenue. Then she dialed and asked for Michael LoTriglio. I shook my head sadly, as in Pathetic. She was clearly hearing the same "Mikey *who?*" that Thighs had got. But she cut the guy off. "You may not know Mr. LoTriglio," she said into the phone, "but he comes into Rosie's every now and then." She sounded commanding, secure, the way a good cop has to sound. "I'd like you to do your best to get a message to him. Tell him that Bonnie Spencer—S-p-e-n-c-e-r—called and said it's urgent that she speak with him." She gave him my number and hung up.

"Good luck," I said.

"Thanks."

I told her I was going to go to the set in East Hampton to try and harass Lindsay into cooperating, and tie up a few other loose ends. I started to enumerate them when the phone rang. I recognized the voice, gravelly, tough. "Get Mrs. Spencer," it ordered. I handed it over to Bonnie.

"Mike?" Pause. "Fine." Pause. "I've missed you too." I stood beside her, tilted the receiver and put my ear right next to hers. "Actually," she went on, "I'm not so fine."

"What's the matter, Bonita?"

"I'm the major suspect in Sy's murder."

"*What?*"

"They issued an arrest warrant for me."

Mikey laughed. Not amused. An incredulous snort. "That is so stupid it makes regular stupid look smart."

"I know. But, Mike, let me tell you what happened."

"You don't need to give me no explanations."

"I know. But see, I was sort of keeping company with Sy again. And the police found evidence of my being at his house right before he died—and we weren't downstairs having tea. So they have this physical evidence from a bedroom, and they have this theory that Sy rejected me or my new screenplay and that I shot him. And that's another problem. They know I can handle a rifle."

"What can I do?" Mikey asked. "You got a blank check with me. You know that. Want me to find a nice, quiet place for you where you can not get noticed? Need money? Want me to . . . Listen, I would never talk to you this way, but what we have here is not your standard situation. So you want me to say abracadabra? Make some rabbit disappear? Name it. You're a sweet girl, a lady, and you were a good friend to my Terri."

"Terri's a lovely woman," Bonnie said. I couldn't believe this conversation. "You're lucky to have each other."

"Thanks," Fat Mikey said. "I tell her she's too good for me, but she don't believe it."

"Mike, let me tell you what I'd like you to do, and please, feel free to say no. You know me. I don't live in a world where people call in IOUs."

"I'm listenin'."

"There's a detective on this case, Detective Brady."

"I met him."

"He's on my side. He's trying to help me."

There was a long pause where Mikey contemplated the alternatives, including, if he had half the brains Bonnie credited him with, a setup. But he trusted Bonnie. He had to, because all he did was ask: "What makes you think he's on your side?"

"He knows it's a weak case, and he thinks he can make a better one." There was silence. "And he's in love with me." I stepped away from the phone and stared at her. She just continued with the conversation, so I stepped back and kept listening.

"The cop's in love with you?"

"I think so. So this is what I'd like, Mike—if you can see your way to doing it. I'd like you to talk to him. Anyplace you say. He seems to feel you might remember something now that slipped your mind during your interview." Mikey gave another one of his laugh/snorts. "He's sworn to me this would be off the record." I grabbed her shoulder, shook my head, but she just kept talking. "If you feel this would compromise you in any way, please don't do it. I know how it feels to have the police after you, and it's not something I'd want for you or Terri or your family. It's a horror."

"Where are you now, Bonita? The truth."

"He's hiding me, Mike. I can't tell you where."

"Tell him to meet me at the Gold Coast restaurant on Northern Boulevard in Manhasset in an hour." I shook my head, made a stretch-it-out signal with my hands.

"I think it will take him more than an hour to get there," she said.

"An hour and a half, then. Tell him to meet me in the parking lot in the back. Get out of his car, walk away from it and just stand there. Got it?"

"Thank you," Bonnie said. "I won't say I owe you one, Mike. But I will say I appreciate this from the bottom of my heart."

"I know you do, Bonita."

*   *   *

"I *love* you?" I said.

"I had to say something."

"Do you honestly think I love you?"

"Yes. Not that it means anything. You've decided you need a life with a Ford station wagon and kids with freckles and trim-a-tree parties and intercourse every Saturday, Sunday and Wednesday. It's preventive medicine, something you have to take to keep from self-destructing. I think you've convinced yourself that passion is a dark side that's too dangerous for you. Well, maybe you're right. Look at my life. Where has passion gotten me? What do I have to show for forty-five years of letting go? One movie nobody remembers and a warrant for my arrest for murder. Listen, you made the right choice. What could I offer you? Two dried-up fallopian tubes and a few laughs? So forget what I said about the love business. I get delusional under stress. Don't think twice: she's perfect. Grab her, marry her. *Mazel tov.*"

The restaurant was a block away from one of those sumptuous suburban shopping centers that attract people who neeed to spend eighty-five dollars for a cotton T-shirt.

Another cloudless day. Heat shimmered off the hoods of the Mercedeses, BMWs and Porsches, distorting the air, making the lot look like a slightly out-of-focus downtown Stuttgart. No Mikey. I'd been waiting for ten minutes, away from my car. All I saw was an occasional woman who had exhausted every possibility in the way of hair, makeup, nails, jewelry and clothes; one of them should have been put in a glass case in the Smithsonian just to show what we had become after eight years of Reagan.

I unbuttoned my jacket; all that accomplished was to allow more hot, humid air to circulate around my sweat-drenched shirt. Five minutes later, as I was loosening my tie, the door of a little red Miata convertible, top up, opened, and Mikey, with all the grace of sausage meat oozing out of its casing, somehow managed to emerge. He waddled across the blacktop. He'd obviously been

watching me since I arrived. We nodded at each other. He was
wearing sports clothes that looked more maternity than Mafia: white
pants and a huge red, blue and purple flowered shirt.

"Nice car." It was all I could think of to say.

"Not mine." I wasn't sure if he meant stolen or just borrowed.
"Take off your jacket and open up your shirt." He motioned me
over to the far side of a garbage Dumpster and examined my chest
and back for evidence of tape or wires. While I was buttoning my
shirt back up, he checked out my holster and patted down my
pants, taking out my wallet, shield and handcuffs to make sure
they were what they felt like. After he finished, he rumbled:
"Wanna go inside?"

I shivered at the frigid blast of air-conditioning. Mikey chose
a table and, without asking me, told the waitress to bring us two
club sandwiches and two iced teas. "You don't got to eat it. It's
for looks," he explained. He had one of those Roman noses that
begin at the forehead, but his nose, like the rest of him, was fat;
you wanted to squeeze it and hear it honk. "So tell me about our
mutual friend."

"I don't think she did it."

"No shit, Ajax." Even his earlobes were fat.

"But unless I find out who did, there's a good chance she'll
go for a long vacation."

"What do they got?"

"Circumstantial crap: a couple of people who'll say Sy wasn't
going to make a movie out of some screenplay she'd written; they
have a witness that he visited her house every day and they were
having an affair. Either way, the D.A. could make a case for a
woman who's been thrown over and who wants to get even." No
wonder no one had ever been able to nail Mikey. He was too smart.
He just sat there, a huge flower-shirted Buddha, but I could sense
him analyzing, weighing alternatives, computing—and all the
while not missing a word I was saying. "The physical evidence is
more of a problem," I continued. "Four of her hairs got caught in
one of those wicker headboards where she was keeping Sy company

no more than a half hour before he was killed. You know about the new DNA tests we do?"

"I know more than you know, Brady. Keep talking."

"They just found another hair, right at the spot where we figure the killer stood when he fired."

Mikey shook his head in disgust. His chins quivered. "Who put it there?"

"It could be Bonnie's."

"You wouldn't be here if you thought that."

"It's not important who put it there. It's important that I get some help. She's going to have to turn herself in by five o'clock, or they're going to declare her a fugitive. That wouldn't be a plus if she has to go to trial."

"Why are you doing this?"

"Look, I have until five o'clock. Either I sit here and talk philosophy with you—I know how you like to talk about Plato—or I try to save Bonnie Spencer's ass."

"Don't talk about her like that. Show some respect." A busboy came over to pour some water. Mikey waved him off. "What do you want to know?"

"You knew about Sy paying Lindsay an extra half million?"

"Sure. The bookkeeper told me, as I'm sure you know. It bothered her, seeing the investors fucked, so she confided in me."

"You bribed her and probably threatened her."

"You're tellin' me about the five o'clock deadline, so don't waste your time on cop chicken shit."

"Did you threaten Sy when you found out about the extra payment? I'm not chicken-shitting you now. I'm trying to figure out his state of mind."

"I didn't threaten him. I just told him what a stupid, fucking dick he was. Okay, I told him in a loud voice, and he was scared of me. I won't deny that. But I never would have killed him or had him mussed up or nothing. We went back too far, and I'm a sentimental guy."

The sandwiches came. Giant, first-generation-rich sandwiches, showy with frilly lettuce, wasteful, so high they were held together with toothpicks the size of small swords. I ate half of mine, Mikey ate all of his and then the other half of mine. I didn't touch the iced tea because I was too jacked up from all the coffee I'd been drinking. Mikey talked and chewed simultaneously. Bits of bacon got spewed, and tomato seeds sprayed out of his mouth, but fortunately his lunch stopped just short of my plate.

"Do you think Sy was fearful of you?"

"Nervous. You know. Ever since we was kids, Sy would pee in his pants if I even made a fist. But he wasn't terrified or nothin' like that."

"Did he say why he was giving Lindsay the extra money?"

Mikey shook his head, rolled his eyes, as if unable to believe mankind's capacity for idiocy. "You wanna shit a brick, Brady? You ain't gonna believe this one. When I was yellin' at him, he broke down. Not cryin', but sittin' in a chair, doin' a lot of cringin' shit. He finally stopped the crap about that Lindsay got a better movie offer and needed a added financial incentive. He told me he gave it to her because she said—you ready?—'Sy, I hate men who hold back. I need a man who can give of himself.' "

"*What?*"

Mikey shoved some potato chips into his mouth and said: "I swear to God. Is that pussy-whipped, or what?"

"That's pussy-whipped," I agreed. "So he was really in love with her?"

"Out of his mind nuts for her. I'd never seen him so hot for anybody."

"Not even Bonnie or his other wife?"

"The first was a stringy, ugly sourpuss wit' no tits and these big, ugly yellow teeth from some old family he married so people would think he was high-class. And Bonnie . . . I could never figure out that marriage. It was like a snake marrying a puppy dog. Probably had something to do with Sy's being all hot to get into the movie business, and she was in it then. And maybe he was tired of being a pretend WASP and got on a Jew kick, and she was a Jew but not too Jewey."

"Do you think he would have married Lindsay?"

"Sure."

"Then how come he took up with Bonnie?"

"Beats the hell out of me. When she called and said she'd been seeing him again, my mouth dropped open ten feet. You want my guess? The Lindsay thing knocked the shit out of him, and he was running home to Mommy." He paused. "You gonna eat your potato chips?" I pushed my plate over to him. He woofed down the chips and the crinkle-cut pickle slice.

"You're telling me interesting stuff but not helpful stuff."

"You sayin' I'm holdin' back?"

"I don't know, but what you've given me isn't going to help Bonnie. Do you want to help her?"

He wiped his chin with the back of his hand. "Don't ask dumb-fuck questions. Okay?"

"Okay."

"I found out about the extra half mil the second week of shooting. I confronted him. He wimped out right away, apologized, like I told you. Next day he messengered over a half mil in negotiable securities to me, and if you try to use that against me, you better hire somebody to start your car every morning."

"Mike," I said quietly, "no threats. I want to help Bonnie. That's all."

"You married?" he asked.

"No."

"Anyways, that was that. Until the Tuesday before he died. He calls me up, says he can't leave the Hamptons 'cause of the movie, but he's *got* to talk with me. He'll arrange for a private plane, or send a car and driver. I told him I don't like aer-o-planes and I don't use drivers because they got ears and mouths, but I'd drive out there because I was his friend. So I get there to his house—Jesus, that was some beautiful house. He tells me Lindsay's acting is terrible, that the movie is in deep shit. I tell him I'd heard that from my sources and so what else was new, and that if I lost my investment, I was sure he'd make good."

"That's a great way to invest."

"The only way. So then he tells me Lindsay is cheatin' on him. I start to say some garbage like 'Too bad,' but he didn't want that."

"What did he want?"

"He wanted her removed."

"Killed?"

"What do you think, Brady?"

"He asked you to get rid of her?" Mikey nodded. His chins, dotted with potato chip crumbs, bobbed up and down. "Did he suggest how?"

"No, because I stopped him right there. Oh, he did say it would be easy: There could be a letter to make people think it was some crazy fan who did it. But I just told him to shut his mouth and keep it shut and don't even think about anything like that. He was an amateur, and he didn't know what the fuck he was doin'."

"Actually, it sounds like he did."

"I got to admit, it wasn't a bad idea. But no way I was gonna tell him that. He wanted to kill her because she was bompin' the director and because he wanted to start his movie all over again and needed the bucks. You think I'd get anywhere near somethin' like that?"

"Did he offer to pay you?"

"We didn't get that far."

"Did he say anything else?"

"No. I got up and before I walked out I told him he didn't have what it takes, that his plan was full of holes, that if he tried to arrange something stupid with some two-bit local hood, they'd grab him in less than twenty-four hours. And then I told him to be a man. If he had to take a fall on the movie, take the fuckin' fall. And then I got the hell out of there. I gotta tell you: you know how I scared Sy?"

"Yeah."

"Well, he scared me. I got a chill down my spine. What the hell's happenin' to this world if guys like Sy Spencer want to kill people? Tell me. What have we become?"

CHAPTER 20

The tennis court of the East Hampton waterfront mansion that was *Starry Night*'s main set had everything: white wood benches, a water fountain, piles of snowy towels on a white wrought-iron stand, blue spruce and cypresses to obscure the chain-link fence. Beautiful. Except no one in their right mind would have wanted to be there. It was at least a hundred in the shade, but there was no shade. Lindsay Keefe and Nick Monteleone were volleying—if you could call it that—in about a hundred-and-ten-degree heat. There wasn't even a hint of cool air. Beyond the court, the foam on the waves made the ocean look as if it were boiling.

Every time Nick swung his racquet, he missed the ball and Victor Santana called "Cut!" Then a sweat-removal brigade would race over to the actors. Production assistants got there first. Some of them held umbrellas over the actors' heads, others held battery-operated fans. Then the makeup and hair people went to work, while still other attendants offered bottles of water with straws so

Lindsay and Nick could sip without getting drinking-glass dents around their mouths.

"One more take," Santana promised me. His dark skin was flushed almost maroon. The color looked great against his Outfit of the Day: green jungle fatigues. All Santana needed was a scruffier haircut, an M-16 and a couple of joints of skag, and he could have passed for one of my old buddies. He went on: "I must get enough footage of Lindsay because Nick . . ." He sighed in weary resignation. "This is going to cost an extra half day of long shots, with a tennis pro standing in for Nick. I simply cannot believe it; we gave him a full four weeks of tennis lessons preproduction."

"Monteleone has zero hand-eye coordination," I pointed out. "He'd need an instruction manual if he wanted to scratch his balls. Now look, Mr. Santana, I know making a movie is the most important thing in the world and it's not easy making a guy who doesn't know a tennis racquet from a pogo stick look like a jock. But I need more cooperation from you than I'm getting."

"Please, just one more take for the master shot." The brigade was walking off the court. "I give you my word of honor."

Lindsay was no natural athlete, but she could place a serve and look beautiful at the same time. Her dark eyes were shaded with a pink sun visor. Her pale hair, done up in some special curly ponytail, began to flutter as some guy in surfer trunks turned on a giant wind machine to the breezy setting. Santana called "Action " one more time.

I watched the crew watching the actors. The guys were taking in the whole scene. But the women seemed to have eyes only for Lindsay. Were they contemplating what life could be like with those breasts, those legs, that perfect ponytail? Were they curious? Jealous? Raging, that such glorious gifts had not been bestowed upon them? I thought about Lindsay's competition—Bonnie.

If Mikey had, in fact, nixed killing Lindsay, could Sy have persuaded his Annie Oakley of an ex-wife to pick up a .22? I'm *aching* to make your movie next, he'd have sworn. But I need some help getting over this rough patch. Or maybe: I want to marry you, bring you to Sandy Court, back to Fifth Avenue. My life will be your life, my friends your friends, my charge cards your charge cards. Remember how it was? Bonnie, darling, it was such a ghastly mistake, our splitting, and I know how profoundly lonely you've been. Let me make it up to you. But first, help me.

Why the hell was I thinking these things? Did I believe Bonnie Spencer was capable of willfully taking the life of another human being?

No.

The compressors in the trailer air conditioners had died under the strain of the humidity, so after Santana gave everybody a twenty-minute break, Lindsay and Nick, accompanied by assistants who, probably by tradition and job description, were paid to grovel, trekked up to the mansion—a modern interpretation of the White House cross-pollinated with the Taj Mahal—and went into two upstairs bedrooms. Before he went into his, my pal Nick gave me a for-your-eyes-only, homicide-cop-to-homicide-cop one-finger salute.

I was about to walk into Lindsay's room, which seemed to be some sort of homage to mosquito netting, but one of her designated toadies tried to shut the door on me. "She needs to recoup," the girl whispered in hospital-corridor tones. I pushed past her, ordered everybody except Lindsay to get out and slammed the door.

Filmy stuff formed a canopy and curtains around the bed. It covered the windows from ceiling to floor. For some reason, odd pieces of it were draped over chairs. There were three chairs and one of those chaise longues in the room, but naturally, given the choice, Lindsay stretched out on the bed. I pulled up a chair and pushed away some stuff, so I wouldn't have to interrogate her through gauze. Right away she started with the lascivious shit, running her hands slowly over her face and neck, arranging pillows so she was angled to achieve maximum tit power.

On the table next to the bed, there was a six-pack of foreign water in blue bottles. She put out a languid hand to take one but couldn't quite reach it. She waited for me to get up and hand her one. I didn't. She got one for herself and drank, not sexily, but with the loud glug-glug noises of a cartoon character.

"I feel sick from the heat," she said. I don't think she was acting. Her whole body was red and covered in a cold sweat.

"It must be a bitch out there."

I guessed she'd fulfilled her courtesy quotient by making a comment about the weather. She snapped: "Well, what do you want?"

"I want you to stop lying. If you don't stop lying, you're going to find yourself under arrest."

"You tried that tactic with my agent. He's old, losing his touch, so it worked. It won't work with me."

"Want to bet? Fifty bucks says before I even bring you in for fingerprinting, you'll—"

"Do you honestly think you can scare me?"

"Beats me. But I do know I can interrupt your moviemaking. And when you come before the judge, I can arrange to have a lot of reporters at the courthouse. You can explain to them how I'm not scaring you—even though I've arrested you for withholding information in the matter of the death of Sy Spencer."

"You are a low-class shit," she said.

"Yeah, but a low-class shit with the power to arrest."

There was a too-long moment of silence. I felt like closing my eyes, relaxing, but in the interests of projecting authority and macho intensity, I glared at her. At last, Lindsay propped herself on her elbow. "Sometimes I like low-class shits," she said, her voice lazy, husky. She extended her hand to me.

"Ms. Keefe, let me be honest with you. As far as I can see, you're not in that much trouble that you have to fuck a cop." She pulled away her hand. "You just have to answer a few questions, and chances are, your answers won't get any further than me. All right?"

"Yes." Brusque. The momentary fake desire was supplanted by her normal disdain.

"Did Sy confront you about your affair with Victor Santana?"

"Yes."

"This isn't Twenty Questions. Tell me about it."

She finished glugging the water and took a second bottle. "He didn't raise his voice, not once, the whole time. He told me, very calmly, as if he were giving me the next day's weather forecast, that I was a whore. That I'd lost my ability as an actor." She stopped. She didn't want to talk to me.

"Keep going," I said.

Finally, reluctantly, she did. "He wanted me off the film. He followed me around the house all that evening and the next morning, calling me Whore, as though that were my given name. 'Going up to bed so early, Whore?' He kept telling me I was ruining *Starry Night*. Always in that calm voice."

"When did this start?"

"The week he was killed. Monday night."

"Was he threatening to fire you?"

"No. He wanted me to quit."

"Why?"

"*Why?*" she demanded. She gave a snort of contempt, as if I'd just asked the stupidest question of the twentieth century. "So I'd be in violation of my contract, that's *why*. So he wouldn't have to pay me. So he could get the guarantors to pay the completion insurance and start all over again."

"Is that possible?"

"Of course it's possible. And then the insurance company could sue me to recover their costs."

"So you wouldn't quit."

"Of course not. It was an insane suggestion."

"Why would he expect you to quit if the consquences to you would be so bad?"

"Because."

"Because why?"

"Because he was trying to make me so upset, so frightened of him, that I'd do anything he wanted."

"What was he doing?"

"Before he told me he knew about Victor, he'd already started being cold. Very cold."

"He stopped sleeping with you?"

She gave me a look that showed her distaste; I was getting off on her sex life. "He wouldn't touch me," she said. "Do you want to know more? Of course you do. When I tried to take his hand, he pulled it away—as though I had leprosy."

"But he wouldn't say what was wrong?"

"Not at first. Just horrible coldness."

"Was he cold in front of other people? On the set?"

"No. That threw me off. He was delightful to me on the set."

"And how were you to him?"

"Oh, grow up. What do you think? That I was going to let everyone know I was having terrible problems with the executive producer? He was acting very loving to me, so I acted loving to him. I thought: Well, he hasn't made anything public; maybe we can work it out. I stopped seeing Victor—in a private sense—on Wednesday."

"You told Santana it was over?"

"No. I never burn bridges. What if I couldn't fix things with Sy? I just told him I was having a messy, painful period. *Very bloody.*"

"That's nice."

"I know men. It works. In any case, I did everything I could to heal the breach with Sy. If not personally, then professionally. But it was so strange. And even when things got really terrible, we were still playing loving in front of everybody else."

"Like the day he was killed, taking a wad of cash from him? Loving like that?"

"Don't make it sound like I was picking his pocket! It was a homey, wifely gesture."

"You said things got terrible. When?"

"Thursday morning. My car came a little before six, and when I left the bedroom to go downstairs, Sy was out there in the hall, waiting." Her face, under the sweat and layers of makeup, went rigid. Her mouth began to move mechanically, like a marionette's. She was somewhere between unsettled and petrified. "He told me—he sounded so detached—that he had all kinds of friends. I didn't know what he was talking about, but I wanted to get away from him. He was standing right up against me. His face was less than an inch from mine. I could see each whisker where he hadn't shaved. He said some of his friends weren't very nice people, but they'd invested in *Starry Night* and they'd heard that the dailies were terrible. They were very unhappy, and they wanted me to quit. If I didn't, Sy said he couldn't be held responsible for the repercussions."

"Did you ask what the repercussions were?"

"Yes." Her body gave a fast, powerful involuntary shudder, almost a convulsion.

"What did he say would happen?"

"Acid in the face."

"Jesus! What did you do?"

"I told him I was calling the police. I marched back into the bedroom and picked up the phone, but he grabbed it from me. I let him take it. The whole scene was so predictable."

"Did he make any more threats?"

"No, of course not. He backed down. I knew he would. He actually lost his cool, the little bastard. Apologized all over himself. *Begged* me to forgive him."

"And what did you say?"

"I told him I'd consider it." Lindsay's lips arched into something like a smile. "I knew how to handle Sy. I'd let him go out to L.A., have his little meetings with Kat Pourelle and the other losers, and by the time he got back on Sunday night, he'd want me again. In his movie. In his bed. On a permanent basis."

"You think he wanted marriage?"

"Oh, he would have needed a week or two to cool down over Victor, but yes. Definitely."

"You think so?"

"I know so."

"Would you have married him?"

"What do you think?"

"I don't know. He was a guy who threatened to have you disfigured. Ruin your life, ruin your career."

"He was a man eaten up inside by jealousy."

"He was a producer who wanted you out of his life, out of his movie."

"Only because I'd wounded him so deeply. I admit it: I made a mistake. A big one. But Sy would have come around. We were so well suited, and he knew it. I'm . . . well, what I am, and he was a brilliant, successful film producer. He cared about serious social issues. *And* he was my intellectual equal. To tell you the truth, as far as the jealousy, I *loved* it that he was finally displaying some real emotion." Lindsay began to rub her bare legs together; she seemed to be getting aroused, not so much by her recollection of Sy's crazy behavior but by the remembrance of her power over him. "Jealousy," she said again, savoring the word. "Sy was *consumed.*"

"You think he loved you?"

"Of course he loved me."

I got up and stood behind the chair. "The killer was fifty feet away from a small, white-robed figure about your size. At the moment the rifle was fired, Sy was supposed to have been flying somewhere over Kansas. And you were supposed to be getting ready to do your late-afternoon laps in the pool."

"No!" The makeup didn't help. Her skin started to lose its color. It took on a waxen cast, like a corpse's.

"Yes." I pushed aside a drooping piece of mosquito net and walked out of the room.

I called Carbone and told him I was at the *Starry Night* set on the off chance Bonnie Spencer had connected with any of the crew members, and also to check if she'd showed up again after Sy threw her off, maybe doing some kind of neurotic, obsessive number. He said that Thighs, Robby and Charlie Sanchez were all out trying to get a lead on her. Casually, as if I already knew what the answer would be, I asked if the DNA results had come in on the new hair sample. It's Bonnie's, Carbone said. Still think she didn't do it?

I told him if he had nothing better to do, to check the evidence record files. Find out the number of hairs we'd picked up that first night, then go down and look in the envelope the lab had returned. He'd find a minus-one factor.

He told me I was losing my emotional equilibrium, that I was projecting something—I forget what—onto Robby Kurz, that I needed a vacation, and if I passed the fancy Italian store in East Hampton to pick him up two pounds of sausage with fennel.

I hung up. Robby *had* to have planted the hair. And for sure, he had spread the drinking rumor, the Steve luvs Bonnie 4-ever rumor. He was out to get her—and me. Sooner or later, he was going to realize that Bonnie had a protector and had gotten some help with her disappearing act. And then he would be at my house.

Gregory J. Canfield was supposed to be in a store in the village doing his job as production assistant, which, in this instance, meant picking up fresh figs, prosciutto, a semolina bread and a bottle of Dolcetto wine for Nick Monteleone since, according to a couple of people on the set, Nick had mumbled that what with the heat, he wanted a light bite, not a heavy supper, and since Lindsay's performance was still so inert, any hope of salvaging *Starry Night* seemed to rest on Nick's well-moussed head, so finally, after forty minutes of consultation between the line producer and the first assistant director (which included a call to Nick's agent in Beverly Hills), a definition of the term "light bite" was agreed upon, and Gregory was dispatched.

But I figured he might stop in to say goodbye to his woman, Myrna the costume lady, and sure enough, they were holding hands in the costume trailer, staring into each other's eyes, giving each other sweet, delicate, pursed-lip kisses of farewell. It didn't seem to bother them that one of Myrna's assistants was no more than a foot away from them, ironing a duplicate of the tennis outfit Lindsay was wearing. And it didn't seem to bother them when I called out "Hey, Gregory!" He gave me a slightly dopey glance, then gazed back into the depths of Myrna's eyes.

The trailer was huge, like a wildly inflated walk-in closet, with rack after rack of clothes, shelves of shoes, and drawers with scarves and underwear and fake jewelry spilling out. I walked to the back and tapped Myrna on the shoulder. "Hello!" she said. "How are you?"

"Fine, thanks." She looked as messy as when I'd caught her in her inside-out negligee. This time she was wearing a long sacklike thing with a parrot design; it looked as if she'd picked it up in Woolworth's in Honolulu in 1957 and had worn it frequently since. "Myrna, I need Gregory for a minute."

"Is anything wrong?" she asked.

"No. Everything's fine. A couple of minor points need clarification." She nodded, released Gregory's hands and gave him a tender nudge toward me.

I took him away from her, outside to where they had a table set up with bagels and cookies and doughnuts with melting sugar and M&M's and nuts and raisins. There was a bowl of red grapes, but they were hot. He gave me a Coke from a cooler beneath the table. "How's it goin', man?" he asked. A few nights with Myrna had turned him from Ultra-Geek into Mr. Cool.

"It's going all right," I told him. It wasn't. It was ten minutes to five; I wanted to get back to Bonnie, but I had nothing worth bringing her. I held the icy soda can against my forehead. "Remember that conversation you mentioned to me that took place in dailies? The 'if lightning struck' conversation."

Gregory nodded. "Sure, sure." He had a thoughtful look. He was probably recalling the graininess of the film and seemed, worse, about to describe it to me. I cut him off.

"Who was there? You said it was late. Most people had gone."

"Ummm," he began.

"Don't 'ummm.' Talk."

"Sy."

"Good. Keep going."

"One of the assistant producers, Sy's gofer. His name's Easton."

"Who else?"

"Me. I think Nick Monteleone. The D.P. Director of photography. That's another term for cinematographer."

"What's his name, Gregory?"

"Alain Duvivier."

"Is he French?"

"*Mais oui, monsieur le detective*. He was there, and his girlfriend."

"What's her name?"

"Monica, Monique. But she's gone."

"How come?"

"He started with the set dresser, Rachel."

"Who else?"

Gregory shut his eyes and, for once, his mouth. He seemed to be trying to re-create the scene. "That was it."

"You're sure?"

"Positive."

"Did Sy hang back to talk to anyone afterwards?"

"I don't know. He sent me out to put pink pages in his leather folder in his car. Revised pages of script. You change color with every revision. First blue, then pink, and then yellow, green, goldenrod, then buff—"

"Go get me Alain."

"I can't. I'm supposed to be in East Hampton, and he's—"

"Get him *now*." Now took two minutes.

One thing about movie people: none of them dressed in a normal, businesslike way. Alain Duvivier looked like a cliché of a French creative type. He was in his mid-twenties, with blond and brown hysterical hair that tumbled over his shoulders, matching heavy eyebrows and one hoop earring. He wore bubble-gum-color shorts and one of those wrestler-style strap undershirts that have practically no sides. He was more the size of a grizzly than a man; beside him, Gregory was almost invisible.

"Hello," I said.

"Alo," he said, then added, with fitting somberness: "Sy. Very, very sad." He sounded so French you half expected him to say Ooh-la-la, but he didn't.

"Mr. Duvivier, I understand you were at dailies the night a certain conversation took place." He was concentrating too hard, so I slowed down. "There were some remarks about lightning and a discussion—a talk—about what would happen if lightning struck—hit—Lindsay Keefe. Do you recall any of that?"

"Lighting Lindsay?" he asked.

"No, light*ning*. It was a conversation about lightning."

"Lightning?"

I turned to Gregory. "What the hell's the word for lightning in French?"

"I took Spanish."

I turned back to Duvivier. "Lightning." I pointed up to the sky and made a streaking gesture back and forth. He glanced over at Gregory a little nervously, and it didn't help when I made a thunder noise and followed it with another lightning imitation.

He blurted out: "Rachel!"

"Rachel?" I inquired.

Gregory said: "His girlfriends translate for him."

"He doesn't understand English?"

"Well, technical terms. And he says 'Alo, pretty girl' a lot."

"*Au revoir*," I said to Duvivier.

"Bye-bye," he responded.

Smart. The sound on the TV was low enough so someone standing outside would never guess anyone was home. I found Bonnie sitting in my recliner, watching a movie. Before she zapped the remote control I saw that even though it was a black-and-white thing, it was something I would watch, with Kirk Douglas or Burt Lancaster; I always got them mixed up.

She pushed herself out of the chair. "Ready? It's five-thirty."

"Relax."

"We have an agreement." She was very subdued.

"Are you all right?"

"I'm fine." She wasn't, but since she wasn't crying, or sullen or angry, I couldn't get a precise reading. "How do you want to go about this? Should I call Gideon first, or do you want to drop me off—"

"Listen, do you trust me? Trust my judgment?"

"Isn't it a little late to be asking that?"

"We've got to get out of here fast, because I have a sickening feeling that fuckface Robby is going to wind up here, looking for you."

"Why?"

"I don't have time now. Let's get out of here. I'll explain on the way."

"On the way home?" She sounded so quiet, thoughtful. Well, she had a right to be. Leaving my house was like picking the Go-directly-to-jail card.

"You're not going home yet."

"You promised me."

"I know, but there's one more shot. Will you have faith in me, give me another half hour?"

"Yes." So hushed, proper, ladylike, even. "I will."

"Then let's haul ass, Bonnie."

She looked past the mud room into the kitchen. The stove and refrigerator were older than I was, and the white porcelain table had deep black craters where it had chipped.

"Where are we?" Her voice was barely a whisper. I realized she'd seen me lift up an unplanted flowerpot and take the key that was under it. She'd assumed we were breaking and entering, and having gotten to know me, she did not appear to be surprised.

"My family's house." I guided her—almost pushed her, be-cause she didn't want to come—through the kitchen, into a hallway that led to the stairs. "My brother was there for that 'lightning' conversation. And he was always around, doing things for Sy. I want to see if he remembers what happened after those dailies, that night or maybe the next day." Bonnie stopped so suddenly I banged into her. "Come on." I gave her a light shove and kept talking. "I want to find out who Sy saw—" She wouldn't move. "—and who he talked to."

And then I saw what she was staring at. A gun cabinet. Plain pine. Familiar to someone who grew up on a farm.

Or to someone who grew up in a sporting goods store, whose old man was the best shot in Ogden.

No, I thought. No. She didn't do it.

CHAPTER 21

Growing up in the house of what had once been Brady Farm, I'd pretty much been able to disregard the slight stink of degeneration. That odor of decay had always been there, but it was elusive, except when I sat on the living room couch long enough. There, at the heart of the house, it could not be ignored.

But if I was just passing through—which, during the years after my father left, was how I thought of myself, a low-class transient who happened to have the last name Brady—I'd smell, instead of underlying decay, the tangy carnation scent of the room spray my mother had boosted from Saks, the stuff they used to smog dressing rooms after ladies with gamy underarms tried on Better Dresses.

On the rare occasions I visited after I'd moved out, I must have made an unconscious shift and begun breathing through my mouth, because I stopped noticing the smell. But as I led Bonnie to the staircase, I got a killer whiff of Mildew Plus.

I was embarrassed. I hoped that someday I could really un-
load, tell her my history, but for now I hoped she'd think well of
my background. I didn't want her to notice the stink of my family's
house, or the dry, blackened edges of the rips in the gray stairway
runner. I wanted her to believe we were poor but nice, not that
we were poor and so bitter we couldn't bestow any kindness on
our surroundings.

When we got to the second or third step, she finally turned
and faced me. "Maybe I'd better wait downstairs." I didn't bother
to answer. What the hell could I do? Offer her a seat on the
Odorama couch? That way, when I heard my mother come home
from work, I'd have to run downstairs in time to say, Mom, this
is Bonnie Spencer, the Jew whose ex-husband was murdered in
Southampton, and my mother could say, Oh, yes, that was the old
Munsey place. Paine Munsey. He's in sugar. They're up in Little
Compton now. They couldn't bear the new element, so they sold.

I put my hand on the small of her back. "It won't take long."
I propelled her a little harder, and she continued up the stairs. I
loved the chance to touch her.

But it was more than wanting her with me. It made sense to
let Bonnie hear what my brother had to say before I let her go.
She was so smart; maybe she could pick up some small, free-
floating fact that could be added to the equation and, finally, make
it balance. Sure, Easton had been in the city the whole day of the
murder, but there might be a snatch of a phone conversation, a
note, a memo—some indication of hostility—he'd absorbed sub-
liminally the day before.

Could he have picked up even a single word—like "rifle,"
"shoot," "pool," "insurance" or "Lindsay"—soon after the "if
lightning struck" conversation at dailies?

I thought: What if one of those words had something to do
with Bonnie? All of a sudden, on the last of those shadowy steps,
I felt what I'd always felt as a kid. Not a memory, or déjà vu. The
feeling itself—empty, and so sad.

I knew she couldn't have done it.

But what if she had? Well, then I would be what I was before. Nothing. My life offered only two compensations: baseball and work. But neither the Yankees nor the Suffolk County Police Department was set up to do the big job, save lost souls. And all the drugs I had tried—beer, pot, peyote, hash, yellows, women, 'ludes, LSD, booze, heroin, more women, more booze, Lynne— in the end had given me no peace either; they'd just taken the edge off for a little while. Only Bonnie Spencer had made me believe that, truly, I might be redeemed.

What if I was wrong about her? What could my future be? I could drink again, and die. Or I could become one of those old retired cops, clutching a felt hat in my hands, keeping busy shuffling between daily Mass at Queen of the Most Holy Rosary and AA meetings, until death came.

But I knew she didn't do it.

When I guided Bonnie into Easton's room, he wasn't the only one who was surprised. Bonnie was. Surprised, angered. Easton had stolen Sy Spencer's ties! Her hands became fists; she could have decked him. There they were—blue ties with tiny stirrups, green with minuscule anchors, red with itty-bitty French flags—laid out on the bed, ready to be packed for Easton's trip to California to meet with Philip Scholes, the director, about his new job. There was no doubt that they were Sy's: Easton could never have afforded them, plus I'd seen dozens of them on special hooks on a section of Sy's giant remote-control revolving clothes rack the night of the murder, when I did a walk-through of the house. And—Bonnie's face was so grim—there were Sy's sweaters, too, on that bed! Cotton knits and cashmeres meant to be fashionably baggy on a little guy like Sy, sweaters that would just, barely, fit Easton. Her expression declared: Arrest this man!

And Easton's expression? Furious, sure, at another of my tiptoed instrusions. He stood legs apart, arms crossed over his chest, maintaining his dignity despite the fact that all he was wearing was one of those shortie shaving robes, and a particularly hideous one. But he was also confused: I know who this woman with Steve is, but I can't place her. And embarrassed too, as all three of us stared at over a thousand bucks' worth of accessories from the wardrobe of the ultra-suave (and ultra-dead) Seymour Ira Spencer.

I suppose my expression was something less than sunny, reflecting my disgust at my brother's penny-ante thievery. I could just see him, hanging around, waiting for us to take down the crime-scene tape and go home, so he could do a search-and-destroy through Sy's closets under the guise of Setting Things in Order. My guess was that if I looked through Easton's drawers, I'd find cuff links, or one of those mini-VCRs, a pocket telephone, or maybe one of those skinny, gold-coin watches on an alligator strap.

I was just about to lighten the atmosphere with some joke about taking Easton in, when he got petulant, affronted by my drop-in with a tall woman of unknown origin in athletic shorts and grungy running shoes. "I'd like to know what all this is about, Steve."

"You would?"

"Yes. I would." Just at that instant, as he was carving out a new niche in supercilious schmuckdom, he recognized Bonnie. Obviously, hers was not a calming presence. Easton began to sidle back and forth alongside the bed, doing an agitated step-together-step, as if trying to keep out of her line of sight—or block her view of her ex-husband's wardrobe. "What is *she* doing here?" he demanded. His gracious-living voice disappeared, replaced by a troubled squeal.

"She's with me. You do know that this is Bonnie Spencer?"

"Yes."

I steered Bonnie over to a straight-backed chair. "Stay put," I told her. I turned back to my brother. He stopped his sideways skedaddling. "You saw her that day at the set, when she knocked on the door of Sy's trailer?"

"Yes." His yeses sounded more like yaps than complete syllables. I thought: He's fucking mortified about being caught red-handed. Steal billions, everybody knows, and you're invited to the best parties; steal ties, and you're a tacky little piece of shit.

"And Sy told her to get off the set, that she didn't belong?"

"Yes."

"Stephen, listen—" Bonnie started to say, in her direct, you're-not-approaching-this-right voice, as though we were husband-and-wife detective partners in some 1937 movie.

"Not now!" Then I asked my brother: "Did you know Sy was having an affair with her?"

"What?" It wasn't an assertion of amazement, as in: I don't believe it! It wasn't even a question. It was more a "Duh" of befuddlement. Easton was on overload; he couldn't seem to get what was going on.

"Answer me," I snapped at him.

I had to know how finely tuned in he was to Sy's private life. How much did he know? What could he guess at? After dailies that night, had Sy made any secret phone calls? When they'd gotten back to the house and Easton was setting out Sy's papers or his pj's or pink pages for the next day, had he possibly picked up another reference to "Lindsay"? "Lightning"? An icy laugh? An intense "I need your help" spoken behind a closed door? Would Easton the Refined actually eavesdrop? Would Easton *not* eavesdrop was more the question. My brother wouldn't recognize an ethic if it snuck up and bit him on the butt.

But still, as I looked at him, I knew he'd make a fantastic witness for the D.A., all blue-suited and white-shirted, with one of his new ties. His fair hair would shine in the harsh light of the witness box, his low-key gentleman's voice would appeal, convince. I thought: Wouldn't it be wonderful if he actually could remember something important?

State your name, the assistant D.A. would command. Easton Brady. I ask you, Mr. Brady, the A.D.A. would say, did you overhear a telephone conversation between Sy Spencer and Michael LoTriglio? The defense lawyer—Fat Mikey's, maybe, although I felt a twinge of regret at the notion—would leap up and object on the grounds of no foundation. The A.D.A. would rephrase the question and inquire, How did you know who was on the phone with Mr. Spencer? Well, I answered the phone and the man said it was Mike LoTriglio and he wanted to talk to Sy *now*. I'd spoken to Mr. LoTriglio before, and this sounded exactly like him, Easton would begin.

I glanced over at Bonnie. Her eyes were riveted on Easton.

I remembered her eyes in that moment when she'd stood before the gun cabinet downstairs. I thought I'd seen a fleeting shadow of pain in them, a recognition of what was behind those doors.

What was behind those doors?

My old man's twelve-gauge shotgun.

And his .22.

And then I knew what Bonnie knew.

Easton seemed to understand that, at last, I knew. He stood quietly, thumbs hooked into his pockets, watching me.

I had to get ready for an interrogation. Oh, we Bradys were so neat. I lifted Sy's folded sweaters from the bed and placed them—one, two, three—gently on the dresser. I was so painstakingly careful you could hardly hear the rustle of the tissue paper between the folds. Then I took my brother by the hand, and, together, we sat side by side on the space I had cleared.

"East," I said.

"Yes?"

"You have something you want to tell me."

"No."

"Come on."

His neck and his ears got fiery red, but he said, "No. Absolutely not."

"I found the rifle." He shook his head. It could be taken to mean: I don't understand. Or: No, you didn't. "I found it, East." I prayed—neat, always put things back where they belong—that he had returned it to the cabinet, that he hadn't done something like take a ride on the Shelter Island ferry to drop it into Long Island Sound. But then I saw I was okay; Easton angled his body away from mine and with the side of his hand was ironing out an imperceptible wrinkle in the blue tie right next to him. I said softly: "It's just a question of time before we get back the results of the ballistics tests." He wouldn't look at me. "We fire the rifle and then compare the markings on the bullet with the two bullets we took from Sy." I was afraid if I looked at Bonnie I'd lose my rhythm, but then she didn't seem to want my attention. There was no sound, no motion; if I hadn't known she was sitting in a chair five feet away, I would not have sensed she was in the room. "The markings will match, East. You know that."

Easton lifted his chin and breathed out sharply, giving his nostrils a scornful, Southampton flare, so Old Society. "I can't believe you can even *think* something like this!"

"How can I *not* think it?"

"You're my brother!"

"I know. Maybe that's why it took me so long to understand."

In the past, when a case finally came into focus, I always got a wild burst of energy, a hunger to *know*. But now I felt heavy, sluggish, incredibly weary. If Easton ran, I wouldn't have been able to go after him; I was on some other planet, with terrible gravity.

"I want both of you out of here!" he ordered. He scowled at Bonnie. "There is nothing to discuss."

"There's a lot to discuss," I said.

"This is totally asinine."

"No. This is very serious and important."

"You have no proof of *anything*."

"I have the murder weapon."

"Oh, don't be melodramatic! Are there fingerprints on it? Are there?"

"There may be, even if you think you took care of that. We use laser technology now."

He shook his head. Either he didn't believe me, he wasn't impressed or he wasn't afraid. "And what if there aren't fingerprints?" he inquired.

"Who the hell else would take Dad's .22 and shoot Sy Spencer? Mom?"

"You *would* bring her into it."

"Relax. Who do you think she's going to blame for all this? You or me?"

I got up and walked toward Easton's closet. A regular closet, not a mahogany-and-brass state-of-the-art architectural space like Sy's. But Easton aspired. Everything was in perfect order: suits, shirts, ties—more of Sy's—slacks, blazers, shoes. Shoes in their cardboard boxes, stacked on the top shelf. The front panels of the boxes had been cut off so you could see each pair. Years of shoes: penny loafers, tassel loafers and oxfords; white bucks, golf shoes and rubber-soled boaters; tennis sneakers, running sneakers, sandals, slippers. And thongs. Ordinary rubber thongs for the beach, the kind you can pick up anywhere. A men's size eleven, my size, my brother's size.

I covered my left hand with my handkerchief. I took out my pen with my right and, carefully, eased the box off the shelf and caught it in my left.

I said, "You hated to bet when we were kids. You know why? I always won. But I'll bet you right now these thongs will match the molds we made from impressions in the grass right near Sy's house, where the shots were fired. A fancy, hot-shit lawn, East. Turf, they call it. It's a special variety of Kentucky bluegrass called Adelphi. The guy at the State Agricultural Extension said it must have cost him a fucking fortune to cover all that ground. But what the hell. The right shade of green makes a statement." I held up the box. "I'll bet you we find a blade or two of Adelphi right in here."

It took a while before Easton could get his eyes off the shoe box. Then, in an I've-got-a-secret boyish manner that my mother would have found enchanting, he gestured me over with his index finger. Without looking at Bonnie, he whispered: "Why is she here?"

"She's been giving me some information on the case. Some insights into Sy."

"Oh." He seemed hesitant about what to do next. His mouth opened, but nothing came out.

"Why don't I tell her to take a hike?" He seemed so relieved. He inclined his head; it was almost a bow.

I walked over to Bonnie and spoke softly. "Can you drive a stick shift? Okay, you know where the nature preserve is, that swamp place, about a minute and a half north of here? Go there. Watch birds or something for an hour and a half. Then take back roads to your friend Gideon's. Don't park too close to his house. Don't call him to tell him you're coming. And make your approach from one of the houses behind his in case they're surveilling his place. Got it so far?"

She was levelheaded, serious and terse. "Yup."

"Explain to Gideon what's happening. Under the circumstances, he won't want you to turn yourself in. So just sit tight."

"Do you need any help? Want me to call anyone?"

"No."

"Promise me—"

"Yeah, I'll be careful. Now look, if for any reason they find you and scoop you up—arrest you—don't make any statements of any kind."

"Okay."

Her eyes darted over to Easton. I knew what she was thinking: There was a good chance that if I didn't nail him, she'd be nailed. And maybe, in the final analysis, I couldn't nail him. Or I wouldn't be able to.

"I trust you." That's what Bonnie said instead of goodbye. Then she held out her hand for my car keys and was gone.

"You killed Sy," I told my brother.

"Please, Steve."

"You killed him."

He lowered himself on the chair Bonnie had vacated. "I didn't mean to." His voice had the emotional intensity of someone caught running a red light. "I'm sorry."

"You meant to kill Lindsay."

"Yes. How did you figure it out? From that one conversation about lightning?"

"Just tell me what happened, Easton."

"You know what's funny?" He kept tugging at the hem of his bathrobe like a woman with lousy legs in a too-short skirt. "You always call me 'East,' and now you're saying 'Easton.' "

"What happened?"

My brother's bright-blue eyes filled with tears. "I want you to know I really loved that man. There was only a sixteen-year age difference, but Sy was like a father to me." He put his hands over his face and wept.

I sat on the edge of the bed and watched him. I wanted to be moved by his grief, but I had too many years in Homicide; I'd watched this movie, *The Crying Killer,* too many times.

People who commit murder are weird, and not just in their willingness to stick out their tongues at God, to steal His gift of life, to commit the one act that is unquestionably and universally wrong. No, what always got to me about murderers wasn't their evil, their distance from the rest of humanity, but their closeness to it. I'd watched mothers sob at the coffins of babies they'd clubbed to death; I'd heard boyfriends scream out in anguish at the funerals of the girlfriends they'd battered, strangled and, postmortem, raped. They were so vulnerable, so wounded, these killers. And I knew what would be coming next from my brother because, for me, this was the hundredth rerun of that scene. His eyes would plead: Pity me, help me, go easy on me, because I, the survivor, am also a victim of this monstrous crime. What a loss I've suffered! Look at these tears!

I played it with Easton the way I always played it. I gave

him exactly what he felt he deserved: sympathy and support. "It must be such hell," I said.

"It is. Complete hell." I shook my head as if I couldn't bear his—our—sadness.

What the fuck right did he have to kill? To fly off, with a new wardrobe of ties, to California, leaving Bonnie to spend the next twenty-five years paying for what he did?

I felt no sadness for my brother's stupid, wasted, empty life, and no guilt, not a goddamn twinge, about not having been a better older brother so I could have given him some values or shit like that. No, I just felt cold and very tired. "Tell me how it happened, East," I urged. Oh, did I sound full of compassion.

"You're calling me 'East' again."

I smiled. "I know. Hey, you're my brother, aren't you? Come on. Let's talk. Tell me what went on. Was there any discussion about getting rid of Lindsay before that night at dailies?" Every now and then I slipped, but I knew to avoid the word "kill" when questioning a killer.

"No. Nothing. I knew they were having troubles. Sy had turned off on her completely, went from hot to cold overnight. But I'm sure you know by now that he wasn't the confiding type."

"But then there was that remark that if lightning struck Lindsay, if she died, the problems with *Starry Night* would be over. What happened after that?"

Easton didn't answer. He yanked at the hem of his bathrobe. It was one of those Saks uglies that my mother had bought on final, maximum markdown and saved for Christmas; it was some sort of strange, long-haired terry cloth, and grayish-brown, the color of a rag used for unpleasant chores.

"Who brought up getting Lindsay out of the picture? You or Sy?"

"I did, but it isn't the way it sounds. I just asked him some questions about the completion insurance. He said that if a star dies, the guarantors will pay to make another movie. If you're on a forty-day shooting schedule and she dies when you're fifteen days into it, the producers will get fifteen days of money. Well, minus a deductible of either a couple of hundred thousand or three days. But Sy said the coverage was quite fair."

"But there was no suggestion he wanted you to facilitate matters?"

"No. Not then."

My brother's face reflected a little hurt, as in why hadn't Sy leapt at his unstated offer right away. I had absolutely no doubt that Easton's questions about insurance were openings to Sy. Maybe Sy hadn't even thought about offing Lindsay before. Who knows? But all of a sudden, there it was, out in the electrified air: if lightning struck.

But Sy was no fool. He knew lightning was dangerous; only an expert could handle it. Like Mikey. Not a jerk like my brother. So he'd bypassed Easton, who was, most likely, doing everything but jumping up and down, waving his arms, calling out: Just ask me, Sy. I'm your boy. I'm your assistant producer. I'll do whatever you think needs doing. Sy, though, had gone to a pro. But the pro had been smarter than both Sy and Easton put together. He just said no.

"When did the matter come up again?"

"Wednesday night."

I sat back on the bed, as though I were getting comfortable, all ready and eager to hear about my kid brother's first day of junior high. "Tell me, how did he bring it up?" I asked.

"That's what amazed me, Steve! He was so unbelievably direct. He said, 'We've got to terminate Lindsay.' He already had the plane reservations and the appointments in L.A., so he wanted it done over the weekend, when he was out there." Easton was talking fast, freely, so I didn't stop him to ask how come he'd done it the day before the weekend. "He didn't say, 'Will you do it?' or anything. He just assumed I would."

"Goes with the territory, right?"

"You don't have to be sarcastic."

"Hey, East, I'm not. But I want us to talk straight, matter-of-fact. No bullshit between us. We're brothers."

"Don't condescend to me, Steve. That's all I ask."

"I'm not. Now, did he plan it out, or did you?"

"He had it all mapped out. He invented this imaginary killer—a crazy fan. He would make believe Lindsay had gotten a letter from the fan, telling her he loved her, threatening to kill her if she didn't write back to him."

"But she'd never gotten any letter like that?"

"Well, she *had* gotten crazy letters. All actors do. That was the beauty of it. She'd talked about them, to her agent, to some of Sy's friends at a dinner party a few weeks ago. Sy said that this murder would just seem to be a horrible extension of those letters. He'd tell the police she'd seemed a little upset about some new threatening letter, but that he'd never seen it. He'd say he kept after her to have one of the private investigation agencies who handle things for public figures look into it, and she kept saying fine, but she was busy with the movie and never bothered. And then *I* was supposed to say—but *not* volunteer it, only if the police asked me—that I'd overheard Lindsay telling him about the letter."

"Was he going to write one for the police to find?"

"No. He said he'd given it a lot of thought, and almost did it, but it was just too chancy. Who knows what kind of scientific tests the police have these days? He didn't want to risk having it traced."

What I couldn't get over was how clever Sy was. In the course of just a couple of days, he'd come up with a brilliant, almost foolproof scheme for getting rid of Lindsay. Except instead of convincing Mikey to carry out the plan, Sy had relied on a fool. So maybe, in the end, he wasn't such a brilliant mogul. He'd executive-produced his own death.

"Who decided on the rifle?" I asked.

"I did. He wanted me to stab her."

"Wouldn't that be a mess?"

"Yes, but it would be very convincing," Easton explained. "Stab her once, to kill her, but then do it again and again, so it looked like the work of a mental case. Except I told him I didn't have the stomach for it." I nodded with great seriousness, trying to show how much I cherished my brother's decency. "But then I told him I'd been a pretty good shot as a kid. And he *loved* it that I already had the rifle, that we didn't have to go out and buy one. He was very edgy about leaving any kind of tracks."

"I don't blame him. We've been checking gun dealers' records going back six months. He was a smart guy."

"Yes, he was." My brother got teary again. He sniffed.

"East, how did you have the balls to pick up a rifle that probably hadn't been touched for years? And then to rely on your being able to bag Lindsay with one or two shots?"

He gave me an I-thought-of-everything smile. "Well, it did take some balls, as you say. But I did some fast planning. Although first I had to find the key to the padlock for the gun cabinet. That took me hours! You'll never guess where it was."

"On top of the gun cabinet."

"You *knew?*"

"Yeah. You should have given me a call. I could have saved you some time." We both went chuckle-chuckle. "So you just took it out, locked the cabinet and went ready, aim, fire?"

"No. I cleaned it."

"Smart. Did you try it out?"

He inclined his head. "I went to a range."

"Which one?"

"The one up near Riverhead."

"Right. I've been there. Where did you get the bullets?"

"At a hardware store right near there."

"Took some target practice?"

"Yes. But I didn't need much. It's like riding a bike. You never really forget it."

"No, you don't," I agreed.

"And from fifty feet, it's so easy."

"Did you and Sy plan where you'd stand?"

"Yes. It had a clear view of the whole pool, but the spot itself was sort of in shadows because of the porch. The only thing I had to worry about was to make sure no one else was around. Sy would be in L.A., the cook would be off. Sy was worried Lindsay would invite some people over for drinks. Or Victor Santana for . . . you know."

"What did he say to do if Santana was there?"

"To wait, see if he'd leave."

"But if not? Get rid of him too?"

"Not on Saturday. If he was there, I should leave and come back on Sunday afternoon. There was a good chance he'd have left by then, to go over the next day's work. She'd be alone. But . . . You want me to be totally honest?"

"I really do, East."

"Well, if not, get Santana too. It would look like the crazy fan saw them together and got jealous."

I stood, walked to the open window, lifted the screen and leaned out for a minute. I pulled a couple of leaves off an overhanging branch. Then I turned back to my brother. "It was a terrific plan."

"It really was."

"So how come it didn't work?"

Easton got real earnest. He crossed his legs, rested his elbow on his knee, braced his chin on the heel of his hand. "That's what's so maddening. It *should* have worked. You know how impossible the traffic is Friday afternoons? I mean, the Long Island Expressway: the world's longest parking lot." This quip hadn't been funny even in 1958, when it had probably been invented, and hadn't improved with either age or repetition. But I laughed as though hearing one of Western Civilization's Great Witticisms. "Well," Easton continued, apparently satisfied with my appreciation of his ability as a raconteur, "the casting director was so crazed—she was casting another movie and two plays—that when I left, I realized she wouldn't have any idea of the time. And then

I got finished at Sy's shirtmaker in about two seconds. So instead of taking the Expressway or the Northern State, I took every obscure east-west road ever built on the Island. I mean, if I'd been in your car, one of those potholes I went over would have swallowed me and the Jag whole!"

I laughed again. Such cleverness! Such superb humor! Of course, I'd done that audience appreciation bit more times than I could count. It was part of the job, not only turning a suspect into your friend but also turning yourself into the one person most able to savor his comic or tragic art. It had never bothered me before, this playacting. But now, every smile, every good-natured nod of understanding I offered, cost me too much.

A couple of times I had to fight down surges of insane vitality—like rushes of a mainlined drug—to go for him, hurt him, kick him off his chair, hold him down and smash his bland, handsome face against the floor. The killer was so civilized; the cop was so savage.

"So you pushed a little and got home earlier than you'd expected?"

"Yes, a little before four. I'd been in quite a state all day, as you can imagine. This was not going to be any ordinary weekend."

"Doesn't sound like it," I said.

"I said to myself: I can't wait. I have *got* to get this over with today. I cannot *stand* the tension. But I was smart. I knew I'd promised Sy to wait until Saturday or Sunday, to make sure he was safe in California. But I called MGM Grand and asked if the plane, the ten-fifteen morning flight, had taken off on time and they said yes, it had, and it had landed in L.A. a little after four New York time. That's how I knew"—he squared his shoulders; so proud—"that he was there!"

"You didn't call him, just to make sure?"

The pride evaporated. Easton seemed to shrivel into a smaller, older man. "I didn't want to seem overanxious, make Sy think I wasn't up to handling it. He said we should call each other, because that would be the normal thing to do, but not to go overboard."

Easton was holding something back. I could tell. He had that insecure, twitchy-tentative Dan Quayle smile, the one he'd put on as a kid when my mother asked him how he was doing at school and he'd say "Fine!" not mentioning that he'd gone through the mail, found the Failure Notice in geometry and torn it up before she got home from work. "You're leaving something out, East," I said good-naturedly. "Come on. What is it?"

"Sy left a message on my machine"

"What did it say?"

"That he was taking a helicopter and going to make the seven o'clock flight instead of the morning flight, and that he'd call when he got to the hotel. But you see, I didn't play back my messages when I got back from the city. To tell you the truth, I didn't even look at the machine to see if I had any. I can't believe I could have missed something so obvious. That's so sloppy. It's not like me to be sloppy. But I just changed out of my suit—"

"Into the thongs?"

"Yes. And a good pair of shorts and a shirt, so I'd look like I belonged."

"Where was the rifle?"

"Oh, once I took it from the cabinet, I kept it in the trunk of my car, in one of those canvas sports duffels. Sy told me to do that, and to fill the duffel up with a bunch of clothes, so if anyone saw me, it would look like I was carrying a full weekend bag, not a rifle. He said carrying a rifle alone might call attention to the bag, make it look funny, bottom-heavy."

"Then what?"

"I did everything Sy told me to do. Drove up to the side of the house, near the garage, to that space where there's room for three or four cars. You can't see it from the front. I opened the window, turned off the engine and sat for five minutes, by my watch."

"He wanted you to make sure you didn't hear anyone."

"Right. Then I got out, took the duffel and walked to that place right under the porch."

"What time was it?"

"Sometime after four. I knew the *Starry Night* crew was doing the scene where Lindsay runs into the ocean, but I was praying she'd be very tired and bitchy and they'd let her go the regular time. They'd done that the last two Fridays."

"Because she was tired?"

"No. Because she was Sy's, and she was spoiled rotten."

"Would they stop filming once she left?"

"No, they'd keep going till six or seven, but they were scheduled to do Nick Monteleone's reaction shots. Most actors want the actor they're playing a scene with to be there so they can have a true reaction, but believe me, Nick would have been *delighted* to have Lindsay go home. I was counting on that."

"You weren't worried about Mrs. Robertson?"

Easton clapped his hand to his forehead. "Oh my God. That's right. It was Friday!"

"Forgot about her?"

"Totally. Did she see me?"

"Come on, East. You know I can't tell you that." I tried to make it sound as though we were kids playing a hot game of Candyland and I couldn't break any of the rules. Before he could think: This is no fucking Candyland, I pushed him further. "So you were at that spot just under the porch. What happened?"

"Well, she was there. Standing alongside the pool, talking on the portable phone. Except it wasn't her."

"You couldn't hear the conversation, I guess."

"How could I? There's always the sound of the ocean, and there was classical music playing through all those speakers."

"And his back was toward you."

"Yes, and he had on a white robe, like the one Lindsay always wears. Well, there are robes like that all over the house, for guests, but it looked like Lindsay. It *did*, Steve."

"I'm sure it did. Short, small—and with the hood up."

My brother looked baffled. "Why would he put the hood up?"

"He'd gone for a swim. His head was wet."

"That was so dumb! If the hood had been down, I'd have known right away."

"When did you know it was him?"

He swallowed hard. "When I got home."

"You shot him and then turned around and drove home?"

"Yes. That's what he told me to do. Drive right home, not too slow, not too fast. As if I could go fast, in that traffic! And then call him at the Bel-Air, and if he wasn't in, leave a message that I met with the casting director; that's if everything went okay. If there was any problem, I was supposed to leave a message that I was Fed Ex-ing another three copies of the script to him." He uncrossed his legs and sat up straight. "I can't tell you . . . those messages on my machine! First playing them back and hearing Sy's voice saying he was taking the seven o'clock flight. And then . . ." There was no doubt Easton was genuinely crying again, but overall his performance stank; he stood, walked over to the wall, rested his head against it and then pounded it with his fist, again and again. It was something Sy would have rejected in one of his movies. Overdone! Sy would have snapped at the director. Lose it! "And then," Easton went on, "there was that kid, that P.A. saying that I 'might want to know' that Sy was murdered at his house. God almighty!"

"I don't know what to say, East. What a trauma."

He turned around and leaned against the wall for support. "What do I do now, Steve?" He wiped his eyes with the lapel of his robe.

I ignored his question and asked one of my own. "What about that screenplay you showed me? That *Night of the Matador* thing?"

"There were bookcases full of scripts in his house. I just grabbed one late Saturday, after the police left. You see, once I realized what I'd done, I wanted to emphasize that I had a wonderful, *continuing* relationship with Sy, that he was my mentor. I wanted all of you to think I could never kill him. Because what would I be without him?"

"Tell me about the Lindsay business," I said. "You were acting like you were crazy about her. You weren't, though, were you?"

"No. Of course not. I saw her for what she was."

"But you pretended you were gone on her. Why?"

"I thought of that afterwards too," he said, brightening a little at the recollection of his cleverness. "If anyone remembered that talk at dailies about it being better if Lindsay was dead, and someone put two and two together . . . Well, they probably wouldn't have gotten four, but I thought if you—if the police— thought I was in love with her, I'd be counted out right away."

"Actually, if we'd been adding and came up with Lindsay as the planned victim, you'd have been suspected right away."

"Why?" He looked annoyed.

"Because you had an emotional tie to her."

"That's stupid."

"Well, that's cops for you. Stupid, unimaginative. The civil service mentality. We do it by the book."

A barely tolerant shake of the head. "Some book."

"Well," I said, "book or no book, we got you. Didn't we, Easton?"

"No!" He rushed over and grabbed the shoulders of my jacket. "Steve, you're not going to do anything?" His mouth and eyes formed huge circles of astonishment. "Steve! Are you crazy? I'm your brother."

"I know."

"How can you even think of doing something so terrible?"

"Get dressed," I said. But he just stood there, right in front of me, still clutching the shoulder pads of my suit jacket. "It's getting late. Come on."

"*Think*. Think about what you want to do. What about Mother?"

"She's due home soon; you can explain to her what's happening. Or if she's stopping off someplace, I'll come back and sit down with her later. After I bring you in."

He let his hands drop to his sides. He spoke softly, his voice full of gentleness and understanding. "Steve, you have to understand. This will kill her." The good son.

"I don't think so."

"I know her much better than you do. She won't be able to survive a blow like this."

"Yes, she will."

"You think she's tough. She's not tough."

"I know she's not. She's empty. She'll survive. Please, don't make me have to act any more like a cop than I'm already doing. Get dressed."

Instead, he sat down in the straight-backed chair. "What would it cost you to let me go?"

"Bonnie Spencer's life."

"No, it wouldn't."

"It would. There's a warrant out for her arrest."

"Then how come she was here with you?"

"Because I was taking care of her. I didn't think she should be arrested." I looked outside. The light was softening, the prelude to dusk.

"Do you want me arrested? Do you want to see me go to jail?" I was still holding the two leaves in my hand. I ran my finger over a stem, up the veins. "Steve!" Easton cried out. "Who the hell is she? How can you want to protect her and not want to protect me?"

"I'm protecting her because she's innocent." I spoke more to the leaves than to Easton.

"But I'm your brother."

"You're a killer."

Easton got up and went over to the window. I inched forward, in case he made a move to jump, but he just stared out at the muted light. "Nothing can bring Sy back now," he said.

"I know."

He turned to face me. "I don't want that woman to go to jail for me."

"Since when?"

"Listen to me. We can work something out. I can give her an alibi." I didn't react. "Wait. Hold on a second. Just listen." Easton rubbed his hands together. "Okay, first of all, I'll tell them that Sy was very fond of her, that things with Lindsay had soured, and that he really seemed to be happy with the ex-wife again— and made no bones about it. All right. I didn't say anything earlier because I had such a crush on Lindsay I couldn't bring myself to say anything that would make her look bad. I'll admit I was terribly wrong. I'll apologize all over myself. So they won't think the ex had any reason to kill him. And I'll say . . . I know! I stopped at a pay phone on my way home from the city and called her about something. Like about her screenplay, and she was there, at home. Answered the phone and—"

"No."

"Why not?"

"Because it's so full of holes it's a joke. Because she's decent and honorable and this fake-alibi crap would make her sick. And because she doesn't have to lie. We have our perp, Easton."

"Is it all so black and white to you? Don't you see any grays?"

"I wish this weren't happening," I said slowly.

"It doesn't have to."

"What choice do I have? I'm a cop. I know there are a million shades of gray in the world. I see them. But I can only act on black and white."

Easton came over and put his arms around me. A real hug. Except for my old man when he was soused, I don't think, until that moment, I ever had an embrace from any member of my family. "Steve," he said, "I need you so much. My life has been one mistake after another. One charade after another. And now this. I don't know who I thought I was, who I was hoping to be, but I botched it. More than that. I did a terrible thing." I stroked the back of his head. His hair was so much softer than mine. "A wicked thing. I know that, but I'm so messed up, so weak, that I didn't have the courage to face up to it. Until now." He let me out of his embrace and backed away. "Just hear me out. Please?"

"Go ahead."

"I know you think I'm useless, and you're right. I never, ever asked myself: What's really important? And even if I had, and came up with love or friendship or something like that, it probably wouldn't have mattered. You know that. I still would have gone for the razzle-dazzle. But now I really have to face the music. I can go to jail for the rest of my life. You *know* what jail is like."

"Yes."

"It's as bad as they say, isn't it?"

"Worse."

"I swear to you, by all that's holy, that I'll spend the rest of my life making up for this terrible thing I've done." He stood before me in that perfect gold and pink and blue light. "I know we've never been close. But we are brothers. I'm not asking for special treatment, Steve, but I am asking—begging—that you give me a chance. Neither of us has ever had much of a shot at happiness, have we? I know I've lost that shot now, forever. But maybe I can have something, at least. Something from you."

"What?"

"Forgiveness."

I looked past him, out at the light. It was the magic hour. It comes and goes so fast. In movies, though, it returns just after dawn again, and then, once more, just before dusk. Twice a day, opportunities for wonder. But in real life, those moments that allow the possibility of grace hardly ever come at all.

If I brought my brother in, that would be the end of him. Forgiveness, he'd said. I could allow him the possibility of finding his own salvation. Because what he said was true: nothing could bring Sy back. And the beauty of it was, I wouldn't even have to stand in shamed silence and let Easton present his twisted, transparent alibi for Bonnie. I could just let him overpower me, escape, and disappear into a new life.

"Can't you forgive me, Steve? Haven't you ever done wrong?"

"Are you kidding? Most of my life has been wrong. That's no secret."

"So? We're two of a kind."

"No, East. Even when I was wrong, I knew there were laws. I knew there was a God."

"But God forgives!"

"I know. And maybe God will forgive you, or has forgiven you. I can't know that. And maybe I, personally, can forgive you. But a life has been taken."

"What are you saying?"

I let the leaves drop to the floor. "I'm saying an apology won't do it."

"You're going to send me to jail?"

"No; that's not my job. My job is much smaller. I'm just going to arrest you for the murder of Sy Spencer."

"That's sending me to jail, damn it!"

"That's doing what I have to do."

"I'll tell them you're setting me up to save that woman!"

"The rifle, East. The ballistics tests. Your rubber shoes with the Adelphi grass."

"Someone else could have stolen that rifle. Or my thongs."

"And put them back?"

"Try and prove it was me."

"There was a man who bought bullets in a hardware store, who took target practice with an old Marlin .22 at a range near Riverhead the day before the murder. A nice-looking man in his late thirties. Don't you think witnesses will recognize his picture? Don't you think they'll be able to point him out in a lineup? In court?" I opened the door of his closet. "Get ready, East. We have to go."

He knew better than to try and fight me. He might have tried to run for it, but being what he was, he just scurried around the bedroom for a few hysterical seconds. Then he got dressed. What else could he do? Rush outside on a Friday night in the height of the season, in a short, ugly, grayish-brown shaving robe? No. My brother had too much class.

CHAPTER 22

In the end, I called Ray Carbone at home and asked him to please come over. I couldn't bring myself to handcuff Easton, lead him through the house and take him to Headquarters. Also, I realized that the fact the perpetrator had a brother on the Homicide Squad should be a single sentence in the last paragraph of the news story, not a nightmare headline—HOMICIDE COP ARRESTS KILLER BROTHER; MOTHER CRIES "MY SON!"

My mother, of course, didn't cry anything of the sort. She came home around seven, a couple of minutes after Carbone arrived. She was a little tipsy from a martini or two with some rich lady with a dog name from her latest charity committee: Skip or Lolly or something. When she finally understood what was happening to Easton, she didn't scream or faint or have a heart attack.

All she did was collapse onto the couch. I got her some water. Right before he left, my brother bent down and kissed her goodbye. He aimed for her cheek but somehow missed and got her nose. He told her he was sorry, for her, not for himself. Carbone said he'd be at Headquarters all night if I needed him and then mumbled a few words to my mother about how bad he felt for her troubles.

I pulled up a footstool and sat in front of her. She was a fine-looking woman, with neat, even features, genuinely remarkable green-blue eyes, large and round, and a slender figure. After that momentary slump into the chair, her Emily Post spine straightened up. Her back was at a perfect ninety-degree angle to her lap. "What should I do?" she asked me.

I told her Easton needed a lawyer. I went into the kitchen and looked up Bill Paterno's number in the phone book. She asked me if he was expensive, and I said yes, but he was very good, and when she called him, to tell him I'd speak to him tomorrow and work something out.

"Does that mean you'll pay for it?" she asked.

"Yeah."

"Not 'yeah.' "

"Yes," I said.

"Do you really think Easton did it?"

Yes, I told her, and explained the evidence we had against him. She asked if I thought a jury would find him guilty, and I said most likely Paterno would work out some sort of a deal with a guilty plea so there wouldn't have to be a trial, but that Easton would go to prison.

"I seem to have made a mess of things," she said quietly.

"No. Easton did."

Her excellent carriage became even more excellent. "I can't understand it. He was never a troublemaker," she said, not mentioning who had been. She looked so fine sitting there. Well, fine, but dated, like a 1952 Republican country club lady brought back in a time machine. Even now, stunned, probably anguished, all she was missing was a Rob Roy with a cherry and an Eisenhower button. "He had no drive, but you can't fault someone for that."

"No, you can't."

"He didn't belong in the movie business," she murmured. No one looked the way my mother did anymore. No one would take that amount of time to produce that strange, dated effect. She set her hair every night on fat wire rollers so it would fluff up and curl under in the chin-length pageboy she'd worn as long as I could remember. She tweezed away most of her eyebrows and redrew them into a thin, light-brown line. Her makeup was pale powder, red rouge and matching lipstick, a little smudged after her martinis. Her nails, filed short and oval, were red too. "He should have gone into banking. Not that he could have been a bank president. I would never deceive myself. But he kept trying to be a salesman, and he couldn't sell anyone anything. And then movies, with all those people. They're so hard. He wasn't cut out to deal with them."

"No, he wasn't."

"I thought he liked that man, though. The one he killed." I explained how Easton had been doing Sy's bidding, how he thought he was shooting at Lindsay. She asked: "Why didn't he just say 'I won't do it'?"

"I don't know, Mom."

"Well, neither do I."

I asked her if she wanted me to make her something to eat. No, she wasn't hungry, and she'd be all right. I knew that meant she wanted to be alone, but I asked if she wanted me to stay the night, or if she wanted to come over to my place. She said no thank you, and yes, she would call me if she needed me. I told her I'd be over first thing in the morning.

"It will be in all the newspapers," she said. "On the television too."

"It will be a bad couple of days," I said. "Well, in terms of publicity. I know it will be bad for you for much longer than that."

"Do you think they'll fire me?"

"No. You're too valuable to them. And I think most people will go out of their way to be understanding."

"They won't understand, though. They'll just be polite. Deep down, they'll all think I did something wrong that made him turn out this way." She stood. "I'd like to be alone now."

"I'm so sorry, Mom."

And then she almost knocked me over. "Why should you be sorry? It's not your fault. You didn't kill anyone. Your brother did." But before I could work up a major case of filial sentiment and possibly reach for her hand, or gush, I'll always be there for you, Mom, no matter what, my mother added: "I'd like you to leave." So I said good night and so did she.

Ray Carbone and Thighs were getting Easton's confession on video-tape, and it was being transmitted, live, in living but somewhat purplish color, on the TV monitor in Frank Shea's office. Carbone was asking, "Did you pay cash for the bullets or charge them?" and my brother, showing how ingeniously he and Sy had planned Lindsay's murder, replied: "Cash. Don't leave tracks: that was our motto."

Shea started to explain to me, "You'll see the beginning of the tape, how we read him his rights. We gave him every chance—"

I cut him off. "A guy wants to talk, you can't muzzle him."

"How's your mother taking it?"

"She's numb." I didn't mention that the condition was prob-ably congenital. But then, because Shea and I had been at each other's throats over the case and there was so much bad blood, I decided I'd better show him I was a decent guy. "I'd be with her now, but she asked me to leave. Really wanted to be alone. I think she probably was going to fall apart and wanted to spare me." That image of my mother going out of control and wanting to protect me had nothing much to do with reality, but it did make us sound like a normal family. Well, until you looked at that talking head on the TV screen who was telling Carbone that yes, he'd cleaned the .22 at home, but when he got to the range the lever was so stiff he could hardly move it, so one of the men there—a black man with a goatee—helped him. I said to Shea: "Listen to him. Jesus, I can't believe we're from the same gene pool."

He got up and walked to the TV. His gold chains clanged.

"I'll catch this later," he said. "Unless you really want to watch, but between you and me"—he was using his Compassionate Leader voice—"I think you should spare yourself."

"You can turn it off," I agreed.

He did and then came back, stood behind my chair and put his hand on my shoulder. "You want to take some vacation time, Steve?"

"Probably."

"You've got it. Ray thinks you ought to see Dr. Nettles, the new department shrink, get some counseling. Preventive medicine. That's up to you. Ray says she's good. I met her. She's got a face like a bulldog." He clanged his way back to his big leather chair and sat down. "Now listen, you've got my apology. The drinking thing. The saying you're in love with that Spencer woman." I started to worry. What if, finally, it had all been too much, even for Bonnie? What if, now that it was over, she wanted to leave it all behind, go back to her mountains? "That fucking Robby Kurz," he breathed.

"Robby's in the squad room," I said.

"I know. Did you have it out with him?"

"No. I didn't even go in. I'm wiped. My fuse is so short I'd blow in two seconds, and I don't want to do that. There are more serious matters than him saying I'm a drunk. And they're your territory, not mine."

"The Bonnie hair," he said.

"Yeah, the Bonnie hair."

He picked up his phone, pressed the intercom and said, "I'd like to see you, Robby. No, now." He hung up and looked me right in the eye. "Listen, I'm sympathetic to what you're going through. A family tragedy. But I won't mince words. The Suffolk County Police Department is a paramilitary organization. You know what that means?"

"You're the captain and I'm not."

"That's right. Sometimes you seem to have some trouble with that concept. Now, you have a personal beef against this guy, and we may have a departmental beef. Guess which gets priority tonight when he walks through—" At that instant, Robby walked through the door. "Sit down, Robby." It was an order, not an invitation, and Robby, after nodding at me, sat. Sitting across from Frank Shea's black-Irish, lounge-lizard good looks, Robby looked even puffier and pastier than usual; he was starting to resemble one of his crullers. "You almost ruined Brady's career," Shea said.

"I didn't mean to."

"So how come you called him a drunk?"

"Because I thought he was."

"Why?"

"I thought he was acting in an erratic manner, and I thought I smelled liquor on him."

"How was I erratic, you weasel son of a bitch fucker?"

"Shut up, Brady," Shea said. Then, remembering I was in the middle of a Major Personal Crisis, he added, "Please." He turned back to Robby. "I won't call you a liar. But I question your powers of observation."

"I know the tests say I was wrong. So I apologize."

No one seemed to expect me to accept or decline the apology, so I just sat back and shut my eyes for a second. I wanted to call Gideon and find out how Bonnie was. I wanted to tell him my back door was open, so they could get Moose, who might need more water or a walk.

"Let's get to the Bonnie hair, Robby," Shea was saying. "We had *everyone* on this case. Our best people. We examine, reexamine, re-reexamine the area where the perp stood." He paused, to indicate that out of deference to me he was not using the perp's name. "We find zip in the hair department. And then the next week: A miracle! Crucial evidence! One of Bonnie Spencer's hairs—with a root, no less, so we can get a DNA reading on it."

"Are you saying I planted it, Frank?" Robby asked.

"I'm saying Ray Carbone checked the plastic thing we got back from the lab and the seal looked a little funny and one hair seemed to be missing. Would you call it a plant?"

"No. Obviously the lab lost a hair. You of all people should know they're not perfect."

I thought: What if Bonnie doesn't want me? What if she thinks I'm too unstable?

"Why would Bonnie Spencer's hair be at the exact spot the perp stood if Bonnie Spencer wasn't the perp?"

"Maybe she just passed by." You could hardly hear Robby's voice anymore. And he was slipping lower and lower into his chair. The only part of him holding up was his sprayed hairdo.

"That's your explanation?" Shea boomed. "She just was taking a stroll around the six acres of grounds and her hair caught on that one infinitesimal little spot?" Robby didn't reply. Shea leaned forward. "Let me ask you something. Do you think you're any better than any of the shits we lock up?"

"I deserve a fair hearing." It sounded like Robby had already talked to a lawyer.

"I'm sure the department will give you one."

"Thank you."

"But as far as Homicide goes, you know what?"

"Frank—"

"Pack up your pencils."

As far as I know, Robby Kurz did not pack up his pencils. He certainly didn't say goodbye. He just left for good.

I took my brother's tinny excuse for a convertible, a Mustang, went back to my house and got Moose. She sat in the passenger seat, raised her snout and let the rush of air blow her hairy ears back. When we stopped at a light, she gave some Manhattan yuppies in a Volvo station wagon the patronizing glance of a glamorous dame who only travels top-down.

I pulled into Bonnie's driveway. At last the bureaucratic wheels were turning: they had discontinued the surveillance. Her Jeep was in the garage. The house was dark, and the front and back doors were locked. I rang the bell a few times, but there was no answer. I knew she had to be at Gideon's, but I was scared. I kept thinking crazy things, like what if she'd gone home, tripped on one of her stupid scatter rugs and cracked open her head and was lying inside, dead. No. Then my car would still be there. But what if she'd hit an oil patch and the Jag went out of control and she'd gone off a bridge, or gone up in flames? The only sounds came from wild ducks, and from the forced laughter over cocktails on the back deck at her neighbor's, Wendy Bubbleface.

It took me about ten minutes to get Moose back in the car. She was home and saw no reason to leave. She took a dump, chased a rabbit, then lay down on the front lawn. I made an ass of myself, clapping my hands and calling, "Here, girl! C'mon, Moose! Oooh, let's go for a ride!" and whistling. She wouldn't budge. At last, I hefted her, all hundred pounds of her, and carried her back to the car.

It was dark when I finally found Gideon's house, one of those renovated barns set back a couple of hundred feet from the road. There was a small sign on a strip of barn siding that said "Friedman-Sterling," but Friedman and Sterling had planted so much fucking English ivy that I drove past it at least five times until I spotted it.

I opened the car door, but before I could get out, Moose leapt over me, then sat, waiting, tongue dangling, for me to join her. But I couldn't get out. I reknotted my tie, then loosened it, then took it off, took my jacket off, rolled up my shirt sleeves, then got dressed again.

Maybe she'd taken an overdose of sleeping pills, thinking I was going to marry Lynne and she'd never see me again.

I wanted to hold her in my arms. I wanted to take her over to Germy's to watch the DiMaggio video and tell him, This is my girl.

I thought, I shouldn't be driving my brother's damn car, since Easton had stowed the rifle in the trunk. Now it had my prints and dog hair. The lab guys would be pissed.

My heart began to pound. She'd be in there, but she'd refuse to see me, and Gideon's boyfriend would stand at the door, his hand on his hip, and sneer: "Bonnie's flying to the Coast tomorrow to sell her story for a CBS Movie of the Week and she's on the phone with her new agent and cannot be disturbed. Ta-ta."

Or she wouldn't be there. She'd be on her way to the airport, to go to Utah. She'd stay with one of her brothers for a while, until her house was sold, then buy a cabin ten thousand feet high in some mountain by a trout stream. She wouldn't answer my letters or phone calls. I'd finally go out there and track her down, but she'd run out the back door up the mountains and wouldn't come back until I'd gone. The next spring, after the thaw, they'd find her. Dead. She'd frozen in February. She'd forgotten how hard winters in the mountains could be. She hadn't chopped enough wood for the stove.

I was so upset by the thought of her decomposing body that I didn't see Gideon until he was right next to the car. "Is Bonnie here?" I demanded. "Is she all right?"

"She's fine," Gideon said cautiously. I guess I looked a little nuts. "She's sleeping." Moose, the town slut, had already transferred her allegiance to Gideon and was licking his hand.

"I guess she must be pretty tired," I mumbled.

"Do you want to come in for a minute?"

For a barn, it was a nice place, with a vaulted ceiling and a lot of beams going to interesting places. Gideon introduced me to his friend, Jeff, who looked like a bouncer in a very rough nightclub. He stayed just long enough to shake hands, say "Pleased to make yo' 'quaintance" and give me a thorough once-over; my guess was he could hardly wait for me to leave, so he and Gideon could launch into an exhaustive analysis.

A giant black iron chandelier hung from the main beam; it had cut-out sheep and cows and pigs all over it. Upstairs, there were closed doors off a landing that had once been the hayloft. "Bonnie's in the middle room," Gideon said, when he saw me looking up. I thought he would tell me not to trifle with her affections or something, but he just said how sorry he was about it being my brother. I told him my mother was calling Paterno, but that my brother had already given a videotaped confession—probably less because he wanted to make a clean breast of things than that he wanted to be thought of as pleasant company. And I told him about Easton's sick pride, that he'd planned the whole thing with Sy Spencer, big shot. Just the two of them. Sy and Easton, partners. I said I couldn't believe my brother had been so willing to let Bonnie take the fall for him. Gideon said, Take it easy. It's over now. He added that Shea had called Paterno and said they were rescinding the warrant and to tell Mrs. Spencer sorry for any inconvenience.

"Do you think she'll be all right?" I asked him.

"She's strong."

"I know."

"But it's going to take a long time."

"Do you mind if I go up and see her?" I asked.

"Once we knew it was officially over, after Bill Paterno called . . ." Gideon hesitated. "Bonnie said you might drop by. She asked me to thank you for all you've done for her, but that you and she had agreed earlier that it would be best if you didn't see each other again."

"I want to see her."

"And I want to protect her." We tried to stare each other down. "It seems we're at an impasse," he said, "and since it's an impasse on my territory, I'm going to have to ask you to leave." He stood.

So did I. "I just want to tell her something."

"I don't think that would be advisable."

"Fuck you, Friedman."

"Fuck *you*, Brady."

I tried to count up to ten, to think of something else to say, but I only made it to two. "Look, I love her."

"You love her?" Gideon repeated. "You must be a very loving man. You love the other one too."

"If it's any of your goddamned business, I don't love the other one, and as a matter of fact and of law, Counselor, the other one isn't the other one anymore and the position is vacant. Now can I go up and see Bonnie?"

"Be my guest," he said.

I could sense her waking as I opened the door. I came in and sat on the edge of the bed. "You're beautiful," I said.

"Sure. It's pitch black in here." Bonnie stuck her hand out and groped for a lamp. She turned it on and squeezed her eyes shut at the light. She looked like Mr. Magoo. "Now say it."

"You're beautiful. I love you. What was the third thing?"

"I'm a truly fine person." The base of the lamp was a big china chicken. She turned it off.

"You're a truly fine person," I said.

"I told Gideon not to let you up here."

"I told him I was going to tell you I loved you, so I became his pal. Anything I want. His house is my house. His chicken lamp is my chicken lamp." I turned it on again and pulled down the sheet a little. She'd taken off my T-shirt.

She pulled the sheet all the way up. "Listen, I guess you'll be hearing this a lot, but I'm sorry about your brother. I'm sure it's going to be very painful for your family, and it's too bad you can't be spared that."

"Thank you. It's too bad you couldn't have been spared your pain."

"Thank you," she said. "I don't want to seem insensitive, but I'd like you to leave now."

"Why? Are you going to cry or something?"

Bonnie gave me an angry nudge. Some nudge. It practically knocked me off the bed. "You want to hang around and watch?"

"Yeah."

"Well, I don't want you to. I want you to go."

"I can't. I promised Gideon I'd ask you to marry me."

"Well, ask me and then get out."

"All right. Will you marry me?"

Somehow, all of a sudden, she knew. She didn't make any

wisecracks about my having a previous engagement. She didn't tell me to leave. She just said "Yes," but then she told me I couldn't kiss her because she had sleep breath. I kissed her anyway. It was a sweet and beautiful kiss. After it was over, she asked, "Am I *really* beautiful? Objectively."

"No."

"Am I *really* a truly fine person?"

"You're not bad."

I stood up, took off my clothes and got into bed.

"Do you *really* love me?"

"More than anything in the world, Bonnie."

"I've known that for years, Stephen."

And together we turned off the chicken lamp, and we began our life.